CRAZY COOL

"Wild nonstop action, an interesting subplot, a tormented-but-honorable and brilliant bad boy and a tough girl, and great sex scenes make Janzen's... romance irresistible." —*Booklist*

CRAZY WILD

"While keeping the tension and thrills high, Janzen excels at building rich characters whose lives readers are deeply vested in. Let's hope she keeps 'em coming!" —*Romantic Times*

CRAZY KISSES

"The high-action plot, the savage-but-tender hero, and the wonderfully sensuous sex scenes, Janzen's trademarks, make this as much fun as the prior Crazy titles." —*Booklist*

CRAZY LOVE

"Readers [will] instantly bond with [Janzen's] characters. Driving action and adventure laced with hot passion add up to big-time fun." —*Romantic Times*

CRAZY SWEET

"Exciting and adventurous suspense with nonstop action that will keep readers riveted. I highly recommend it, and can't wait to read more."
—*Romance Reviews Today*

LOOSE and EASY

TARA JANZEN

A DELL BOOK

LOOSE AND EASY
A Dell Book / September 2008

Published by
Bantam Dell
A Division of Random House, Inc.
New York, New York

This is a work of fiction. Names, characters, places, and incidents either are the product of the author's imagination or are used fictitiously. Any resemblance to actual persons, living or dead, events, or locales is entirely coincidental.

Dell is a registered trademark of Random House, Inc., and the colophon is a trademark of Random House, Inc.

ISBN 978-0-440-24469-1

Printed in the United States of America
Published simultaneously in Canada

www.bantamdell.com

OPM   10   9   8   7   6   5   4   3   2   1

CHAPTER ONE

Johnny Ramos knew the sad-looking little hooker limping her way down Seventeenth Street in two-inch black patent-leather platform heels. Her fishnet hose were torn in the back, revealing the bottom curve of her ass under what could only be described as a supermicrominiskirt. Red lace and leather and having seen better days, the skirt was barely seven inches wide from top to bottom and matched her red lace gloves. The cheap white vinyl tote bag slung over her shoulder was almost as big as she was and looked like it had seen better days, too. The white Lycra T-shirt laminated to her upper body had more heart-shaped cutouts and pink sequins than material. He could see a red push-up bra doing its job under the shirt.

Esme Alexandria Alden, he thought, East High School's valedictorian the year he'd graduated. *Geezus, how the mighty have fallen.*

"Easy Alex" hooking in LoDo, Denver's lower downtown district; it was enough to boggle the mind. Nothing about what he was seeing made sense: that sweet little size-four ass in torn fishnet; the twisted-up pile of ratted and heavily sprayed blond hair he'd only ever seen in tight and tidy braids; the smartest girl he'd ever known turning tricks.

He slid his gaze over her again, from the shoes to the French twist falling out of its pins. At seventeen, he'd have given anything to get her hair loose and falling down. Those long blond braids of hers had driven him crazy. He'd wanted so badly to undo them. Hell, he'd wanted to undo everything on the girl, from her prim little button-down shirts to her carefully tied and spotlessly white tennis shoes, but there hadn't been anything easy about "Easy Alex." That had been the joke. She'd never had a date in high school, not one, not even the prom. He knew, because he'd been the guy she'd turned down.

She couldn't possibly be a prostitute. No way in hell. Back then, she hadn't known what the word "sex" meant. He'd gotten more off of her than any guy in East, and it had taken him years of pursuit and most of one hot summer night to even get to second base.

She'd been sweet. Yeah, he remembered. Sweet and scared, mostly of him, he'd guessed, and of herself, of her reaction to him. He'd been one of the city's bad boys, and she'd had the lock on the title of Little Miss Goody Two-shoes.

He'd loved it, loved the challenge of it, but she'd

been too good to let him get in her pants, which is where their party had ended that night, with him aching and her panting, and neither of them getting what they'd needed.

Fifty bucks said he could get whatever he wanted off her tonight. Hell, maybe it would only take twenty, but with her looking rode hard and put away wet all he wanted was the story, the explanation, the "What in the hell happened to you?"

Yeah, that's what he wanted. No way should Esme Alden be limping down Seventeenth with her ass hanging out of ripped fishnet. After graduating from high school, she'd been slated for the University of Colorado on a scholarship, full ride.

She got to the corner at Wazee and started across the intersection, heading toward the Oxford Hotel. When she was partway to the other side, the Oxford's valet signaled her, and Johnny swore under his breath.

"Geezus."

She'd been called in to service some guy staying at the hotel, and he had to wonder, really: How many doormen and parking valets in Denver had her name in their little black books?

He hated to say it, but he would have thought any girl working the Oxford would look a little classier than what Esme had pulled off tonight.

None of his business, he told himself, not for any good reason on God's green earth, and yet he stepped off the curb from in front of the Blue Iguana Lounge, where he'd been having a beer, and crossed Seventeenth. He wasn't following her. He was just checking things out, doing recon, getting the lay of the land, and he'd been thinking about heading this way anyway, and maybe stopping by an art gallery next door to the Oxford, the Toussi Gallery.

He'd gotten home from his last tour of duty, this one in Afghanistan, two weeks ago, and was still waiting to be reassigned to General Grant's command, specifically into Special Defense Force, SDF, an elite group of operatives based in Denver and deployed out of the Pentagon. Until his official orders came through, he was on leave, on his own, hanging out in his hometown and looking to stay out of trouble.

Or not.

A brief grin twitched the corner of his lips. Easy Alex had never been anything except trouble for him, starting in Ms. Trent's seventh-grade social studies class, where he'd come up with her nickname and ended up in detention. Decking Kevin Harrell for pushing her up against a locker in a back hallway in East High when they'd been juniors had gotten him suspended for three days. He'd been protecting her honor.

And now she was hooking?

No. He wasn't buying it. Not the Esme he knew. Something else had to be going on, no matter how much of her ass he could see—except when she got to the sidewalk, the damn valet handed her a room key.

Johnny came to a sudden halt. *Geezus, a friggin' room key.*

Okay, this really wasn't any of his business, and honestly, he didn't really want to see what she was going to be doing in the hotel, or who in the hell she was going to be doing it with, or doing it to, or any damn thing about Esme Alden "doing it" at all.

Which was why it took him another second and a half to get moving again. Halfway across the street, he paused as a sleek black Town Car turned the corner and cruised to a stop in front of the hotel's main entrance. The doorman stepped forward and opened the Lincoln's rear door, with the valet close behind.

Johnny detoured around the front of the car, but made a point of glancing back. A distinguished-looking gentleman got out of the car, mid-forties, slender build, very elegantly dressed, and wearing a fedora.

A fedora in Denver, in August? That was unusual, but nothing compared to the exotic Asian woman following the man out of the limo. She was gorgeous, wearing a black and white dress, heels, and a drop-dead stare that withered each of the hotel employees in turn.

Yikes. He'd hate to be the peon on the receiving end of her bad days.

Interestingly, after letting the woman out, the man in the fedora got back in the car. The dragon queen turned to say something to him, and that was the last Johnny saw. He pushed through the door into the hotel. Inside the lobby, he caught sight of Esme just before she disappeared up the stairs.

He didn't hesitate. Taking the damn things two at a time, he easily made it to the second landing in time to see which door she opened with the key—number 215. She slipped inside and the door closed behind her, and there he stood like an idiot, at the end of the hallway, wondering what in the hell he was thinking.

The seconds ticked by, and he was still standing there. When a whole minute had gone by, he knew he should leave—but he didn't, he just kept staring at the door to room 215 and telling himself not to go anywhere near it. Good advice he might have taken, if he hadn't heard a loud thump come from inside the room, a sound like somebody falling, or getting knocked over.

None of his business—right—except it was Easy Alex in there, and he didn't want to be reading about her in the morning papers. He'd "been there, done that" with too many people in his life, so better judgment be damned, he started down the hall.

When he got to the door, he could hear some guy with a German accent spluttering in indignation and anger from inside the room.

"You...you...goddamn *Shiksa*. You...you can't do this to me."

Johnny pressed his ear closer. None of his business, absolutely none—*dammit*. He wasn't cop of the world, not here. He should be enjoying the reprieve, not jumping in the middle of a fifty-dollar trick.

"*Shiksa* yourself, mister," a cool, sweetly feminine voice replied. And yes, it was definitely Easy

Alex. He remembered the slightly cultured accent, the honeyed tone, the instinctive edge of authority. *Christ*. She'd always had the edge of authority, usually with her hand in the air, fingers waggling, her arm stick-straight, going for all the height she could get—*Hey, hey, teacher, I know the answer, I know the answer*. Hell, she'd always known the answer.

"That's not . . . this isn't," the guy kept spluttering, his voice starting to sound a little strained. "This isn't what I asked for . . . I wanted Dixie. I was told to ask for Dixie, and . . . and you're not Dixie."

No, Johnny thought, a little taken back. She most certainly wasn't. Anywhere in Denver north of the Sixteenth Street Mall, the name Dixie bandied about in that tone of voice by some guy in a hotel could only mean one thing: a diminutive forty-year-old dominatrix with a quirt. She'd been a permanent fixture of the city's nights for as long as Johnny could remember, which did nothing to answer the questions of why Esme Alden was taking one of Dixie's calls, and what in the hell she'd just done to the guy in 215.

Somebody in the room let out a strangled sound of distress, and he knocked, twice, hard and solid, a pure knee-jerk reaction that clearly said, "What in the hell is going on in there?"—and the room went silent. He could have heard a frickin' pin drop in the hall, and he could just imagine the two of them frozen in some sordid S&M act, their gazes glued to the door, wondering who in the hell had knocked.

"Housekeeping," he said, loud and clear. "We have your towels."

Towels?

Esme tightened her grip on the handcuffs she'd used at Otto Von Lindberg's request to secure his hands behind his back. He was facedown on the floor, her knee planted firmly and deliberately in his back, pressing hard. Her other hand had a strong grip on the dog collar the German had also been so kind as to provide already in place around his neck. She had the attached leash tied to the bed frame—and there was somebody at the door, somebody she'd bet didn't have any towels.

Dammit. Releasing her hold on the collar, she swiveled on Otto's back, and used one of his other leashes to hog-tie his flex-cuffed ankles to his wrists. He was old, and his ankles looked frail, considering his well-over-two-hundred-pound girth, but she wasn't overly concerned about Otto's skinny ankles. They'd been carting him around for sixty-some years. More than likely, they'd hold up under a little hog-tying.

"*Nein . . . nein,*" he gasped and struggled—to no avail. She'd had the bastard cold from the instant he'd let her lock him into the cuffs.

Let her? Hell, he'd begged her. It was part of the game.

She finished off the knot on the leash and jerked it tight. *Geez.* Germans and dogs—it was always the Germans with the dog paraphernalia. She'd seen it half a dozen times in her line of work, which despite her outfit didn't have a damn thing to do with prostitution.

Esme Alden, Master of Disguise—yes, sir, that was her, all right, when the situation called for it, and old Otto had laid himself wide open to get taken by a hooker tonight. She'd known he would, and she'd known exactly what kind of girl he'd be looking to hire. Fifty bucks to the parking valet hadn't gone to naught. The call for Dixie had come to her instead. She might have to make up the missed trick to the aging dominatrix, just to keep peace on the street, but a couple hundred bucks ought to cover it, which left her with the night's potential profit margin still hitting at the required eighty-two-thousand-dollar mark.

And it wasn't enough, not even close, not for the risk she was taking, not if she didn't make a clean deal of it and an even cleaner getaway.

Esme rose to her feet, leaving Otto to cuss and squirm on the floor. He'd left his suitcase open on the bed, and it took her about thirty seconds to search through his clothes and the rest of his dog collars. He had a penchant for spikes and studs.

She had a penchant for fine art, the stolen variety, and she wasn't finding any packed in his suitcase. Oh, hell, no—that would have been too easy.

"Wh-what are you looking for?" he stammered. "What do you want? Money? More money?"

Actually, bottom line, yes, and the art was the means to that end.

"You . . . you shouldn't be doing this. Not . . . not

to me," he rattled on. "You don't know who you're dealing with."

Oh, yes, she did. She knew exactly whom she was dealing with.

"I am a *very* important man."

True. Damned important to her, for now, or she wouldn't be in this damn hotel room, wearing a damn stupid outfit, with a damn fat old German at her feet.

Some nights, life just got quirky on a girl. She was sure as hell redlining the Quirky-O-Meter tonight, which she could handle. No problem. As long as the Shit-Hitting-The-Fan-O-Meter stayed well on the low end of the scale.

Reaching into a narrow pocket on her skirt, Esme pulled out a knife and thumbed it open, and next to her on the floor, Otto went dead silent. Suddenly, there wasn't a peep, or a squeak, or a twitch coming out of him. She could almost hear the gears in his head grind to a halt in sheer, unadulterated terror.

Yes, old boy, she thought, *this is the masochist's risk, that the game gets out of hand.*

Not bothering to reassure him of anything, let alone his safety, she leaned farther over the bed and started in on the suitcase—and in her opinion, his relief, heralded by a sharp expulsion of breath and a general collapse of his body against his restraints, was overly optimistic. He was in it up to his neck for this night's work even if he was safe from her blade.

"Wh-what..." he finally stammered, when he'd

gotten his breath back. "Wh-what are you doing? I don't . . . I don't understand."

Oh, yes, he did. He just needed to think it through a bit.

She kept to the edges of his suitcase, inside and out, running the blade close to the frame and carefully pulling back the linings and fabric covering.

No art.

Specifically, no Jakob Meinhard's 1910 *Woman in Blue,* a small Expressionist masterpiece last seen in Munich in 1937 as part of the *Entartete Kunst* exhibit, the Degenerate Art exhibit, and believed burned in Berlin in 1939. Her father had been on the painting's trail since word of its survival had surfaced four years ago. Or more accurately, he'd been on the trail of the reward money offered by the painting's rightful owner, Isaac Nachman, a wealthy, eccentric Denver industrialist. A good friend, Burt had always called the man, which in the jargon Esme knew meant Mr. Nachman had loaned her father money—quite a bit over the years, as it had eventually come out, with their "friendship" and their business overlapping almost one hundred percent of the time in Mr. Nachman's favor.

Esme hoped to even that number out a bit before the night was through.

"You . . . you are crazy," Otto said under his breath. "A crazy American whore."

Not really.

"You will regret this, *Shiksa*," he swore sotto voce, having apparently found a theme. "You . . .

you crazy American bitch. I . . . I will find you, and beat you . . . beat you to death, you crazy whore."

Fat chance. Old Otto couldn't catch her on her worst day, but he wasn't the one she was worried about, not on this deal.

"I don't know what you are looking for," he went on, "but there is *nothing*, I tell you, *nothing* here."

Yes, there was. He hadn't hauled his butt to Denver empty-handed. He'd come to make a deal, expecting to walk away with five hundred thousand dollars for a painting worth two million, if it could have been sold at a legitimate auction.

Sitting back on the edge of the bed, she quickly quartered the room, looking for an art case, or a mailing tube, or something, anything, that might hold the Meinhard.

Four years of following the painting. Six months of following Otto, including the four weeks since she'd gotten involved, the four weeks needed to set up a "sale" in Denver, and about five minutes in a hotel room to put seven decades of loss right—not to mention saving her dad's butt. Again.

If she could find the painting.

Dammit. Esme let out a short sigh and closed the knife, her gaze searching the room again, more slowly. All Otto had brought with him, that she could see, was the suitcase and the clothes on his back.

She dropped a glance at the mostly-naked man trussed at her feet. Without the black leather thong he'd strapped on with all its buckles and snaps, he'd be completely naked.

She was so grateful for the thong.

The rest of his clothes were in a neatly folded stack on a chair next to the bed—except for his suit jacket.

She looked to the open armoire near the door leading out into the hall. Sure enough, he'd hung up his jacket, and it was looking very tidy. *Very tidy, indeed, and rather stiff.*

Pushing off the bed, she walked over to the armoire and reopened the knife in a single smooth move.

"No," Otto said from the floor, panic rising in his voice, his understanding of the situation finally dawning. "No. No. No, you...you crazy whore. *Nein.*"

Oh, yes, she thought.

"Y-you can't. You don't know. You can't...no, no. Not the Meinhard."

Yes, the Meinhard. She came to a stop in front of the armoire.

"*Sí, policía.*" The man outside the door was talking again, the guy with no towels.

Policía? Hell, it was possible, she guessed, and the last damn thing she needed was to get busted for vice.

"*Puedes abrir la puerta? Es muy importante—por favor,*" he said.

Puerta was door, and even she knew *importante* meant important. *Por favor* was another no-brainer—please.

Without a doubt, her time was running out fast. He was obviously speaking to somebody with a key, and given his choice of language, she was guessing one of the maids. Everybody manning the front desk spoke English.

Without rushing, she didn't waste a second, taking hold of Otto's suit jacket and neatly slicing open the side seam. Her hand went in between the silk lining and the English tweed, and her smile came out—*voilà!* Success.

On the floor, Otto was apoplectic, twisting and turning, struggling against his bonds.

"*No,*" he insisted. "You cannot...*cannot* leave me like this. Cut me loose...*goddamn* you."

She slipped the painting free from its hiding place and closed her knife. Bold strokes of red, orange, gray, and green on copper were visible beneath a protective sheath inside a narrow frame, a blue dress, a woman's face smudged in pink—she'd done it, recovered the Meinhard.

Pocketing her knife first, she began unsnapping the latches on the thin case she'd brought with her in the white vinyl tote. She was heading toward the window that opened onto the alley even as she was sliding the painting into the case.

"*Du verstehst nichts!*" the old man all but growled in frustration.

Whatever.

She met his eyes for a brief moment as she passed him, then wished she hadn't. Otto was so hung up in his leashes, he'd had to twist himself to an unnatural angle to pin her with his gaze—and he was melting in fear, the sweat running off him, following the fatty folds of his body.

"*Sie kommt . . . lass mich lohs, du Hündin!*" He pulled against the leash tied to the bed. "*Sie kommt sofort!*"

He was afraid. She understood that much, if not his actual words, and yeah, she would have been afraid in his situation, too.

The Oxford was an old historical hotel, and the windows did open. In room 215, where fifty bucks to the reservation clerk had guaranteed Otto would be put, the window not only opened, it opened onto an old fire escape which she'd personally checked out two nights ago. It had held her then, and it held her tonight.

By the time she heard the commotion of the no-towel-guy and the maid discovering a dog-collared, thong-clad foreigner short-leashed to the bed, she was in the alley, disappearing into the shadows.

CHAPTER TWO

Sonuvabitch, Johnny thought when the maid finally opened the door. He took the room in with a glance: one mostly naked guy wearing a dog collar leashed to the bed; one destroyed suitcase sliced open every which way; absolutely zero size-four hookers; and one open window. His gaze slid over the suit jacket hanging in the closet and the neatly split seam, and he guessed Easy Alex had gotten whatever she'd come for—and she'd gotten it quick.

Behind him, the maid let out a small scream and ran back down the hall. He understood perfectly.

He also understood the next thing he heard, spoken by a woman the maid must have run into on her headlong flight.

"*Entschuldigung*," the woman said in a high, light voice with a singsong accent not normally associated with the German language. *Excuse me*.

Johnny crossed the room in five long strides, heading for the open window and reminding himself never to buy a black leather thong. Dudes did not look good in black leather thongs. All the proof he needed was squirming around on the floor, swearing in German, handcuffed and hog-tied.

Geezus, and he'd thought he'd seen it all. Fifteen years of running wild on the streets of Denver, four years of busting his butt in the Steele Street garages, and another five working hard in Uncle Sam's army, most of it spent fighting in the world's hottest spots, and yeah, he'd seen some pretty disturbing shit, the kind that stuck with a guy.

And now this poor slob on the floor wearing a spiked dog collar—*fuck*—Johnny figured he was going to be stuck with that damn image until he drew his last breath.

A small grin curved the corner of his mouth. *Geezus. People.* They never failed to amaze him. And Esme, good God, she'd frickin' *hog-tied* this guy in damn near record time. He could have used her in Afghanistan.

He got to the window and checked the alley.

Sure enough, the little size-four hooker was hoofing it toward Sixteenth, still limping, her two-inch black patent-leather platform heels snap-snapping on the alley asphalt.

Johnny didn't hesitate. He was through the window and heading down the fire escape before she could get away from him. Dog-boy was the hotel's problem, not his, and if they wanted to track down the hooker, they could start with the valet, a fact of street life they knew as well as any vice cop on the force. He just wanted to get to her first.

At Sixteenth, Esme turned northwest and went half a block to Wynkoop before turning southwest again. There were plenty of people on the streets in LoDo on a Friday night in August. It was easy to blend in, keep his distance, and still keep her in sight. When she turned into an alcove on the east side of Wynkoop, he closed in.

She wasn't going to be glad to see him. He didn't have any illusions about that. She'd hit the skids, turning sadistic tricks and stealing from her johns for a living, and he'd become one of the most elite and highly skilled soldiers in the world. It was the only reason he'd been tagged for SDF, not because he'd grown up in Denver and knew the guys. The personal association was a bonus, not a prerequisite. Johnny knew who and what he was, and so did Dylan Hart. Dylan knew how he'd been trained, where he'd been, what he'd done, and how he'd survived. It was more than enough to earn him a slot on the team—and Dylan knew that, too.

Methamphetamines, Johnny guessed, crossing Sixteenth at Wynkoop. Maybe crack cocaine, maybe heroin. Whatever had derailed Esme Alden's life was probably something she was popping, putting up her nose, or shooting into her veins. He'd seen enough drug-induced destruction to know the score, and nothing else could have sunk her so low.

At least that was his best guess until he reached the alcove.

Two glass doors with transoms were set back from

the sidewalk, with the words *FABER BUILDING* and a date, *1937*, chiseled in stone on the lintel above them. Flanked by an Oriental rug store on one side, and a pizza place called The Joint on the other, the doors each opened onto a long set of stairs leading up to the building's upper floors—two doors, but there wasn't any guesswork involved in which one she'd taken. B & B INVESTIGATIONS, ROBERT BAINBRIDGE, PROP. was painted in gold letters on the north door, along with three other businesses.

Yeah, Johnny remembered her old man had been a private investigator working for Bainbridge, and he remembered one day back in high school when Christian Hawkins, the SDF operative known as Cristo on the streets of Denver and Superman everywhere else, had let him know some gumshoe from B & B was snooping around, asking questions about him. Her old man's instincts had been good. Johnny had definitely had designs on the PI's daughter. He never had known, though, what Mr. Alden could have come up with, other than the same facts everybody already knew about Juan Ramos—that he'd spent time in juvie, dropped out of school twice before he'd decided to stick it out, and that he'd been with his older brother the night Domingo had been killed in City Park, capped by a Parkside Blood in a turf war.

Old news.

But Esme Alden dressing up like a hooker to do some work for her father—well, that was good news, in a bad sort of way, if that's what had been going on at the Oxford. And if that was what had been going on, what the hell was her old man thinking? Sending her to deal with guys like that German? For that matter, what the hell was Bainbridge thinking? Of course, Robert Bainbridge had to be in his eighties by now, maybe even his nineties. He'd been older than dirt since forever, so maybe he wasn't thinking too clearly about anything anymore.

Johnny stepped back onto the sidewalk and looked up. Of the eight windows stretching across the second floor above the rug store, two were lit. He stepped back into the alcove and pressed all the intercom buttons next to the north door.

"Carlson Services," a man answered one of the intercoms.

"Delivery," Johnny said, giving it his best shot, and a couple of seconds later, the door buzzed.

Esme closed the door of B & B Investigations behind her and immediately pulled the heart-and-sequin shirt off over the top of her head. The gloves came next. She didn't bother to turn on the lights. The streetlamps on Wynkoop gave off enough light for her to see the main office, not that there was much to see beyond a bunch of old filing cabinets, a couple of beat-up desks, and a couple of mismatched, overstuffed chairs she knew were tucked in the corners somewhere. A door flanked by two bookcases led into another, smaller office, Robert Bainbridge's private office, otherwise known as her father's storage room. There was no Robert Bainbridge at B & B Investigations anymore. Failing health had landed him in a nursing home a few years back, and his business had been hanging by a financial thread ever since, a situation that had taken an even sharper downhill turn since her father's ill-fated involvement with the Mountaineer Dog Track, a badass bookie in town named Franklin Bleak, and the truly hapless Otto Von Lindberg.

She had the painting now, though, and that was a start toward sorting this mess out. Once she made her delivery of the painting to Isaac Nachman, Otto wouldn't have any choice but to hightail his deviant butt back to San Francisco to deal with his boss as best he may. Esme didn't envy him the job. Erich Warner didn't suffer fools gladly, and he suffered losers even less well.

Tossing the shirt and gloves onto a chair, she checked her watch.

Eight-thirty. The night was still young, and she was on schedule—a ridiculously tight schedule. Getting all her players in place in time to meet Franklin Bleak's deadline had left her with a very small window of opportunity.

The sudden buzzing of the intercom on the security system brought her to a standstill, all her senses on alert. Then the intercom in the office next door buzzed. When she heard Pete Carlson buzz back, she relaxed.

Pizza delivery, she thought. Pete liked his Friday night pizza, The Joint's version of Chicago-style. She'd gone over and shared it with him more than once as a kid, when her dad had been working late and her mom had been pulling the night shift at the hospital. Nothing had changed there either. Her mom still worked the night shift at Denver General.

Bending over, she released the straps on her platform heels and kicked them off her feet. Timing was everything tonight. As long as she kept moving, she could pull this deal off. On her way across the office, she lowered the zipper on her skirt and let it fall to the floor.

It hadn't been Otto on the intercom. She knew that for damn sure, and if by some chance, for whatever reason, somebody had been tailing her tonight, they were hell and gone out of luck if they thought they were going to find a shopworn hooker with a limp in the Faber Building. That girl was disappearing fast.

As she passed her desk, she leaned over and hit the play button on the phone, then continued on to the bathroom, where she did turn on a light. She set the white vinyl tote on the floor, keeping it close, and left the door open, so she could hear the messages come off the machine.

The first one was dearly predictable.

"Esme, you're not answering your cell, honey, and I need you to stop at the Sooper's to pick up your father's prescription and a watermelon. Aunt Nanna forgot to get a watermelon for the twins' birthday tomorrow. Everyone is just thrilled that you were able to get home for the party. And that's the Sooper's just off Federal, not the new one. Oh, just a second..."

The line went quiet for a moment, then her mom came back on. *"Okay, honey, I just pulled into the hospital, and I've got to get to work. Don't forget the watermelon. Thanks, baby."*

Geezus, her mother was so clueless, so sweet and clueless, and that was for the best. Burt Alden worked hard to keep her in the dark, with varying degrees of success, and far be it from Esme to shine a klieg light on her father's less-than-kosher activities. She loved her mother too much for that—but a watermelon? Honest to God, there was a helluva lot more at stake tonight than a damn watermelon, and she sure as hell hadn't come all the way from Seattle for Danny and Deb's seventeenth birthday party. Not that she didn't love them, but *geez*.

The answering machine beeped for the second message.

"Burt, this is Thomas in Chicago. I have the name you're looking for. Call me."

Score, Esme thought, kneeling down and reaching into her tote for her personal cell phone. She'd needed that name days ago. She'd left her anonymous, prepaid phone in the tote, the one whose number she'd given to the Oxford's valet.

The machine beeped again, and a third recorded message came on.

"This call is for . . . BURT ALDEN . . . A courtesy reminder for your dental appointment on . . ."

She punched a couple of buttons on her phone, speed-dialing her dad. Then she tucked the phone between her ear and shoulder and began shimmying out of the fishnet hose.

"...*MONDAY, AUGUST 23, at* . . . *two o'clock* P.M. . . . *with*. . . *DR. STEVENS* . . ."

"Dad," she said, when he answered. "Thomas called from Chicago. He's got the name we need. Call him. Then call me back."

She pulled a black half-slip off the towel rod and pulled it up to her waist.

"Did you get the Meinhard?" he asked, his voice tense with the strain of the last few months. His deal with Otto had hit the fan in San Francisco, and he'd been playing a game of high-stakes pickup sticks ever since—and losing, up until she'd come on board.

"Yeah. I got it," she said, pulling a meticulously tailored black skirt off one of the hangers on the door and stepping into it.

"And Otto Von Lindberg?" he asked.

"Compromised." She finished zipping the skirt and shrugged into a shoulder holster, slipping it on over her red push-up bra.

"And you're okay?"

"Yeah, Dad. I'm okay." He knew what her plan had been—and he knew she'd been right, no matter how much he'd disliked it. "Get the name and call me back."

She ended the call and set the phone on the sink.

There was no way to play nice and come out ahead, not in this game, and still, Von Lindberg had gotten off lightly. He was alive, a condition she wasn't putting any money on him maintaining, not once Warner found out old Otto had lost the Meinhard. She'd gone up against Warner before, a couple of times, and both times had been intensely educational. Hard, hard lessons had been learned.

Like in Bangkok eighteen months ago.

Yeah, she thought. That had been a real damn touch-and-go situation, real damn touch-and-go. If there was any one reason to permanently get out of the art-recovery game, its name was Erich Warner.

Christ. She instinctively squeezed her right hand into a fist, feeling all five fingers band together— and she was grateful, so damn grateful. The scars on her right shoulder were another matter. There was no getting away from them, no fixing them. They were a brand, the price she'd paid for not being quick enough to make a clean getaway.

So what was she doing here, getting within a thousand miles of another of Warner's deals? He'd kill her this time, if he caught her, and that was if she was lucky. If she wasn't lucky, if he was in a bad mood, which she had all but guaranteed by stealing his Meinhard, well, then things would get messy again—damn awful messy, and then they'd get worse.

Geezus. What in the hell *was* she doing here, dressing up like a hooker and hog-tying some guy in a thong and a dog collar at the Oxford Hotel? The act itself was at the top end of her EZ scale, but the fallout—hell, the fallout could be her very own personal nightmare, the one that snuck up on her in her dreams when her defenses were down.

She swore softly under her breath. Burt Alden had a lifelong habit of getting in over his head and more often than not sinking like a stone. But he'd never been sunk the way Warner could sink him— and that was why she was well within Warner's thousand-mile limit. Her father didn't have a clue what he was up against. Bainbridge would have known. Robert Bainbridge would have connected the dots on the Meinhard deal, realized Otto was no more than a messenger boy, and been on the lookout for the big fish, the shark, but Burt didn't consult with Mr. Bainbridge anymore.

Burt hadn't consulted with Esme either, not until he'd been going under for the third time, and the minute he'd mentioned Otto Von Lindberg as his connection to the Meinhard, she'd known exactly what he was up against, and exactly who he was dealing with—and she'd known she had to get in on the deal. She was the Alden who kept her head above water. She never sank.

Not ever.

She'd come damn close in Bangkok, closer than she ever wanted to be again, but even with the pain, and her guts churning, and her brain edging perilously close to panic override, she hadn't slipped beneath the waves.

She was here tonight to make sure her father didn't either. A month ago, she'd taken his Meinhard fiasco and started turning it into an operation, a mission, with her in charge. It's what she brought to the table, the ability to conceive of and execute an effective plan. It was why the people who hired her paid top dollar for the privilege. It was why she ran her own investigations out of Seattle with a partner she trusted down to the marrow of her bones, far away from her dad's day-to-day peccadilloes.

Except for today.

Today was Burt Alden's last outing as a PI. She was putting him out of business. Today, she tied up all of his loose ends, cut him out of the loop, and set him on the road to retirement. All she had to do was deliver the painting to Isaac Nachman, redeem the bad paper Nachman was holding on her dad, walk away with what was left of the reward money, and pay off the bookie Burt had hocked his soul to, the badass Franklin Bleak.

Last, but far from least, she had to convince Mr. Bleak to call off his dogs instead of following through on his threat to make an example out of Mr. Burton Alden, kind of a body-slamming, bonebreaking, bloody-beating example, or even something more lethal if Mr. Bleak got the urge. Apparently, overdue payment on bad bets was all it took to give Franklin Bleak the urge to commit any number of sins—and that was her dad's personal nightmare.

Between the two of them, it was looking like a real rough night all the way around. *Geezus.* It was going to take every last favor she had to get her dad out of this mess. With luck, the only losers tonight would be Otto and Warner, which was a crazy bad choice of enemies to make, but neither Otto nor Warner had ever heard of Burt Alden.

It was the only smart move her father had ever

made, to work under the auspices of Robert Bainbridge, and since Bainbridge had been out of the game, to trade on the old man's reputation by actually using his name. Every bookie in the northern hemisphere knew her father, but Otto Von Lindberg thought he was working with Robert Bainbridge. Esme was doing her damnedest to keep it that way—and if it all went to hell, she had backup. She had Dax Killian.

Before she put on her jacket, she slipped her Para-Ordnance CCW .45 out of the vinyl tote, checked the chamber, and slid it into the holster. She immediately felt better. She didn't like "carrying" in a purse. She liked her pistol on her, in a holster. For the kind of people she'd be dealing with tonight, she needed protection, and she wanted it close. Reaching back into the tote, she pulled out her knife and slid the clip inside the top of the skirt.

She shrugged into the suit's matching jacket and checked the drape, making sure it fell in an unbroken line to her waist, concealing her weapon. The jacket was low-cut, the lapels meeting at a set of two buttons that she'd had tailored into snap closures. Buttons were too slow.

The machine beeped again and ran some static, indicating a hang-up caller.

She reached for a pair of black high heels. The suit was supremely elegant, expensive, couture, and so were the heels. Tilting her head to one side, she removed a pair of cheap silver-toned hoops from her ears. She replaced them with diamond studs, then slipped a string of pearls around her neck.

The static came to an end on the office answering machine, and it beeped.

"Hey, bad girl, all good on this end ..."

Her gaze shot to the phone at the sound of her partner's voice, deep and easy. That was Dax Killian, cool, calm, collected, and the best damn cousin a girl ever had. She needed to give him a call as soon as she got off the phone with her dad.

"I'm leaving Colorado Springs now, ETA Denver at twenty-two-hundred hours. See you soon."

She checked her watch again. He was on the road and on his way.

Thank God, she thought, finishing with the clasp on the necklace, then reaching up into her hair and starting to pull the pins out of her mussed-up twist. She was on schedule, and things were going exactly according to plan, but she had a feeling, a nagging kind of unease way deep down inside that had been building all day. Normal tension, she'd told herself, the kind that keeps you sharp. But the longer it had gone on, the more she'd gotten to thinking it was a damn good thing Dax had come home with her to Denver, old stomping grounds for both of them— because her uneasy feeling was telling her she just might need all the help she could get to get through the night in one piece.

She pulled another pin out, and then another.

Dammit. She hated it when she had that feeling.

CHAPTER THREE

There was a God.

Johnny had never doubted it, not really. He was a good Catholic boy, one of the best, but verifiable instances of divine grace and intervention were still welcome and only helped cement his faith.

He was currently in the midst of one of those instances—*Shimmy, shimmy cocoa pop. Shimmy, shimmy rock.*

Fishnet.

Coming off into a pile at her feet.

It was a gift, with Easy Alex stepping into a black satin slip and about half coming out of her red push-up bra, and if she wasn't the earthly embodiment of divine grace, he didn't know what was.

Red lace panties.

He hadn't known. The hem of her hooker skirt had just covered them. But he'd seen them now, reflected in a double-hung window overlooking Wynkoop, the one closest to the B & B Investigations office bathroom where she was doing her reverse striptease.

She couldn't know—not that every move she made was revealed in the window glass, just like a mirror, and she couldn't know someone was standing in the low-lit hallway with a clear view through the window in the door.

And he wasn't the guy who was going to tell her, not that he'd seen her in her underwear, but he was going to let her know he was there—in a minute, once she got herself dressed. His hand was raised, closed in an easy fist, ready to knock on the door as soon as she put on the suit jacket he could see reflected in the window.

But the jacket wasn't what she went for next.

Amazingly, what she slipped into next was something he slipped into on a regular basis. Nothing could have surprised him more, that he and Esme Alden wore the same thing under their clothes— and he'd never been within a hundred miles of slipping on a pair of red lace panties.

Well, actually, he had kind of gotten tangled up in a pair one night in the rear bucket seats of a 1960 Chrysler "Letter Car," a 300-F. The car had been a brute, beautiful and black, sleekly menacing with its 413-cid wedge-head V-8 and tail fins. The girl had been a pure heartbreaker from the get-go. She'd slain him in the back of that car, teased him to the point of no return and then taken him straight over the edge. That she'd only done it once and dumped him for a premed student at the university up in Boulder had damn near driven him crazy.

He was so goddamned glad he wasn't nineteen anymore. Not that he felt overly in control of his re-action to seeing Easy Alex doing her Victoria's Secret model impression.

She'd filled out a bit in the last few years. Quite a bit. What he was looking at couldn't all be the push-up bra—though he did love a push-up bra. The only thing better was no bra.

When she pulled an autoloading pistol out of her ratty white tote bag and checked the chamber be-fore slipping the gun into her shoulder holster, he lowered his hand. The girl was carrying, "cocked, locked, and loaded."

Johnny instinctively checked the hall, looking in both directions. Carlson Services was behind him, down at the end of the hall closest to the stairs. The other offices were dark, but Esme Alden was ex-pecting trouble.

He returned his gaze to her reflection in the win-dow. Or maybe, like him, she made a habit of being ready for trouble whether she was expecting it or not.

Extra ready, he thought, watching her slide a folding knife inside the waistband of her skirt. She was starting to look dangerous—damned danger-ous.

So what was this all about tonight, he wondered, with her and her weapons and the German? What had she been after in the Oxford Hotel?

And did he really want to know? That was always

the sticking point. Johnny'd learned a long time ago not to ask questions he wasn't prepared to hear the answers to, good or bad. Life was funny that way, real life. A guy could be so goddamned sure of what was going on, and then get an answer straight out of left field.

It happened.

And given what he'd already seen tonight, Esme Alden owned the lease on left field. *Geezus*. The German in the Oxford had been strapped into a leather thong, and she'd leashed him to the bed— short-leashed. No wonder the guy had sounded a little strained.

Walk away, a voice in his head said. *Back up,* chingaleto. *Get your ass down the stairs and back out on the street.*

He knew that voice. He'd heard it hundreds of times. It was the voice of reason, and he was a reasonable guy.

And yet he didn't budge an inch. He stayed right where he was and continued watching her.

She shrugged into the black jacket, slipped on a pair of black high heels, and changed her jewelry. He could hear the murmuring of the answering machine running through its messages.

Busy girl, he thought.

A little black suit, "catch me, fuck me" heels, and a string of pearls—she looked good. Damn good.

Too good for him to walk away. She was Esme Alden, the hot crush of his teenage years, and he'd

just seen her in red lace panties and a push-up bra.
No guy was walking away from that.

He raised his hand again and knocked.

Geezus. Esme's heart damn near stopped. Then it
occurred to her that it was probably Pete at the
door with his pizza, coming over to share.

Geezus. She took a breath and finished putting
the last bobby pin in her sleek new twist before
turning off the light and stepping to the edge of the
bathroom door.

Peeking around the side, she noted a couple of
things right off the bat: They needed better lighting
in the hall, and it wasn't Pete standing out there.

Picking her phone back up and slipping it into
the pocket on her skirt, she looked back to the office door. She couldn't see the guy very clearly
through the window, but she could see the outline
of his body, and she was guessing five feet ten,
maybe five eleven. Pete topped out at five six, and
with years of Friday night pizza under his belt, he
was as big around as he was tall.

This guy was long, lean, and broad through the
shoulders. He was also unknown and unexpected,
two things she didn't take any chances with under
the best of circumstances. Tonight hardly qualified
for the best of anything except pure, unadulterated
trouble.

Crap. Walking quietly and quickly across the
room, she stopped to hit the off button on the answering machine, and then she made a beeline for

the back office. Tucked into the end of the hall, Bainbridge's old lair made the short end of the "L" of the two-office suite. From the window in his private entrance, she'd have a clear view of who was standing in the hallway.

An advantage that proved unnecessary when the man knocked again.

"Esme? Hey, it's John Ramos."

She stumbled to a stop and whirled around to stare at the door. *Geezo freakin' crap. John Ramos? Johnny Ramos?* The name registered instantly, along with a face.

"From East High School. We graduated together."

Totally unnecessary information. She hadn't forgotten Johnny Ramos, oh, hell, no. Not in this lifetime, she wouldn't.

"I, uh, heard you were working with your dad now. Thought I'd drop by and see if you could help me with a problem," he said from outside in the hall.

Good God. Johnny freakin' Ramos. Out in the hall.

Of course, out in the hall. Hell, he'd spent half his life out in the hall, especially at Campbell Junior High, especially during seventh-grade social studies class. She'd gotten sent out in the hall with him once, her one and only time in the hall ever, the two of them put there to "work things out," and her poor little thirteen-year-old heart had barely survived the experience.

Ms. Trent had banished them to a pair of desks

on either side of the doorway, leaving a bare three feet between them, thirty-six inches, not enough distance to insulate Esme from Johnny's dark-eyed gaze and the heat that seemed to come out of nowhere and slam into her whenever their eyes met. There sure as hell hadn't been any "working things out" going on. She hadn't opened her mouth, not once. He'd been so bad, dangerously bad, even at thirteen, given the crowd he'd run with, especially his older brother, Dom Ramos, and for reasons she hadn't understood, out of all the girls in the seventh grade, he'd chosen her to torture and tease.

Of course, eventually, she'd figured out what he was after—certainly by the time he'd asked her to the prom at the end of their junior year. Maybe even before that, like when he'd punched out Kevin Harrell in the locker bay—and for sure by the summer after graduation, when she'd ended up in the backseat of his car, a hot green, incredibly fast old-style muscle car he'd called "Roxanne." Oh, yes, by then she'd definitely figured out what he'd wanted, and if she'd had any doubts, he'd pretty much cleared them up in between unhooking her bra and unzipping his pants. He wanted her, wanted her to be his girl, and he'd wanted it since the first time he'd laid eyes on her in Ms. Trent's social studies class way back in seventh grade.

And he was out in the hall.

She took a breath. Roxanne. Yeah. That was right, a Dodge Challenger, 1971, very hot, very fast, and completely underappreciated by her at the time, but she'd long since learned how rare and wonderful the car had been, and exactly what Johnny Ramos had saved her from by putting himself between her and Kevin Harrell that day in the locker bay.

Kevin, a current resident of the state penitentiary in Canon City, had been twice his size, but there had been no contest in the brief, violent encounter. The older boy had shoved her up against the lockers, pressing his body against hers, talking trash and trying to jerk her skirt up to her waist, and for a few seconds, she'd been frozen in fear, the breath knocked out of her. Then someone had called him out, their voice harsh, the words insistent, spoken in gutter Spanish and full of threat.

Kevin had turned to face his challenger, and it had all been over. One punch, brick hard and lightning fast.

An iron fist, her dad had called it, being able to knock out somebody that size with one hit. Johnny had also had a tattoo, she'd discovered in Roxanne's backseat, a tattoo with its own claim to iron.

God, that had been an experience. Definitely. Being in the backseat of a car with Johnny Ramos had been the single most educational experience of her life up to that point, and maybe even a little bit beyond.

Iron tattoo, iron fist, a reputation crossing over into misdemeanors edged in felonies, if the rumors about how he'd "acquired" the Challenger were true—and he was standing out in the hall.

Unbelievable.

And what in the hell was she going to do about it? He obviously knew she was in here—which just opened up a whole other can of worms, one she was simply going to ignore, like how maybe his was the voice she'd heard outside the door at the Oxford, like maybe she had been tailed, which made her more than a little irritated with herself, a whole lot more. It also meant he had way more information about her than she was comfortable with him having—like the whole hooker scene. *Dammit*. Dax had taught her better than that.

"Esme?"

Hell. She couldn't wait him out. She had a schedule to keep, which only left her with Option B: Play along with his "heard you were working with your dad" line, and get rid of him.

Yeah, that's what she'd do, say her hellos, hand him one of her dad's business cards, give him the office hours—without actually telling him she was shutting the place down—and shoo him along, back out onto the street, which is where she'd heard he'd ended up—out on the street. Someone she'd known in high school had mentioned it, about how so-and-so who worked in LoDo had seen Johnny Ramos going in and out of the alley called Steele Street. As she had recalled, the only thing in that alley was an old garage, a place that at one time had been the most notorious chop shop in Denver.

Esme'd hoped for better for him. He'd been a smart kid, far smarter than his academic record had implied, but a lot of things can go wrong when a person grows up wild—and Johnny Ramos had been running wild for as long as she'd known him. His older brother hadn't even made it to twenty before he'd been gunned down in City Park.

God, that had been awful, she remembered, especially for Johnny. He'd been there when it happened.

"I actually could use a little help here tonight, Esme," he said, still trying to talk his way inside, and she wondered how in the world she'd failed to recognize his voice in the Oxford, the calm edge of it, the deep, feathered undertones, the easy, measured cadence. Those hadn't changed. For all the craziness in his life, he'd had a steadiness about him, even at thirteen.

"All right, all right," she said, stepping over to the door, making sure her voice carried. "Hold your horses. I'm coming."

Yeah—play along and get rid of him. That was the best plan.

Taking a deep breath, Esme pulled the door open—and got hit by a freight train.

Full speed.

No brakes.

Two engines in front, and two engines in back.

No caboose.

Diesel powered. All locomotion.

Johnny Ramos, in the flesh, all grown up and looking like the stone-cold definition of every big bad boy she'd ever known, except better, harder, and like the last thing he needed was help, with anything. Oh, hell, no. One look said it all: This boy could take care of himself—in spades.

Criminy. Her breath was actually caught in her throat, an unprecedented reaction to a guy since . . . well, since the last time she'd seen him, naked in the backseat of the awesome Roxanne.

Perfect.

She couldn't breathe. Her heart was racing. He was standing in the hall, and all she could do was stand there in front of him, clutching the doorknob and praying for her brain to kick in.

CHAPTER FOUR

Oh-kay, Johnny thought, looking at the stunned expression on Esme Alden's face. *This is good...I think.*

Sure. Shell shock was good. It meant he wasn't what she'd expected, and that could only be good, considering that everyone from his parish priest on down to his guidance counselor had expected him to end up in prison before his twenty-first birthday.

"Esme. Hi. Good to see you." He gave her an easy smile and stuck out his hand. "You don't mind if I come in for a minute, do you?" Low-key, friendly, but not too friendly—that was him.

She responded automatically, putting her much smaller hand in his. Her grip was firm, her skin warm.

"John...Ramos, yes, well...come in, yes." She was slightly breathless, but given the night she'd had so far, he didn't blame her.

When she stepped back, he stepped into the office, and since she hesitated about what to do next, he did it for her, taking hold of the door and quietly closing it behind him, which left them in the dark—not such a bad place to be with a woman wearing red lace panties and a push-up bra.

But that wasn't why he was here—or maybe it was. He wouldn't have followed Liz Malone, a great girl from his twelfth-grade chemistry class, or Benita Montoya from calculus, or Janessa Kaliski from English...okay, he might have followed Janessa Kaliski, if he'd seen her on the street dressed in next to nothing and platform heels. But he wouldn't have followed her into a hotel, climbed down a fire escape, and jogged through an alley to catch up with her.

No. He'd done that because it had been Easy Alex he was trailing.

"I...uh, guess I should explain right up front," she said with an absent gesture, carefully backing her way toward one of the desks in the office, one high-heeled step at a time. "I don't *actually* work for my father."

There were two desks in the office, two bookcases, and four filing cabinets, another door besides the bathroom door, two overstuffed chairs, and enough light coming in the windows for him to see it all.

"Well, I do, *actually*," she was going on, "but I don't do my dad's kind of work. I do secretarial stuff...like filing...and stuff...so, I, uh, don't know how I could help you...with anything, I mean...like a problem."

Yeah, right. Every secretary he knew made a habit of checking the chamber on their .45 before they filed the day's invoices. So now he had the German, the hog-tying, the theft, the weapons, and the first lie.

The night was definitely getting interesting.

"But I can, uh..." She paused for a second as she leaned over the desk and switched on a lamp. "I can give you one of my dad's business cards."

"Thanks, that'll be great," he said, and she gave him a bland little weak sort of smile, before turning and rummaging through a catchall box on top of the desk.

Behind her back, he grinned. She'd always been the queen of the bum's rush, and it was nice to know some things never changed, but she was hell out of luck tonight. Any woman who needed a .45 after hog-tying a guy in a hotel room was probably more trouble than she was worth. As a matter of fact, he was absolutely positive of it, and yet he was hooked, like a big old fish with the bait stuck in his gullet.

Little Miss Goody Two-shoes packing a pistol. That was his line of work, his territory, and he couldn't help but wonder what she was doing in it. Back when they'd been in school together, the closest they'd gotten to common ground had been in the backseat of Hawkins's 1971 Challenger, a beautiful beast named Roxanne. He hadn't seen Esme since, and in between then and now, she was supposed to have become some kind of kick-ass accountant, or corporate lawyer, or at least have saved the whales. She'd always been going on about saving the whales. Never in a million years would he have guessed "gun-toting hooker" would end up on her resume, or even "gun-toting hooker impersonator."

"Somebody told me you'd moved to Seattle," Johnny said, looking around the office, and there was just no denying it. The place was a dump, frayed on every edge. "I think it might have been Toby Eaton."

"Toby Eaton," she repeated, still rummaging through the box. "Sure. I...uh, remember him. Good old Toby. Wasn't his dad the one who owned the hardware store over on Thirteenth?"

"Did," he said. "They lost their lease on the building a few years back. It's all condos on that corner now, and Toby is selling used Subarus up on Sheridan. Funny, isn't it."

She looked up from her search. "Funny?"

"How life can throw you a curve," he explained. "Toby always thought he'd be working for his dad, selling screwdrivers, not shilling Subarus up on Sheridan."

One of her eyebrows arched briefly, a nonplussed expression passing over her face before she dropped her gaze back to the desk.

"Yes," she said. "That's...uh, too bad, old Toby getting a rough deal like that." Her tone implied otherwise, like the difference between selling screwdrivers and Subarus could be summed up in one word—tonnage—and probably didn't have a damn thing to do with fate or thrown curves or legitimate bar-stool philosophy.

"Kind of the opposite of you, I guess."

"Me?" Esme's gaze came back to his, but with a definite wariness in it this time.

"Yeah," he said. "You're the last person I would have thought would end up working for their dad. So this must be your desk over here." He moseyed over to the corner of the office. "The one next to the filing cabinets, for when you do your filing."

Yeah, he said it with a straight face, even though the cabinets didn't look like anything had been filed in them in the last hundred years. They were four of the junkiest damn things he'd ever seen, gray metal, dented, heavily scratched, a couple of broken handles. Everything in the office looked old and beat-up, except for the sleek black laptop set precisely in the middle of a cleaned-off area on top of the corner desk—and her.

Up close, she looked amazing. The girl had great lines, about five feet five inches of mind-bending curves wrapped in a suit that fit her like a glove, and he was upping the ante on her ass to a very nice size six. All that leg in fishnet had skewed his first calculation, but bent over a desk, hell, he didn't make mistakes when a woman was bent over a desk.

Actually, he didn't make mistakes when a woman was bent over anything. He had that contingent covered. Literally.

Size six. He was putting the bank on it.

He picked a pen up off the desk. It had a picture of a pinup girl on it, and when he tilted it upside down, her clothes slid off. Glancing over, he caught Esme still watching him, but with something a little more calculating than wariness in her eyes.

"You can keep the pen, if you like," she said. "Compliments of B & B Investigations."

He looked down at the pen again and noticed the lettering going down the side, next to the girl—"B & B Investigations—Your One-Stop Undercover Shop—We Snoop 4 U"—and a phone number.

It was the tackiest damn thing he'd ever seen.

"Catchy motto," he said, looking back up.

"My dad's a marketing genius, comes up with all sorts of things," Esme said, straightening from the desk, the elusive business card in her hand. ·

Johnny just bet he did. Burt was her dad's name. He remembered now. Burt Alden. And it looked to Johnny like the man had come up with everything except a decent living.

Esme was doing all right by herself, though— doing something somewhere other than this second-floor dump in the Faber Building. She was wearing couture. He'd bet the bank on that, too. He had a friend, Skeeter Bang Hart, former street rat, current kick-ass operator and high-class fashionista, who bought designer clothes the way kids bought candy, and in Skeeter's world, shoes had names. He was betting Esme's shoes had a name. He didn't know what in the hell that name might be, but from the looks of them, it probably started with Kate, or Stewart, or Manolo.

"Here's his card," she said, extending her hand. "He usually has the office open by ten A.M."

"Thanks." Johnny stepped forward and took the card—and there they were, standing close to each other, with traffic noise coming up from the street, and the desk lamp bathing her face with soft creamy light.

"I'll . . . uh, let him know to expect your call."

"Great." Maybe they were standing too close.

Yeah, he was sure of it, because he was having a little trouble taking his eyes off her, and because suddenly he was remembering the satiny texture of her skin, the way she'd tasted that night in Roxanne, and the way she'd felt in his arms—nubile.

Yeah, she'd pretty much defined the whole erotic concept of being nubile, at least for him. He'd heard the word a few times, and after those few glorious hours in Roxanne, he'd gone and looked it up. The actual definition had been a bit lacking to his way of thinking, but the word . . . the word itself was fine, extremely accurate. The way it felt in his mouth lined up precisely with the way she'd felt lying up against him, the give of her in his hands, the silky strength of her body—fulsome, curved, resilient, a force to be reckoned with, and yet tender, and so very soft.

And that image pretty much confirmed the excellent condition of his memory. He was running at a perfect one hundred and ten percent, all systems go. Great.

"Yes . . . well . . ." she said, her voice trailing off.

Well . . . yes . . . He needed to think here, come up

with something fast, or she was going to have him back out on the street in no time.

"Thanks...uh, for stopping by," she said. "We can always use the business."

Obviously, he thought, but he kept it to himself.

"I'd like to take you to dinner, if you haven't eaten, or buy you a drink, if you have." It wasn't original, and he just kind of blurted it out, but it was solid, something a girl could count on.

"Actually, I have an appointment, and I'm running a little late." She made a point of checking her watch. "So if you'll excuse me..."

An appointment? At nine o'clock on a Friday night?

Actually, he was going to have a little trouble excusing that, and if Esme Alden *actually* turned out to be some kind of high-end call girl, he was going to have to sit down and sort through the unsettling information with Christian Hawkins—Superman, second in command at Steele Street, owner of the beauteous Roxanne, and SDF's unofficial but widely used therapist. Hawkins knew things about women all the other guys could only surmise. Dylan was certainly useless in that capacity. He and Skeeter had been married for—hell, Johnny didn't know how long, a few years, and it didn't look to him like the boss had figured out too much about women, or he might have noticed he'd been holding the reins a little too tight on his girl. If he wasn't careful, Skeeter was going to flat-out break loose.

Kid was holding on to his wife, too, holding on

for the ride, but who could do anything else with Nikki? She was an artist, like quicksilver. Johnny had posed for her completely buck naked, the first time a couple of years ago, and a few times since, and he still wasn't sure if he'd ever quite recovered from the experience. He liked the paintings she'd done though, most of them dark angel paintings with him looking pretty badass. He liked them a lot. Nikki did, too. She'd picked one of the paintings of him for the poster of her latest exhibit, the Ironheart Angel. It would probably impress the hell out of Esme.

Sure it would—and he just happened to have the announcement Nikki had left for him at Steele Street in his back pocket. She and Kid had left for Los Angeles this morning, and he knew she was hoping he'd stop by the gallery and just sort of be there—getting stared at.

Right—just one of the perks of posing naked for a famous artist, having women show up to check you out. Not that they needed you there. Nikki didn't leave anything to the imagination, but Johnny had wondered if she kind of added a little something extra here and there. Even with paintings of himself to look at, the verdict was still out on that one.

"Well, maybe after your appointment then," he jumped back in, reaching around and checking his back pocket. Sure enough, he had the postcard announcement next to his wallet. "You could give me a call." He pulled out the postcard. He wasn't really floundering. This was a plan. "A friend of mine has some paintings showing at the Toussi Gallery on Seventeenth. There's going to be wine and cheese, that kind of stuff, tonight, and these things always go late. So, if you like, we could go and look around, check out the artwork, whenever you were free. It wouldn't matter what time, not really. I know the owner." He handed the postcard over to her—and if her answer had even a hint of "I'll be busy the rest of the night," he was heading straight back to Steele Street and knocking on Hawkins's door.

"You know Suzi Toussi?" Her eyebrows went up again, her expression slightly disbelieving.

Okay. More than slightly.

He wasn't insulted. There was no reason on earth for her to think he'd turned into anything other than the street gangster his guidance counselor had predicted.

"Yeah, I know Suzi, and she's still involved with the gallery," he said. "But the woman who owns it now is named Katya." Katya Hawkins, Superman's wife and mother of three, with another one on the way. Johnny wasn't the only one at SDF who was beginning to wonder if Christian and Katya were going for some kind of record.

"Uh, sure...Toussi's, that sounds like fun," Esme said, after another few seconds of looking him over. Then her gaze dropped to the postcard.

He didn't expect her to recognize him, not as the blood-streaked, tragically heroic angel Nikki had made him. For the postcard, Nikki had only used a portion of the painting, zooming in on his jaw and shoulder, with part of one wing showing. The feathers in the wing were broken and torn, and he didn't know why, but that was the part that disturbed him the most—not what Nikki had done to him, how she'd made him look so brutalized, but what she'd done to his wings. It just looked so fierce, like some maelstrom had gotten ahold of that angel and shaken him to his core—which, if he remembered correctly, and he did, was exactly how he'd felt when Nikki had gotten hold of him.

He guessed she was a pretty good artist. In fact, he knew she was an amazing artist.

"This is good . . . very good," Esme murmured, quietly echoing his thoughts. "Um, sure"—she looked up—"why not. Why don't you give me your number?"

She set the card on the desk and pulled her cell phone out of a pocket on her skirt. He recited the ten digits, watching her punch them into her phone's memory along with his name—and all the while, he knew she was lying through her teeth.

She wasn't going to call him, and suddenly it wasn't just curiosity motivating him, and it wasn't just his heated memories, or his teenage crush. Suddenly, she was a woman with a gun and something she'd stolen off a man in a hotel room, and she had an appointment she was damned serious about keeping.

Whatever was going on, Johnny had a feeling it had to do with her marketing genius of a father, and it was a bad feeling. He knew her. He'd spent six years in school with her, and he'd been paying attention, probably too much attention—but, man, she'd held it hard. She'd been more than book smart. She'd been able to think her way around things, book things, sure, but people and situations, too. East was a tough school. She shouldn't have lasted a week in those hallways, not looking the way she had, all cute middle-class white bread. But she'd done three years, and the only time anyone had ever gotten to her had been in that locker bay with Kevin Harrell—and that bastard hadn't gotten far.

She'd been the valedictorian of their class for a reason, and none of those reasons would have led her here. No way in hell did she work in this dump, and no matter where she worked, she didn't have pens with naked women on them lying around on her desk.

Christ. She had stolen goods, a .45, and an appointment. There wasn't a thing in that combination that didn't spell trouble in capital letters, and the one thing she didn't have, the one thing he hadn't seen anywhere since he'd first seen her up on Seventeenth, was backup.

He let his gaze drop down the length of her, and when he got to her feet, he stopped, his attention arrested. By whatever quirk of fate was out there, when she'd stepped over to the desk, she'd stepped right on top of her hooker skirt. It was under her slinky black high heel, and as he watched, she quietly and deliberately slid her foot across the carpet, dragging the small slip of leather and lace with her, until she could give it one small last push and make it disappear under the desk.

And she did it all without a word.

When she pulled her foot back from the desk, he looked up and caught her gaze. She knew he'd tailed her from the Oxford. She knew he knew about the German, the leash, the dog collar, and probably about the suit jacket she'd cut open, and man, oh, man, it didn't faze her in the least. Butter wouldn't have melted in her mouth.

Oh, she was a cool one, all right, but not cold. Her hair was warm honey gold, swept up in a Holly Golightly twist. Her mouth was softly pink and glossed, and her eyes were gray, a dozen shades of it, any one of them callable at will—and the one she was currently calling up was clear. Not storm gray, not arctic gray, nothing to do with ice or an emotion—just clear, pure, simple, clean gray. Pure and simple "I know what I'm doing, so don't get in my way" gray, and he was impressed as hell. What he'd seen in room 215 was none of his business. She couldn't have made it any plainer if she'd painted it on a billboard in big block letters: "Back off, big boy."

He knew women like her, had been in love with them most of his adult life, women like Skeeter Bang and the bodaciously dangerous Red Dog. Those two knew exactly what they were doing, and they really didn't need his help, especially if they had each other.

But Easy Alex had taken on the German alone, and nobody had been waiting for her in the Faber

Building. She was running a private game here—
and she was cutting him loose, pushing him out the
damn door. He had an emotion for that, but he
really didn't know what in the hell to call it.

Bottom line, though, this was her call, not his,
no matter how skeptical he was about her father,
her gun, and how she'd leashed that guy to the bed.
She was done with him, and he wasn't going to
learn anything more by hanging around the B & B
office, getting in her way and holding her up.

"If you want to get your things, I'll walk you out."
He didn't ask. It wasn't a question. He was walking
her out, end of story, and unless she threw herself
at his feet and begged for his help when they hit
the street, he was going to go back to his beer at the
Blue Iguana.

From the looks of her, he figured the odds on her
begging him for anything were zip and none.

Esme hesitated, but only for a second, before she
walked back to the bathroom. She knew what time
it was, and she knew she didn't have any to waste.
Good God, Johnny freakin' Ramos.

She had a handheld black light already in the
bathroom, and once she closed the door, she
turned it on. It would only take her a minute to
check the painting. The last thing she wanted was
to show up at Nachman's with a fake. The
Meinhard was her bargaining chip. She needed to
know she had a solid opening hand.

Reaching into the white vinyl tote, she removed

the thin metal case containing the Meinhard and popped it open. With a small screwdriver also from out of her tote, she loosened the wooden frame on the painting and lifted off the protective covering. One slow pass with the black light was all she needed, and as soon as she was finished, she reassembled the painting and the frame and put the piece back into the case.

The metal case measured precisely two by ten by fifteen inches, and when she got back to her dad's desk, she slipped it neatly inside a black leather messenger bag she'd designed for a courier contract she'd taken last May. The job had been to transport a rare manuscript from Presque Isle, Maine, to Bern, Switzerland, and it had gone without a hitch.

She zipped the interior pouch on the bag closed, securing the case inside, then buckled the outside straps.

John Ramos, standing right there next to her. That was a bit of a hitch, maybe more than a bit. *Cripes.* She'd seen the way he'd looked at her red leather skirt, and she didn't have a doubt in her mind that he'd been the *"policía"* at the Oxford, or that he'd followed her through the hotel room, or that he knew exactly what she'd done to Otto Von Lindberg.

Hell, for all she knew he *was* a policeman, undercover, off-duty, whatever. It was enough to make a girl sweat, if a girl ever sweated. Thank God, Esme didn't, never, not on the job.

The messenger bag had been constructed with a

net of very fine steel mesh sandwiched between its lining and the thick latigo leather. It also had a cipher lock connected to a steel cable running through the flap. She engaged the lock before slipping the bag's shoulder strap over her head and adjusting it across the front of her body in a manner that insured it wouldn't get in the way of drawing her pistol. Nobody could get the bag without taking her with it, which suited her just fine. This was a four-part deal with three parts left—Isaac Nachman, Franklin Bleak, get the hell out of Denver. That was the plan, and she was still damn close to being on schedule, despite Johnny freakin' Ramos.

He walked ahead of her into the hall and waited while she locked up.

Hell. She probably needed her head examined for opening the door to him. She should have waited him out, toughed it out, gone out the window—something.

Jiggling the key in the lock, trying to get the dead-bolt to slide home, she hazarded another quick glance at him, and got hit by that freight train all over again, which brought her train-wreck quota for the last ten minutes up to an even dozen, easy, *dammit.* She felt the collision the same place she'd felt all the others, in her throat and her upper chest, a pure respiratory reaction—as in he took her breath away. It was ridiculous. She was too old for this, too jaded. She'd had real lovers since him, with real sex—and never ever had a man gotten her so hot in a backseat or anywhere else that all she could see on her horizon was complete and utter annihilation. It was the only thing that had stopped her from losing her virginity to the baddest of the bad boys that night—fear of destruction. Everything between the two of them had been so hot, and wild, and edging on frantic, the windows of the car steamed over, his body like corded sinew, all muscle and bone and warm skin, his dark hair so silky, and so tangled from her fingers, his mouth on her everywhere.

Everywhere.

Dammit. Her fingers slipped on the key, and she chipped a nail on the jamb.

Dammit.

She glanced at him again—and got hit by the memory train one more time, except the collision was closer to her solar plexus, and a little lower down.

He'd been naked that night, the first naked boy she'd seen, and she'd never seen another one like him, naked or otherwise, until ten minutes ago.

Perfect.

What an absolutely perfect image to have slide out of her memory banks—John Ramos naked. *Cripes.* With another couple of tries, she finally got the deadbolt locked.

Dropping the keys into an outside pocket on the messenger bag, she headed for the stairs, and he fell in beside her.

She took a breath, calm, easy. About two more minutes and he'd be firmly back in memory land, a blast from the past that was behind her. She took another breath and kept walking.

He had definitely filled out since high school. He was broader through the shoulders, broader through the chest, taller—just plain bigger all the way around. His hair was thick, and dark, and cut short, shorter than she'd ever seen him wear it. The style made him look older than she knew he was, and the thickness of it made his hair stick up a little, and altogether, combined with the lean, carved lines of his face, he looked tough, like he'd just walked out of the LoDo alley where he'd been seen, like he was still running wild on the streets.

Oddly enough, he also looked like he'd just walked out of an Abercrombie catalog. Clean, softly worn, button-fly jeans; expensive boots, tactical boots like Dax owned; a dark gray T-shirt; and over the T-shirt, a black, collared shirt, worn unbuttoned and untucked, the long sleeves neatly buttoned at the cuff. He'd slipped the naked-girl pen in his pocket between a mechanical pencil and a small spiral notebook—whatever in the world he needed those for on a Friday night in LoDo. She could also see the top end of an envelope peeking out of the pocket. In another life, if he'd grown up another way, this close to the Auraria Campus, he could have been taken for one of the university's graduate students. As it was, she'd never seen a college boy with that hard a gaze, so much "Don't fuck with me" stamped in the way he carried himself.

Maybe he really was a cop.

Or maybe, the gang his brother had been fighting for the night he'd been killed, the Locos, maybe

Johnny had climbed to the top of it, made himself the shot caller.

Honest to God, she didn't know which would be worse, cop or gang lord. For her sake, it would be better if he wasn't a cop. She didn't want to show up anywhere, officially, as having been in Denver, and she sure as shoot didn't want to get arrested, but everything in her hoped for his sake that he hadn't followed in Dom Ramos's footsteps, that he'd done better by himself.

At the bottom of the stairs, she felt a moment's regret. This was it. Her dad's car was parked on the street, right out in front, so as soon as they walked out of the Faber Building, that would be it. *Sayonara. Adios. Ciao.* He'd go his way, and she'd go hers.

Too bad.

This close to getting rid of him, she could admit it. Another time, another place, under different circumstances, she might have taken him up on that drink, just to catch up with him, see what he was up to, see how he'd really turned out. But tonight, she was on a mission: return the painting, get the reward money, buy off the bookie, full speed ahead—up until they came out onto the sidewalk and her mission came to a sudden screeching halt.

She couldn't believe it.

Parked next to the curb in all its cheap-ass, middle-of-the-road, minivan glory was her dad's car, right where she'd left it, but somehow, for some unknown but probably easily deducible reason, sometime in the last twenty minutes, between when she'd walked in with the painting and was now walking out, the cops had booted it.

Big, heavy, and clamped to the rear wheel, the hunk of bright orange metal said only one thing to her: She wasn't going anywhere, not in her dad's damn minivan.

CHAPTER FIVE

Dressed to kill and driving a minivan?

Johnny double-checked the direction of her gaze and ended up right back at the same POS minivan he'd thought she was looking at—the butt-ugly brown-and-tan one with the license plate number LVH3590 and the big orange boot on it.

From her crestfallen expression, she knew that baby wasn't going anywhere tonight. To her credit, the news only waylaid her for about three seconds, before she turned and stuck out her hand to him.

"Well, it was great to see you . . . really," she said, giving his hand a firm shake when he took hold of hers. One shake, then she let go of him. "Good luck with my dad tomorrow. Maybe we can have that drink sometime."

Sure they could, he thought, watching her take off across the street, dodging the traffic. Talk about a bum's rush.

From the other side of Wynkoop, she hailed a cab, but the cabbie passed her by. That was her problem, not his. His problem was...hell, he didn't have any problems. He'd done three combat tours and gotten away with nothing worse than a sprained ankle, a bajillion flea bites, and a few stitches once when a round hadn't quite missed him.

He didn't have any problems.

Except for the skinny, blond-haired guy getting out of the passenger side of a Buick LeSabre about halfway up the block on her side of the street. Two things bothered him about the guy. One, Johnny knew him. His name was Dan Smollett, more often known as Dovey, and he worked for a bookie up in Commerce City named Franklin Bleak. Two, Dovey was looking straight at Esme as he was getting out of the car, which made this as close to a high school reunion as Johnny had ever gotten— him, Dovey Smollett, and Easy Alex. They'd all graduated from East the same year, and apparently, only one of them had gone straight. Surprisingly enough, it hadn't been the class valedictorian.

Dovey closed the door on the LeSabre and started toward her, and Johnny felt another knee-jerk reaction coming on. *Goddammit.*

Civic duty, he told himself. They were in the middle of lower downtown, Esme had not yet seen the scumbag zeroing in on her, and Dovey was coming up on her strong side. The element of surprise could really work against old Dovey in this situation, given that Esme had a .45 strapped under her arm, and from the extra little bit of adjusting she'd given the messenger bag, Johnny was guessing she practiced drawing out of her shoulder holster, which had the potential of making her fast.

Not that he thought she might accidentally shoot old Dovey. No, he figured if she shot somebody, it probably wouldn't be by accident.

Kee-rist. He stepped off the curb, checking the traffic both ways, and made his way across the street. She saw him coming, he made sure of it, and she didn't look happy about it, but that was just too damn bad.

He headed for her left side, to put himself between her and Dovey, and no doubt, Dovey was going to see him, too, and no doubt he'd tell Franklin Bleak what and who had happened to his bird, which meant Johnny was going to have to call Sparky Klimaszewski and have him put the heat on Franklin to set things right and get the bookie off his ass.

It was amazing really, how quickly life could get complicated, amazing just how quickly a guy without any problems could acquire a whole boatload of them.

Case in point: Being in debt to Sparky usually required felonious restitution. Sparky was only interested in one thing, cars and the grand theft auto thereof.

Hell. Johnny hadn't stolen a car since he'd been fifteen. Okay, seventeen, but that had been a strictly one-off job for the last time he'd needed a favor from Sparky. But fine, he could deal with Sparky, because Sparky, for all that he ran more cars through Denver than any other chop shop, was not an undersized psycho who tried to compensate for his lack of physical stature by committing violent acts of retribution against losers who didn't pay and anyone else who got in his way.

Franklin Bleak was all that and more, a verifiable freakazoid. He had a very nasty reputation, well earned, for doing very bad deeds—and he'd sent his errand boys to pick up Esme Alden.

Johnny didn't particularly bother to explain all this, or himself, to her when he stepped up on the curb on the other side of Wynkoop.

"Let's go." The command was short, succinct, and impossible to misinterpret, his specialty, and before it was even out of his mouth, he had ahold of her, one of his arms going around her back, his hand gripping her upper right arm, his other hand going across his front and taking hold of her left biceps. Without expending too much effort, he had her under control, half lifted off her feet, and heading back across the street.

"Wh-what in the . . . who do you think . . . wh-what in the hell?"

"Incoming at nine o'clock." He kept walking, hustling her along. Given half a chance, she might have resisted, but he didn't give her half a chance. He'd grabbed her, and they were moving back through the traffic, fast, too fast for her to get any leverage against the hold he had on her.

"Incoming? What the . . . *dammit* . . . This is a *bad* move, Ramos," she said in a tone of voice that reminded him that besides the .45 he could feel through her jacket, she had a knife, that she had a knife for a reason, and that he'd just become one of those reasons.

Sonuvabitch. That was not the sort of information he was used to forgetting. That was the sort of information he was used to hardwiring into his brain.

"Do you remember Dan Smollett?" he asked, his grip still very firm on her, very close to a death grip. He couldn't afford to have her squirming away just yet, or going for one of her weapons, or doing any damn thing, not in the middle of the street, or anywhere else for that matter. He was in charge, and that was for the best almost one hundred percent of the time.

"Dovey?"

Obviously, she did remember the cretin.

"He's thirty yards behind us and closing."

She let out a short sound of disgust. "If you're on the run from Dovey Smollett, that's your problem, not mine."

"No. It's your problem, babe." They reached the other side of Wynkoop, but he didn't relent with his grip. He kept her moving. He had a plan, and it didn't involve letting Dovey Smollett catch up to them.

"The hell it is. I don't give a damn if Dovey Smollett is in LoDo, or if he dropped off the edge of the earth. Now let go of me, you . . . you . . . *jerk.*" She tried to twist out of his grip, and got exactly nowhere—for a damn good reason. He was well trained in the ways and means of physical restraint, and he could bench-press Esme Alden, all hundred-and-what pounds of her.

Hell, he could bench-press three Esme Aldens.

"Can you run in those heels?"

"Yes." She didn't hesitate with her answer. "But—"

"There's no but," he cut her off. "If I say run, you keep up. Got it?"

"Go to hell." Short, succinct, and impossible to misinterpret—he had to give her credit for that much.

He opened the next door they came to and pushed her inside ahead of him, straight into the crush of people jamming O'Shaunessy's back bar.

"Excuse me...sorry..." Johnny edged his way through the crowd, keeping one hand wrapped around her waist, keeping her close. Nobody was getting to her without going through him first, and the only people in this town who could get through him were on his side.

She could thank him later—but he wasn't going to hold his breath.

"*What the...oh, cripes.* You've got a...a...*dammit,*" she said, her voice low.

Yeah, he had her pulled real close to his right side, and he'd wondered when she would notice the pistol riding under his arm.

"*Dammit,*" Esme swore again. "I don't believe this. I can't believe I...*dammit.*"

"Just keep moving."

The crowd thinned out at the service end of the bar, and after getting the two of them tucked into the dark corner between the waitress station and the kitchen door, he took a moment to check and see if Dovey had followed them inside.

Geezus. Franklin Bleak. Whatever she'd gotten herself into, she needed to get herself out, or she was going to end up wishing she'd picked a different line of work. The stories he'd heard about Franklin Bleak weren't just grim; they were gruesome.

"Dammit, Ramos. If this is your way of getting a girl to have a drink with you, I can see why you're alone on a Friday night." He had her about half behind him in the corner, and her voice was close to his ear and very sharp-edged, understandably so. He'd pretty much railroaded her into O'Shaunessy's.

Which in no way fit in with his plan to head back to his beer at the Blue Iguana, despite the fact that she had in no way begged him for help.

No, there had been no begging. That was too big of a stretch, even for him. It had been a clean snatch-and-grab all the way.

"And now, if you're finished *manhandling* me," she continued, starting to push by him, "this party is over."

No, it wasn't.

"Stay put," he said, shifting his body sideways and holding her in place, while keeping his gaze on the crowd of people.

"You're out of line, no matter what you're packing under your shirt," she whispered, her voice even closer to his ear.

"And you're in more trouble than you seem to realize."

At that, she let out a short, surprised laugh. "And how in the hell do you figure that?"

"For a secretary, you've got some real bad guys after you."

"Like you?" The comeback was vintage Easy Alex, pure smart-mouthed.

"No. Dovey," he said, turning to face her. "He's what we call an undesirable element, no matter where he is—in LoDo, dropped off the edge of the earth, or sitting at home on his couch."

A flash of something darkened her gaze, but only for a moment, and it took him another second to realize what it had been: alarm, the first instance of it he'd seen in her since he'd spotted her up on Seventeenth.

"Don't worry. I'm not going to let Dovey get within ten feet of you." The skinny numbers runner was no match for a U.S. Army Ranger, not on his best day with three of his buddies.

"It's not Dovey I'm worried about," she said, giving him a carefully measured look, holding the moment for the space of a breath before she continued. "So what's with the 'we' and the 'undesirable element' lingo? You sound like a cop."

Her tone implied it would be the worst damn thing in the world, which did nothing to reassure him that she was up to anything except no good.

Geezus. She'd hog-tied that poor sap in the Oxford. She'd stolen something from the guy, and Mr. America here had been going to let her just walk away from the crime. He wasn't sure he even wanted to know what was up with that. Just because he'd liked a girl in high school did not make her a saint, although he had seemed to fall for the saintly ones, the good girls, the ones who wouldn't give it up in a backseat.

No wonder it had taken him so long to get laid.

Thank God, he'd expanded his horizons since then. Saintliness didn't even make the cut on his top ten list of attributes to look for in a woman anymore. As a matter of fact, given what he'd learned of human nature, any woman aspiring to saintliness was highly suspect in his book.

Which, of course, under her current circumstances, made Esme Alden look like the perfect girl for him all over again, except this time from the dark side—very dark, if Franklin Bleak was after her.

"No. I'm not a cop. I'm the guy who just saved you from getting shook down by Dovey Smollett and maybe getting thrown into the back of that Buick LeSabre parked on Wynkoop."

Her reaction was almost imperceptible, a slight, extra stiffening of a body already strung tight, but without another dose of alarm. He knew the difference between readiness and fear—and she was ready.

Ready for the likes of Dovey Smollett, and alarmed by the police. That didn't look good or set well.

"What's it to you who shakes me down?" she asked.

Her cool little attitude didn't set too well either. Neither did the fact that he didn't have an answer to her question. What the hell was it to him who shook her down? None of his business is what it was—and yet here he was, jammed into the back of O'Shaunessy's, up close and personal with her for no damn good reason.

"If you tell me why he's after you, maybe I can help." And maybe that was enough, the whole "damsel in distress" motif. Although, from what he'd seen so far, she was doing pretty good on her own, and if it hadn't been for Smollett and Bleak, he might have let it be.

But it was Smollett, and it was Bleak, and if she knew what he'd heard about Bleak, she wouldn't be quite so nonchalant.

She seemed to consider his words, weigh his offer, and see what it might be worth.

"I saw the LeSabre," she finally admitted. "But I can't imagine any reason for some guy from high school to get on my case, let alone abduct me—present company excluded, of course." The last was delivered with the arching of one delicate eyebrow.

He got the point.

Smart-mouthed Easy Alex didn't mince words, and she was right. He had abducted her off the street, and done a damn good job of it. He had her, and Dovey Smollett was sucking air out there on Sixteenth and Wynkoop.

"Dovey was staring at you so hard when he got out of his car, I'm surprised your hair didn't start on fire. He had a tractor beam on you."

"Guys stare at me all the time." She was stating a fact, not dabbling in vanity, and he didn't doubt her for a second. Hell, he'd hardly taken his eyes off her since he'd spotted her up on Seventeenth.

But he shook his head. "He was waiting for you, parked on Wynkoop with a good line of sight on the Faber Building. If you hadn't been dressed in your flavor-of-the-week getup, I'm guessing he would have recognized you when you first went to your dad's office and tried to pick you up then."

"Are you *sure* you're not a cop?"

"No, I'm not, but I know a stakeout when I see one."

"Congratulations. So do I, and you've been following me since the Oxford. But we're done." She looked up at him from underneath her lashes. "Right here, right now. I'm walking out of here, and if you touch me one more time, I'm going to take deep, personal offense. No more nice girl just because we're old school chums. Do you understand me?"

Well, when she said it like that, he guessed every guy in the bar would understand her.

"Yes, ma'am."

Her eyebrow arched again, and she started to step by him—but he stopped her with a simple lift of his hand, being damn careful not to deeply and personally offend her.

"I just have one more question," he said. "Do you know who Dovey Smollett works for?"

"No." She shook her head and gave him a small, indulgent smile. "Dovey and I haven't kept up."

She started to move again, but his hand stayed where it was, blocking her path, but still not touching her.

"I do."

Her look said she wasn't impressed and didn't give a damn.

"He's a local guy," he said anyway, whether she wanted to hear it or not. "He makes book up in Commerce City, a guy named Franklin Bleak."

CHAPTER SIX

Esme's heart caught in her throat, and for a moment, she was frozen in place. But just for a moment.

Bad news, she told herself. *Take the hit, and move on, very carefully.*

Goddammit. Franklin Bleak.

Commerce City, five A.M., a warehouse on Vogel Street—the payoff had been set. So why was the bookie pooching the deal?

Only one reason came to mind, and the bad feeling she'd had in the office suddenly got a whole lot worse. Strong-arming people for money sometimes required a little extra leverage. A wife or child, or both, worked pretty good. A guy who might be willing to sacrifice himself could usually be spurred a little harder to come up with cash when his other choice was having his family take the hit for him, possibly quite a bad hit. If they owed money to

Franklin Bleak, the prognosis could be elevated to "definitely bad." The Commerce City bookie had a very unsavory reputation, and thus the .45 for tonight's work. Even with the money to pay her dad's debt, she'd known presenting herself to Bleak in her father's place entailed a certain amount of risk. For her own peace of mind and to keep potential problems at a minimum, she'd purposely left her dad out of the night's proceedings.

But now. Hell, the risk factor had just gone through the roof—which in no way meant she didn't still have to deliver the money. It did mean she couldn't afford even one loose end, not so much as a thread out of place. She needed to tighten up her plan, get her contingencies in place and lock them in, and for that she needed the name Thomas had promised her father, and she needed Dax. She hadn't planned on walking into a Vogel Street warehouse with eighty-two thousand dollars without guarantees. If the name Thomas delivered didn't do the trick, the information Dax had gone to Colorado Springs to get was her backup—and if that didn't work, then it would be just her and Dax, and that was as close to an ironclad guarantee as a girl was ever going to get.

At least it had been. Now she had to wonder if the only guarantee was to walk away. Come up with another game plan.

Dax had gotten her out of Bangkok—but it had cost him. She didn't know what. He'd never said, not in eighteen long months, no matter how many times she'd asked, no matter how obliquely she'd approached the subject—but the price of her freedom, whatever back-room deal he'd cut with Erich Warner, had cost him, and now this damn deal was twisting in her hands.

That bastard Bleak had sent somebody to snatch her off the damn street, and if it hadn't been for John Ramos, that somebody might have succeeded.

So what did Bleak want here? His damn money? Or blood?

Goddammit.

Something had gone wrong somewhere, and she needed to find out what.

"Are you sure it was Dovey Smollett you saw?" She wasn't surprised to hear Dovey had taken to a life of crime. Hell, half their graduating class had been headed for a life of crime. And she wasn't surprised to hear that Dovey worked for Denver's most dangerous bookie. What made her head spin was the screwing of the deal eight hours before it was supposed to go down.

That was all bad, all dangerous, all totally disastrous, and she was running out of time, standing around in a bar.

"Look for yourself," John Ramos said, making a slight gesture toward the door where they'd entered.

She turned to look, and swore under her breath. He hadn't been lying, and he hadn't made a mistake. It was goddamn Dovey Smollett coming into O'Shaunessy's off Sixteenth—stringy blond hair, pockmarked face, narrow shoulders, a cheap suit.

He hadn't changed nearly enough since high school.

"I think he's working the room with somebody," she said. Dovey had a phone to his ear.

"Check out the Chicago Bear at two o'clock."

She turned and looked in the direction he'd given.

"Yeah. I see him."

Dammit. The guy coming in O'Shaunessy's front door was big, brutish, dark-haired, bulbous-nosed, and needed a change in football team affiliation. Denver was a Broncos town, all the way, and this guy was wearing a Chicago Bears jacket. Esme didn't know him. She didn't have to know him. All she had to know was the look of somebody's untrained chump looking for somebody else, and this guy had it—gaze blatantly quartering the room, phone to his ear, standing straight and tall, neck craned. He might as well have been wearing a sign that said, "Can you help me? I'm looking for ___." Fill in the blank.

"I think . . ." God, she couldn't believe what she was about to say.

"What?" he asked next to her.

"I think we should get a cup of coffee."

There, it was out, and from the shit-eating grin forming on his face, Johnny Ramos knew exactly what she meant—inside joke, all the way. A person had either double-dog-dared their way through Campbell Junior High, or they hadn't.

She had, and he'd been the one double-dog-daring her—him, and Mason Maxwell, and Ruben

Sabino, and Janessa "the jerk" Kaliski. Esme had only taken the stupid dare because of Janessa. The girl had been ridiculously infatuated with Johnny Ramos, and Esme hadn't wanted him to think the skinny brunette with the big boobs was tougher than her.

So, yes, she'd taken the dare, and she'd made it to the coffee shop, and Janessa Kaliski had chickened out. The other boys had rushed over to rescue "the jerk" where she'd gotten hung up in the bridge over the alley—but not Johnny. He'd been watching her, Esme the Miraculous, make her triumphant climb up onto the roof of what had once been the Wazee Warehouse. From there it had been a short drop and a five-story high walk to the fire escape down to street level. Half of another block southeast had dumped them out on Wazee, right in front of the Cuppa Joe coffee shop.

Their first date—that's what she'd always called how that little escapade had finished up, a date. Her and Johnny Ramos, with his silky dark hair and tight T-shirt, the two of them sitting at a table next to the window overlooking Wazee, watching the traffic, waiting for Mason and Ruben and Janessa to show up—and not a damn thing to say to each other.

It had been excruciatingly embarrassing—but still an official first date. She'd put it in her diary that way. Date number two had been in the backseat of the Challenger, and now here they were on date number three. Like date one, date two had been a little low on conversation, so by comparison, date three was on a roll, a real chatterfest. Most of it bitchy on her part, true, but still conversation.

And they were in the exact spot where the Cuppa Joe double dog dare began, between the waitress station and the door into the kitchen of O'Shaunessy's Bar and Grill. The first trick for a junior-high-school-aged kid being to get into the back bar to begin with. Anybody could get into the main bar. It was part of the restaurant. But the back bar was for the after-work crowd, the sports crowd, and the drinking crowd—no kids allowed.

"You're wearing heels," he said.

"You knew that when you brought me in here and shoved me into this corner." Yes, she'd immediately recognized the spot where he'd corralled her, and recognized his tactics for what they were, a way of ditching a tail with a built-in escape route if the ditching failed. "Don't worry, I can do the alley bridge in heels."

"Then we only have one problem," he said, his gaze going back toward the middle of the room. "Make that two problems."

"Two?" She tried to turn and look, but he'd already started moving her toward the kitchen door.

The back bar end of O'Shaunessy's kitchen was the storage area, and therein lay the secret of the double dog dare—the entrance to the O'Lounge. At the far end of shelves laden with cans and boxes and fifty-pound bags of flour and beans and rice, was a smaller pantry where the chef kept the good

stuff, the specialty goods, and in the back of the
pantry was a small wooden door, no more than four
feet high. There wasn't a busboy, dishwasher, or bar
back who'd ever worked O'Shaunessy's who didn't
quickly learn about the door, or the dark, rickety little staircase that led four stories to the southeast
corner of the roof and the open-air O'Lounge.

The last time Esme had been up there, in high
school, someone had gotten a couch up the staircase. She didn't know how. The first time she'd
been in the O'Lounge, the day of the dare, it had
been furnished with produce crates, a couple of
broken chairs from the restaurant that somebody
had duct-taped back together, and an amazing
number of empty beer bottles, "handles," and for-
ties. How the O'Lounge had lasted all these years
without some drunken kid accidentally pitching
himself over the side of the roof was beyond her.

Johnny pushed the kitchen door open, and she
got hit with bright light and chaos. In a big place
like O'Shaunessy's, on a Friday night, the kitchen
was a madhouse. Dozens of people were moving in
dozens of directions, orders flying, flames on the
grill flaring, cooks yelling above the din, waiters going every which way.

Nobody asked them if they needed help, or particularly took notice of them. Johnny knew how to
walk through a room like he belonged there, and
so did she. They stayed out of the action, keeping
close to the storage shelves. It wasn't very many
steps to the pantry, just enough for him to take the
small spiral-bound notebook and his mechanical

pencil out of his shirt pocket and look exactly like a delivery guy checking an order.

She, on the other hand, made a point of looking like his boss—expensive and unhappy.

"Two problems?" she repeated, when they reached the pantry. She kept her attention on the door, with an occasional glance at his notebook. She did not look around the kitchen.

"I think Dovey Smollett did this dare back in seventh grade."

Oh, crap. He was right. Dovey had been a Campbell Junior High kid, and like every other outcast, which at Campbell had just about encompassed the entire damn seventh grade and half the eighth-graders, Dovey had laid himself on the line for double dog dares. On the whole, ninth-graders were too sophisticated for double dog dares. By ninth grade, sex, drugs, and gangs had taken them.

But Dovey, she remembered, had gotten suckered into a few sketchy moments and gotten hurt on the Larimer Square dare, a bit of "on the hoof" pickpocketing of the chichi LoDo crowd. Dovey had been too heavy-handed for the deed and been knocked into next week by the guy whose wallet he'd tried to lift.

Esme had bypassed the Larimer Square dare, out-and-out thievery being beyond her comfort zone at the time, way beyond, though she'd obviously since adjusted her parameters. Johnny, as she recalled, had been quite comfortable and surprisingly skilled at picking pockets. He'd gotten a couple of wallets the night he'd done it. Fourteen years old and running freaking wild on the streets.

It was a wonder he'd never gotten arrested. Or maybe he had been. Hell, for all she knew, he was an ex-con on probation, which made her wonder what in the hell she was doing going to the O'Lounge with him.

Getting away from Dovey and the Bear, and staying out of Franklin Bleak's clutches—the answer really was straightforward, and honestly, it didn't matter how many crimes and misdemeanors John Ramos had committed as one of the city's more skilled juvenile delinquents, or at any other time. He'd already redeemed himself by rescuing her off Wynkoop.

And wasn't it funny how quickly a girl's perspective could change, from abduction to rescue.

She walked into the pantry after him, looking concerned and serious, and like any number of the most expensive items in her entire inventory had been misplaced by one of her delivery drivers—up until he closed the door.

"We better—" he said.

"Yeah," she finished his thought, looking around. The pantry was small, the shelving high and narrow, and there was a step stool pushed up against a crate.

She shoved it toward him, and he lodged it between the wall and the shelving unit closest to the door, then further reinforced the blockade with two five-gallon tubs of Greek olives. By the time he was finished, she'd moved three cases of premium mixers for the bar away from the small door in the back of the room.

"There's a—" she said, noticing a lock on the door.

"I've got it." He took his mechanical pencil and shoved it hard between the hasp and the door. When he pulled, half the hasp and its screws came out of the wood, and the door swung wide.

She was impressed.

She ducked inside the door and started up the stairs. "Steel pencil?" It had to be.

"Titanium."

Very cool. Dax had a titanium pencil. It had saved his life once, when he'd buried it in . . .

Her thought trailed off for a second. The narrow stairwell was dark, and it took her a couple of seconds to get her flashlight out of its pocket on the messenger bag. There were a few things she never went anywhere without; a small flashlight was one of them.

What Dax had buried his titanium pencil in was some guy's throat. He'd recommended she get one for the same reason. She'd decided to stick with her knife instead, and even then, even with the training she'd had, she wasn't sure how effective she'd be if the moment ever came for the throat-burying move. Not because her training wasn't good, but because she hadn't had enough of it—yet. Working with Dax meant there was plenty more on her horizon.

And Johnny Ramos had a titanium pencil and had been giving her directions likc "incoming," and "two o'clock," for the last five minutes. Possibly, he had risen above street level.

The stairs were short, not up to code, and she was taking them two at a time, quickly, following the pool of illumination cast by her flashlight.

"You said there were two problems."

"Yeah...two." He was right behind her on the stairs, coming on fast, keeping her moving.

"So what's the second problem?" she prompted, when he didn't explain. Franklin Bleak was on her ass. She needed all the information she could get, and she needed it immediately, and she needed to get ahold of her dad again, her dad who had *not* called her back yet. *Geez,* he knew what she was up against tonight, and now she had this little sidebar into O'Shaunessy's, and then the damn second running of the double dog dare. It was all just plain eating into her schedule. She needed to get to Nachman's and get that damn money or the whole damn night was a bust, and her father was going to have to pack his bags for a one-way trip to Siberia.

Sure, she could get her dad out of town, and her mother...and Aunt Nanna, and Danny, and Deb, and Uncle Tim, and about forty other family members.

Crap.

She got in another half dozen stairs before Johnny spoke two words guaranteed to get her attention.

"Kevin Harrell."

Well, that sure as hell stopped her cold. She

whirled around, and landed smack dab up against him.

Her first realization was very physical, and very profound: Johnny Ramos was built like a slab of granite.

Her second realization was how amazingly angry she still was at the idiot who had dared to slam her up against the lockers in East High.

CHAPTER SEVEN

Johnny caught her close, bracing himself to keep the both of them from tumbling. It didn't take much. If he hadn't been following her so closely, she could have done her "spinning top" imitation without making any contact with him at all.

Thank God he'd been following her so closely.

She smelled great.

He hadn't had a chance to notice when he'd been hauling her across Wynkoop and into O'Shaunessy's, what with the cars, and the noise, and Dovey hot on their tails—kind of like now. But in the dark quiet of the stairwell, with the building's walls coming up close on each side, with the two of them plastered together, and her just one stair above him with her face and neck right there in front of him, it was all about the scent of summer gardens and honeysuckle.

"That *sonuvabitch* is out of prison?" she whispered, her voice harsh.

Honeysuckle and summer gardens wrapped around one very angry woman, he realized.

"And he's in the *bar*?"

Yes, he was. Johnny hadn't forgotten what Kevin Harrell looked like, even if he had changed his hair color to blond, and the asshole had walked into O'Shaunessy's and headed straight for Dovey. Franklin Bleak must have recruited him right out of Canon City.

"We need to—" he started.

"I know," she snapped, and in the next second, she was moving back up the stairs, almost at a run, bitching under her breath.

Good. He liked a woman who knew how to prioritize, and escape always trumped a temper tantrum. But he had to wonder, for just a moment, while he was climbing up the stairs behind her, if he'd missed something all those years ago when Kevin Harrell had slammed her up against the lockers.

Had that sonuvabitch actually had the time to do something to her that he didn't know about? And really, if he thought about it, just how far up had her skirt been when he'd called Kevin out? And where had that asshole's hands been?

And what in the hell was he doing, really, chasing Easy Alex up to the O'Lounge, hoping Dovey Smollett wouldn't remember about the damn double dog dare, all so he could get her out of this frying pan and throw her straight into the fire.

She still had an appointment to deliver whatever

she'd put in the messenger bag bandoliered across her chest. He hadn't forgotten.

This girl ... he thought, taking the damn short stairs three at a time. *This girl is nothing but trouble, scary trouble.* Scary for her. He wasn't scared of anything, except of letting his men down, but his men, the guys in Third Platoon, weren't in O'Shaunessy's outrunning three mopes from Commerce City, and his men weren't his anymore. They were back at Benning, most of them, and he was heading to his home team, SDF.

Most, but not all—the thought skirted the edge of his mind, and he just let it go. For now, all he could do was let it go.

But hell, this girl—he should have played hardball with her right from the start, right when she'd first let him into her dad's office. He should have called for backup as soon as he'd seen that damn German. He should have gotten somebody into that room and found out what was going on.

He should have called Creed. The jungle boy was in residence at Steele Street, and the German might have appreciated someone with a big, sharp knife to cut him free—and if having Creed standing over him with a knife in his hand hadn't given the old guy a heart attack, Johnny would have figured the German was tougher than he'd looked tricked out in a thong and a dog collar.

On the other hand, General Grant was due in Denver tonight, a real short-notice visit, and even though Johnny wasn't officially part of the team yet, and probably wouldn't be part of any meetings, he was pretty damn sure he didn't want SDF's commanding officer to get the impression he was the kind of guy who chased hookers out of hotel rooms filled with deviant foreigners. Or actually, considering the slot he was hoping to fill, being able to run a "honey trap" wasn't such a bad skill. Far worse to Grant would probably be that he was running around the streets of Denver and heading for the rooftops with a woman without knowing why. Even with the thought he'd given it, he wasn't precisely clear about his motives.

Not precisely clear at all.

Yeah, that didn't look so good on an operator's resume.

What he should have done was call Loretta, Lieutenant Loretta Bradley of the Denver Police, and let her clear up the mess at the Oxford. He would have plenty of intel to work with then.

A sudden pounding sound coming up from below told him Dovey had remembered plenty about the O'Lounge, and that he was going to get another chance to play hardball real damn quick if he and Esme couldn't outrun these jokers. From the sound of the grumbled cursing he heard between the scraping open of the pantry door and the sliding of the olive tubs, it was going to be Mr. Kevin Harrell up first at bat, which suited him just fine.

Johnny's money was still on Esme. The girl was in shape with a capital S. They'd just passed the second landing and were on their way to the third, and even in heels and a tight skirt, she hadn't so much as blinked, let alone slowed down.

She'd hitched her skirt up to give herself some room to run in, and her flashlight gave off enough illumination for him to catch a glimpse of her legs about every other step. He shouldn't have noticed. Under their current circumstances, hoping to see up her skirt was just another dumb-ass move the likes of which had gotten him into this mess in the first place. *Geezus*, it had barely been more than half an hour since he'd sucked down the last of his beer at the Blue Iguana and gone outside to decide where else he could go and spend a couple of hours.

Anything to keep from going home—yeah, he knew he was avoiding it. But hell, his place at Steele Street's Commerce City Garage was just too damn quiet to face alone.

Way too damn quiet. He just got in trouble when he was trapped with that much quiet. Red Dog and the Angel Boy lived upstairs, but they were out more often than they were in, and they'd been out for the last two weeks, running the security on a senate subcommittee's junket through Bolivia.

Still, the O'Lounge was so far back in his memory banks, it wouldn't have occurred to him in a week of Sundays as a place to go, let alone as a place to meet up with Kevin Harrell and Dovey Smollett for old home week.

Easy Alex was a different story. He actually thought about her quite a bit for a girl he'd never actually had sex with—or maybe those were the girls a guy tended to mull over in his mind, the ones who'd gotten away, especially the ones who'd barely gotten away.

Heavy footsteps started up the stairs below, accompanied by a fair share of swearing. Kevin and the Chicago Bear had to be scraping both sides of the narrow stairwell. Those boys were pushing well over two-fifty each, and it wasn't all muscle, not even close.

He'd actually thought about Esme once in the middle of a firefight during this last go-around. It had startled the hell out of him at the time, that little lapse in his concentration. He'd been in a bunker in the Kunar Province of Afghanistan. They'd been getting pounded by enemy machine guns, and an image of Esme had flashed in front of his eyes, a really sweet image of her looking over her shoulder, smiling at him, wearing a little summer dress that barely covered her ass, her blond hair cascading down her back—hips swaying, her dress lifting in the breeze, sunshine lighting her like a halo.

It had unnerved the crap out of him. Third Platoon had already gotten hit seven times in twelve hours that day, and she'd shown up in the eighth firefight, like a messenger from God, an angel come to tease him with a vision of home, or maybe a Valkyrie waiting to claim a fallen warrior.

Nothing else strange had happened, just that little, almost hallucinatory vision of Easy Alex in the middle of the fight. Third Platoon had continued to get hammered into the night, which had been standard operating procedure during the Kunar deployment, but most of them had come out okay by morning, when an MRE and a couple of cups of coffee had set him straight—at least straight enough to face another day of the same.

He could probably use a couple of cups of coffee right now, and honestly, he didn't need to see up her skirt. He already knew what was up there—red lace panties and a sweet size six.

Geezus.

They came out onto the roof, and Esme didn't even break stride. She knew exactly where she was going.

She pointed to a couch up ahead under a canvas tarp rigged as a sunshade. "Should we—"

"No," he cut her off. Blocking the door with the couch wouldn't do any good. It would take Dovey and friends less time to push past it than it would take him and Esme to move it.

Better to keep moving, and she did, cutting off the beam on her flashlight as she continued at a jog toward the edge of the roof. There was enough streetlight to see where they were going, and no reason on earth to carry around a spotlight for Bleak's goons to follow.

Tactically, he was impressed, even more so when she rounded the O'Lounge and came face to face with the alley bridge. It had been a few years since he'd been on the roof of O'Shaunessy's, and sometime during those years, some manager must have decided the gig was up on the double dog dares. To limit his potential liability and cut down on the number of junior high school students trying to sneak into his bar, he'd had somebody's old wrought-iron security door welded to the near end of the alley bridge, and then put a big steel padlock on it. The Wazee Warehouse was still only fifteen feet away, but now it was prohibitively difficult to get to—unless your name was Easy Alex.

Stopping in front of the scrolled wrought-iron door, and without missing a beat, she cut the beam of her flashlight back on, stuck it in her mouth like somebody used to working alone, and reached into another of the messenger bag's outside pockets.

She was just so freaking smooth, all of her moves calibrated, with her thoughts always one step ahead of what she needed to do. He was impressed as hell. He was also impressed by what she was doing, although if he'd blinked, he would have missed the whole thing.

Johnny knew lock picks and the guys who used them. He knew Superman, who was one of the best and who had taught him—and she was better. Two seconds flat and she was turning off her flashlight, repocketing her tools, and opening the door onto the alley bridge. He followed her through to the other side, and she turned and closed it behind them. Then she refastened the padlock on their side.

For anybody to get through was going to take some doing, which meant, after some possible milling around and cursing his bad luck, even a less-bright guy like Dovey would realize the only chance he had was to pick up their trail on Wazee Street.

Johnny was still putting his money on Esme. From the sound of what he'd heard going on behind him in the stairwell, Dovey and his two bull elephants weren't negotiating four flights of acutely angled stairs with nearly the grace and speed that he and the catlike Easy Alex had managed. By the time the bad guys got themselves turned around and back down the stairs, he and Esme would be halfway to Steele Street and hopefully some answers.

The bridge over the alley four floors below hadn't improved with age, but neither had it deteriorated to the point where he felt like they needed ropes and carabiners. Esme was across in seconds and climbing the iron ladder bolted onto the side of the Wazee Warehouse.

A cat, that's what she was, sinuous, leggy, sleek, graceful. Add skilled, fearless, decisive, efficient, and wary of the cops, and suddenly he got an even clearer picture of her: cat burglar.

Esme Alden, LoDo hooker, he couldn't buy, but Esme Alden, cat burglar—yeah, he was afraid that one was all too easy to believe.

In minutes, they were across the warehouse roof and heading down the fire escape to the street, and so far, on his scoreboard, it had been one helluva night.

CHAPTER EIGHT

"What do you mean you didn't get the goddamn girl?" Franklin Bleak said into his phone. "How many lives do you think you've got, Dovey? Twelve? You think you've got twelve goddamn lives?"

"No, sir, Mr. Bleak."

"Good, because you don't. I can fucking guarantee you that much, Smollett." Franklin settled back into his cordovan leather chair and lifted his feet to set them on his mahogany desk. The wallpaper in his office was richly flocked, a black rampant lion pattern on hunter green. The rug covering his hardwood floor was straight out of the Arabian Nights via hand-knotted New Zealand wool, a rich tapestry of gold, ivory, and cinnabar red. He had two richly upholstered chairs in his office, and a matching settee in a pattern called Rutherford. The material was wool, the frames were hand-carved beechwood stained to a rich cherry. Amber sconces and a crystal chandelier bathed his private lair with warm, luxurious light.

The room was richly colorful, but then, Franklin Bleak was a richly colorful guy, leaning heavily on the "rich" side of the equation. He owned Commerce City and everything north of Speer Boulevard in Denver. His empire stretched southeast to Aurora and north into Brighton. He stayed the hell out of Boulder, that crapshoot of liberalism and panty-waisted, tree-hugging, small-carbon-footprinted do-gooders to the west, but he did run a few games and some girls in Thornton. He'd stayed away from moving a lot of drugs, because drugs were such a dirty, fierce business, very dangerous. Girls were easy to keep in line. Game scores, race numbers, and the money never lied. But the drugs put a guy directly in the line of fire and could get him killed. To do drugs well, a guy needed layers, a lot of layers, between himself and the street. The safest place to sell drugs was from the top, and even then, some douche might decide to blow up your house, or take out your whole damn condominium building, just blow it the fuck up while you were asleep inside.

Drugs were a crazy business, not like the betting game and girls. Franklin Bleak left drugs to the Denver gangs, especially the Locos, who seemed to have their fingers in every kilo that ran through the city. He had no beef with the Locos, and for the most part, he'd worked hard to keep it that way.

But inevitably the three got mixed—girls, bets, drugs. You had girls who did drugs, and losers who wanted to pay in drugs, and winners who wanted to place in drugs, and guys who'd lost their ass who needed drugs, and guys in drugs who just wanted to make you a deal because you were Franklin Bleak, kind of a famous, colorful guy.

He had resisted all such offers, until the deal of a lifetime had landed practically in his lap three months ago, more of a middle-man transaction for him than outright involvement, a conduit situation of some high-end cocaine for which the demand was through the roof via a high-end dealer who only dealt with very select, high-end clients in Vail and Aspen and Beaver Creek.

And Franklin was talking incredibly select and high-end clients, famous people.

People on television and in films. Movie stars.

Colorado ski towns were Mecca to those people, and Franklin controlled a hefty portion of the front door into those towns, so naturally, when Hollywood had gone looking for a guy to bring in one of their loads from Chicago, Hollywood had found him. He had friends in Chicago. He was known. He had the ways and means . . . but he did not have the goddamn Alden girl, and he needed her to make sure her crapola father didn't welsh on his bet one goddamn more time.

Bleak was done with the stupid bastard. He needed his money by five o'clock tomorrow morning, before the frickin' crack of dawn, before the Chicago cocaine and its handlers got to Denver for the deal at nine o'clock. If Alden didn't have his money to him by sunrise, there was literally going to be hell to pay, and then he'd give the guy two more hours. If Alden failed again, the bastard would wish he was dead, and then Franklin would make it so, putting the jerk out of his misery—and he'd be goddamned if he ever took a bet from anybody named Alden ever again.

"I don't want to hear how you lost her, and I sure as hell don't want to hear about O'Shaunessy's. That O'Shaunessy bastard has given me nothing in forty years. Nothing. You hear me?"

"Yes, sir, Mr. Bleak."

The whole lower downtown crowd was nothing but assholes. They thought they were better than Commerce City. They thought they were high-end, but Franklin was going to show them high-end. Lunch, that's what Graham Percy, the Hollywood agent and his connection, had promised him—lunch with Katherine Gray, the hottest "It" girl to hit late-night cable in the last six months, his kind of girl, all legs and long red hair. Franklin liked a girl with some pizzazz, and Katherine Gray had pizzazz up the yazoo.

He looked over at a picture of her he'd cut out of *Starlets* magazine and framed for his desk. She was gorgeous. She'd made it. She knew what it took. She was that kind of girl, and he was that kind of guy. He knew what it took—and it was going to take the damn Alden girl to insure he got his money, and he needed his money, all eighty-two fucking thousand dollars of it to get him through the Chicago cocaine deal tomorrow. No money, no deal—no lunch. And he wasn't letting Burt Alden screw him out of Katherine Gray and his lunch. Everyone else he'd shaken down these last two months, pulling in *all* his bad debts, had been giving it up, no matter what it took, or they'd kissed their ass good-bye. Alden was going to give it up, too, or Bleak was going to personally check the bastard out—as in *out*, done, finished, dead.

"You stay on the lookout for her, you hear me? You ask around down there. You know people. Use them. Where's the Chicago guy, Bremerton?" Vernon Better-Watch-His-Shit Bremerton. Franklin didn't like fucking watchdogs, and Bremerton was a watchdog, sent by the Chicago boys to make sure Franklin held up his end of the deal—the assholes.

"With me," Dovey said.

"Good. You keep him with you. I don't like him down here, staring at me all day like some dumb piece of Chicago pork. Put Kevin on the B and B office. Tell him to stay put."

"I've got Kevin checking the coffee shop on Wazee," the kid said, like he'd come up with a good idea.

Franklin was not impressed.

"And why in the hell would you do that? With three guys chasing them, I don't think they're going to stop for a goddamn cup of coffee. Do you?"

"No, sir . . . well, yes, sir, not stop exactly, but go by there because—"

"Because nothing, Smollett. Get Kevin back on the B and B office."

"Yes, sir."

"Eliot is on his way to her old man's house, so

we're covered there, but if she shows up at that office again, you tell Kevin to get her and bring her to me. No more screwing up."

"Yes, sir."

"And you tell him to keep his hands to himself. I want her in one piece." He wanted Burt Alden to get one last goddamn good look at what he was going to lose if he didn't have that money, and if it got to the point where Franklin had to take the girl apart, he didn't want her old man missing any of the action, not so much as a single piece of it.

He hoped it didn't get to that. He really did. In his heart, he did. The girl was a looker, plenty of pizzazz, and that created options. She wouldn't be worth eighty-two thousand dollars, not right off the cuff, but he could play her, parlay her into something to hold the damn deal together—a smart looker like her, and he could teach everybody in goddamn Denver a lesson while he was at it.

"Yes, sir."

That was the great thing about Dovey. The kid knew the two most important words in his vocabulary were "Yes, sir." That's all Franklin ever wanted to hear out of him.

"You find her, Dovey, or it's gonna hurt you. Do you understand?"

"Y-yes, sir."

Good, Franklin thought, *a little hesitation is good.* It meant the kid was thinking.

But Dovey Smollett thinking wasn't always that much better than Dovey Smollett not thinking.

Franklin ended the call and speed-dialed another number.

"Mitch," he said, when the call was answered. "Are you and Leroy still at the Jack O'Nines?" The Jack O'Nines, a dump of a strip club in downtown, was sometimes referred to as Denver's little Chicago, because of the three Chicago boys who had cruised through there a few years ago. One of them had gotten himself gutted, right there in Jack's back bar, and the other two had been capped, with all three bodies dragged out into the alley, thrown in a truck, and blown to bits in an explosion out at the old Stapleton Airport. At least that was the story.

Bremerton better watch his ass. Denver wasn't always so good to Chicago boys.

"Yes, boss."

"Dovey is at Sixteenth and Wazee, looking for the Alden girl. She's on the run. I want you and Leroy down there yesterday. See if you can pick her up."

"Yes, boss."

"Call Dovey for his last sighting."

"Yes, boss."

"Did you get my money out of that prick Abrams?"

"Yes, boss."

Good.

"How hard did you have to work for it?"

"We leaned on him enough to let him know that being late wasn't a good idea, but we were careful. We didn't break anything on him, just roughed him up a little."

"Good. Then get your asses down into LoDo." He hung up the phone and took another long look at Katherine Gray's photo, before he pushed away from his desk and walked over to the window at the far end of his office. With a twist of a rod, the blinds opened to reveal the main floor of the Bleak Enterprises warehouse.

Paper products, that was his legitimate game, supplying paper products to businesses up and down the Front Range—paper towels, toilet paper, napkins, cleaning supplies, specialty containers, bags, boxes, whatever his customers wanted, Bleak could get, including Lady's Pride in the seventh at the Downs, but that part of his business was run out of the back of his building.

He walked to the other end of his office and opened up another set of window blinds. A private set of stairs led from his office to the room below. Most nights, he had two guys on computers and cell phones and a digital whiteboard hanging on the wall down there. Most nights, he ran a lot of bets through that room, with most of the transactions running smooth as silk, but every now and then, something went wrong. He was a good guy, and if somebody had a sure shot they wanted to play big, but not the cash to do it, they could count on Franklin to cover it for them. But sure shots seldom were, and no matter how the damn bet turned out, the piper had to be paid.

He caught sight of his reflection in the window and narrowed his gaze. That damn hairstylist at Mirasol's had done him no favors with this last cut.

At seventy dollars a pop, he'd think a damn hair-stylist could cut a guy's hair without cutting it all off. He still had plenty on the sides. He always had plenty on the sides, and it was the plentiful side hair that was supposed to make up for the barely noticeable thinness on top. But the damn stylist had cut him too short.

Using his fingers, he combed a few more strands off the side and up over the top. He was done with Mirasol's. But the girl did give good color, nice and dark with just a touch of a warmer shade. That's the way she described it, and Franklin agreed. His hair looked real natural, like he was a guy who got out in the sun.

He wasn't.

Franklin Bleak was an inside guy, all the way; he was also the piper, and one way or another, Burt Alden was going to pay, starting with the middle-aged blonde handcuffed to a chair in the corner of the betting room. She was alone down there in the half-lit room where he ran his bets. Her first name was Beth, according to his information and her name tag, and she looked terrified—rightly so. She was a done deal. Twenty years ago . . . hell, even ten years ago, Franklin might have been able to cop a deal on her, but not now. She was worthless to him, except as leverage, her best years long behind her.

She was also in complete disarray—the top of her nurse's uniform ripped up one seam, as if she might have put up a fight when Eliot had grabbed her out of the parking lot at Denver General Hospital. Her cotton pants were torn and dirty, as if she'd perhaps fallen in the parking lot and Eliot had dragged her to his car. Most of her hair had fallen free of her ponytail band and was hanging in a knotted mess to her shoulders, as if Eliot might have had a fistful of it while he was dragging her across the pavement. And one of her shoelaces was missing out of her sensible shoes.

That was a new one on Franklin. He'd never seen a woman lose a shoelace in a struggle. He'd seen them lose their shoes, but it had always been whole shoes, not just a lace.

Live and learn, Franklin thought, turning his back on the frightened, smallish woman and walking toward his desk, *live and learn*—unless you were Beth Alden. Her time ran out on both those options at five A.M.

CHAPTER NINE

The state of Colorado was known as the Centennial State, having been admitted to the Union in 1876, one hundred years after the War of Independence. The state bird was the Lark Bunting. The state flower was the Columbine. The highest mountain was Mount Elbert at 14,433 feet, and the fastest fish was the barracuda.

Not many people knew that last fact. Dax Killian did. He knew it, he'd built it, he'd run it up at Bandimere in the quarter mile and forever laid claim to the title—fastest fish in the state.

Fourteen years later, he didn't have a doubt in his mind that the pure stock Plymouth drag title was still holding at 11.897 seconds @ 119.46 mph. Her name was Charo, because she could shake, like jelly on a plate, with a Shaker hood scoop feeding air to 426 cubic inches of hemispherical engine, the old King Kong of power plants bolted under the hood of his 1971 Plymouth Hemi 'Cuda. Every car that had ever gone up against her had gotten sent to the house.

Charo was shaking now, stuck in idle in the parking lot called Interstate 25. Four lanes heading north, and all of them were stopped cold.

The traffic in Seattle had won "Worst on Planet" on some oddball list he'd seen last year, but Dax had to wonder if the list makers had checked out trying to get from Colorado Springs to Denver on a Friday night. He and Easy were on a schedule, and he was screwing up his end.

That was unusual.

Dax usually had everything under control. So did Easy most of the time, with a couple of notable exceptions—*very* notable exceptions. Bangkok came to mind. That one had cost him, but he couldn't have left the girl to Erich Warner.

A favor, that's all Warner had asked for letting her go, an unnamed favor due and payable upon request—and then the German had offered a little something to seal the deal. Eighteen months later, and Warner still hadn't asked for his favor, and Dax and Easy were back in Warner's business, stealing the man's Meinhard.

Sometimes life got too interesting. Dax didn't mind, not really. He figured it beat the alternative. On the other hand, a guy needed to think about things like an open-ended debt to the likes of Erich Warner.

So every now and then, he gave it a thought,

while trying at the same time not to think too much about that little something Warner had offered.

He checked his watch—a Chase-Durer Pilot Commander Alarm chronograph. He wasn't a pilot. He just wished he were when he was stuck in traffic with nothing but rolling hills, pine trees, and prime Angus on either side of the highway. He thought this might be a phenomenon unique to the Front Range of Colorado—interstate traffic stopping dead in the middle of nowhere. He had an aunt who lived north of Denver, in Fort Collins, and he'd heard her complain about the same thing happening whenever she drove south toward the city, the whole interstate grinding to a halt in the middle of nowhere.

The Honda Civic in front of him slowly inched forward, and Dax followed suit, easing up on Charo's clutch and brake to get the 'Cuda rolling. They went all of ten feet before they stopped cold again.

He leaned over and popped open the glove compartment. At this rate, he was going to need Patsy and a smoke to see him through. There was only one Patsy, but he had a choice on the smokes, a jockey box full of half-empty cigarette packs, menthol, nonmenthol, filtered, straights, clove, no kidding, compliments of some girl, and those things had almost killed him. He had chewing tobacco, loose tobacco with papers, a pair of handcuffs, and cigars in every size, from corona to robusto, but no presidentes, which was fine. This was not a presidente moment.

No. It was Patsy and a panatela.

He unwrapped the long, thin cigar and cut the end before firing up his lighter and getting it going.

Puffing, he thumbed through his case of CDs until he found what he wanted. Charo was a driver, not a concourse car, and he'd been only too happy to change out her eight-track for a Bose sound system.

Patsy sounded good on Bose.

The panatela smoking, he snapped his lighter shut.

Ahead of him, the Civic rolled another ten feet and Dax followed, easing up on the pedals until he was back on the Honda's ass.

Sucking in a mouthful of smoke, he lifted his hips partway off the seat and slid his lighter back in his pocket. Then he slid the divine Ms. Cline into the CD player.

It was a hot summer night in the most beautiful state in the lower forty-eight, a perfect night for "Walking After Midnight." That's what he and Patsy did a lot—search for love in the lonely dark hours. As a pair, they were a couple of losers in that regard, and that's probably why he loved her so much.

It was nine-thirty, and he knew where Easy was supposed to be—Isaac Nachman's. She should be pulling into the guy's Genesee Park compound in the mountains above Denver right about now. The old guy had built a massive hunting lodge back in the fifties, instantly creating a Colorado landmark, but Dax wasn't at all sure the girl was there. She had not checked back in with him yet. The last he'd heard from her was right after she'd gotten the call from the valet at the Oxford, the call that should have gone to Dixie.

She'd told him when she was going in, and she should have called and told him when she was coming out. Standard operating procedure called for turning cell phones on silent mode for the duration of any contact with the opposition. Certainly, frisking old Otto Von Lindberg out of his contraband qualified as hostile contact. But Easy should have had her phone back on normal ring by now and been taking his calls.

He had three into her.

Settling deeper into Charo's driver's seat, he took another long draw off the panatela.

Dixie the Dominatrix. Her real name was Jolene Talbot. She'd been a few years ahead of him in school, and putting out even way back then. She hadn't been the only girl doing it, of course, but she was the only one he knew who'd gone professional.

It was a rough life. He didn't remember her being bad, or even all that wild, just real down on her luck. She'd had a friend whose luck had been even worse than hers, a girl named Debbie Gold. Debbie had started turning tricks young, too, and ended up floating in the South Platte River, her body washing up near Confluence Park one summer about eighteen years ago.

There'd been another murder that summer. Poor Debbie had barely gotten a mention in the papers, but Jonathan Traynor III, a senator's son, had gotten plenty of play. Both murders had remained unsolved for most of those years, up until the Traynor case had gotten busted wide open and the Gold girl had been found to be a piece of collateral damage to the main event.

Dax had seen and heard about incidents a lot worse than those two murders in the intervening years, but Gold and Traynor had died in his neighborhood while he'd still been young enough to be horrifyingly awed by violence, with both murders being lurid enough to have instantly attained the status of urban legend and seal themselves in his memories—gang rape, heroin, a little strangulation, and a bullet to the brain. Right in the heart of Denver.

Life was funny. Dax had known the guy who'd gotten sent up for Traynor's murder, wrongly it had turned out, had known him a whole lot better than he'd ever known Jolene Talbot. Hawkins had been his name. They'd boosted a couple of cars together with a kid named Quinn as part of a crew running out of lower downtown. Then that whole crew had gotten busted and sent up to juvie on a job Dax had been slated to work. The bust had pretty much scared him straight on the car boosting business.

Fortunately, there'd been plenty of other trouble to get into, and he was pretty sure he hadn't missed any of it, right up until a Denver police officer, Loretta Bradley, had suggested, strongly, that the U.S. Army might be a better place for him than the streets of Denver or one of her jail cells.

Apparently, from what and whom he'd seen in a lot of far-flung places over the intervening years, she'd given that advice to a lot of lower downtown's grand theft auto wizards.

Loretta was a lieutenant now, and she'd been right. The army had been a good place for an eighteen-year-old kid who'd been on the verge of upgrading into felonies beyond his successful, and therefore undocumented, forays into boosting cars.

The Honda moved again, and Dax kept up. He could see the lights of Denver spread out across the horizon and spilling onto the dark plains to the east, but no matter how much sprawl the suburbs provided, Denver was a small town, especially if you'd grown up running her streets.

Hawkins, Quinn, and a guy named Creed—he'd crossed all their paths at some point during his time in the army and during his last few years in the Middle East, before he'd gotten out of the military. He hadn't seen Dylan, though. From a few oblique asides, he'd surmised that the boss of the chop shop had gone a slightly different route. More spook than operator, it didn't appear that Dylan Hart spent much, if any, time in BDUs.

The one guy he hadn't seen since he'd left Denver was J. T. Chronopolous, but he'd heard the rumors about a couple of operators on a black op in Colombia a few years back, about one of them having three scars across the top of his shoulder—and he'd thought of the car thief he'd used to know. Given what the other guys had ended up doing, he'd always kind of figured there was a fair chance that guy in Colombia had been J.T. He hoped to hell what he'd heard hadn't happened to anyone he knew, though, especially someone from the Steele Street crew, especially J.T. But someday, he was going to have to check it out and get the real story.

Hell, they'd all been running so damn wild on the streets as kids way back then.

Not all the wild kids were on the streets, though. He'd found a whole passel of them in a private prep school in Colorado Springs, Folton Ridge Academy. He'd been down at the school taking pictures of four of the students, all girls, all about seventeen years old, all brunettes, all on the Folton Ridge Flyers field hockey team. He'd gotten their names by matching the photos he'd taken with those in the school's yearbook, and then gotten to know each of the girls up close and personal through their on-line profiles and the accompanying chitchat messages posted between them and their friends.

If Dax ever had kids, he'd only have two words for the on-line chitchat, post-your-picture-so-your-friends-can-find-you Web sites: no way. Not if hell froze over. He knew the one girl's bra size, which was not the information he'd been looking to gather. On the plus side, by sifting through their messages, he'd determined that two of the girls were pretty nice kids. Three of them were good students. All four complained about their coach. One of them had freckles and thought they made her look fat.

Dax thought that maybe it was the extra twenty

pounds she was carrying that made her appear plump, but he was no expert on teenage girls and didn't want to be. He'd survived that territory once by the skin of his teeth, as a teenage boy, and he wasn't going back except in the driver's seat, though truth be told, he'd never met a father yet who thought he was in charge of his teenage daughter's life. Quite the opposite—teenage girls seemed to rule whatever planet they were residing on, which was exactly how he remembered high school being: girls in charge, boys going in circles standing still.

Of the four Folton Ridge girls, both of the nice ones had been in their rooms last night. The other two had started out in the boys' dorm with a fifth of vanilla vodka and ended up half-naked in a hot tub at a private house near the Broadmoor Hotel with a whole bunch of Folton Ridge boys, half a dozen townies, and, from the uniforms he'd seen littering the deck, a couple of cadets from the Air Force Academy.

Dax knew hell-bent-for-disaster when he saw it, and the two Folton girls had been leading the pack. They were wild ones, a fact he had thoroughly documented with the long lens on his camera.

Four Folton Ridge field hockey players, varsity, and one of them was the girl he needed. He wouldn't know for sure which one until Easy got him the name from Burt's Chicago connection. They should have had it before he'd ever gone to Colorado Springs. If they didn't have it by morning, he and Easy were going to be walking into the payoff with Bleak without their ace—in which case he'd be winging it.

Nothing new there, but he preferred the sure shot when he could get it.

Sure shot, hell. Uncle Burt had never had a sure shot in his life, and this mess Dax and Easy were trying to pull him out of had been screwed up from the get-go. They hadn't been able to get Otto to commit to coming to Denver any earlier for the "deal of a lifetime" they'd concocted strictly to set him up, and they'd held Franklin Bleak off as long as they could. That bastard was done with Burt Alden. Tomorrow, five A.M., was the drop-dead date on the money Easy's father owed, and she and Dax had ended up in the middle of the time crunch.

Never again, that's all he could say. Esme wanted her father paid up, shut down, and exfiltrated. Ex-filleted was more like it as far as Dax was concerned. He didn't care where Burt Alden landed, the old man was going to find a bet, and a scam, and trouble—and probably a little stolen art. Uncle Burt was good at that. Dax had to give him some credit.

His glance slid to the folder lying in the passenger seat. He'd found the girls—four girls, four sets of photographs, and endless pages of on-line chitchat. He'd combed through all of it, compared the photographs to the pictures he had of Franklin Bleak, and he had a guess as to which of the varsity girls called Franklin "Daddy"—and Daddy Franklin wasn't going to be happy to see the photographs Dax had taken of his girl in that hot tub.

Bottom line, though, Dax could have photographed her serving tea to the queen, and it would have been enough to push Franklin Bleak off center and off Burt Alden's back. No one was supposed to know Franklin Bleak had a daughter. The facts of the girl's connection to him had been buried deep, and for good reason. Franklin was the kind of guy with a lot of enemies and no known weaknesses to exploit—except her.

The prep school girl was no love child, no by-blow from one of Bleak's many mistresses over the years. No, the chubby, dark-haired, freckle-faced teen with the penchant for vanilla-vodka shooters and topless hot-tubbing was the real deal, Bleak's only legitimate offspring, heir to his fortune—the blood running true. Seventeen years and nine months ago, after a violent rise up the ranks in the Chicago rackets, Franklin had bought himself a high-society wife off the East Coast who'd done her duty and then locked him out cold. There'd been no divorce. But the wife hadn't stuck around either. She'd taken his money and his kid and hightailed it back to the coast. The only thing she'd left behind was his name—Bleak.

Without the name, the kid had been little more than a rumor, but a damned persistent rumor with enough clues to get Dax and Easy wondering why Franklin Bleak, a man with no previously observed altruistic tendencies, had endowed a little-known school in Colorado Springs and gotten himself appointed to the board of trustees. On top of which, for the last three years, he hadn't missed a single

Folton Ridge Flyers field hockey game. He was also the sole donor of the Flyers' new uniforms, which they got every year—this information having been unearthed by Easy while she'd been chatting up the coach during an afternoon practice a week ago.

It had all fit, and despite having to witness a lot of adolescent hot-tub groping and the one girl up-chucking the night's libations, and despite being stuck in a traffic jam and running out of time, Dax was sitting easy.

He had Patsy.

He had the panatela.

And up ahead, at the top of the next rise in the road, he had an exit ramp to get him back on an open road heading into the hills. He wasn't that far out from the city. He'd find his way into lower downtown, no matter how many cows he had to pass.

CHAPTER TEN

This couldn't be right.

Esme looked at the car Johnny had stopped next to, a low-slung wreck in primer gray with a few haphazardly applied swaths of navy blue paint and one black stripe going up over the hood and down the deck, a fastback with a badly dented rear end and dirty whitewalls. The badge on the side panel said Cyclone.

She couldn't have agreed more. The car looked like something that had been spit out of a hurricane and then rolled down a cliff.

"This is your car?" She had one hand pressed to her rib cage, trying to ease the stitch in her side. They'd sprinted the two blocks from Wazee up to Market, after making it down the warehouse fire escape.

"Yes." He pulled a set of keys out of his pocket, checking the street in both directions, not at all winded. She was in shape. She went to the gym. She didn't know where he went, but if it was a gym, he was living there.

"I thought you used to steal cars." She checked the street, too, looking to see if Dovey and his crew were rounding a corner or pounding up the sidewalk.

"I did once…maybe twice," Johnny admitted after a short pause.

Yeah, maybe twice. Maybe more than twice.

"Maybe you should have kept one of them." The rear bumper on the Cyclone was held in place with a few wraps of baling wire and a length of twine and was still half falling off.

The look he gave her was unreadable—but it was definitely a look.

"It was just a suggestion." *Geez.* The Challenger he'd picked her up in that long-ago summer night had been a beautiful car, and so freaking fast the takeoff had stolen her breath and jump-started her pulse. He should have kept that one.

He slid the key into the hunk-a-junk's passenger-door lock and gave it a twist, but nothing happened.

Big surprise, she thought.

She looked back down toward Wazee and saw a guy running up the street—*cripes.* It was Dovey. Smollett hadn't forgotten anything about the damn double dog dare.

"Hey," she said, thinking she should give Johnny a heads-up.

"Yeah, yeah, I see him."

Okay, but did he see—

"Yeah."

Good. Great. Kevin and the Bear guy were lumbering after Dovey, shoving their way through anybody not smart enough to get out of their way.

What in the hell was she thinking? she wondered. Any advantage they'd had was in speed, and the Cyclone didn't look like it had any—even if he could get in the damn thing.

And even if he did get in, she shouldn't.

No, that wasn't the smart move.

He jiggled the key, then jiggled it again, and she felt her tension rising with every little shake and wiggle.

Sure, logically, if he could get in and get it started, a car could outrun a guy, especially a guy like Kevin or somebody like the guy in the Bear's jacket—but Dovey was looking pretty quick. He was gaining ground.

She glanced back at Johnny. He'd taken the key out and was shoving it back in very gently, very slowly.

Good God. If the suspense didn't kill her, Franklin jerk-off Bleak might.

She needed to move.

"I'll just go ahead and get a cab," she blurted out, taking a step up the sidewalk. "Uh, thanks. For everything. Really. I'll call you—"

The key turned.

"Get in the car," he ordered, swinging the door wide.

He didn't wait for her to obey, just stepped

around her and headed for the driver's side of the wreck.

Shit.

She grabbed the door and glanced down the street again, then slid her gaze back to Johnny, who was already dropping in behind the steering wheel, the ignition key in his hand.

If the Cyclone started, so help her God, she was getting in. Dovey had hit the sidewalk and was moving in fast—and she had to wonder, really: Just how damn badly did Bleak want her? And if he wanted her as badly as it looked, sending three of his boys after her, then, chances were, it would definitely be to her advantage to—

Geezus holy mother—the beat-up old car came to life with one twist of the key, sending a body-rocking vibration up through her hand, up her arm, and down her body all the way to her toes—and in that instant, inside of a heartbeat, the Cyclone ruled the street.

The hunk-a-junk was alive and well, tuned and timed to a rumbling roar of horsepower and headers, growling low in its throat like a feral cat, shaking like a wet dog, and making the glass rattle in the door frame.

She didn't hesitate.

In one move, she was in the car, dropping into the passenger seat, reaching for the seat belt with one hand, and slamming the door behind her with the other. Johnny instantly spun the wheel, his feet working the pedals. Shoved up into first, and then second, the Cyclone slid fast and sleek into a break in the traffic.

She craned her head around, looking back toward
Wazee, only to see Dovey standing stock-still on the
sidewalk, his gaze riveted to Johnny, his mouth
hanging half open.

Damn, damn, oh, double damn.

"I think Dovey has definitely recognized you,"
she said, feeling beholden to warn him. For whatever reasons, he'd just saved her ass—again.

"Good," he said, the word succinct. "It'll give
him something to think about."

She arched an eyebrow in his direction, surprised at the coldness of his voice.

In high school—sure, Dovey would have definitely thought twice about messing with Johnny
Ramos. In fact, he would have thought about it
until he'd changed his mind. But Franklin Bleak
wouldn't, and Dovey worked for Bleak—at least according to Johnny, the guy in the driver's seat, the
one momentarily in charge.

Very momentarily, if she so chose.

She looked him over again, from the thick dark
hair cut short on his head, to the lean, chiseled
lines of his face. There was no "give" in the way he
looked, no softness. His shoulders were broad under his shirt, his hands large and strong on the
steering wheel, the way he moved filled with intent.
He wasn't the wild kid she'd known in school. He
was something else. She just didn't know what. No
shot caller for some gang—she'd bet the house on
that, and no errand boy for Franklin Bleak, setting
her up for a takedown. Something about him was
too straight. She felt it. Something emanating from

his core, and it filled him with a confidence she'd only seen in a certain kind of guy. Guys like Dax.

Yeah, that was it, and she knew damn well where her partner had gotten it from—the crucible of combat and years of exacting training engaged on a level that was recognized in all quarters as elite, those teams where the percentages of acceptance were measured in single digits, with only two or three men out of a hundred already toughened soldiers making the cut. Dax belonged in the life-and-death game of war played by the "for real" big bad boys, not the sagging gangbangers, not the mall rats and the street punks, but the ones who'd "been there, done that" in far-off places under circumstances few men could survive.

And Johnny Ramos reminded her of that.

It was enough to make a girl think.

No, he wasn't setting her up for Bleak, and she knew for damn sure he wasn't part of any fallout from Otto. She knew Erich Warner's guys, and Johnny wasn't one of them. Whatever he was up to, following her, getting involved, he was up to it for his own reasons—and she couldn't help but wonder what in the hell those were.

They cruised up Market Street in the Cyclone, weaving through traffic at just over the speed limit, just fast enough to give them an edge without getting a ticket, leaving Dovey and his crew behind, which was all great and good, except for one thing.

"We're going the wrong way." She didn't mean to sound ungrateful, but it was the truth.

"Excuse me?" He slanted her a quick glance across the darkened interior of the car.

"Wrong way," she repeated, pointing out the windshield. "We're going it."

"We're on a one-way street."

"I know." And she did. She knew Denver like the back of her hand, and she knew he did, too. "We need to get up on Larimer and back down to Speer, or you need to pull over and let me out somewhere up here, so I can catch a cab."

"Sure," he said, nodding his head, his brow furrowing. "Right. Good idea. I'll get right on it, right after you settle down for a minute and take a breath, and maybe, just maybe, tell me what in the hell is going on."

He downshifted for a light, and they sat at the corner, rumbling and rocking in place.

"Is this thing street legal?" It didn't feel street legal.

"Not in fourth gear."

Whatever that meant, though she thought she had an idea. Just like she had an idea of what was making his jaw so tight. Just like she had an idea that he wasn't really considering her suggestion to pull over and let her out.

"I have an appointment," she explained. She didn't dare put it any plainer, or make it any clearer, and her appointment was in the other direction.

"So you said." He kept his attention on the street, his gaze checking the intersection and the Cyclone's rearview mirror. "But you didn't say who with, or what it's about, and frankly, given who's chasing you, I think we'd both be better off if I knew the answers to both those questions."

She thought about his request for a nanosecond, and gave him the only possible reply.

"You can think whatever you like."

It was a summer night in August, in the middle of the city, but the temperature in the Cyclone dropped forty degrees in a heartbeat, with the Ice Age starting on his side of the car. She didn't bother to turn and see what kind of look he was giving her. She could figure it out on her own—glacial, with a side order of pissed-off. So what—she had a job to do. That was her bottom line, and he wasn't part of the job.

While they waited, two cop cars came down Eighteenth, heading northwest, passing in front of them at a good clip. A second later both cars hit their lights and sirens. Another siren sounded somewhere behind them, the noise fading north.

Typical Friday night in the city, she thought. Trouble everywhere, and her in the middle of more than she liked. She had to get to Isaac Nachman's. Her schedule wasn't flexible, her plan was not optional, and Johnny Ramos wasn't part of either.

The light turned, and they cruised up another block and stopped at the next light with cars on either side of them. He slid the Cyclone back down into first gear.

"I saw that guy you hog-tied at the Oxford," he said, not sounding any too happy about it.

She didn't blame him. Otto Von Lindberg hog-tied in a black leather thong and leashed to a bed frame was one of those haunting images she was afraid she was just going to have to live with, probably for quite a while.

There were worse things, though, far worse, and if John Ramos was anything close to what she thought he might be, he knew it.

"So?" she said, refraining from a sigh. She wasn't going to squirm. Regardless of how sordid it all must have looked to him, she'd done a damn good job in the Oxford. She'd gotten in with the least amount of effort possible, a seamless pretext that had required nothing more of her than fifty bucks to the valet and slipping into a short skirt and a cheap shirt. She'd controlled the situation from the first instant of contact until the last. Old Otto had never had a chance. She'd had one hundred percent mission success, verified by the Jakob Meinhard currently residing in her messenger bag.

And she'd gotten the hell out without a hitch—except for the close to six feet of tight-jawed bad boy sitting behind the Cyclone's steering wheel.

He was a hitch. No matter how she worked it around in her mind, the truth was she'd gotten herself tailed and caught.

"I heard him say he'd called for Dixie," he said. "He was expecting the dominatrix."

Oh, great. He'd been right there on her ass practically the whole time, and she hadn't had a clue.

"Dixie's pimp is a guy named Benny-boy Jackman," he continued, after her first moment of silence built to a second, and a third, and a fourth.

She cleared her throat—very discreetly.

"If he finds out you've been trading on her name, he'll come after you big-time and not play nice when he catches up with you."

Yes, she knew, and wasn't that just what she needed, one more thing to worry about, but it wasn't like she hadn't figured Dixie and Benny-boy into her night's profit margin.

"I'm prepared to shell out some cash to keep the peace," she said.

"Fair warning, babe. Benny-boy may want more than cash. He's got a reputation to maintain, and it ain't pretty."

She held herself still, refraining from giving in to another, even heavier, sigh. She knew all this. Didn't everybody the hell in Denver have some damn reputation to maintain? That was her whole frickin' problem, men's egos and their badass reputations. She knew how the streets worked, and they didn't work with some middle-class blonde getting away with stealing "Dixie" Talbot's tricks— but no matter what in the hell Benny-boy Jackman wanted, she had much bigger problems than a Mile High Sixteenth Street pimp.

"Tough," she said, and she meant it. "If he wants more than that, he'll have to get in line."

Get in line?

Benny-boy Jackman could just get in line?

Yeah, Johnny thought. Benny-boy could get in line behind Franklin Bleak and his goons, and probably that German guy, too, if he'd gotten out of his cuffs yet. That ought to be a real party and a half, and just how the hell many of these guys did she think she could take on and still come out in one piece?

Oh, she was a cool one, all right. Too cool for her own good, and he was just about ready to tell her, when he saw a delivery van pulling into the traffic behind them off of Eighteenth and onto Market.

Fuck.

"You're buckled, right?"

"Right."

He checked the street ahead of them again, waited for a truck to clear the intersection, then shot across against the light and kept going.

She twisted in her seat to look out the back window. "What? The LeSabre? I don't see it."

"No. A white panel van in the right lane." He took a sharp left into an alley and slowed down just enough to keep the Cyclone from hitting the Dumpsters and packing crates pushed up against the sides of the narrow opening.

"Why? Who's in the van?" She sat back a bit, facing him.

"I don't know who's in it, but it says Bleak Enterprises on the side."

"*Geezus,*" she breathed the word, looking back out the rear window—and for the first time, he thought maybe she was getting a little unnerved by what he considered to be a damned unnerving situation.

At the end of the alley, he crossed Blake, then

continued on through the alley, until he was back to Wazee and turned north.

"No-no-no-no," she said. "South. We need to get to the interstate."

"No, we don't," he said, continuing north, the Cyclone roaring up through its gears. A few more turns had them back on Market and headed into the danger zone.

LoDo quickly disappeared behind them, the neighborhood going downhill fast once they passed Park Avenue, and he kept going, past the rail yards and into the boondocks, until he pulled into another, even narrower alley. He quickly eased the Cyclone down into second.

She looked around at where he'd brought them, and when recognition settled in, he felt her stiffen.

Her gaze rocketed back to him.

"You've got to be kidding."

The only answer he gave her was to shake his head. He wasn't kidding, not in this place.

Stretching his arm out the driver's side window, he closed a circle with his ring finger and his thumb, and holding the Cyclone to a crawl, he drove through an open iron gate into the no-man's-land of the Locos' hideout.

CHAPTER ELEVEN

Scotch.

General Richard "Buck" Grant dropped his duffel at the end of the bed in the guest suite at 738 Steele Street and walked over to the long row of windows overlooking the seventh-floor garage. A bottle and two glasses were waiting for him on a table next to the windows.

The Scotch at Steele Street was always the best of the eighteen-year-olds. Hart and Hawkins made damn sure of it.

He poured himself a short shot and took his first sip. For a long moment, he let it sit in his mouth, let it infuse his senses. For a long moment, he waited, wondering if anything could disguise the taste of betrayal.

No, he decided, swallowing. Not today.

Fuck. He tossed back the rest of the shot and poured himself another.

Everything at 738 Steele Street was the best, up to and including the operators. Hart and Hawkins made damn sure of it, and there wasn't a goddamn one of them who didn't deserve better than what he'd brought with him to Denver.

Fucking CIA.

Below him in the bays, Creed and Skeeter had their heads under the hood of one of Steele Street's most infamous American muscle cars. The Chevy Nova's name was "Mercy" because she had none— so the story went, and Buck knew it for a fact. He thought Dylan had ordered the beast drawn and quartered years ago. The 1969 Yenko 427 Nova did her 0 to 60 mph in under four seconds. Buck had been in her once when she'd done it with Quinn Younger, SDF's jet jockey, behind the wheel, and once had been enough. He hadn't checked, but he was pretty sure he'd left part of his stomach and half his hair on the starting line. He didn't like to admit it, but he really couldn't afford to lose half his hair, so he kept it short, regulation buzz. What was left of it was one hundred percent iron gray, a hard color, on a hard guy, with a hard job. That was him—Hard-Ass Grant.

Geezus. He set the glass aside, still full. This was so much bullshit, the reason he was here, and what he'd been sent to do.

He lifted his hand to his face, covering his eyes, and he swore again. Shit like this is what gave guys like him ulcers.

And apparently, ulcers didn't like their Scotch neat.

He let the pain run through his gut, rode it out, and took a breath. Then he picked up the glass and dosed himself with the second shot of whiskey.

His gaze shifted from Creed and Skeeter and the cars on the garage floor to his duffel. There was a very official folder inside from the Department of Labor containing photographs and a letter from William J. Davies, who'd been the Assistant Secretary of Defense for Special Operations and Low-Intensity Conflict when Special Defense Force had been created and put under Grant's command. Davies had long since been kicked upstairs to an undisclosed position in an undisclosed government agency that didn't have a damn thing to do with the Labor Department. The chain of command hadn't really changed for Buck and SDF, but it had sunk deeper into the black water of the Potomac as the years had gone by, the wars had gotten more costly, and the necessary deeds had become less publicly palatable. Still, the chain of command had never been as deliberately obscure or the orders as black as what he'd gotten this morning. He'd opened the folder as soon as it had arrived in his office in the Marsh Annex east of Washington, D.C. He'd read the letter inside once, looked at the accompanying photographs, put it all back in the envelope, and immediately hitched a ride out of Andrews Air Force Base to Colorado.

The photographs had been damned startling, damned unnerving, and Buck had seen it all in his fifty-four years. He just hadn't seen anything like this.

Davies had told him what to do. He hadn't told him how to do it, and Buck had wanted to do it in person. Some information just shouldn't be delivered over the phone, no matter how secure the line. He'd also figured if he was on deck with them when he briefed the team, he could manage the fallout. He'd also wanted to be on board during the initial planning phase of the requested mission.

Mission—he hated even putting the word to the deed. It was a goatfuck, a gut-wrenching goatfuck. Sometimes, being in this man's army took almost more than he had to give. Everyone on SDF was going to know what that felt like and have to deal with it by the time they finished looking at those photographs, by the time he laid out the operation. The only alternative to dealing with it was anarchy, to willfully disobey a direct order, and the only alternative to mutiny was to lock the whole damn team up in some goddamn high-security prison and throw away the key until the mission had been accomplished by someone else. But then, that had been the problem, hadn't it? No one, *no one,* had even gotten close to accomplishing the mission. Tasking SDF with the deed was about as desperate an act as he'd ever seen the government's snoop-and-spook apparatchiki reduced to miring themselves in—and they were "in," the whole goddamn alphabet-soup boatload of them. Not that anyone would ever take responsibility for what had happened. In cases like this, the buck got passed around faster than a hot potato, getting kicked under tables and buried in crap, until everyone who had ever heard of it was either dead, exiled, or promoted out of the line of fire.

Politics was such a goddamn dirty business. It made war look like a cakewalk. Politics was such a goddamn dirty business; it made him sick.

He checked his watch. It had taken forever to get to Denver from Peterson Air Force Base, and there wasn't a whole lot of the night left. He'd contacted Dylan in New York and asked for a meeting at Steele Street first thing in the morning. Besides Creed and Skeeter, Hawkins was in residence. Grant knew Dylan had told them to stay put. Zachary Prade was already on his way from Podunk, Montana, or wherever the hell his wife's family ranch was located.

Trace, that was it. Trace, Montana, in Chouteau County.

Kid had done a flip-flop in Los Angeles, barely getting there before the word had gone out for him to come home. Quinn would be down from his mountain home in Evergreen before dawn. Smith would be getting into Peterson a little after midnight. Buck hoped the traffic between Colorado Springs and Denver had cleared out by then. The damn interstate had been a parking lot when he'd been on it.

And they needed Smith. He'd be good to have on board, a cool head, a cold heart. Smith could be counted on to keep appropriate emotional distance between himself and what the others would be feeling no matter how professionally they'd always conducted themselves. This damn situation would test them all.

There was no pulling Gillian and Travis off their mission. Politics again. Protecting senators on junkets in Third World countries, this one Bolivia, took precedence over just about every other damn thing. The trouble was, Dylan would instantly recognize the advantage of having Red Dog and the Angel Boy on the outside, if everyone on the inside found the mission parameters unacceptable and chose to exercise their marked instincts for independent thought—and who could blame them? Not Buck, not on this deal.

But neither was he going to condone or allow it.

His job was going to be to convince them not to abandon ship, to stay inside the system, to stay inside the rules. Working together, they could keep the sacrifices to a minimum. They were soldiers. He knew them. They would comply. He'd be damned if he lost his whole team due to a situation the CIA should never have allowed, let alone allowed to get so damn far out of hand that it had become a priority-one national security issue.

On the upside, he'd also brought the team something they needed: Juan Aurelio Ramos. The kid had proven himself in combat over and over again in his three tours of duty. Even with his last go-around in Afghanistan having gotten a little tight in places, and damn rough in others, Ramos had pulled through. He'd made it home in one piece, inside and out. Hawkins would take care of the rest, getting him trained up for the type of missions SDF took on. Training never stopped for any of them. It was the order of the day, every day. Ramos was officially SDF's now—and Grant's. All Buck had to do was keep the team alive long enough to use him.

Snagging the pair of highball glasses with the fingers of his right hand, he grabbed the bottle of Scotch with his left and walked out of the guest suite to the main elevator in the office. It was a hot summer night in Denver, and he was heading to The Beach—a couple of lawn chairs and a ratty piece of Astro Turf nailed to the roof of 738 Steele Street. With a bit of luck, he wouldn't be alone up there for long.

CHAPTER **TWELVE**

Old fears die hard. Legitimate old fears don't die at all, hard or otherwise. Driving into the Locos compound off north Delgany was a fairly well-grounded old fear in Esme's book, an old fear with a new, unexpectedly current infusion of adrenaline.

Fight or flight—she was feeling it with every leap of her pulse.

"This isn't cool." It was crazy. She had enough trouble tonight without him adding a boatload of gangsters to the mix.

"No, it's not," he agreed, which didn't do a damn thing to calm her nerves.

"Then why in the hell are we here?"

"I need some information. Baby Duce will have it."

Oh, perfect. Baby Duce. She knew the damn hierarchy and history as well as any inner-city kid. Baby Duce ran the Locos. He'd been running them since Carlos had gotten killed in some turf war, and before Carlos, it had been Dom Ramos, who, as she most certainly remembered, had also gotten killed in some turf war. The Locos had been a lot smaller crew under Dom, very tight-knit, and they'd mostly run their business and their wars on the other side of the river. This north-downtown stuff had all started with a pipeline cocaine deal Baby Duce had brokered during the first year of his reign. The whole Locos sphere of influence had done nothing but expand since then. They owned both sides of the river now, ran most of lower downtown and downtown, and had made heavy inroads into the eastern suburbs.

Johnny freakin' Ramos—crown prince of the Locos by blood and heritage. Maybe she'd been wrong about him.

Crap.

Of course she'd been wrong about him.

Esme could see shadows moving in the shadows of the buildings and houses on each side of the alley. They were coming in the back door of a very sketchy neighborhood, a very well protected neighborhood, and they were running a gauntlet of its guards, with every shadow a potential threat.

Within the space of a couple of blocks, she and Johnny had left the hip and happening part of lower downtown and cruised into what Realtors referred to as River North, or RiNo, a "mixed use" area. In this case, the mix of use included ultra-low-end residential crammed in between no-longer-in-use industrial and retail buildings, a good breeding ground for vice. Not for long, though. Developers had already made headway in the area, optimistically hoping they could turn it into a "front door" neighborhood.

Hell, get a couple of developers holding hands with a few Realtors and guaranteed they'd start turning pigs' ears into silk purses, and RiNo into the next LoDo—for a price, usually a pretty pricey price.

But for now, this block and half a dozen others belonged to Baby Duce, and she and Johnny were right in the middle of his River North territory.

Halfway down the alley, Johnny stopped the Cyclone and took the key out of the ignition. To her right, a haphazard array of garbage cans flanked a padlocked iron door with the words Butcher Drug Store painted on the cinderblock above it.

Geezus. Butcher and drugs in the same sentence were enough to send a chill down her spine, especially when, to her left, a chain-linked, barbed-wire fence was all that stood between her and the Locos' north-side crib. A pair of lights on the back of the ramshackle old house lit up the yard and part of the alley.

Yeah, every guy in Denver had some badass reputation he was working to uphold, and Baby Duce was no different. So now she had Bleak on her ass, Baby Duce on her left, Benny-boy staring out of her near future, Erich Warner and Otto Von Lindberg hopefully not bearing down on her from out of her past, and Isaac Nachman nowhere in sight, because she was stuck in this goddamn alley, in a car with no key.

"Wait here." Johnny opened his door and was about halfway out when she stopped him with a word.

"Five," she said.

He hesitated for a second, then glanced back at her over his shoulder.

"Five?"

"Five minutes, and then I'm walking out of here." And she meant it.

He considered the pavement at his feet for a couple of seconds, then finished getting out, closed the door, and leaned down through the window. "In that case, I'll be back in four and a half."

Straightening up, he slapped the roof of the car twice, saying something in Spanish to the guys who'd come up from both ends of the alley and were stationing themselves along the fence.

Esme had taken French in high school, thinking it would make her more refined. It hadn't, and now she was clueless about what he'd said, except it was probably something like "don't steal the tires off this awesome car," or "don't strip the huge, mother-freaking engine I bolted under this hood," or hope-fully, maybe, "don't harass the dumb blonde who let me hijack her into this alley."

Not that the girl was going to stand still for too much harassing.

Still, hell—she watched him step through the gate into a weed-choked yard and walk to the back door of the house. A tall, muscular guy covered in tattoos met him there, and they talked for a few moments, with the guy looking at her most of that time, then he and Johnny disappeared inside, and she sat back in her seat. There were five guys milling in the alley, and each and every one of them was staring at her, too—*dammit*.

She checked her watch. Four and a half minutes—just enough time to do a little housekeeping.

She pulled her phone out of the messenger bag and found three missed calls, all from Dax, and nothing from her dad. This time, she didn't refrain from a heavy sigh. She gave into it, just to get it off her chest. This whole damn night was because of him, and all she'd asked for was the name of Franklin Bleak's daughter. Burt had promised her his good friend Thomas in Chicago would get the name weeks ago, but like everything else with her dad, it hadn't worked out like he'd planned. She'd given him one simple job to do, and he'd blown it.

Big surprise.

Esme Alden, Private Investigator—she was smarter with strangers. She expected more. But her dad—hell, she definitely had issues with her dad. Someday she was going to grow up and stop trying to make him into something he was not, like responsible, smart enough to take care of his family, and strong enough not to court financial ruin on every damn toss of the dice, and every dog race, or every horse, or the damn Denver Broncos.

Today was obviously not that day.

She scrolled down her address list to his name

and pressed the call button. After seven interminable rings, she got her folks' answering machine.

"Hi. You've reached the Aldens, Burt, Beth, and Esme," her mother's sweet voice said. *"Leave us a message, and we'll call you back."*

Esme figured when and if she ever got married, her mother would finally take her name off the family answering machine.

"Dad," she said. "If you're there, pick up. If you're not, you should be, and either way, call me as soon as you get this message. The clock is running here, Dad."

She hung up, and hit Dax's number.

"Go," he answered halfway through the first ring.

"I'm on my way to Isaac Nachman's with the Meinhard." And she was...sort of, in a roundabout way.

"Good going, bad girl, congratulations." She could almost see him smile. "But you should have been at Nachman's fifteen minutes ago."

"I got hung up."

"At the Oxford?"

"No. Back at the office."

That slowed him down for a second.

"Your dad's car didn't start, right?"

He'd warned her against using her dad's car, all but insisted she get a rental, but no, she'd had to use the old man's minivan, so he could feel like he was contributing to the team.

The old man was going to get her killed.

She could see that coming now. His incompetence had always been contagious. It was why she'd worked so hard in school, and so hard keeping her ducks in a row, keeping her clothes tidy and her shoes clean and her homework done and her braids tight, and her pants on, just to have some goddamn control over something besides the missing grocery money, or the hocked television, or the men who sometimes had come to the house—men very much like Franklin Bleak and Kevin Harrell. It was why she'd moved to Seattle to work with Dax—to get away from the rolling inevitability of her dad's disasters.

She'd begged her mom to come with her, but her mom had said no, she couldn't leave Esme's father—and if that was love, Esme didn't want a damn thing to do with it.

"No. The minivan was starting for me all day. I didn't have any problems with it until the cops booted it on Wynkoop."

"*Cripes,*" he swore under his breath. "So where are you? In a cab?"

"Actually, I'm in Baby Duce's backyard, sitting in a Cyclone."

"Baby Duce? The Locos Baby Duce?" he asked after a moment, not exactly an innocuous question under the best of circumstances, and these weren't anywhere close to the best, and she could tell by the tone of his voice that he'd figured that much out in a heartbeat, and that his mood had taken a sudden, understandably steep dive.

"Yes."

"In a Cyclone?"

"Yes."

There was another slight pause.

"A '68?" he asked.

She'd known he wouldn't be able to resist that one.

"Probably. It's fast, got a lot of engine in it, but it's really beat-up."

"A sleeper," he said.

Sure, she thought, a sleeper, the kind of car no one would suspect of having more power than Godzilla.

"You're sitting in a sleeper in Baby Duce's backyard." It wasn't a question. "Who's holding the pink slip on the Cyclone?" That was a question, and she was going to get around to answering it pretty damn quickly, right after she assured him she was still doing her job.

"I'm only here for another couple of minutes, then I'm heading straight for Isaac Nachman's." One way or another, with or without Johnny Ramos.

"Answer the question, Easy, and then tell me you got the name of Bleak's kid from your dad."

What did she have to offer him, really, except a damning silence. Fortunately, with Dax, a damning silence was about all it took.

She heard him sigh.

"You know what this sounds like, Easy," he said, his voice slipping down another notch into the "very unhappy" category.

"A royal screwup."

"Like it's time to close up shop and figure out another plan."

"No. We're still a go here."

"Your dad—"

"I know."

She heard the Dax Killian version of an angry outburst, which sounded a lot like a softly muttered *"for the love of God and Patsy Cline."* Burt Alden was the family curse. The fact had been highly documented over the thirty-year course of her parents' marriage.

"What aren't you telling me, Easy? Start at the top, and don't forget the Cyclone."

It was situation report time—sit-rep—or confession time, depending on a person's point of view and level of guilt, and he wasn't going to like this part any more than she did.

"I was recognized at the Oxford by a guy I went to high school with, John Ramos. He followed me to the office. We talked for a couple of minutes and walked out. When I saw the van was booted, I crossed Wynkoop to get a cab, and the next thing I know, he's hauling me up Sixteenth, because Dovey Smollett, Kevin Harrell, and this other guy look like they're out to snatch me off the street. So we do the O'Shaunessy's–Cuppa Joe double dog dare, lose them, and end up here in one of Baby Duce's alleys in Ramos's Cyclone."

It was quite a story, even in the retelling, a royal screwup, just like she'd said, but all Dax said to her was, "Kevin Harrell."

"I know." Kevin Harrell had been hovering near

the top of Dax's "Guy's Who Don't Want to Meet Me in a Dark Alley" list for years.

"Is Dovey Smollett Greg Smollett's little brother?"

"Yes."

"And why in the world would a Smollett be after you? What—did you break his heart in junior high or something?"

She wished it were that simple. She really did.

"He works for Franklin Bleak."

Dax took Patsy Cline's name in vain again under his breath. Three times on the Patsy business, and Esme knew the shit would hit the fan.

"I want you out of there now. Go back to the office, and—no, on second thought, skip the office. They've got that covered. Go to Mama Guadalupe's. I'll meet you in the bar."

"I'm not meeting you anywhere, until I see Nachman and get the cash. We stick to the plan, Dax. Nothing has happened here, except for a half-hour delay." More like an hour, actually, by the time she made it to Isaac Nachman's mountain mansion, but the Denver industrialist was her next call. She'd smooth everything over, make the delivery, get the money, and meet Dax back at the Faber Building as planned.

"A half an hour and Bleak pooching the deal, bad girl. You know what this means. Bleak is looking to put the squeeze on your dad. And who is John Ramos?" Dax said. "What's his angle? How do you know he's not working for Bleak, too? What was he doing? Staking out the office, and then he follows you over to—oh, wait a minute here . . . ah, hell, Easy, don't tell me John Ramos is Dom Ramos's little brother."

Okay, Dax. Her lips were sealed.

"He's Dom Ramos's little brother, isn't he?"

"Well, Dax, I'm sitting here staring at five Locos in an alley off north Delgany. I'm not at a warehouse in Commerce City staring at a few hundred cases of toilet paper and fiesta napkins."

"What are you doing on Delgany?" Dax's voice took on an added edge. "I thought Baby Duce worked out of the Aztec Club."

"The Aztec burned down a few years ago. To the ground. You really need to keep up."

While she watched, one of the Locos pushed off the fence and started for the car, and all she could think was—*Oh, baby, don't go there.* Nothing good could come from backing her into a corner, absolutely nothing good.

She very discreetly slipped her open hand up against the snap on her jacket. From that position, she knew exactly how far she was from her pistol— less than a second away—but she wouldn't draw unless she made the decision to shoot. An unarmed blonde in a beat-up old car had a zero threat quotient to a gang of five Locos, and that's exactly what she wanted all of them to keep thinking—that she was no threat to them. Once a gun was brought into play, all the rules would change.

"I keep up enough," Dax assured her. "You tell Duce you're with me. That dude owes me from way back. He won't have forgotten."

"Sure. If it gets to that, I'll drop your name." She wasn't going to ask what Baby Duce owed him for, but she didn't doubt the debt was real, or that Baby Duce would remember both it and Daniel Axel, Dax, Killian. All the time she'd spent being good in school and keeping her ducks in a row, Dax had spent running wild and making a name for himself. Dax's ducks wouldn't have known a row if it had snapped up and bit them in the butt.

"Have you called Isaac Nachman?"

"He's next on my list. Trust me, there won't be any trouble. He wants the Meinhard. You know how he is about his paintings. Me being even an hour late isn't going to change anything or put us out of the running."

"Call me when you get to Mama Guadalupe's."

"Can do. It should be about eleven," she said, keeping her eye on the young Loco. He smiled at her, showing off two rows of pearly whites with his incisors capped in gold—vampire-style. *Geezus.*

"If there's any trouble, any at all, I want you—"

"Nachman knows the drill," she interrupted. There wasn't going to be any trouble, not with Isaac Nachman. "Dad's done amazing work for him over the years. Geez, Dax, Dad's the one who tracked down Nachman's Renoir. In sixty years, no one else even got close to it, and with me on board now, the Meinhard is another clean transaction."

Disasters and general failures aside, her dad did have a real flair for finding stolen art, especially if it had been stolen by the Nazis, which encompassed most of the Nachman family's missing pieces.

Hitler's ambassador to France had personally absconded with three hundred and forty-eight paintings and drawings out of the Nachman family vault. To date, one hundred and twenty-three had been recovered, over forty of those by her father, including, as of tonight, the Jakob Meinhard.

"So what's your ETA?" she asked.

"Ten-thirty to eleven o'clock on the outside. I'm on the back roads in the boondocks south of Denver. The interstate is a traffic jam," Dax said. "If you get to the bar first, don't have a margarita. Just wait for me. When I get there, we'll decide whether or not we need a new plan for dealing with Bleak. And answer your darn phone when I call."

"Can do." She started to hang up, but he stopped her.

"Easy, wait."

"Yes."

"So what's the deal with Dom's little brother? What's his stake in this? What does he want?" Dax asked.

"I haven't figured that part out yet. He said he came to the office to hire my dad, but I don't think that's it."

"He tailed you from the Oxford without you knowing it?"

Talk about rubbing it in.

"Yes."

"And he saw Smollett before you did?"

And that was even worse.

"Yes."

"And he got you out of there."

"Yes."

"Take him to Nachman's with you."

No. Her plan was to dump him and catch a cab.

"Dax, I don't—"

"Easy," he interrupted. "You've got Bleak looking for you, and I'm not there to watch your back. Whatever this guy's reasons for tailing you, I'd rather you kept him close. Maybe he'll come in handy. So far he's made pretty good moves."

"Dax, I'm sitting in Baby Duce's backyard with five Locos staring me down." And one of them was moving in.

"You're there with Domingo Ramos's little brother, sweetheart, and that blood runs deep. Ain't nothing going to happen to you on Locos turf, and this John guy knows it."

Sure, she knew it, too, except even the oldest gangster in the alley was too young to have run with Dom, and the one moving in on her might not even remember Carlos, and Johnny's time had run out about a minute ago.

"Well," she said. "If I don't make it to the bar at Guadalupe's, remember, the body will be just off Delgany, behind Butcher Drug Store."

"If I believed that for even a second, I'd be calling in the cavalry."

Esme felt herself blanch. "Uh . . . no. No cavalry. Honest, Dax. I'm fine. You're right." The last damn thing she needed was Dax's idea of Denver cavalry, which could be summed up in two words: Lieutenant Loretta. The woman had been a beat cop long before she'd made lieutenant, and if there was a kid on the street she hadn't scared straight, that kid had probably ended up in Canon City.

She'd scared the crap out of Esme. One little incident of being in the wrong place at the wrong time had been all the delinquency Esme had been able to handle.

Lieutenant Loretta was a big woman, reddish hair, large nose, amber-eyed, kind of lovely . . . maybe, if a person wasn't shaking in her shoes, looking straight up at her. Esme had been shaking like a leaf the night she'd run up against the lieutenant, and she was going to skip the cavalry tonight. Loretta Bradley didn't forget, ever. That was the urban legend, and Esme wasn't about to put it to the test.

"Hola, chica." The gangster with the gold incisors finally reached the Cyclone and leaned down in the driver's-side window, all flash and swagger. Two spiders inked into his skin covered the back of his right hand. Not black widows, she didn't think, not tarantulas, but brown recluses—with fangs. *Cripes.*

"Gotta go, Dax."

"Watch yourself."

"Check." She hung up the phone and gave the gold-toothed, spider-inked wonder a contemplative look, wondering how much longer Johnny was going to leave her here, holding down the fort in the damn alley, and whether or not it really was in her best interest to get out of the car and start walking.

Somehow she didn't think so.

The longer she held his gaze, the wider the boy's grin got.

"You see somethin' you like, *gatita*?" he asked, leaning a little farther into the car.

Not really, especially since two of the other guys had pushed off the fence and were heading toward the Cyclone. She didn't like seeing that at all.

"Maybe." She smiled back. "Do you like . . . uh, Vermeer?" She was floundering, making conversation, passing time, and hoping she could just slide her way through the next few minutes without having to make a big deal out of saving her ass.

But these guys weren't going to touch her. No way. Not when this one was flashing vampire teeth and arachnids.

"Sure, *chica*." He nodded his head, very cool, very laid-back. "I love Vermeer. *Me gusta mucho.* You got some? You wanna party?"

"Me gusta Vermeer, también," another of the gang members said, leaning down to look in the driver's-side window. He, too, had spiders tattooed on the back of his right hand.

"Kiko," the guy with the gold teeth said, "wasn't that Vermeer boom we were smokin' at Rosario's?"

"Yeah," the third Loco confirmed. "That was Vermeer." She couldn't see his right hand, but her money said he was sporting a spider tat.

"That was good shit, man."

"Yeah."

Yeah, Vermeer was good shit. Adolph Hitler had *me gusta mucho*ed it so much, he'd stolen a piece from the Rothschilds in 1941, an exquisite painting done by the artist in 1668, *The Astronomer*. To the benefit of everyone, the piece currently resided in the Louvre.

On the other hand, she was currently residing in this damn Cyclone, and Johnny Ramos was now two minutes late.

"So, *chiquita, cómo se llama?* What's your name?" vampire boy asked.

Esme didn't give it a second thought.

"Margaret Mead." That was the name she was going by in the alley tonight.

"Ah, Margarita." They all chimed in, charming as hell, and why not? She was no threat to them.

Yes, Margarita frickin' Mead.

"*Arañas, qué tal? Eh?*" She heard Johnny make his way through the crowd around the driver's door, and all she could think was that it was about time.

"*Juanio.*" The boy with the gold teeth greeted him, giving him a sign that Johnny returned.

"*Ramos,* your girl." One of the other Locos made a kissing sound. "*Se me empalmó.*"

The other guys laughed. The banter continued, and from the sounds of it, Esme was glad she didn't speak Spanish.

Behind Johnny, from somewhere in the yard, she heard a guy shout out. She glanced through the windshield and saw the tall, muscular man with all the tattoos—Baby Duce. Within seconds, the Locos had melted back into the alley, returning to their posts.

Crisis averted, thank God.

"You're late," she said, when Johnny finally got inside the car.

"And you're Margaret Mead?" He slid her a highly skeptical look.

"Margarita Mead," she corrected him.

"Shifting your anthropological research from the indigenous tribes of New Guinea to the inner-city tribes of Denver?"

She lifted one eyebrow, nonplussed. This boy was no gangster. She didn't care how tight he was with Baby Duce.

"Uh...gang culture is highly regarded as a legitimate field of academic inquiry with a number of direct correlations documented between it and more traditionally recognized tribal customs and affiliations." It was the truth. More than one dissertation had been published on the subject.

"Yeah," he agreed. "Right. That's what I've been studying for the last few years, too, tribal culture."

For no good reason, she believed him, even if she did get the idea that somehow they were talking about two different things.

"Well, I mean, of course, aside from the violence of the gangs," she added, wanting to clarify that she understood there were some inherent differences.

He let out a short, humorless laugh. "There's no 'aside' about the violence, Esme. It's front and center and always coming up behind you when you're not looking, and I can guarantee there isn't a gang in America that has anything on the 'more traditionally recognized tribes' when it comes to sheer, mind-numbing brutality. It's a war zone out there, babe, every day, in every way."

The casual bluntness of his words struck a chord, giving them a hard validity.

"Voice of experience?" she asked, curious as hell.

In answer, all he did was hold her gaze, clear and steady. By the time he looked away, she had all the answer she needed.

CHAPTER THIRTEEN

Voice of experience? Sure, Johnny thought. Tribal culture experienced and studied from the stock end of an M4 carbine in Iraq and Afghanistan—a curriculum otherwise known as war, which, according to Duce, was where Franklin Bleak was headed, if the bookie didn't get back on his side of the fence and stay there.

Johnny slipped the key in Solange's ignition, but held off starting her up. Solange the Cyclone—he'd named the car after Quinn Younger's mother, the most beautiful woman he'd ever seen. She was fifty-four now, and as far as Johnny was concerned, just hitting her stride in the gorgeousness department. The guys at Steele Street had teased him unmercifully when he'd first started calling his ride Solange—but they knew. Each and every one of those *pendejos* knew Quinn's mother was hot.

Fast-backed, 4-stacked, and radial-tracked, the

1968 Mercury Cyclone GT was plenty hot, too, but only under the hood. He'd never taken a torch or a hammer to her body. She wasn't rusted or pitted, so he'd left her alone, let her be the sleeper.

Esme was hot, but he sure as hell hadn't left her alone. Oh, no. He couldn't have jumped into the middle of this disaster any quicker if there'd been money in it.

Duce had noticed her, and he'd had plenty of questions about the blonde Johnny had left in the car, especially after Johnny had asked him about Franklin Bleak.

He started to turn the key, then stopped and took a breath.

Had it really only been an hour since he'd been sitting at the Blue Iguana drinking a Corona and minding his own business?

He checked his watch. Barely an hour—*dammit*.

Leveling his gaze at her from across the inside of the car, he very seriously asked himself if he needed to back off. She certainly hadn't asked him to get involved; quite the opposite.

But there she was, tucked into Solange's passenger seat, and there were a few things she needed to know, whether he backed off or not.

"Baby Duce wanted to know if you were Bleak's Chicago mule," he said. "Bringing in a few cakes of ice for this deal Bleak's got going down tomorrow."

That got her attention. Her eyes widened and locked onto his.

"I told him I didn't think so," he continued. "So then he asked me if you were one of Bleak's girls, and I told him the whole Dixie-tricks-at-the-Oxford-Hotel scene, and he suggested I call Benny-boy Jackman personally and grease those wheels before anybody had a chance to get themselves all worked up and maybe go gunning for trouble."

Her eyebrows rose at that, which he considered a good sign. Little Miss Cool as a Cucumber needed to know these guys were heating her up.

"And then he tells me Bleak has been shaking down all his losers for the last couple of months, shaking them hard, hurting a few. A couple of guys have even gone missing, guys who placed bets with Bleak, but bought their blow from the Locos. All bad for business, as far as Duce is concerned. He understands the need to protect profits, and God knows, he's not above hurting people if that's what it takes to make his point, but, according to Duce, it's not like his and Bleak's customers are stellar examples of humanity, especially Bleak's, according to Duce. Shit is gonna happen, he says, and a guy who wants to stay in business just has to roll with it."

For a moment, she just stared at him, and he could almost see the gears churning in her mind, organizing the whole boatload of information he'd just uploaded into her system. He could definitely see the worry suddenly darkening her eyes.

Good. She had reason to worry.

"So what do you think?" he asked.

"I think that's a . . . uh, surprisingly philosophical view from somebody who didn't get past the eighth grade."

"Yeah," he said. "That's what I thought, too. And then I thought, hey, maybe Duce is right, maybe Esme's getting shook out for some bad money."

When she didn't say anything, he kept going, pushing ahead.

"So then I ask myself, Johnny, what do you think? You think it's the ponies she's running? Or do you think it's the dogs?"

He saw her slide her hand farther around the messenger bag and pull it closer.

Yeah, he was going to get to the bag in a minute.

"And then it occurred to me that a girl who'd gotten herself in trouble, a girl who didn't want to turn a few tricks to get herself out of a jam, or a girl who didn't want to transport a few kilos of coke in lieu of the cash she didn't have, might take on another kind of job to pay her debts. She might steal something her bookie wanted, like whatever is in that bag you're so damned determined to deliver to somebody. Except if you'd stolen it for Bleak, and he was your appointment, why in the hell have we been running from his guys for the last half hour? At least that's what I asked myself, while Duce was asking about you."

She still didn't say anything.

"You can fill in the blanks here anytime, Esme. Just go ahead and jump right in."

Still, he got nothing.

"Did I make a mistake when I got between you and Dovey Smollett?"

No. She shook her head. He believed it, but she still wasn't talking.

Okay, he thought. *Fine.*

"Why don't you show me what's in the messenger bag." If it was cocaine, the party was coming to a screeching halt. It was going to hurt. Really, it would, but if Duce had called it right, the best thing he could do for Esme was turn her in before somebody turned her six feet under. He sure as hell wasn't going to step aside and let a kilo of coke hit the streets and watch her get hurt in the process. No fucking way. That was the Boy Scout in him, and for someone who had never been a Boy Scout, he seemed to have a helluva lot of it.

But, *geezus,* that was going to hurt, if she'd really sunk that damn low.

She looked down at the leather messenger bag she had clutched in her lap—and he waited.

"My partner suggested that I stick with you tonight," she said after a long, weighted silence, right about when he was going to insist on seeing what was in the bag. "That with Bleak pooching our deal, you were doing a good job of watching my back and keeping me in one piece, and I should take you with me to make my delivery, if you were willing to go."

Well, talk about a boatload of information. *Geezus.*

He sat back in his seat and looked at her for a moment, and for every second of that moment, he only saw one thing: trouble. It was probably tattooed on her ass. In caps.

"What's your deal with Bleak?" Start at the top. That was the best place.

"I pay him the money he lost on my dad, or he breaks my dad into a couple dozen pieces, a process my dad may or may not survive. It doesn't matter to Bleak either way."

Straightforward. Brutal. Predictable.

Fucking perfect.

"And your partner thinks I'm the guy to help you out with this transaction?" What kind of asshole had she hooked up with, to leave her on her own to do a deal with Franklin Bleak?

But she was shaking her head.

"Then what?" he asked.

"My first delivery is up in Genesee Park, to meet a man named Isaac Nachman. He'll give me the money in exchange for the property I recovered off the German you saw in the Oxford. Nachman's property. My dad's been working on this deal for over four years, and I've been on it a month, getting everyone in place for tonight, and now I'm running late, about half an hour late, getting to Genesee and getting the money."

Recovered—now there was a nice word. Johnny had "recovered" a few things in his younger days, and he wasn't talking upholstery.

"And when are you meeting Bleak?"

"Five A.M., but my partner will be here by then. We'll do the final deal together."

"Partner in what?" Crime? Some kind of scam they were running on rich guys living up in Genesee? Out and out idiocy?

"Private investigations. We're based in Seattle, and mostly do a lot of Pacific Rim stuff, specializing in property recovery and finding people, especially people who don't want to be found. Sometimes we work in South America, and people who need help down there know to come to us."

"Private investigations." That was a nice catchall, and the whole Pacific Rim thing sounded so professional, and she was just so sure of herself, rattling all this information off—and yet, here she was, sitting in this dump of an alley with him, back in the old neighborhood, with a lowlife like Franklin Bleak threatening to bust up her deadbeat dad. "Did you major in that up in Boulder, at the university?"

He wasn't being a smart-ass about it, really. He was curious. She'd been the best and the brightest, and guys like Franklin Bleak shouldn't be in her vocabulary, let alone breathing fire down her neck.

"Look," she said, a bit of an edge coming into her voice. "I really don't need help delivering the property. I appreciate everything you've done, but all I really need is a cab. I can take it from here."

"Where's your partner?"

"On his way up from Colorado Springs."

"You sleeping with him?" That was the question, rude or not. If he was in, he was in, and he wanted to know where all the lines were. A few thin bricks of cash delivered to Bleak? Hell, he could do that in his sleep. Esme didn't have to be part of it at all. Duce could grab a couple of his crazy spider boys out of the alley, his elite *Arañas Locos*, and the four of them could go over and visit Mr. Bleak. The whole damn thing wouldn't take more than five minutes. Johnny knew how the street worked, and whatever beef Bleak had with Burt Alden wasn't going to be worth pissing off Baby Duce, not once the bookie got his money.

And Duce owed him. Duce would always owe him, until the shot caller pulled his last breath. There was no walking away from the places they'd been together.

"No," she said. "Not that it's any of your business."

She was right. It was none of his business.

"Are you sleeping with anybody?" That wasn't any of his business either, but the question stayed where it lay.

"I don't see what that has to do with anything," she said, giving him a look that said he was way outside the bounds of propriety.

She was wrong. He and propriety had reached a truce a long time ago—and the question still stayed where it lay.

"Yes, you do," he said.

And she did. She knew exactly what it had to do with everything. It was why he was sitting here in the dark with her, instead of back on a barstool at the Blue Iguana with a shot and a beer in front of him. It was why at five A.M., no matter how she answered the question, he'd be staring across the table at Franklin Bleak with the bookie's cash lying between them.

"I don't think . . . well, think that . . ."

Yes, she did, and he could prove it.

Without moving from his side of Solange, he lifted his hand and gently cupped the lower part of her face, spreading his fingers across her left cheek and letting his thumb rest on her lips.

Softly, ever so softly, he brushed his thumb across her mouth—and watched her grow still.

He could have stopped there, could have stopped with her eyes darkening under his gaze, with the heat rising between them at his touch. But she was the impossibly not-so-easy Easy Alex, and for this one moment, he literally had her in the palm of his hand.

So he kissed her, simply leaned forward and opened his mouth over hers—and she let him, exactly as he'd known she would. Nothing had ever been finished between them, and *God,* her mouth. She had the softest lips, the slightest overbite, and a taste that went straight to his groin. She didn't move away, not so much as a millimeter. She held so perfectly still, her breath seemingly caught somewhere between them, her lips parted just enough to allow him entry, a hesitant welcome that warmed with every slow thrust of his tongue into her mouth.

She was sweet, and hot . . . and careful, exactly as she'd always been. He almost grinned. Somehow, somewhere, sometime tonight, the carefulness had to go. But for now, he'd take her careful kiss. He'd take the soft, hesitant giving way of her tongue to his, take her gentle exhalation inside himself, and imagine what it would take to make her groan.

Not much, he decided, when she made a soft sound deep in her throat and turned into the kiss— but not all the way, still holding back. Still keeping her hands to herself. Still not committing, not submitting—and that's what he wanted, what he needed. Submission. He knew how incredibly sweet it could be, and he wanted it from her.

God, she'd made him work for it the last time they'd been kissing in a car, too, never giving away too much, until toward the end, when she'd been so close to giving it all up for him.

So close ... so close ... but then no closer.

Tonight would be different. He hadn't chased her down to lose out in the end. And that's exactly what he'd done—chased her down, hooker skirt and all. He'd been sitting in the Blue Iguana, checking out the women, wondering about them, idly fantasizing about a couple of them, and wondering why the old "threesome in the back of the bar" fantasy never seemed to happen to anybody in real life, and at the same time he'd been wondering why he wasn't putting more effort into at least saying hello.

Nothing ventured, nothing gained in the pickup game. One of the women in the bar had definitely noticed him, smiled even, and still he hadn't made a move, just watched the crowd, and waited, and wondered what in the hell he was waiting for, an engraved invitation?

No, he realized now. He'd just been waiting for something more, anything more than what he'd seen and felt in the bar. So he'd left and gone out onto the street, and there on Seventeenth, with her ass peeking through torn fishnet and her hair ratted up into a blond pile on top of her head, he'd finally seen something he wanted, and he was making his move now.

Slipping his hand around the back of her neck, he opened his mouth wider over hers, pushed his tongue deeper, and let her know he wanted her, pulling her tighter and sliding his other hand up her thigh, under her skirt, but stopping short of the red lace panties. Her skin was satin smooth beneath his fingers, her half slip a silky drape across the back of his hand.

And she was trembling, ever so slightly, but he could feel it.

Good. That's all he'd needed to know.

He slowly broke off the kiss, taking his time, breathing her in and letting his mouth rest on hers, before he finally pulled away.

"Stay put," he said, opening the car door and swinging his feet out onto the pavement. "This will only take a minute."

In whole, it took more like five before he was settling back in behind the steering wheel.

"Genesee Park?" he asked.

"Yes." She nodded. "And, well . . . whatever you're thinking . . . well, it's probably not . . . I mean I just wanted to say, uh . . . well . . ."

He turned in his seat, and with one arm draped over the steering wheel, gave her his full attention.

"Well, what I wanted . . . to, uh, say, I guess . . . was, that, I, uh . . ."

She was stumbling over her words and having trouble meeting his gaze, and yeah, he remembered her doing that before when he'd kissed her. It was sweet. But she needed help here.

"Yeah, me too," he said, hoping that would clear up any confusion she might have. He'd loved it. She'd loved it. And trying to play it any other way wasn't going to fly, not in his car.

Reaching for the ignition, he gave it half a twist, and the beast that was Solange fired up, all eight cylinders of pure Cobra Jet.

Genesee Park, a cold-cash deal in exchange for an undisclosed piece of property "recovered" off a seminude German, and Esme Alden sitting in his Cyclone, looking downright dumbstruck—the night was looking up, even if they were in a back alley in RiNo, surrounded by crazy spider boys, with a pimp trolling the streets looking for a Dixie impersonator who looked just like her, and a bookie and his goons looking for Burt Alden's daughter and the guy in a Cyclone who'd saved her.

Was he willing to stick with her with that kind of night stretching out in front of him?

Oh, hell, yeah.

CHAPTER FOURTEEN

Lieutenant Loretta Bradley of the Denver Police Department surveyed the scene in room 215 of the Oxford Hotel with a jaundiced eye. Friday night was definitely getting off to a strange start.

Damned strange.

"What we've got here isn't the bloodbath we expected," Connor Ford, her newest detective, said. "It's just a bloody mess." She'd snagged the sandy-haired, gray-eyed youngster from the Boulder Police Department about a year ago, and he was working out pretty damn well—so far.

"Yes, I can see that," she said, letting her gaze range across the elegant hotel room one more time before it settled on the victim and the EMT patching him up with a little first aid. "So what did he do, panic and roll around on every single surface he could find?"

"Seems like it. He's a little upset," the detective said.

"Oh, yes," she agreed. The old guy, one Otto Von Lindberg from San Francisco, was definitely upset, grumbling and complaining under his breath, giving them all the evil eye, wanting everyone to leave, just leave. "And what in the hell is that?" She gestured to the symbol someone had very carefully carved into the old guy's back. He was bleeding, but he was in no danger of bleeding out. He'd been cut deep enough to maybe leave a scar, but not deep enough to kill, not even close. The EMT was using steri-strips and butterfly bandages, not stitches, to hold the guy together.

It was all damned strange.

Especially the black leather thong the old guy was wearing. It had snaps on it, and spikes, and ... oh, hell, she'd seen it all in her twenty-five years on the force, but this was one of those things that was going to stick with a person, seeing this old fart in his leather thong, sporting a dog collar around his neck. According to Connor, he'd been handcuffed with his hands behind his back, flex-cuffed around the ankles, hog-tied, leashed to the bed, and bleeding profusely when the manager had found him, after being alerted by one of the maids.

Interestingly, the maid had not seen any blood or wounds when she'd first glanced in the room. But by the time the manager had calmed her down enough to understand what she was talking about and gotten up to room 215, the guy had definitely been bloody and writhing around on the floor. The 911 call had been dramatically overstated—with three squad cars bearing down on the hotel in award-winning response time... *"Blood everywhere, it's a massacre."*

Not quite a massacre, Loretta thought, shaking her head and looking the old guy over. He did have blood running down his back into his butt crack, though, and *geezus,* she would have just as soon skipped that part.

Half of a leash was hanging off the guy's dog collar and trailing down the front of his chest, with a cleanly cut end, and the other half was still tied around the bed frame. He'd been easy pickings for whoever had cut him up and then cut him loose.

Sometimes Denver was an interesting town—too interesting.

"I don't remember Dixie ever taking a knife to anyone," she said.

"Dixie's involvement was a misunderstanding on our part," Connor said. "The guy was pretty wound up when we arrived, jabbering away in English and German, and it took a while to figure out he wasn't saying 'It was Dixie.' He was saying 'It wasn't Dixie.' Kind of a miscommunication thing... maybe."

Loretta gave her new boy a long look. "I want Dixie anyway, and I want Benny-boy Jackman, and I want them both at the precinct before I get there."

"Yes, ma'am."

"And if it wasn't Dixie, who was it? Maybe this guy blew into town on his own and found a knife-wielding dominatrix hawking it on Colfax. Or maybe somebody helped him out. The doormen here at the Oxford usually have their little black book vetted better than this, but if someone in the hotel was involved, I want to know who."

"The new valet," Connor said. "He was approached a couple of days ago by a blond-haired woman who wanted him to make sure she got this trick instead of Dixie. The woman also requested that Von Lindberg be put in this room—two-fifteen. I think because of the fire escape. She paid the valet fifty bucks, and the reservation clerk fifty bucks."

Loretta looked to the open window and the curtains blowing in the light breeze. Okay, she thought, the Boulder boy was earning his keep.

"And how was the valet supposed to steer this john to her?"

Connor flipped open his notebook and showed her the top page. "She left her phone number."

Loretta grinned. "Find this blonde and bring her in. I can't have hookers carving their initials into their customers."

"It's not her initials, Lieutenant. It's kanji."

"Kanji?"

"Japanese characters. At least the middle part of it looks like a distinct character. The angled lines around the outside of it might just be for decoration."

Whatever it was, she didn't want decorating fat old Germans with the sharp end of a knife to become a new trend in Denver.

"And what's the kanji on this guy mean?"

"I'll know here in just a minute," he said. "I had the tech clean him up a bit and took a picture of it to send to—"

"Skeeter," she interjected. Who else? Skeeter Bang Hart was a mutual friend, *manga* artist, and former kick-ass street punk turned good. The young woman had become part of a Defense Department black-ops team Loretta was very glad to have based in Denver and on her side. She'd saved most of the operators' butts at one time or another as juveniles, and they made a habit of returning the favor when they could, sometimes quite handsomely. For reasons on both sides, their unspoken alliance remained just that—unspoken. They had each other's numbers and weren't afraid to use them. It was enough.

"Yeah." The detective showed her the photograph on his phone, and Loretta was impressed. His phone took better pictures than her camera. Hell, she could hardly keep up with personal technology anymore.

"Well, let me know as soon as she . . ." Her voice trailed off, and she reached for Connor's phone. Holding it one way into the light, and then the other, she swore under her breath. There was no doubt what she was looking at—*dammit*.

"What?" Connor asked.

She handed him back the phone.

"Swastika," she said. "Those angled lines? That's a swastika, radiating out of the kanji in the middle."

Connor looked at his phone, then looked over at the German.

"Hell," he said softly. "So what do you think? Aryan Nation?"

"Or just plain old Nazis," she said. "Either way, I don't like it. What's Otto Von Lindberg been saying?"

Connor gave her a resigned glance. "Nothing except he wants us out of his room. He paid good money for the room and seems to have plenty left, and he wants to be left alone."

Loretta gave a short nod. Von Lindberg had a fistful of hundred-dollar bills clutched in his right hand.

"Robbery would have been too easy," she said.

Getting attacked and robbed was a nice, straightforward crime. Getting cut the hell up, while wearing a dog collar and a thong, and being tied to a bed, and *not* getting robbed—that was complex.

Most days, Loretta thrived on the complex, but she had a late date tonight, and a damned early morning tomorrow, and she wasn't in the mood for ranting Germans.

"We've got a definite crime scene here, Lieutenant," Connor said. "But Mr. Von Lindberg is saying he did this to himself."

"Handcuffed and tied to a bed, he cut a swastika and a kanji into his back?"

"Yes, ma'am," Connor said. "That's his story."

"It's a little weak, wouldn't you say, Detective?"

"Yes, ma'am. I've definitely heard better."

So had she.

"Take him into protective custody. We'll hold

him as long as we can, see what we come up with. I want the window dusted. If the blonde paid for an escape route, I'm sure she used it."

"And maybe the guy with the maid did, too," Connor said. "Nobody saw him go back out the lobby, but there's almost half a dozen ways out of the hotel. He could have used any of them."

"Guy?" Loretta asked. "What guy with the maid?"

The detective had the wisdom to blanch slightly. "Sorry, Lieutenant." He flipped over to the next page in his notebook. "I thought Weisman filled you in on the way up."

"He did, but he didn't tell me about any guy with the maid."

"Young guy, in his twenties, five ten, maybe five eleven. Taller than the maid's husband, she says, and her husband is five eight," Connor said, consulting his notebook. "Hispanic, clean-cut, wearing jeans and a black-collared shirt, gray T-shirt, told the maid he was the police and asked her to open the door of this room for him. She did open the door for him. He walked in. She took one look, saw Von Lindberg tied to the bed, and ran the other way."

"But this guy came in the room?"

"That's what she says."

"Did she see if he was carrying a knife?"

"No such luck," Connor said. "But she did say he had a hard look about him, serious, very much in charge. She didn't doubt for a second that he was a policeman."

"In jeans and a black shirt."

"She thought he was undercover."

"Did he flash any identification?"

"No, ma'am. Not according to her."

"And she goes around opening room doors for every Tom, Dick, and Harry who comes along?"

"If he says he's a policeman, it seems so, yes, ma'am."

Perfectly legitimate, Loretta thought. If she were an illegal immigrant shifting the sheets around in an upscale hotel, she wouldn't be second-guessing anybody calling himself a policeman either, especially if he had a solid air of authority. It sucked, but that was the way of it.

"Take her in, get her an artist. Let's find out what this clean-cut police impersonator looks like."

"Yes, ma'am."

The detective's phone beeped twice, signaling a text message, and they both looked at the screen while he opened the file. The sender was Skeeter, and only one word came up on the screen: HERO.

"Nazi hero," Connor said, putting the two symbols together.

Well, that just about took the cake in Loretta's book of crap she didn't want to deal with on her beat, which was the whole damn city.

"I don't like it," the detective said, shaking his head, still looking at the screen on his phone.

"Neither do I, Connor," Loretta agreed. "Neither do I."

She was going to die.

Her mind was going in circles, thoughts racing.

Her heart was pounding, pulse racing. Her legs were shaking, arms trembling, her stomach churning, lips quivering. She hated it all. She hated it so much—and yet she couldn't stop any of it. She was going to die. She knew it with a dread certainty.

For no reason, she was going to become one of those horrifying statistics, an unsolved crime, a victim of senseless, random violence.

She only had one edge, and she was holding onto it with a death grip, using every ounce of her strength to keep her emotions frozen, to keep from crying.

The awful, terrifying man who had kidnapped her had taped her to a chair, her ankles taped to the legs, big, wide, gray duct tape, her wrists handcuffed to the arms. He'd stuffed something foul in her mouth and taped it in place, and it took every ounce of her strength not to gag. She hurt everywhere, especially where he'd hit her, backhanding her in the face, punching her in the stomach, where he'd pulled her hair out and wrenched her arm backward. She could see her blood on the front of her uniform shirt. He'd taken her name tag. She didn't know why.

She didn't know where he'd brought her, or why. It had all happened so fast. The huge, frightfully strong man had come out of nowhere, his attack so fast, so brutal, so unexpected, she'd never had time to react. One second, she'd been walking across the hospital parking lot, and in the next she'd been in the middle of a nightmare, caught in the maelstrom of violence, a random act of violence perpetrated by some pervert, some woman-hater.

She felt sick. She was so frightened, and she knew beyond any shred of a doubt that her situation was very, very unlikely to improve.

CHAPTER FIFTEEN

"Yes, Mr. Nachman . . . No, Mr. Nachman . . . Absolutely. I have it with me now, and it is beautiful. I'm quite thrilled, and I know you will be, too." Smoothing feathers, that's what Esme was doing, smoothing eighty-two thousand feathers, and after her last stammering bit of embarrassed idiocy in the alley, she was also doing everything she could to avoid having to talk to Johnny Ramos ever again for the rest of her life. "Within the hour, yes, sir. I'm leaving downtown now."

But despite her dearest wish to remain utterly occupied while in Ramos's car, there was only so much verbal genuflecting she could manage, and with her last "yes, sir" she'd met her quota.

She should have gotten a damn cab, and the reasons she hadn't were reasons . . . well, they were reasons she wasn't going to examine too damn closely. She knew they wouldn't pass any test of actual reason, so she wasn't going to put them to the test. Given the night she was having, she figured she deserved a break, and it sure as hell didn't look like the universe at large was going to give her one.

"Thank you, sir. I'll see you shortly." She ended the call and checked her messages, hoping for some, especially one from her dad, but there was nothing, which left her at a momentary loose end— *dammit*.

"Solange and I have made the run to Genesee in half an hour, if you need to be there quicker," Johnny said to her from his side of the car.

Solange? She glanced over at him.

Who in the heck was...oh, she got it. The Charger had been named Roxanne. Solange was the Cyclone, and yes, she supposed if a person sort of squinted and didn't look too closely, possibly the "sleeper" looked French. Good God.

"I think regular speed will be fine," she said. "It's why I told Mr. Nachman an hour, in case there were any...uh, any more extenuating circumstances."

Extenuating. Right. She guessed that was one way to put the night so far, one damned unexpected extenuating circumstance after another.

"Even if there is a delay, we should be okay." Yes, she'd just said that. "We shouldn't hit traffic, though."

And that was it.

"Not at this time of night," she added, and that really was it. Nothing more needed to be said, which left her at another momentary loose end—*dammit*.

While Johnny downshifted for the next stoplight, she busied herself with rummaging through the pockets on her messenger bag until she came up with her PDA. She really needed to upgrade to an all-inclusive system. A quick check of her calendar proved she was heading in the right direction, toward Genesee, but running a little late, over half an hour. No news there.

She let out a very quiet sigh, which in no way indicated her current level of stress.

He'd kissed her, and on top of everything else she had going wrong tonight, she'd liked it—a lot. So everything was A1 perfect: running late, Bleak gunning for her, Dax in the boondocks, and she'd liked kissing a guy she'd known in high school who, despite her initial hopes, had turned out to be a street gangster.

She had to be certifiable. She didn't have a love life, true, and she resented that she'd all but told him as much, but on those nights when she dreamed about having a love life, she usually dreamed a little bigger than old muscle cars with big engines, and bad boys with big . . .

Oh, for the love of God and Patsy freakin' Cline—she brought her hand up to cover her face. She couldn't believe she'd just thought that, about his . . .

Oh, hell—there she was again, remembering his . . .

"Are you okay?" he asked, and under her hand, she felt her face turn hot with a blush.

No, she wasn't okay. She was mortified. He was the first boy she'd ever seen naked, and in her naiveté, she'd thought all guys were built like him.

They weren't.

Not even close.

"Esme?"

Not that size mattered, really, at least that's what everyone said, but how in the hell would she know? Every guy she'd ever been with had been about the same, size-wise anyway, and she'd never been with him, not really, not with him actually . . .

Oh, geez, Esme, she told herself, *grow up, get a grip.*

But there was no way to get more grown-up than the thought she'd just had, of him inside her, of everything she remembered about him, and everything she'd learned about men since. The combination was sheer, erotic meltdown, a wall of heat crashing into her and washing through her body, triggering a deep, sensual reaction that was going to be her undoing, right here in his bucket seat.

He'd kissed her, and she'd been poleaxed, frozen in place, because his mouth had felt like coming home. The taste of him, the smell of him, the sound of his breath—the slow slide of his tongue over and around and down the length of hers, it had all said, "Here's your place, girl, here with me."

Wrong. Impossibly wrong. It just simply couldn't be.

He'd done a great job tonight, and it had been a

good decision to stick with him for the delivery to Isaac Nachman's, but beyond that it was crazy.

Crazy to want to kiss him again, right now, while the warmth of him was still in her mouth.

Crazy to feel desire like a weight on her chest, a longing she wasn't getting past, even though it had only been a kiss.

Just a kiss.

One kiss.

"I'm...um...feeling a headache coming on. It'll pass. They usually do. If I just rest quietly." And don't talk to guys who get me hot.

She was pitiful.

Of course, not talking to guys who got her hot was her signature modus operandi. That was the problem. Almost one hundred percent of the time, she was only ever in the company of guys who didn't get her hot—and now she knew why. Johnny Ramos was the guy who got her hot, and she hadn't been in his company since high school.

Good God.

"Here," he said, and she heard him lift something into the front seat from the back.

She glanced up from beneath her fingers, then reached over and took the small red canvas pack he was handing her.

The stoplight changed, and with a press of the gas pedal, the Cyclone ramped back up to chassis-shaking life. *Geezus,* she felt it everywhere, the slow, deep rumble curving around her in the seat, the sound of it sliding down her spine.

"Look in the mesh pocket inside," he said, shifting into second gear. "You'll find aspirin and Motrin. Take your pick. Have you had anything to eat lately? Like in the last three or four hours?"

"Uh, no." Breakfast had been coffee. Lunch had been light, and dinner had been nonexistent.

"Well, open this up." He stretched his arm into the backseat again and brought up the last thing she'd expected to see.

She lowered her hand from her face to take the package he was offering.

"Um, thanks." It was an MRE—Meal, Ready to Eat. She glanced into the backseat. Four more MREs were stacked in the corner—government issue, no commercial resale allowed. A guy couldn't just go to the grocery store and buy a few MREs to keep in his car. She should have noticed them before, and she might have, if she hadn't been so busy noticing the Locos in the alley and trying to keep them all in view.

She had noticed how nice he kept the interior of the Cyclone. The dash looked as if it was regularly detailed with a toothbrush. Every knob and dial gleamed. There wasn't so much as a gum wrapper in sight, and if she wasn't mistaken, the upholstery on the seats was new. Considering what a wreck his car looked like from the outside, he took surprisingly good care of it on the inside.

He'd been taking good care of her, too. Dax had been right, and she'd noticed. Even taking her to Baby Duce's hadn't been a bad idea. It had given her a chance to catch her breath someplace safe—

and not much could have surprised her more than that she'd been safe in Locos land.

At a clear place between a couple of cars, he pulled over to the curb and put the Cyclone in neutral before engaging the parking brake and reaching into the backseat again.

"You should have this, too. The more of it you can get down, the better you're going to feel. I can guarantee it," he said, bringing up an eight-pack of a bottled sport drink.

Electrolytes, just what she needed.

She let out another small sigh, watching him pull a bottle out of the plastic ring harness and unscrew the lid for her.

"Thank you," she said and took a sip—grape, her favorite.

This was crazy.

He lifted the red pack out of her lap and unzipped the main compartment, revealing an incredibly well organized first-aid kit, of all the darn things.

Watching him, she screwed the lid back on the bottled drink, curious as hell.

"Blowout kit?" She read the label off a sealed plastic pouch in the pack. The pouch was only slightly smaller than the MRE.

"In case one of the good guys gets hurt, me included," he said, moving aside a package of sterile bandages set above a number of elasticized bands and pockets, each of them fitted with some kind of medical supply.

"What about the bad guys?"

He let out a short laugh. "I don't spend a whole lot of time worrying about saving the bad guys."

A little harsh maybe, or maybe not—MREs, blowout kits and first-aid supplies, a pistol he carried concealed in a shoulder holster, for crying out loud, and the way he had of taking charge... *especially* the way he had of taking charge.

"Do people get hurt a lot in your line of work?"

"Sometimes, yeah," he said, unzipping one of the kit's mesh pockets.

"And what is that exactly? Your line of work, I mean." They'd been rolling through lower downtown pretty much at a dead run for the last hour together; she figured it was time to ask, probably past time.

He gave her a brief glance, and without missing a beat said, "I'm currently between assignments."

Oh, right. Between assignments. Sure. She'd been there.

Well, actually, she'd never been between assignments, but she could see how some gangster from RiNo could end up "between assignments."

Bull.

He'd just given her a perfect example of misinformation by omission if she'd ever heard one—and she'd heard plenty. Some days in the private investigation business were just chock-full of all the things people *weren't* telling you.

"You're not one of the Locos, are you?" She just couldn't get that to line up, him being a street thug, a gang member. It didn't fit with what she'd been seeing since he'd walked into her dad's office, no matter how easily he'd fit in with those guys in the alley off Delgany.

He pulled two small brand-name packets out of the mesh pocket and held them up. "Aspirin or Motrin? What do you want?"

"An answer to my question."

He held her gaze, and, after a moment, handed her the aspirin packet. The Motrin went back in the kit. Then he took the MRE out of her lap and ripped open the top.

"Drink more of your drink," he said, pulling a tightly sealed package out of the MRE and ripping it open as well.

She unscrewed the lid on her bottle and took another sip, and when he handed her a four-inch-square cracker, she took a bite.

"They're a little dry," he warned.

No kidding.

When she had about half the cracker washed down, he nodded at the aspirin packet she still had clutched in her hand.

At any time during the exchange, she could have told him that she didn't really have a headache, but she was rather ridiculously enjoying his attention—emphasis on the ridiculous.

She took the aspirin, and when she was finished swallowing, she let her gaze slip to his mouth.

She was doomed.

It had only been a kiss, she told herself, a kiss that made her want more and more, until the more became more than just a kiss.

Her gaze drifted lower, down the strong column

of his throat, down the gray T-shirt covering his chest, to his lap, to the zipper on his jeans. It had been a long time for her, since she'd been with someone, which she was absolutely positive would never have come into play tonight—except he'd kissed her, and now everything was in play, especially her response to him.

He'd grown quiet on his side of the car, and when she looked up, she found him watching her, his gaze darkly serious, his attention focused on her face.

Another wave of heat washed through her. Johnny Ramos, all grown-up, the promise of what he could be completely eclipsed by what he'd become—harder, calmer, with a solid confidence she felt coming off him with every breath he took. He wasn't running wild anymore. He wasn't running dice in the school parking lot or dope on the corner for the Locos. His world had gotten much bigger, whether he was between assignments or not.

"You don't answer to Duce," she said, so sure of it. He didn't look like he answered to anyone who wasn't at least as mentally strong and physically tough as he was—which she knew for a fact narrowed the field down to a couple of very specific skill sets, law enforcement and the military. He was either a cop or a soldier. It was in his bearing. She'd been picking up on it since her dad's office, but she hadn't put her finger on it until now. The businessmen she dealt with didn't move like he did. They thought tactically, but their tactics revolved around making money, not survival. Lawyers jockeyed for position in court, not on the street. Accountants, like Pete Carlson, the guy whose office was next door to her dad's in the Faber Building, or even her own accountant back in Seattle, spent their time anticipating the cost-benefit ratio of tax laws, not threats like Dovey Smollett.

Johnny moved like Dax, who would have seen Dovey zeroing in on her in a heartbeat.

"No, I don't answer to Duce," he admitted, handing her the other cracker from out of the package.

She took the cracker, but what she noticed was the ink peeking out from under the cuff of his shirt.

"Oh," she said, surprised, but then quickly remembering. "I'd forgotten about that one."

She reached out, her fingers making contact with the letter *L* inscribed on the inside of his wrist. Almost as quickly, she felt the warmth of his skin.

"This was before Dom got killed, wasn't it?"

It took a moment, but when he answered, it was in the affirmative.

"Yes."

"Can I see it?"

She glanced up, and after a moment, he silently obliged, unbuttoning his cuff and pushing up his sleeve to reveal the word "LOCOS." The letters were styled in Old English, all capitals, ornately strung along a knife blade with "XX2ST" and "C/S" written on the hilt, all of it inked into his skin, the tattoo going from his wrist to his elbow.

Oh, yes. She remembered this.

She slowly ran her fingers up the inside of his left arm. "You were fourteen when you had this done," she said. "We were both in Mr. Hawthorn's American Literature class that year. I remember asking you if it hurt, and you told me no."

"I lied."

"Yeah, I figured as much." A grin tipped the corner of her mouth. His tattoo was elegant, professionally done, far better than what some of the other boys had put on their bodies. "I thought you were so tough."

"Still am."

Her smile broadened. "*C slash S,*" she said, reading the hilt. "*Con safos,* you told me, protected by God, and the *XX2ST* is for Twenty-second Street."

"You remembered." He sounded somewhat surprised.

She remembered everything about him, not that he would know it, and if at all possible, she was going to keep the news flash to herself.

"I think everybody who grew up around here remembers that the Locos started on Twenty-second Street." His skin was soft, his arm so hard to the touch, the veins running down the length of it a confluence of strength underlying the elaborate design and stylized script of his tattoo.

He'd been marked hard by his heritage.

"Yeah, way back in the day."

"Yeah," she said. "Back in the day."

Silence fell between them again, a silence underscored by the low growling rumble of the car—and anticipation. She felt it descending like a curtain, hot and silky, around them. He'd kissed her, and she wanted him to kiss her again—Esme the Desperate.

Oh, babe. Johnny looked down at the top of her head where she was bent over his arm, her fingers still warm on his skin. She had no idea how beautiful she was; she never had. Being smart, that had always been her personal claim to fame, and she'd completely missed what everybody else understood—that she was gorgeous.

She didn't know it, but Kevin Harrell hadn't been the first guy he'd fought for her. A number of young punks had set their sights on her over the years, *la rubia,* the blonde, starting way back in seventh grade. He didn't know about the jerks in grade school, but he'd never doubted for a second that there had been a few. Lucky for them, he'd been at St. Catherine's while Esme had been at Bennington. The playground had been safer for it.

Despite his chosen profession, violence wasn't ever his first choice for conflict resolution, unless it was armed conflict—then violence came swift and hard. Winning was the only parameter in armed conflict, in combat. But the whole guy thing with girls was so physical it naturally lent itself to physical confrontation. Guys *always* wanted to get in a girl's pants, and other guys knew this, and that's why they got so pissed off. So when a thirteen-year-old *cholo* at Campbell Junior High had started talking like he'd had her in the band room, Johnny had called him out. It hadn't taken more than a little half-assed scuffling to solve the problem, but a pattern had been set.

There was more than one reason she hadn't had a date in high school. Most of it had been her reluctance, and her shyness, and her holier-better-smarter-than-you attitude, and the rest of it had been him. He'd traveled the world with the U.S. Army, but from the first moment he'd laid eyes on her, in Ms. Trent's class, his reaction had been pure barrio boy, and he'd never outgrown it, not where she was concerned.

Esme Alexandria Alden, the Unattainable One—when he'd left her in the car in the alley at Duce's, he'd made it clear to the *Arañas* not to touch her. Next time he would be adding "Don't breathe on her." Those *cholos* had been breathing all over her by the time he'd gotten back to the Cyclone.

Yeah, he knew exactly why he'd followed her into the Oxford. He knew exactly what he wanted.

And now here she was, so damn close he could smell her, and not just the honeysuckle and summer garden scent of her perfume. He could smell *her*—the underlying female scent of warm skin and soft breath, of the back of her neck and the lace of her lingerie, a push-up bra and panties curved around just about everything he wanted to get his mouth on.

And she wanted to be kissed.

With Solange rumbling beneath them, and desire building between them, with the night in front of them, and long years of fascination behind them, she wanted to be kissed.

Geezus. He didn't know if he had it in him—to kiss her. To just kiss her. He'd done it in the alley, but he'd barely touched her, and this time she was already practically in his lap, the heat of where she was touching his arm quickly and inexorably spreading, covering the whole front of his body, a good portion of it settling in his groin, which wasn't going to do either of them any good parked at the side of the street with traffic going by.

And yet . . . and yet if he tilted his head slightly to one side he could see down the front of her jacket, and there wasn't a barrio boy alive who could resist such a beautiful pair of *tetas.*

She was so lovely, the lace demicups of her bra working overtime, the nape of her neck exposed, golden tendrils of hair sliding loose from her up-twist and lying like a path to be followed across her skin.

He lifted his free hand and cupped the tender line of her jaw, but this time when he lowered his mouth he pulled her close, really close, meeting her more than halfway across the console and sliding his other arm around her waist, under her jacket, and yeah, he had to skirt her shoulder holster, and yeah, he was being damn careful, but he was also kissing her flat-out, tongue to tonsils, baby, his mouth angled over hers, teasing her, and tasting her, and sucking on her just enough to let her know this was not finished between them, not tonight.

Geezus, she had a beautiful mouth. He loved the way her teeth fit together. He loved the softness of her tongue. He loved the way she was kissing him back.

Yeah, she'd grown up in the years since they'd gotten hot and heavy in the mighty Roxanne. She knew where they were going this time, and from the way she was clinging to him, she knew he was the guy to take her there.

First, though, *dammit,* he had to get her up to Genesee, and get the cash to neutralize Bleak. But in between Genesee and Bleak, he was taking her to his place in Commerce City.

Yeah, with a soft, hot blonde by his side, with Easy Alex next to him, he could face it. He could face going home.

CHAPTER SIXTEEN

"That goddamn Cyclone sleeper, you mean?" Bleak said into the phone. "Yeah, yeah, Dovey, I've seen it running through Commerce City. Hell, it's been in this town longer than I have. I've seen it parked at that damn garage over on Vine and Hoover. What the hell is Esme Alden doing in a big old Merc like that? Who's this guy with the car?"

"His name is Johnny Ramos, Mr. Bleak," Dovey said. "He's one of the Locos. His brother, Dom, used to run the gang."

Not what Franklin wanted to hear.

He swiveled around in his chair, taking his feet off the desk and planting them firmly on the carpet.

"Is she fucking him, Dovey? Is that what you're telling me?" That some-fucking-how, this little bit of information about Burt-fucking-Alden's daughter being the girlfriend of one of Baby Duce's boys had not been unearthed some-fucking-where along the line?

This was not good. Crossing Baby Duce was out of the question. That was how guys got whacked.

"I don't know, Mr. Bleak. I didn't get a clear look at him until they got to his car, and then I recognized him, and yes, sir, maybe they're dating or something. They used to have a thing going in high school, and he sure grabbed hold of her and started hauling her around like she belonged to him."

Not what Franklin wanted to hear.

He sliced his gaze to the photograph of Katherine Gray on his desk. She was a first-class looker. There wasn't a man on earth who wouldn't recognize her for what she was—a grade-A, first-class looker. But maybe a piece of late-night cable TV ass was going to be pricier than Bleak was willing to pay.

Not that it mattered now. *Goddammit.* He was already into this deal up to his neck, whether he got to have lunch with Katherine Gray or not. The Chicago boys were going to be pulling up in front of his damn warehouse at nine o'clock tomorrow morning, and Franklin needed to be waiting for them with cash in hand.

Which he had, except for Burt Alden's eighty-two thousand dollars.

Goddammit.

"Mitch and Leroy are on this car now?"

"Yes, sir. They caught a look at it on Market, then lost it, so I told 'em to head over to Delgany, to Duce's, and just see if that's where Ramos had gone. He'd sure been heading in that direction, and it's Friday night, still early, time for the homeboys to check in."

Franklin pushed out of his chair and walked over to the windows overlooking his betting room.

"The car was there, in the alley, but I told them not to take her at Duce's," Dovey said.

No shit, Franklin thought. The last damn thing he needed was a confrontation with Baby Duce and his damn Locos, especially on their own territory. But he needed that damn girl.

"And now it's parked a couple of blocks from there," Dovey continued. "They've still got eyes on it, but I told them to hold off, until I talked to you."

Dovey with a brain, it was a miracle.

"Good, Smollett. That's good thinking." Mitch and Leroy were driving one of the Bleak Enterprises vans, and that's how guys got whacked. A couple of wiseguys tumble out of a van with your goddamn name written all over it and rough up one of Duce's boys and steal his girl.

Deader'n a doornail by dawn. Oh, yeah, Franklin could see that happening. He wouldn't have to worry about the damn eighty-two thousand dollars then.

But Franklin Camilo Bleak didn't go down that easy.

"You follow them, Smollett. You still got Bremerton with you, right?"

"Yes, sir."

"He's a big guy." From out of town. "Use him. You follow that damn sleeper until you can get it pulled over someplace outside Duce's territory, then send in the Chicago boy to get the girl. He's packing a damn .45. Tell him to use it." The last thing Denver would ever miss was another damn gangster. The city was crawling with them, all of them swinging pistols around and killing people.

Yeah, that was a great idea—to let the Chicago guy kill Duce's boy and just keep the name Bleak out of the whole damn mess.

Esme Alden dating a member of the Locos, somebody should have known that. Somebody should have figured that into the night's plan.

Well, it was figured now.

"You do this right, Smollett, and it'll look real good to me. Real good."

"Yes, sir, Mr. Bleak."

"You bring me that girl, Dovey, and there'll be something in it for you."

"Yes, sir, Mr. Bleak."

"Just bring me the girl, Dovey." He ended the call, and speed-dialed Mitch.

The guy picked up on the first ring.

"Yes, boss?"

"Dovey's on his way to pick up the tail on the Cyclone. When he gets there, you get the hell out of there. I don't want Baby Duce seeing my van crisscrossing his goddamn neighborhood all night."

"Yes, boss. I'll head back and get another car."

"Damn straight, you will, and then get right back on this Cyclone's ass. I want the damn girl, Mitch, but I want Bremerton's face on the deed. Back him up, if he needs it. All I want is the girl, but I want her to just 'poof' off the planet, plain disappear. I don't want no hearing about Duce looking for the guys who stole one of his boys' little *putas*. I don't want him looking for Franklin Bleak."

"No, boss."

"Don't fuck this up, Mitch."

"No, boss."

Franklin ended the call, but didn't go back to his desk.

The woman down there in the betting room, Beth Alden, the one his guys had bound and gagged, and cuffed and taped to the chair, she wasn't crying. She should have been a blubbering mess by now, but there hadn't been so much as a sob out of her.

She was bleeding. Eliot had been a little rough, but that was what Eliot did—get rough with women. It was his specialty.

Franklin let his gaze drop to the woman's shoes. That damn shoelace thing still made him grin. He didn't know how in the hell she'd lost a shoelace. She must have struggled like hell to do it, and to get the bruises starting to show on her face. Eliot must have loved that. He liked struggling women.

Personally, Franklin didn't go in for the rough stuff. He liked a woman to spoil him. Tying them up and knocking them around didn't make any sense to him. Plus, it was just too damn much work—except when it was business. Taking some bitch apart to get her old man to pony up his money—now that made perfect sense to him, and he couldn't say he hadn't enjoyed it a few times, even more than a few times.

The daughter, Esme, was a smaller, younger, cuter version of the woman in the chair, and Franklin had the idea that between him and Eliot and the two women, things could get damned interesting before dawn. Not interesting enough to make up for the eighty-two thousand if Burt didn't come through, but interesting nonetheless.

Yes, he could see it, him and Eliot tag-teaming a mother-daughter combo. More importantly, he'd make damn sure Burt Alden saw it, that the damn stupid bastard saw what he'd done to his women.

CHAPTER SEVENTEEN

Solange stretching out at twenty-five over, riding a hundred, city lights streaming through the darkness, growing fainter in the rearview, making the run up into the mountains, the run up to Genesee—Johnny had done it more than a few times on a hot summer night like tonight, escaped the city for the cooler air of the high country.

And yeah, sometimes he'd had a girl with him. There were a few places up here in the hills where a guy could get pretty busy with his sweetheart. There was even a map of some of the better places tacked to the garage wall on the third floor at Steele Street, put there by the SDF guys back in the day when they'd all considered themselves backseat urban legends. Some of the places had hash marks by them and stories attached to the hash marks, some of which had been alluded to a few times over the years, mostly when the guys had gotten back from some particularly hairy mission and ended up hanging around, working on cars and downing a few beers—some pretty good stories, actually, mixed in with a lot of remembered teenage bull and bravado.

Johnny had put a hash mark up on the map one time, and Skeeter had walloped the holy hell out of him. He'd kept his sexual exploits to himself after that. For being such a badass operator, she was still such a girl. Red Dog had more edge on her, and even though she was smaller than Skeeter, there wasn't a guy on the team who'd take a bet on himself going up against her, not even Superman, and Christian Hawkins was the guy who'd trained her.

Johnny couldn't help but wonder who had trained Esme. He didn't know if she had any hand-to-hand combat skills, but she'd certainly handled her .45 like she knew what she was doing.

He downshifted into third, pulling one of the big hills out of Denver, heading into the darkness of the mountains. With one hand on the steering wheel and the other staying on the gearshift, a grin curved his mouth. She'd kissed him. Esme Alexandria Alden had kissed him like she'd wanted to eat him alive, twice—all grown-up and wearing red lace panties.

Not such a bad night after all, he decided.

The Bleak business didn't have him too worried. When he'd gone back in the house on Delgany to talk with Duce, the Locos' boss hadn't hesitated to sign on to the Bleak payoff. Good for business, Duce had said, letting Bleak know he wasn't pulling anything off on the Locos moving his load of cakes out of Chicago. Duce might even do the guy a favor and cop a couple of points off the top of the keys, take his tribute, put his mark on the deal, and keep the Parkside Bloods from turning Mr. Bleak inside out, literally, for thinking there was room on the north side for another dealer to be bringing in coke. Those rights were won the hard way, and Bleak hadn't even skirmished for them, let alone gone to battle—which was more information than Johnny had wanted to hear. He knew how it all worked, the drug and turf wars. Dom had died in his and Duce's arms during battle with the Parkside Bloods—and man, he hadn't ever been within spitting distance of any goddamn drug ever again, not any illegal substance, and he didn't want within spitting distance of Bleak's cakes.

Cash-delivery boy was probably more than he should have signed on for, more than he wanted General Grant to know about, but there wasn't any way for him to stand by and let Esme do the delivery. He was seriously thinking about stringing her dad up from the nearest light pole and leaving him there for a week or two. What was the bastard thinking? Letting his daughter do his dirty work for him.

When they'd been growing up, Johnny had known Esme's home life had gotten a little sketchy at times. By the time they'd reached high school, he'd also figured out why she was so damn careful with all her little personal parts, like her hair, and her buttons, and her shoes. He could have told her that keeping her buttons buttoned and her shoes clean wasn't going to change a damn thing about running out of groceries, and neither was having all her homework done with extra credit, not in the short run, but he figured, in her heart, she'd probably already known that. He and Dom had always just hustled a little here and there and slid by the rest of the time, but Johnny knew that sliding by and hustling didn't work out the same for girls.

She'd turned out great, though. She'd gone to college, and whatever he thought about her private investigation business, it obviously afforded her some very nice underwear. There were worse jobs.

He couldn't think of any off the top of his head right now, not for the smartest girl in school, considering where she'd ended up tonight and who was after her, but he knew there were worse jobs.

"We're about a half an hour out of Genesee, tops," he said. "You want to tell me what's in the bag, what we're delivering, and maybe everything you know about this Nachman guy we're delivering it to?"

Even a private investigator had to realize that information, intelligence, was the key to success. It wasn't to her advantage to leave him in the dark, not about everything, or anything, for that matter.

"Isaac Nachman," she said, obviously understanding. "Seventy-nine years old, born in Germany, lost his father, a brother, and two sisters to the Holocaust. His mother was American, from here in

Colorado. She and Isaac came home to visit his grandfather back in 1939, shortly after the German invasion of Poland, and they never made it back to Europe. Isaac took over his grandfather's tire business after the war, put his name on the masthead, and made millions."

"Nachman Tires?" he asked, taking Solange back up into fourth gear.

"That's the one."

Johnny let out a low whistle. Multi, multi, multi-millions, Nachman had to be the richest guy in the state. Everyone used Nachman tires—the auto manufacturers, the government, the military, the Indy cars. Nachman rubber hit the road every day of the week from L.A. to New York, and from Baghdad to the Midnight Doubles.

He slanted Esme a quick glance. No wonder she was dressed to kill in couture with diamond earrings.

He didn't have to look at himself. He knew exactly what he was wearing, what he was always wearing. If it wasn't a uniform, it was jeans, a shirt, a T-shirt, and a pair of boots.

It worked, that's about all he could say about his wardrobe.

"There's going to be a helluva security system on his house." That was the second thing to pop into his mind.

"Fortunately, we're not here on a B and E, to break and enter," she said, her tone a little dry, which was a good sign. She was regaining her composure. "We're invited. We're here on business."

She had her legs crossed in the passenger seat, and her skirt was riding up, and for all that he was thinking about getting up to this rich old tire guy's house and doing the contraband-for-cash dance, he hadn't for a second forgotten where he was taking her after that—to bed, his bed. At least he was going to give it his best shot. He wasn't passing Go. He wasn't collecting anything.

"*You're* invited," he clarified. "I'm unexpected."

"It won't be a problem. He might not even . . . uh, particularly notice that you're there. He'll be pretty focused on the property I've recovered. He's a very, uh, very gracious man, but just a tidge eccentric. I've dealt with him before, with my dad."

That got her a lift of his eyebrows. Her dad? What in the hell was a guy like Isaac Nachman doing hiring a guy like her dad? It didn't make sense. Multimillionaires usually had their own people on staff to do anything, including investigations and security. He could see where Nachman would hire a brilliant, classy private contractor like Esme for a specific situation, maybe something she specialized in, but her dad, what Johnny remembered of him anyway, and certainly from what he'd seen tonight, was a jerk with about as much class as a ten-cent hot dog.

"Your dad . . ." he started, then let his voice trail off, hesitating. Her dad was a royal fuckup kinda guy, but it wasn't Johnny's place to say it like that, not to her. He'd save his unvarnished opinion for the guy who needed to hear it the hard way—her dad.

"Actually, he has a good reputation when it comes to art recovery," she filled in his pause with another surprising piece of information.

"Art recovery? You mean he finds stolen art?"

She nodded. "Yes. The Nachman family lost over three hundred paintings to the Nazis during the war, including a Renoir my dad helped them find and reacquire, and they've never stopped looking for the rest of them, especially Isaac."

Nazis. Germans. The guy in the Oxford Hotel with a sliced-and-diced suitcase and a neatly cut-open suit jacket—Johnny's gaze landed on the messenger bag.

Geezus. He was such an idiot.

"You've got a painting in there." Of course, she did, a damn small painting stolen by Adolf Hitler and, somehow, miraculously recovered by Esme Alexandria Alden and her deadbeat dad.

Easy Alex wasn't anybody's drug mule. Hell, no. He should have known that down to his bones—not that knowing it would have necessarily gotten him thinking of stolen art. Nikki McKinney, now she got him thinking about stolen art. One of her "ascending angel" pieces had been stolen in transit to Los Angeles a few years ago, and it had opened up quite a lengthy discussion at Steele Street, and a little personal private investigation on SDF's part. Dylan had been the one to find the piece, and Hawkins and Kid had gone and gotten it back.

No one had said much more about it, other than Johnny knowing it hadn't been the first or the last time the guys had done a little inside work off the record. Things came up with friends and family, and the guys had skills. They'd been superlative car thieves at sixteen, and had become absolutely world-class burglars of anything and everything General Grant tasked them with getting in the ensuing years.

"An incredible painting," Esme confirmed. "Jakob Meinhard's *Woman in Blue*, an Expressionist masterpiece. He painted it in 1910, and up until a few years ago, people thought it had been burned in Berlin in 1939, or possibly in the Tuileries in 1941. Hitler had thousands of pieces destroyed in those two fires. The führer hated modern art. He thought it was degenerate, an abomination undermining the character of the state."

Johnny hadn't known that. Not any of it. Nazis and art had never collided in his educational experiences. Land navigation—he had that down cold. HALO, High Altitude, Low Opening jumping out of airplanes with a ram-air square parachute—*no problema*. Small-unit tactics—he'd studied those hard, given them his all. But the Nazis were way before his time, and the only art education he'd ever had was hanging buck-ass naked from Nikki's studio ceiling while she'd filmed him in angel wings in the middle of a lightshow and music maelstrom.

"And you and your dad found this Meinhard painting?"

"Just my dad. He tracked down its whole history, from when it was initially smuggled from Germany into France via a diplomatic pouch, to its inclusion

with a score of the Rothschilds' collection at one of
their castles in the Loire, to when the Nazis discovered the cache of paintings and seized them all.
He's good, he really is, but he's best at finding the
paintings, and not so good at actually getting them
back. In the case of the Meinhard, he'd set up a
deal, but it fell through in the clutch, and he lost
the cash he'd brought for the exchange without
getting the painting. I took over the investigation a
month ago and managed to get the seller back into
place."

"The guy in the Oxford?"

"Yes. Otto Von Lindberg."

"You knew exactly how to set him up, didn't you,
exactly how to play him?" And that was a sobering
thought.

"Otto and I go back a few years," she said coolly.

And there was another sobering thought. She
played hardball on this court all the time. *Geezus.*

"So what was your dad up to, trying to buy the
painting back from Von Lindberg? Was he working
for Nachman, being a go-between?"

She let out a short breath. "Initially, yes, but Dad
has a way of getting into trouble. He gets in over
his head, and then it's just one big Ponzi scheme
for him, robbing Peter to pay Paul, and making
deals and promises he shouldn't, hoping it will all
turn out right in the end."

"He gambles," Johnny said, and she agreed.

"With everything."

Which Johnny couldn't have cared less about,
except this time, Burt Alden had gambled with

Esme's well-being, with her safety, and frankly, that pissed him off—royally.

"Can I see it? The painting?" He'd sure like to know what all the fuss was about, because the night had been full of fuss.

"Sure," she said, reaching down and opening the messenger bag.

He concentrated on the road, until he heard her snap open the metal case she'd slipped into the bag at the office.

He glanced over to where she had opened the case. It was dark inside Solange, but Esme had taken out her flashlight and had it shining on the small piece of art inside its protective covering.

"That's not canvas, is it?" The painting was too solid, too stiff.

"No. Meinhard painted this piece on copper. It's one of only three pieces he did on metal. One is in the Louvre, and the other was with the Rothschild collection. It hasn't been seen since 1942."

Johnny could see it, even under its covering. Sure he could, and he supposed if a person liked red, orange, gray, and green with a big smear of blue and a little dab of pink—well, yeah, he could see that if a person liked that, well, then they would like Jakob Meinhard's *Woman in Blue* on copper.

Alrighty, then. Now he knew. Their asses were on the line, and the one thing that could save them and old Burt was an eight-by-ten-inch brightly colored piece of copper that didn't look anything like a woman—and yes, it was called art. He wasn't a complete heathen. He didn't doubt for a second that the thing was worth all the trouble everyone had ever gone to for it. But by flashlight light, in a moving car, under its cover, it was a stretch to see the "masterpiece" part of the Expressionist masterpiece.

It was plenty expressionistic, though. He could give it a perfect ten for expressionism.

"Very cool," he said, and yeah, he knew that was about a low-end one on the art appreciation verbalization scale, but for all that he'd posed for Nikki, he'd never really picked up the lingo.

"Cool?" Esme sounded a little disappointed in his opinion.

He was, too. Truly.

"Yeah, cool. Very, uh, colorful. It kind of looks like Solange, with the blue and all, and the curves, and that thicker swath of gray straightaway. The red could be her taillights."

"Solange, your car?"

"Yeah, very curvy, very female, I guess, when I look at it a little more. I never heard of Jakob Meinhard, but the painting looks like it could be worth quite a lot of money." He was telling her the truth. The long slinky lines and the colors reminded him of the Cyclone, but as far as opinions went, that one probably didn't have many redeeming qualities either—a fact she conveyed quite succinctly with her closing of the painting into the case.

"It is," she said.

And there he was, back in high school, in

another classic Esme Alden moment—in over his head.

"The word masterpiece alone implies a certain value." That sounded a little better—maybe.

Hell, if she wanted to talk art, she needed to be talking to Hawkins. Superman could even outtalk Nikki about all the "this and that" of art, and he'd married a woman who owned art galleries, for crying out loud.

"Yes, it does."

He heard her snap the case shut.

"How much *could* you get for it on the open market?" he said, cutting to the chase. There probably weren't any additional redeeming qualities in that question either, but he wanted to know.

"There is no open market, per se, for works of this quality if they're stolen," she said, sliding the case back into the leather messenger bag.

Fair enough.

"How much on the black market?"

"Half a million."

Quite a hell of a lot of money, just like he'd said.

"And if it wasn't stolen and could be bought legitimately?" he asked.

"One point five to two million."

He didn't whistle at that. He just kept driving.

Two million dollars, sitting in his car.

He'd known life was going to be interesting, being back in Denver, being part of SDF, or at least almost part of SDF, but, man, he'd come up with Esme Alden and a two-million-dollar painting all on his own. And any girl dealing in two million dollars' worth of art had done damn well by herself, her screwup dad aside. Private investigations on that scale were a few cuts above following errant spouses around with a long lens, or tracking down the guy who hadn't paid his construction lien.

The sudden vibration of his phone had him reaching in his pocket to pull it out. He automatically looked at the screen before he answered.

"Skeets, wazzup?"

"General Grant, Johnny-boy. He's here, up on The Beach with a bottle of Scotch."

Johnny sat up a little straighter behind the wheel. *Oh-kay.*

He might not have been an official member of the SDF team yet, but he'd been working at Steele Street and living in the annex at the Commerce City Garage for almost ten years, and of the few times that General Grant had come to Denver, he'd only gotten plastered up on The Beach once, when he'd come to mourn J. T. Chronopoulos, one of the original chop-shop boys and one of the original members of SDF.

"Did someone die?" It was a hard question, an awful question, the kind a guy felt in his gut, but with a few of the operators out on missions, anything was possible, and the hard questions always needed to be asked first.

"No. I ran everybody down as soon as I realized where Grant had gone and that the Scotch was missing from the guest suite," Skeeter said. "He's called a meeting for the A.M., and he wants everyone here."

"Red Dog and Travis—" Johnny started, but she cut him off.

"They won't make it. Senators rule, SDF drools when it comes to fact-finding tours of Third World countries. They stay put."

"Smith?" C. Smith Rydell was the other operator currently deployed.

"Arriving at Peterson in a couple of hours. Everyone else is either driving in or flying in before dawn, and we're all meeting up here. Your name is on the guest list."

The news set him back for a second. He'd expected it, sure, but to hear it.

Hoo-yah . . . he grinned—except if Grant was here to deliver good news, what was up with the Scotch?

"Yeah, I'm wondering the same damn thing," Skeeter said, reading his mind—business as usual with SDF's spooky long-legged blonde. He'd spent enough time with her under the hood of a car not to be surprised when she knew exactly what he'd been thinking.

"Exit," Esme whispered, pointing up ahead to an exit ramp.

He nodded and pulled over into the right-hand lane.

"Who all's at the garage?" The building at 738 Steele Street had thirteen floors, seven of which housed cars, mostly American muscle from the sixties and early seventies.

"The jungle boy and I have been working on Mercy all night, and Superman is here."

"And the meeting?"

"Eight A.M., everybody on board, front and center. Creed and I will be hosting. The coffee will be Jamaican, hot, and strong, and the doughnuts will be fresh from Sugarbombs."

Excellent. Everything was excellent. He and Skeeter had been living on Sugarbomb doughnuts since he'd gotten home, and Creed's coffee could stand in a corner without a cup, which was just the way Johnny liked it.

And the timing was perfect. Eight A.M.—plenty of time for him to do the Bleak deal for Esme and still get to Steele Street with time to spare. No one at SDF need ever know he'd spent the night skirting some pretty sketchy edges.

"I'll be there at seven-thirty," he said.

"Good. Are you still at the Blue Iguana?"

"Not quite."

That gave her a little pause.

"Did you get lucky, *chico*?" She was grinning. He could tell.

"Not quite."

She let out a short laugh. "Well, if you run out of places to go, come here before you go home. Creed and I could use some help with Mercy's—"

The rest of her words were lost in static, and then he lost the whole connection.

It happened in the mountains. He could call her back later.

Putting his phone back in his pocket, he slipped

off the interstate onto the exit—Genesee, Isaac Nachman in sight, Bleak on the horizon, and in between, him and Easy Alex finally getting where they'd always needed to be, naked in bed.

Yeah, he needed that. He'd needed it for a long time, and never more so than since he'd gotten back from his last tour of duty.

CHAPTER EIGHTEEN

Standing in the doorway between the hostess desk and the rest of the restaurant, Dax checked out the people sitting in the bar at Mama Guadalupe's. Then he checked his watch. Charo had made good time once he'd gotten her off the interstate. He was early.

He let his gaze go back over the people filling up the tables. The place was packed on a Friday night, with music blaring, folks dancing, drinking, eating, and talk, talk, talking. Jazz was the music, Santa Fe gourmet was the food, and Mama Guadalupe's was obviously the place to be. Mama herself was working the tables at the front of the house, charming the diners and snapping her fingers at the waitstaff to keep them moving. Dax knew it was all for show. The young men didn't need the added incentive. They had to work long and hard to get out of the busboy crew and into the ranks of Mama's howling-wolf waiters. Not only did the job supply them with plenty of ready cash, there wasn't a girl on the west side who didn't want to date one of Guadalupe's waiters. The job was cool, always had been.

"Sir? Mr. Killian?"

He looked down at the young, dark-haired hostess standing at his elbow. She couldn't have been more than fifteen or sixteen and was dressed very neatly in a black skirt to her knees, a white button-up shirt, and a black vest with a name tag pinned to it—Dulcinea.

He agreed. She looked real sweet with her hair swept back in a pair of tidy braids, her warm smile, and her Holy Cross earrings.

"Yes?" he answered, only slightly surprised to hear his name. The city of Denver would have to undergo a pretty dramatic population change for him not to run into people he knew, especially in this part of town.

"Señor Rick requests your company for a drink." She pointed to the far dark corner of the long bar, and Dax grinned. He'd be damned. Rick Graydon, the only gringo in the place, was still in the place.

"*Gracias.*" He smiled at the girl before heading across the room.

"Dax." The bartender greeted him with a smile, a bright flash of false teeth. Dax knew Rick kept the choppers by his bed at night in a cup of peroxide with a touch of water and a whisper of bleach—shaken, not stirred. The guy was seventy, if he was a day, still lively, but definitely old enough to be a piece of Denver history, and he very freely shared the secret of his blindingly white smile with anyone willing to listen.

"Rick." Dax reached across the bar and shook the guy's hand. The older man's grip was still strong, like an ox. Rick was rightly infamous for his mescal margaritas. "Good to see you still working."

" 'Til I drop, Dax. 'Til I drop, probably right here behind the bar."

Dax slipped a five across the bar, and Rick reached under his side and slid a pack of cigarettes back over to him.

To Dax's knowledge, Rick was the only importer of Faro cigarettes in the state. He was also the only importer of Oaxacan mescal. Both sidelines were illegal, Rick's idea of a pension fund for his old age. Considering how long he'd been in the "import" business, Dax figured he must have quite a fund sitting somewhere—knowing Rick, probably buried in his backyard.

"Can I get you a beer? On the house."

"Not tonight, thanks, but will you keep an eye out for my cousin? I'm supposed to meet her here, but I have another stop I need to make."

"You mean that little Esme gal?"

"Yeah, that's the one, but you be careful with her, Rick. She's all grown-up now and meaner than a junkyard dog."

Rick burst out laughing, and Dax grinned.

He wasn't kidding, not really.

"Sure, Dax. I'll watch for her, let her know you've been in and want her to stay put."

"Thanks, Rick."

A couple of minutes later, he was back in Charo and heading toward Speer Boulevard and LoDo. He hadn't wanted Esme going by the office, in case Bleak still had some jerk staking out the place, but Dax wanted to go by the office, in case Bleak still had some jerk staking out the place. He'd given it quite a bit of thought on his way up from the Springs, and getting his hands on one of Bleak's guys seemed like the most expedient method available for gathering intelligence on tomorrow morning's deal, some real hands-on, in-your-face, up-close-and-personal intelligence gathering.

Dax's grin returned. Without a doubt, that was the best way to find out what kind of setup Bleak had in mind for the meeting.

"Lieutenant?"

Loretta looked up from hanging up the phone on her desk. Connor Ford was in her doorway. "What is it?"

"We found Dixie and Benny-boy Jackman."

She tilted her head and looked around him, through the window into the squad room.

"Where?" she asked. "I'm not seeing them."

"Denver General. In the emergency room. Seems like Benny-boy had a run-in with another rock-and-roll star over by Five Points, over a new girl they were both trying to recruit."

"Recruit?" she asked. "Is that what they call it now?"

"When they're talking to the cops it is," Connor

said. "What we know for sure is that during the negotiations with the girl and her current pimp, Benny-boy got cut. Dixie was with him, and after all the prerequisite theatrics and threats, she drove him over to Denver General. They've been there since about five o'clock this evening."

And there went the easy theory, right down the drain.

"Is Benny-boy going to pull through?"

"'Fraid so."

"Well, maybe our luck will be better tomorrow." She glanced at the phone before going back to her paperwork. A grin flitted across her mouth. She had a strange job sometimes, damned *intriguing*. Hell.

A sigh replaced her grin. Her shift had been over two hours ago, and she'd like to get going. She didn't have much of a personal life, but what little she had, she liked to enjoy.

"Actually, Lieutenant, our luck is looking pretty damn good right now."

That got her attention.

She glanced back up. "What have you got?"

"The phone number the blonde gave to the valet at the Oxford?"

"Yes."

"We've located the phone through its GPS emergency signal. It's not too far from the hotel. I thought you might like to go over with us and see who's there."

"In case it's a knife-wielding hooker?" She wasn't smiling, not yet. Nothing was ever this easy.

"If we're lucky, yes."

"And if we're not lucky, we end up standing next to a Dumpster in some LoDo alley, digging through trash, trying to find a phone our S and M expert tossed."

"Yes, ma'am. We call that detective work."

He was right, of course, and she needed to get her mind back on her business and off her social life.

"We've got a good lock on it, though, Lieutenant," he continued, "and it looks like the phone is in the old Faber Building."

Dammit. There was nothing like some really great news to screw up a person's schedule.

She looked at her watch. She could have skipped Dumpster diving and just let the boys and girls in blue have at it—but if they'd tracked the phone to the Faber Building, well, hell, then she ought to be there, in case there was a person still attached to the damn thing.

"Lieutenant?" Officer Weisman leaned into her office, holding a sheaf of papers. "Gail came up with a portrait the maid positively identifies as our police impersonator."

"Let's see it." Loretta held out her hand.

Weisman crossed her office and gave her the drawings the artist had done on the computer. "The top one, Lieutenant. That's the one the maid says is closest."

Loretta took one look and swore under her breath. *Goddammit.* Somebody better have an explanation for this.

Fortunately, somebody did, and she knew exactly who that somebody would be.

"Connor?"

"Yes, ma'am?"

"Get Skeeter on the phone, and ask her what in the hell Johnny Ramos was doing at the Oxford Hotel tonight, impersonating one of my fine Denver police officers."

CHAPTER NINETEEN

Lost. Rangers were never lost. Never.

Johnny could have been dropped in the middle of a damn desert blindfolded, and with a compass and a map, screw the GPS, have known where he was on the planet in a couple of minutes. Guaranteed. Rangers were the ultimate Eagle Scouts.

But he'd been on more than one mission in the Middle East where they'd had a local guide, and sometimes, those boys had gotten lost. The Rangers would still know where they were. The trick was in knowing where they were supposed to be, or finding a target that wasn't where the guide had "known" it would be.

No target, no mission.

That's where he and his current guide, otherwise known as Esme Alexandria Alden, were: off target. According to her, Isaac Nachman's mansion was humongous, fifty thousand square feet of castlelike log-and-stone lodge set on a thousand acres.

And the girl couldn't find it, even with her directions in her hand. Even with having done her recon work less than seven days ago.

So how, he wondered, did a person forget the coordinates of a fifty-thousand-square-foot castle? There was only one way—by never knowing them in the first place.

She'd counted on the roads, and remembering where to turn, without measuring distances and mapping them out. That was the big difference between the pros and the amateurs, between the big boys and the—well, he hated to say it, but between the big boys and the girls.

Esme was all girl, and she was lost, and she'd dragged him with her.

And he wasn't the only one.

In the traffic on the interstate, he hadn't noticed anybody following them, but he knew the rear end of a 1968 Mercury Cyclone had a distinct vehicular signature even at night. It would have been easy to follow Solange's taillights—and somebody had done exactly that, because he and Esme weren't alone out here in the wilderness.

Every now and then, he saw another set of headlights cutting through the darkness below them. He wasn't too worried, because the other car was losing ground, falling further and further behind. Nachman's place was in the back of beyond of Genesee, with dozens of roads snaking off into the night in every which direction.

Rangers were never lost, though. Never. And despite all the twists and turns, and all the roads, Johnny knew exactly how to get back to the interstate. If Esme could just remember how to get them to the lodge, he could get them home.

"There." She pointed out the windshield. "To the right. Just beyond those two big trees."

Two. Big. Trees.

Right. There weren't two big trees on this mountainside. There were thousands—thousands and thousands of big trees.

"Esme—"

"You just missed it."

Missed what?

He looked back over his shoulder—and he'd be damned. There was a road, or rather a track between two big trees.

"A thousand-acre hunting preserve with a fifty-thousand-square-foot lodge on it, and the entrance is a dirt track no more than eight feet wide?" In his limited experience, guys like Nachman liked to announce their munificence with elaborate gates. There wasn't so much as a string of barbed wire across the track.

He threw Solange into reverse and backed up a couple of feet.

"The road widens out in a mile. The first thing we'll see is a massive wall running for about a quarter mile in either direction off a huge gate. It's like the Great Wall of China. There'll be a gatehouse and a guard to call us in. This road is meant to throw off the day-trippers."

A guard—he'd expected as much.

"You're carrying a sidearm," he said, stopping the car and shifting back into first. "Were you armed the last time you were here?"

"Yes, and I kept my weapon with me the whole time, if that's what you're asking."

That's exactly what he was asking.

"Does Nachman's staff make a habit of frisking uninvited male guests?" There wasn't a doubt in his mind that he looked more dangerous than her.

He eased the Cyclone onto the rutted path, heading for the Great Wall of China. It was possible Isaac's security staff simply hadn't considered Esme a threat. She was short, blond, cute. Actually, with the right training, she'd make a helluva bodyguard for somebody.

"It's possible we won't see any staff, other than the guard at the gate. They're there. They have to be. The lodge doesn't run by itself, but the other two times I was here, with my father, I never actually saw anyone at the house except Nachman."

Well, that was damned odd. Maybe the staff was just incredibly discreet.

"If you button up and tuck in your shirt, though, it won't look so much like a gun drape," she added. "That might help, if you're concerned."

He left his shirt unbuttoned and untucked so he'd have easier access to his weapon if he needed it, but she was right. To anyone who was aware, it was a dead giveaway that he just might be packing a pistol, almost as bad as a guy with a fanny pack.

Slowing Solange back to a stop, he put her in

neutral and engaged the parking brake, then followed Esme's advice, stepping out of the car and buttoning up his shirt and tucking it into his jeans. He wasn't in the mood to have his weapon confiscated for security reasons. But neither was he in the mood to be stuck in the car while she went inside alone—and he knew those would be his choices, if Nachman's security guys were paying attention and doing their jobs.

And whether she'd seen them or not, he agreed with her; they had to be there, probably half a dozen of them, along with maids, cooks, gardeners, and housekeepers. Guys like Isaac Nachman didn't live alone.

He stood corrected.

In the middle of the biggest foyer he'd ever seen, a foyer the size of a cathedral, open to the rafters, all open-beamed, three stories high with a giant staircase sweeping up one side, floor after floor, with huge landings and galleries overlooking the foyer, he stood corrected.

The place was empty. He felt it in every bone in his body. Other than him, Easy Alex, God only knew how many dozens of stuffed animal heads from every continent, and the wizened little old man standing in front of them in slippers, socks, and a striped silk robe, and please dear God, something— anything—underneath it, the place was empty.

They'd been passed through the gate by a guard

at least as old as Nachman, maybe even older. Decrepitude seemed to be the order of the day at the hunting lodge, ancient decrepitude.

And yet, Isaac Nachman's eyes were alight.

He'd had Esme open the case on a small table next to the sweeping expanse of stairs, and he'd been riveted to the painting since first sight.

"My dear, my dear." He almost hummed the words, his excitement was running so high. "My dear Miss Esme. This is a rare day for the Nachman family, a rare day."

"Yes, sir, Mr. Nachman," Esme agreed. She was very relaxed, which was more than Johnny could say about himself. The place creeped him out. A Cape buffalo was eyeing him from across the room, its black glass eyes seeming to stare straight at him. Four stuffed cheetahs stalked across the wall opposite the staircase. A pride of lions silently roared and motionlessly stalked unseen prey in a room across the way—a whole pride, taxidermied for posterity and somebody's overwhelming ego.

The rich could be too rich.

And without a doubt, they could be damned strange. He couldn't believe Esme's partner had expected her to come up here into the middle of freaking nowhere, to this huge, empty mansion full of dead animals, to cut a deal with this eccentric old geezer all by herself.

He wouldn't have wanted to do it alone, and he was carrying a .45.

So was she, and he didn't doubt that her partner knew it, and truth be told, she could probably take

Isaac Nachman and the guard at the gate with one hand tied behind her back.

But still.

"She's been missing from our home for a long, long time," the old man crooned. "It's time for her to join her sisters."

Okay, now he was *officially* creeped out.

"I know she's happy to be home, Mr. Nachman."

He slanted Esme a very askance glance. *Geezus*.

"If only we had the Monet, Miss Esme," Nachman mused. "I remember the Monet from when I was a child in Berlin."

"My father is working on the Monet, Mr. Nachman."

"Yes, yes. Burt will find it. Burt never fails. He and Bainbridge never fail."

Johnny kept his mouth shut. His lips were superglued. He had nothing to add here.

"No, sir, Mr. Nachman. My father never fails."

He looked at her again, his gaze narrowed. She was watching the old man, the way his hand hovered over the painting, a few centimeters from the surface, like he was channeling the woman in *Woman in Blue*—and she believed what she'd just said. Her dad never failed. Burt Alden, the guy whose motto was "We Snoop 4 U."

"He has a gift," Isaac Nachman said.

"Yes, sir. He does."

"I've never seen anything like it," the old man continued. "We had hired so many people over the years. Had our own people on the hunt, and then, like a miracle, we found your father. He has out-done them all."

"A gift," she agreed, and Johnny had to wonder, really, just how much of a Burt Alden celebration this was going to turn out to be, and he had to won-der who this "we" was that old Nachman was talk-ing about. There was no "we" that he could see. The mansion was as quiet as a tomb, except for the creaking of the timbers, and the sound of the wind sloughing past the windows.

The wind was new. There hadn't been any wind when he and Esme had walked up to the massive front door.

If thunder started to roll, and lightning to flash, if it started to rain, he was grabbing Esme and get-ting the hell out. He wasn't going to do the whole "dark and stormy night" thing in this freaking weird place.

"And yet . . ." Nachman said.

And yet Burt Alden was a verifiable screwup. *Geezus*. Franklin Bleak was going to deep-six him in the river, if Burt didn't pay off his gambling debt. Whatever gift he had for finding art that had been missing for more than half a century, it sure as hell didn't extend to finding a horse in the fifth.

"And yet . . ." Esme repeated.

"One must be sure, Miss Esme," Nachman said.

"One *must* be sure," Esme again repeated what the old man had said.

Maxing out on the creeping out, Johnny thought, releasing a long breath. He glanced back over at the Cape buffalo. Yeah, that thing wanted to eat his lunch.

"Shall we, my dear? Mr. Ramos, you may await us here." Nachman started walking toward the room with the pride of stuffed lions loping over an artfully designed patch of sub-Saharan Africa.

"Of course." Esme picked up the painting and started after him.

Johnny stopped her with a touch of his hand on her arm.

"It's okay," she said. "Mr. Nachman and I are going to authenticate the painting."

"Yes . . . yes, my dear." The old man had stopped and was looking over his shoulder at her, a very odd and discomfiting smile playing about his lips. "Authenticate to my satisfaction."

Bullshit.

"We'll all go together," Johnny said.

"There won't be room." Isaac Nachman shook his head. "There won't be room, I tell you. Not in the closet."

Closet?

"We'll make room," he said. Fifty goddamn thousand square feet of house and this guy was taking her into a goddamn closet?

Esme gave him a look that clearly said she had it covered, but he didn't care. The look he gave her back said *he* had it covered—his way or the highway.

She rolled her eyes and turned back to Isaac Nachman. "Mr. Ramos has been with me for a number of months now, but is still relatively new to the art-recovery business, Mr. Nachman, and he would, no doubt, benefit from being present at the authentication."

No fucking doubt.

"My . . . my dear, I must . . . well, you *know*."

"I will vouch for him, Mr. Nachman, personally, upon my utmost honor. His association with our family goes back many, many years, and his security credentials are impeccable, acknowledged and accepted by my father."

His security credentials were vouchsafed by a helluva lot more reliable and exacting sources than Burt Alden.

"Well, my dear, if your father . . . well, then, I must, I suppose, *accommodate,* then . . . if Mr. Ramos must," the man said, clearly flustered, which only reinforced Johnny's position. If there were anything worse than being stuck in a closet with an old geezer wearing a silk bathrobe, it would be being stuck in a closet with a flustered old geezer wearing a silk bathrobe.

What in the hell did the old guy think he was going to get away with? Grabbing her ass? Worse?

Well, it wasn't going to happen. Not on his shift. And for the record, in his book, Burt Alden was still a bum.

With a decidedly pinched and vapid expression of duress on his face, Isaac Nachman led the way through the lion room, shuffling along in his slippers. Esme followed him, and Johnny followed Esme, bringing up the rear.

The house was amazing, even with so many

stuffed animals everywhere. It was all log walls and giant stone fireplaces, and expensive wood paneling with incredibly thick rugs carpeting the floors. But the place didn't make sense, and it took him passing through a couple more rooms to figure out why.

There was no art. None. *Nada*. Nothing. Not on the walls, not on the tables, not anything anywhere. No exquisite paintings, no vases, no intricately carved tribal masks, no sculpture, no wall hangings, no tapestries. Only stuffed animals, a bunch of which, on closer inspection, looked a little flea-bitten, like they'd been hunted down and killed a long, long time ago.

Minute after minute passed, with the three of them still walking, heading toward the back of the house, room after room, until Johnny began to wonder how in the world people lived in a place this big. Fifty thousand square feet was unmanageable.

After a couple more turns into beautiful wood-paneled hallways, they took a short flight of stairs down to a lower level with recessed lighting, always with Isaac Nachman in the lead and Esme carrying the painting, until they came to an elevator.

Johnny didn't mind the ride down even though it seemed to last a helluva long time for being part of a house. He had no problems with elevators. But when the door opened, he did have a problem.

They weren't in the house any longer. The elevator had opened onto a tunnel dug deep into the mountain, like a mining tunnel, with raw earth walls shored up with lumber. Lights hung from a rock ceiling, a string of lanterns snaking into the far darkness, but Johnny didn't really give a damn. Lights or no lights, he had a problem, and fighting the urge to draw his pistol and slide up against one of the walls took everything he had.

He clenched his left hand into a fist to hold himself in check, to make sure he didn't do it.

In front of him, Isaac Nachman shuffled out of the elevator and headed down the tunnel. Esme Alexandria Alden followed the old man, and he, Johnny Aurelio Ramos, stood stock-still in the elevator and started to sweat.

CHAPTER TWENTY

This was just too perfect. Dax's luck couldn't possibly be running this good. Kevin Harrell standing across the street from Burt's office, looking like the stakeout king of Dumbsville with his linebacker build and his highlighted blond hair. Of all the jerks Bleak could have put on the Faber Building, Kevin would have been Dax's first choice. He had some unfinished business with the guy.

He cruised around the block, looking for a parking spot and finding one half a block north of Wynkoop. For what he had in mind, it would be better if Kevin came up to the office, rather than the two of them having their little discussion on the street.

Pulling up to the curb, he turned off Charo's ignition and took the cuffs out of her jockey box. He dropped the restraints in his pocket, then checked his watch—ten-thirty, and all was well in lower downtown. People were still bar-hopping and piling out of the restaurants. There were a couple of cops around—more than a couple, actually. He could see a squad car in the alley coming off the back of the Oxford Hotel, and another one parked up on Wazee.

He swung out onto the street, sliding the Folton Ridge folder inside his jacket, then turned and locked the 'Cuda. Kevin Harrell was still standing on Wynkoop, eyeballing the Faber Building, like he could get it to ignite if he just gave it his all.

Fat chance. The guy didn't have those kinds of chops.

Knocking a Faro out of the pack he'd bought off Rick, Dax checked the street in both directions. Another cop car was parked on Wynkoop, which seemed excessive even on a busy Friday night, and which he hoped to hell didn't have anything to do with Easy and Otto Von Lindberg.

It shouldn't. She'd finished with Otto two hours ago, should be finishing with Nachman right now, and then be on her way back into town. When he'd gotten to Denver, he'd called and left her a message to call as soon as she did the same. Phone reception could get sketchy up in the mountains, but once she made it back to the interstate, it should be all systems go.

Walking down toward Wynkoop, he stuck the cigarette between his lips and reached for his lighter, and at the corner he took a moment to fire up the Faro. There were plenty of people on the sidewalk, but he was the only one staring straight at Kevin Harrell across the street, and it didn't take the guy long to feel it.

When he was sure he had Mr. Harrell's attention, he took one more long drag off the cigarette, holding the guy's gaze, hard and steady. Then he exhaled, taking his time.

Yeah, *pendejo*, take a good look at your midnight cowboy over here.

Dax wasn't shy about his looks. He wouldn't have given a dollar for them either, but he knew the value of a well-cut jacket over a hand-tailored dress shirt, a pair of 501s that fit like a glove, and a pair of custom-made cowboy boots.

Finished exhaling, he dropped the Faro on the sidewalk, crushed it with his boot, and headed into the Faber Building.

It was a come-on, sure enough. One he didn't think Harrell would be able to resist. There was a reason the jerk had gotten rough with Easy that day back in high school, trying to prove how tough he was, trying to prove his manhood. It was because he had plenty to prove, and nothing he *could* prove, not in a month of Sundays. Big old brawny Kevin Harrell was gay.

Dax didn't hold personal sexual orientation against anybody, but he sure as hell held Kevin Harrell's treatment of Easy against him. Besides the incident in the locker bay—and, yeah, suddenly, he remembered *exactly* who John Ramos was, which only reinforced the wisdom of having

Esme stick with the guy—well, besides that incident, there had been some verbal harassment that
had even included Esme's mom, his aunt Beth.

And now here was the idiot, leaving himself wide
open on the off chance he was going to get lucky.

Lucky, hell.

Dax used his key on the building's outside door,
and used the doorstop just inside to keep the door
open. He was going to make this as easy as possible
for Harrell.

Once inside the door, he stepped back in the
shadows and waited.

It didn't take long.

Harrell no sooner stepped inside the door than
Dax spun him around hard and slammed him into
the wall even harder. In the instant Harrell was
stunned, Dax cuffed his hands behind his back,
and in the next instant, he had a 1911 jammed up
against the back of the guy's neck, right on the old
brain stem.

"Come on, asshole. Get up the stairs." Dax
jerked the guy's hands higher up behind his back.
"I'd just as soon drop you as talk to you, so don't
fuck with me, Kevin."

"You . . . you broke my fucking nose," the guy
blubbered between gasps for air.

Tough.

Dax moved him even faster, getting them out of
the stairwell as quickly as possible.

Harrell stumbled, shaking his head, and Dax
damn near lifted him off his feet, keeping him up-
right. "Move."

At the door to the B and B Investigations office, Dax forced Harrell to his knees.

"Stay put." He kept the automatic pistol pressed against the guy's neck with his left hand, while he unlocked the door with his right.

"You . . . you asshole. You broke my . . . my nose."

Yeah, yeah.

"Get inside."

Harrell lumbered to his feet and stepped inside the office. Dax closed the door behind them.

"Have a seat." He shoved Harrell toward the client chair in front of Burt's desk.

The big guy dropped into it with a groan.

"Who the hell are you?" Harrell asked, looking up from under a fringe of streaked blond bangs.

Dax had a hard time with questions like that one. The urge to overdramatize was damn near irresistible. Really great lines came to mind, like "Your worst nightmare," or "The last thing you're ever going to see."

He refrained.

"Esme Alden's cousin." That was his business with Kevin Harrell, the high school thing. "That makes me Burt Alden's nephew." And the Franklin-Bleak-wanting-to-beat-the-crap-out-of-and/or-kill-Uncle-Burt problem. The two items were more than enough reason for Dax to get in Harrell's face. Those two reasons, and that Bleak had sent this goon and Dovey Smollett to snatch Easy off the street. He'd break them all for thinking that was a good idea. He knew more than enough about Bleak to know sometimes the people he made a point of getting up close and personal with never made it out of the meeting alive.

Like he said, he'd break them all before he let them get their hands on his bad girl—and it wasn't because he was such a family-orientated guy. He had relatives, everyone did. But Easy? She'd struck a chord with him a long time ago. Skinny? *Geezus*, she'd been a skinny little kid. She'd also been smart, controlled, self-possessed, and self-contained—all that at eight, and he'd noticed. Out of all the ragtag bundles of energy and mischief that had made up the cadre known as "the younger kids" in his family, she'd stood out.

And then three years ago, fresh diploma in hand, she'd come and asked him for a job. To date, he'd never had a regret for taking her on. Not even with that damn Bangkok thing hanging over his head.

"Burt Alden owes my boss money, a lot of money," Harrell said belligerently, as if the fact gave him the moral high ground.

He was mistaken. Dax owned every last inch of the high ground, and he wasn't giving any of it up.

"You put your hands on my cousin once," Dax said calmly, leaning back against the desk and sliding his pistol back into his shoulder holster. "Don't do it again. Ever."

He reached over and hit "play" on the answering machine.

"Do you understand?"

Harrell's hard brown gaze didn't waver. "I understand you're gonna be in deep shit with Bleak, if you don't let me go right now, you asshole."

The first message was Aunt Beth, and Dax pressed the skip button. The next message was a good one, from Thomas in Chicago—but he wanted a callback. He didn't leave the name.

Geez, Dax thought. What was it with these old guys? Why couldn't Thomas have just left the damn name?

"What were you doing out on Wynkoop?" he asked, picking up a postcard lying on the desk. It had a picture of an angel on the front, and Johnny Ramos's name and some loopy-looking girl handwriting on the back. He stuck it in his back pocket. "Waiting for Esme? Waiting for Burt?"

"Fuck you."

"Burt's a problem. I'll grant you that, but we're going to take care of it." Uncle Burt's dentist came on line next, and Dax hit the skip button. "On the other hand, if I ever hear of you waiting anywhere for Esme ever again, I'll fuck you, and not the way you're hoping, Kevin."

Some static ran on the answering machine, and Dax let it play, in case there was a message in it somewhere.

"F-fuck you."

Spoken like a scholar.

The next message was his to Easy. He skipped it, and then hit pay dirt.

"*Burt,*" the same male voice as before came over the answering machine. "*It's Thomas. Why the hell haven't you called me back? I'm not going to be here much longer, so you better get a pencil...Lindsey Larson...that's it, Burt. Her friends call her Lucky.*"

Lucky Larson kinda sounds like a hooker, doesn't it? That's funny, given what her old man does for a living. It sure is. Call me."

Dax watched Harrell while the message played, and the names Lindsey Larson and Lucky Larson didn't register on the guy's face at all. Dax wasn't surprised. He'd have been more surprised if Franklin Bleak had bandied his daughter's name about with his peons. The important thing was that the name registered with Dax, it registered with all the impact of half a dozen vanilla-vodka shooters.

Bleak's daughter had about as much class as her dad.

Dax pulled the Folton Ridge file out of the inside pocket on his jacket and leaned over the desk to turn on the B & B Investigations paper shredder.

Burt had a few more messages piled up on the machine, one from a betrayed spouse wondering if he'd gotten the photos from the Bluebird Motel, another from some guy named Joe wanting to borrow fifty bucks, one more from a guy named Brad who wanted to borrow a hundred.

Walking around behind Harrell, Dax flipped through the file folder. When he reached the other side of the desk, he stopped and started shredding. One by one, he got rid of Nancy Haney, Jessica Durst, and Kim Stiple, the last two being the good girls. That left him with the photos and chat room chitchat of dear Lindsey, Bleak's baby.

"So what were you doing out there on Wynkoop, Kevin? What's Bleak want here? His money, or something else?"

He'd known it was "Lucky" Lindsey. She had her dad's nose, and the same low forehead, and she wasn't an inch over five feet—short, like her dad.

"He wants his damn money."

"He'll have it at five o'clock tomorrow morning. Do you want to go back to the warehouse and remind Bleak the deal is set?"

"Alden's said that before and not delivered. The bastard never delivers. Everybody knows that."

Dax looked up from the Lindsey file at the guy. Kevin Harrell was nervous, rightly so. Broken nose, handcuffed, bleeding, sweating, he was two hundred and thirty pounds of pure helpless. He was shaking in the chair, a low-level trembling. He also had a tattoo on the back of his neck.

"How long have you been out of Canon City?" Dax asked. The tat was classic prison ink, one capital C interlocked with another, the two letters sitting on top of a pair of dice showing snake eyes.

"Fuck you."

"Ah, come on, Kevin," he said, modulating his voice to a slow drawl. "We might still have a party here. I just need some information."

The guy went still in his chair, and after a second, cast a glance back at Dax.

Dax met his gaze without flinching.

Weaknesses—he had a few, but unlike Kevin Harrell, he wasn't telegraphing his in pink neon, and sex was just too simple. Nobody should get taken for sex.

Okay, for the sake of honesty, Dax needed to retract his last knee-jerk opinion. He'd been taken for sex, more than once, but he'd never given up the bank for it. Consolata Rodriguez had definitely taken him for sex. He'd given that girl everything he'd had at seventeen. He'd even let her drive his car, let her use it to impress her girlfriends, right up until she'd hit a stop sign with it—head-on, no brakes, no blinker, no sense. His ardor had cooled a bit after that, and he'd gotten away thinking he'd learned something about women, not the least of which was that they couldn't goddamn drive.

Yep, he'd learned his lesson, right up until the next woman, Debbie Thanatos. She'd left his car alone, but she'd sure taken him for a ride. Adriana, Bridget, the car-wrecking Consolata, Debbie—he hadn't covered the whole alphabet, but in retrospect, and he'd given his love life plenty of retrospective consideration, he'd probably gotten taken for sex more often than he wanted to admit.

Still, Harrell must have been an easy mark in prison. He sure as hell was an easy mark here on Wynkoop in the Faber Building.

"Two weeks," the guy said. "I been out for two weeks."

"Check in with your parole officer lately?"

"Yeah." The guy nodded, then cast another furtive glance back at Dax. "I've been right on time."

Two weeks wasn't long.

"How long have you been working for Bleak?"

"This is my first job. A friend of mine called me this afternoon and got me on, said I can do real good with this outfit. He told Bleak I knew this girl he wanted, that I would recognize her real easy, from high school, and be a good guy to have around."

Well, that was a helluva resume—"I knew this girl in high school." And in other words, Kevin Harrell was a bust. He didn't know crap about Bleak. It was possible he'd never even met the bookie.

"Is your friend's name Dovey Smollett?"

"What's it to you?" Kevin shot back, rallying in defense of a buddy.

Okay, Dax would give him that, the whole honor-among-thieves thing that never really held up very well, not for very long, not under pressure, not with guys like Kevin, and not with guys like Dovey.

There were guys who would give up their lives before they gave up a buddy. Dax knew a lot of them, but the tie that bound wasn't friendship.

"So what's Bleak want with Esme?" Dax continued. "Insurance?"

Kevin shook his head. "I don't know. My friend says Bleak is done with Alden. He's got some kind of important deal he's working, and I don't know, maybe he wants to impress somebody."

"Impress how?"

"I don't know." Harrell shrugged. "But Bleak's a big deal. He runs a lot of girls, and guys know to come to him if they want something special." He shrugged again. "Esme always had a lot of class, and my buddy told him, told Bleak, that Alden's daughter was really hot, like maybe she'd be worth something on the side. So maybe Bleak thinks he can get something for her."

Sure. Maybe Bleak was thinking something like that.

Maybe Bleak was in more trouble than Dax had originally thought. Maybe Dovey was in way more trouble than that even.

And maybe Uncle Burt had better skip the next family get-together, because it was going to be a long, long time before Dax would trust himself in the same room with Easy's dad.

"Whatever," he said, coming back around the desk and leaning against it with his hip. He wanted to be eye to eye with old Kevin for a minute. "Right now, I'm more interested in you and me, Kevin. Are we square on Esme? You and me?" He didn't want there to be any doubts in Harrell's mind about appropriate distances and things like that. "You know she should never see your face again. If you see her, you go the other way. Okay? Are we square?"

"Yeah." The guy was nodding his head. "We're square. But, like, what's your name, dude?"

Dude?

Kevin Harrell was sitting there in handcuffs with blood running down his face onto his shirt, and he was calling Dax dude?

Oh, yeah, Dax bet the guy had been a real hit in prison.

"Well, *dude*, I've got a lot of names." None of which he planned on telling Kevin Harrell, but what stopped him was the sound of people coming up the stairs—more than one person, maybe three, maybe four, which was more business than B and B Investigations had attracted in months.

He pushed off the desk and headed for the door.

"Stay put," he said to Harrell, drawing his Springfield 1911 and holding it in a low ready position. Keeping the gun cocked, locked, and loaded was his standard operating procedure. It never varied. Flipping off the safety was an automatic part of his draw.

Through the unfrosted part of the glass on the door, he identified three people coming down the hall. Two men and a woman, with one of the men dressed in a police uniform.

He smoothly reholstered his weapon, concealing it underneath his jacket, and glanced back at Harrell. That wasn't going to look good to the cops, a guy handcuffed and bleeding.

"Get in the bathroom," he said, pointing to the open door at the far end of the office. "Get in there and stay quiet. It's the cops."

He didn't have to say cops twice to get the guy moving. Dax didn't care how many times Kevin had called his parole officer, the guy didn't want to be face-to-face with the police.

"Uncuff me," he pleaded on his way across the office, sounding appropriately desperate. The guy was in a tight spot for sure. "Come on."

Dax shook his head. He stayed cuffed. Dax did follow the guy over and close the bathroom door once he was inside. He didn't turn on the bathroom light, though. Harrell could tough it out in the dark.

CHAPTER *TWENTY-ONE*

Loretta was glad she'd come. Tramping around the ratty old Faber Building looking for a "cute little blond hooker"—the parking valet's description, not hers—was just her cup of tea when she was two hours into overtime she wasn't ever going to see on a check.

Weisman, the uniformed policeman carrying the signal receiver, stopped in front of the last door in the hall: B & B INVESTIGATIONS, ROBERT BAINBRIDGE, PROP.

That was good news, and Loretta's mood actually perked up a bit. Robert Bainbridge had always had a solid reputation in town. As a former detective with the police department, admittedly about fifty years ago, he'd been a real go-to guy for the department well up to when she'd been a rookie and just starting out.

But fast on the heels of her good thoughts about

Bainbridge came the memory of the most recent time she'd seen the name B & B Investigations and the current facts of the business's situation. It had been on a long sheet of names attached to a vice case, next to the name of a man who didn't have a solid reputation, Burt Alden.

Her mood dipped.

Oh, hell. She didn't like it, this new turn. It could be indicative of a serious complication. Mr. Alden had gambling problems, which inevitably created other problems for him. She knew he was in to Franklin Bleak for more money than he could raise in a year, and she knew Bleak was calling in his debts faster than lemmings disappeared into the sea, which is apparently what had happened to a few of Bleak's customers over the last couple of weeks—they'd disappeared.

"Did you get the warrant, Connor?" she asked. "We're not exactly on a mission of mercy here."

"We're covered, Lieutenant."

"Good."

"Weisman, you're sure this is the place?"

"Yes, ma'am."

She turned to Connor then and gestured at the door. "Detective?"

The door was opened on Connor's first knock, and for a couple of seconds, all Loretta could do was stand there and think *sonuvabitch*.

For one second, maybe two, that was the only thought she had—*sonuvabitch*.

The next thought came straight out of her mouth.

"Mr. Killian." It wasn't a question. She knew

exactly who had opened the door. It sure as hell wasn't whom she'd expected, not in her wildest dreams, but she knew who he was—in her line of work, it paid to know guys like him, Daniel Axel Killian, Dax Killian.

She'd be damned.

"Lieutenant Bradley." He smiled, and Loretta had to fight the cheap-ass thrill that went through her. She not only knew who he was, she knew what he'd done, but really, she was too old to be getting cheap-ass thrills off big bad boys just because they were big and bad. "It's good to see you."

She just bet, but she kept it to herself.

"I heard you turned out okay," she said, taking his hand when he held it out. "That the U.S. Army found a use for you."

"Yes, ma'am, they sure did." His grin broadened, and so did that cheap-ass thrill running through her.

Get a grip, Loretta, old girl, she told herself, ending the handshake.

"I've got a warrant to search this office, Mr. Killian," she said, gesturing at Weisman. "If you've got a cell phone, we'd sure like to see it."

"And I'd sure like to see your warrant." A reasonable request, and one she was happy to grant. She'd have been disappointed if he hadn't asked.

"Detective?" she said, holding out her hand.

For the record, Daniel Axel Killian had gray eyes and dark hair. For the record, he was five feet eleven inches and a hundred and ninety pounds of rock-solid Denver boy done good. For the record, his sideburns were a little long and the rest of his hair a little short, and for the record, he hadn't shaved this morning. On him, the light shadow of stubble looked damned good—and that was for the record.

Connor produced the document, putting it in her hand, all signed and sealed, and she handed it to Killian.

He looked it over, then stepped aside, letting them in.

"Would you mind showing me your cell phone, Mr. Killian?"

He pulled it out of his pocket, handing it over to her, and in turn, she handed it to Weisman.

"Do you live around here, Mr. Killian?" Surely, she would have known if Dax Killian had moved back into her neck of the woods. Surely, somebody would have told her, somebody like General Buck Grant. Buck wouldn't have let that slip by her.

"No, ma'am," he said, walking over and turning on the lamp sitting on a desk next to the filing cabinets. "I'm visiting."

"From?" The added light was only somewhat helpful. It didn't really help the place look any better.

"Seattle, ma'am."

Weisman stepped forward and handed the phone back. "This isn't the one we're looking for, Lieutenant."

The officer walked further into the office, turning the receiver from side to side.

"GPS emergency signal?" Dax Killian asked, slipping his phone back in his pocket.

"Yes, sir." She looked around the office. "Has anyone else been up here in the office tonight?"

"Not that I've seen."

"And why are you here?" Everything looked fine, for a dump, but she wouldn't have expected better considering who was running the business now.

"Burt Alden is my uncle. He offered to let me use the office."

"For?" Burt Alden and Dax Killian related? Talk about a swan getting in with the odd ducks. She wouldn't have guessed it, not in a million years.

"To work in while I'm in town."

"And you're working on a Friday night?"

"Yes, ma'am."

Good enough. She was working, too.

Dax Killian—she hadn't kept track of every kid she'd ever directed into the armed forces. She hadn't actually kept track of him, but a few years ago, a story had drifted back to Denver, of this guy from Colorado, a shadow soldier. There'd only been the one story, and never another, and no name attached to the story she'd heard, but for some reason she'd thought of him. Even at his worst, as a teenager running wild on her streets, he'd had a way of keeping to himself, of running under the radar, and those kind of skills had fit the deed in the story.

She'd long since discovered the truth, compliments of Buck Grant—and looking at Dax now, she was even more intrigued to know the story was his.

And he was back in her city, in what she considered an unusual situation. She sure as hell didn't think he'd cut "Nazi hero" into the old German, no more so than she thought Johnny Ramos had done the deed, though Skeeter hadn't been able to verify Ramos's current whereabouts, not since he'd left the Blue Iguana, which was practically across the street from the Oxford.

Regardless, she still didn't think Johnny had cut up the old German—but somebody had, and Dax Killian was standing in the place where the clues had led.

"I'm looking for a blonde," she said, putting a little of the story on the line, to see if he bit. "A hooker who cut up one of her clients with a knife over at the Oxford Hotel earlier this evening."

Something flickered in Mr. Killian's eyes, but Loretta couldn't get a reading on it, which was unusual. Reading people was her job.

"Kind of a cult thing, we think. Do you know what a kanji is, Mr. Killian?"

"Yes, ma'am."

"Well, that's what this woman cut into this German guy over at the Oxford, a kanji and a swastika. Sliced it right into the old guy's skin, across his back. Not deep enough to kill him, maybe not even deep enough to leave a scar, but sure as hell deep enough to disturb me."

Something definitely went across Killian's face that time, and she knew exactly what it had been—a flash of alarm.

Interesting.

"Would you know anything about something like that, Mr. Killian?"

"No, ma'am."

Loretta didn't mind when people lied to her. She usually learned more from their lies than she ever did from their plain, unvarnished truths.

"I do have one lead. Detective Ford?" She held out her hand again, and Connor gave her the drawing of Johnny Ramos. "This man was seen going into the German guy's room at the Oxford, at about the time the attack took place. Have you seen him around the neighborhood at all tonight?"

She handed the drawing over, and watched Killian give it a quick once-over. In less than a couple of seconds, he was handing it back.

"No, ma'am. I haven't seen him."

"His name is Johnny Ramos. Have you heard of him?"

"No, ma'am."

Dax Killian was a pretty good liar, but he was still a liar. He was probably pretty good at evading surveillance, too, but he'd just bought himself a night's worth of it.

"Lieutenant?" Weisman said, standing outside a door in the corner of the office. "I think I've found our phone in there."

"Open her up." She didn't ask permission. She didn't need to ask permission.

Weisman opened the door and turned on the light. It was a bathroom with a wide-open, floor-to-ceiling, double-hung window. She walked over and leaned a little ways out the window, far enough to see the street two floors below.

It had been a night of open windows.

"Is it in there, Weisman?" she asked, looking back at the officer kneeling on the floor next to a tote bag.

"Yes, ma'am," he said.

"What's that bag made out of?"

"Looks like vinyl to me, Lieutenant."

"Vinyl," she said. "Let's get it back to the precinct without contaminating it, Weisman. I bet we can lift at least one good set of prints off it, and probably another real good set off the phone. What do you think, Detective Ford?"

"Yes, ma'am," Connor said. "At least one good set off each."

"Good." She turned back to Dax Killian. "The phone in the bag belongs to that blond hooker I'm looking for, a dominatrix, maybe one with a knife. If she comes back here, looking for it, you watch yourself, and I'd appreciate it if you'd give me a call." She handed him one of her cards.

"Yes, ma'am." Without a second's hesitation, he took her card and slipped it in his pocket.

"And if you see this Johnny Ramos guy, I'd appreciate it if you'd give me a call."

"Yes, ma'am."

And if Dax Killian gave her a call any time in the next forty years, she'd eat Weisman's hat.

Sonuvabitch—that was the only thought Dax had, watching Lieutenant Loretta Bradley and her boys exiting the office. *Sonuvabitch*.

He closed the door behind them, threw the lock, and pulled his cell phone out of his pocket.

"Come on, Easy, baby." He speed-dialed the bad girl and put the phone to his ear. "Answer."

Geezus. Erich Warner was in Denver, and he'd brought his favorite witch with him, the blade queen of Bangkok, coming straight out of Tokyo: Shoko. One name, innumerable knives.

A kanji and a swastika? Shoko had practically patented the design. She'd sure as hell perfected it on half a dozen people that he knew about, and who the hell knew how many more that he didn't know about.

He strode into the bathroom and leaned partway out the window, scanning the sidewalks and the street. Kevin Harrell had made a helluva jump for a guy in handcuffs. Dax was amazed he wasn't splatted all over the sidewalk below the window.

But he wasn't. Oh, hell, no. He was off and running somewhere, and if the cops didn't pick him up, somebody from Bleak's outfit probably would, not that Harrell mattered anymore. Dax had gotten what he needed out of the guy.

When Easy's voice mail picked up, he left a very succinct message. "Warner in town. Shoko with him, fully loaded. Stay out of Denver. Stick to Ramos like glue, and call me. I'll meet you."

Geezus. He looked at his watch. Five o'clock was looking a helluva long way away.

He dialed Burt, ready to read him the riot act if he answered. But Uncle Burt didn't answer, so he left another very succinct message. "If you're not at

Bleak's warehouse when I get there at five A.M., I'm going to come looking for you, Uncle Burt, and you ain't gonna be happy when I find you. *Don't* disappoint me."

It was a threat, yes, but it was also the truth. The plan had been to leave good old Uncle Burt out of the deal, keep the fat out of the fire and that sort of thing, but Dax had changed his mind. The fat was going in feetfirst. Uncle Burt, God help him, was going to be his backup on the deal. It was Easy he was kicking off the team. He didn't want her within a mile of Franklin Bleak. Even with Lucky Lindsey Larson in his arsenal of tricks, he didn't want the bad girl anywhere in Bleak's sight.

She was already in enough trouble.

And now Shoko. *Christ.*

Easy had a cool head on her shoulders, one of the coolest, but the Bangkok bitch had hurt her, marked her for life, and Dax knew the bad girl still had nightmares about it—which really pissed him off. He'd been waiting a long time to get Shoko in his sights, but it wasn't going to happen tonight. Even more than the Bleak deal, he still owed Warner, and more than the debt was the prize Warner had offered, the little something. The German had information Dax wanted, the kind of information that was going to have him doing just about anything Erich Warner asked, short of treason, a designation that could get damned slippery, depending on how much the information proved to be worth on the E-ring in the Pentagon.

Closing the bathroom window, he wondered how

in the hell he and Easy were going to talk their way out of this once the cops lifted her prints off the phone she'd used to set up her contact with the parking valet. A lot of people could place her at the Oxford at the right time for an assault with a deadly weapon charge at the very least, including Johnny Ramos.

Yeah, that guy. The one whose picture Lieutenant Loretta was flashing around. He had to be trouble, and yet Dax's directive stood—he wanted Easy sticking to the guy like a hot lamination. Dom Ramos had been a punk, but he'd been a punk Dax had liked, a straightforward guy, no bullshit.

He reached in his back pocket and pulled out the angel picture postcard. It was an invitation for a showing at an art gallery over on Seventeenth, the Toussi Gallery next to the Oxford Hotel, and it had Ramos's name on it. No address, just the guy's name where the address would be, along with the note written in a loopy female hand Dax took the time to decipher this time—"Come be the star that you are, sweetie. Love, Nikki."

He flipped the card back over to the angel side, and sure enough, the showing was for an artist named Nikki. That was all the postcard said, Nikki, like Picasso, or Rembrandt. From the looks of the painting on the front of the card, one name might be enough. She was good.

And this woman thought Johnny Ramos was a star.

Dax figured he better go find out if she was right.

CHAPTER TWENTY-TWO

Afghanistan, Nuristan Province, not the Kunar—Johnny was looking right at it. He could smell it, feel the dust sifting down on him. There had been so many tunnels cut into the mountainsides, and Third Platoon's job had been to search a section of them.

He knew better than to reach for his pistol. He was in Colorado, not a war zone, but the sight of the tunnel, actually being in one again, unnerved him.

It shouldn't. He hadn't been unnerved in Nuristan, not even the first time, when they'd gotten rocked by mortar fire on their way out. They'd spent another four weeks clearing tunnels, and he'd never broken a sweat—until now.

Shit.

He was still in the elevator, and Esme and Nachman were heading around a corner. He wasn't going to let that happen, for her to go off in the darkness of a damn tunnel with a strange old man, and him just stand here and watch her disappear.

Shit.

He was a U.S. Army Ranger, had been for five years, and there wasn't anyplace he was afraid to go.

Sucking it up, and more than a little embarrassed that he had to suck it up to get off a damn elevator, he stepped into the tunnel. The feel of the dirt beneath his boots was uncomfortably familiar, the short deadness of the footfalls, but he kept going, one step after the next.

After about twenty feet, the tunnel branched off in two more directions. One glance at the additional corridors snaking off into darkness, and he drew his gun. *Fuck it.* Whatever he was going to be looking at, he was suddenly absolutely positive he wanted to be looking at it through the tritium dots on his gun sights. What the hell did he know, really? Anything could be down here, a bear, a mountain lion, anything, and a Ranger would be ready.

So he was ready.

Right.

With a .45 in the sub-subbasement of a multimillionaire's mansion in the Colorado Rockies.

And there was Esme, up ahead, cool as a little cucumber, raising tufts of dust with her high heels.

And him, sliding along the wall behind her, knees bent, muscles tense, his trigger finger laid flat along the pistol's slide—ready to slip inside the trigger guard, ready to rock and roll.

He checked his six, looking back toward the elevator, moving his pistol with his line of sight—ready—and when he turned back around, gun lowered again, he was facing Esme, stopped in the middle of the tunnel and looking at him with an expression of confusion, fascination, and maybe a little plain old "you've got to be kidding me" surprise.

Her gaze dropped down the length of him in less than a second, then took another one to come back up to meet his eyes. Her expression didn't change. Everything was still in play as she stood and watched him, watched him calculate his odds—the odds of running into an enemy fighter, Taliban, al-Qaeda, Egyptian, Arab, Pakistani, an Islamic insurgent from anywhere who'd come to battle the coalition forces. Anyone who'd come in country to go up against him and his guys.

Zero, he decided. It was zero odds down here in Isaac Nachman's sub-subbasement. Sure. He knew it was zero, or damn close to it.

Convinced, he slowly straightened up, flipping the safety back on his pistol before he slid it into its holster.

"PTSD?" she said, one of her eyebrows lifting a bit, adding a serious dose of flat-out curiosity to her question—more curiosity than the question itself implied.

Post Traumatic Stress Disorder, he knew what the initials stood for.

"No." He shook his head. "Instinct."

Pure instinct, the survival kind. A lot of soldiers struggled with PTSD in varying degrees and with a variety of symptoms. He knew it for a fact. He'd seen it on deployment and seen it each time they'd come home, and he knew that wasn't his problem, not full-out anyway. Hell, he'd been in "combat" most of his life, fighting on street corners and in back alleys, and the night Dom had died, fighting it out in the lush, green expanse of City Park.

He'd seen a lot, done a lot, or so he'd thought until his first combat tour. When he'd come back from Afghanistan the first time, he'd come back with an unsolicited and unexpected realization about the night in the park: Dom had died clean.

It had seemed like such a bloody mess at the time, with Dom gasping in pain and gasping for breath, with the blood pumping out of him, out of the hole one of the Parkside Bloods had put in him. One shot, not even a well-aimed shot, just one *unlucky* shot had killed his brother. A bunch of Parkside gangsters waving their pieces around and pulling their triggers had managed to actually hit Domingo Ramos.

In real combat, death could be a lot different. First, the shots were better aimed. When the shooting started, a guy could be assured that his enemies were shooting at him, not just around him, shooting to kill, and that every guy out there with a scope was using it to target him, that every set of iron sights was leveled at him. Soldiers didn't wave their guns around or hold them slanted on the side. That was only for dumbass gangsters and people in the movies.

The Rangers had most definitely taught him how to shoot.

The second thing about death in combat was the ordnance. Dom had been killed by a single 9mm round, a damn unlucky shot that had hit him square in the heart. But in combat, people got blown apart—into pieces. Some people still got shot, and it was never pretty, but guys also got literally blown to bits, and sometimes those guys looked like the lucky ones.

That was the third thing about death in combat— a warrior's death wasn't the worst way to go. Dead wasn't the worst way to leave a battlefield. Johnny hadn't known that until he'd been in combat and watched people die, and watched the people who hadn't died.

He didn't move his hand, but suddenly he could feel the envelope in his pocket, feel it like it was hot—not hot enough to burn, he wouldn't give himself that. He wasn't the one who had been branded by combat.

But he felt the heat, and he felt guilt—building in his chest and twisting in his gut and sweeping up to make his face hot, and suddenly, he wanted the hell out of this goddamn tunnel.

"What are we doing down here, Esme?" His words were short, his voice curt.

"Mr. Nachman keeps his collection down here in a vault, his art collection," she said, very clearly, holding his gaze steady with her own. "There will be a black light in the vault, and we'll use it to verify that the Meinhard I've brought him is exactly what I told him it is—the original painting, untouched, exactly what he's paying for. Then he'll give me the money, and we'll leave."

Okay. There was an end in sight.

"Let's go," he said, gesturing for her to lead the way.

No, he didn't have PTSD, but neither had he come down from his last deployment. His instincts were still on high alert, which meant "weapon ready." He hadn't decompressed. Two weeks at home wasn't enough to bring him back down, and neither was one beer in the Blue Iguana.

Dammit. He shouldn't have drawn his pistol. Instincts were good; giving into irrational impulses wasn't. But this place, this tunnel . . . he was sweating, and it was cool down here.

Unfinished business, that was his problem, and he needed to finish it. He'd been carrying the letter in his pocket around with him for months, and he needed to deal with it.

Great. Now he had it all figured out—for about the hundred millionth time. He knew what he had to do. He just hadn't found the guts to do it, and now he was in this damn tunnel, unnerved.

Nachman was ahead of them, still shuffling along in his slippers, until he came to a heavy steel door set into solid rock. Johnny couldn't even imagine what the whole setup had cost, but when Nachman opened the door, he knew whatever the vault had cost, it was nothing compared to the value of what was inside.

Geezus.

He glanced at "Miss Esme" and realized she'd been here before. She'd expected all this. She wasn't struck dumb with amazement, and he was damn close.

"Welcome to my closet, Mr. Ramos," Nachman said, letting the steel door swing open.

Closet was a misnomer, but Johnny understood what Nachman had meant about there not being enough room for him. The place was huge, but it was also completely packed, floor to ceiling, wall to wall, with art, an unprecedented sight, utterly unique. It was a warehouse of masterpieces, old masters and new.

"Have you heard of the Alt Aussee, Mr. Ramos?" Nachman asked, leading the way inside, keeping his hand on the door.

"No, sir."

"It's a salt mine in Austria, southeast of Salzburg, a veritable labyrinth."

When Johnny and Esme were inside with him, standing in one of the only clear areas Johnny could see, Nachman slowly pushed the heavy steel door closed behind them.

Johnny heard a lock fall into place.

Perfect.

Not exactly nightmare material, but close— being locked inside an underground vault deep inside a mountain.

Very close, actually.

Maybe even a little closer than Johnny wanted to admit.

Dammit.

But the art was stunning, and there was a museum's worth of it, two museums' worth, hundreds of paintings, pieces of sculpture both large and small, decorative items, vases, jewelry, glassworks, plaques, artifacts, ceramics, and more paintings—some of them massive, upward to eight or nine feet high and nearly as wide—all of it carefully and meticulously organized on racks and in cases, filling the cavelike vault. The ceiling of the room was more than twenty feet above them, the far end of it beyond where Johnny could see. Everything that should have been hanging on the walls and displayed in the mansion upstairs was down here in Nachman's temperature-and-humidity-controlled "closet." He'd felt the difference in the air immediately upon entering the stone depository.

"The Nazis used the Alt Aussee to store their plunder, literally thousands of pieces of stolen art," Nachman said, "all of it nearly destroyed toward the end of the war, when the Germans set explosives inside the salt mine. Fortunately, the plot was discovered by the resistance fighters, and the bombs were never detonated. Some of those saved paintings reside here, now, Mr. Ramos, some of them awaiting proof of provenance so that I can return them to their rightful owners, many of them here because their rightful owners wish them to remain hidden from the world and safe, and a few of them rightly mine. And yet..." Nachman turned and looked at Esme.

"And yet some of Mr. Nachman's most cherished pieces are still missing, pieces like the Monet," she said.

"Pieces like the Henstenburgh," the old man added.

"Yes, the Henstenburgh," Esme echoed.

"And the..." Nachman's voice drifted into a soft whisper.

"We don't have to talk about it," Esme assured him, and from the look on the old man's face, pained and distressed, Johnny thought Esme probably had the right of it.

"No," Nachman insisted. "Mr. Ramos should know the depth of our loss."

Not necessarily, Johnny thought, wondering how in the hell he'd ended up in this place, in this strange situation, with this very strange little man wearing a bathrobe, when he'd started out the night with that beer at the Blue Iguana.

"There was a Rembrandt, Mr. Ramos," Nachman continued. "And...and another, *the* other. They're both priceless, utterly priceless, and they belong here." The old man made a sweeping gesture with his arm, including the whole vault—and Johnny couldn't fault his opinion, not too much anyway. A Rembrandt, any Rembrandt, had to be amazing, but he wasn't sure what the value of something was if no one ever saw it except one old man.

"Isaac," Esme said gently, when Nachman

simply continued to stand there, his arm outstretched, his gaze distant, his lips quivering.

Johnny had a grandma, and her lips quivered sometimes, especially when she was getting emotional and about to cry, which was quite often.

Please, he thought. *Please spare us Nachman's tears.*

Sobbing was only going to make things worse, besides making him personally uncomfortable. Nachman was old, yes, but he was still a guy underneath that silk bathrobe, which was as far as Johnny was going to take that thought.

He looked to Esme, silently asking her to "get on with it," whatever "it" needed getting on with.

"Isaac," she said again. "May we continue with the authentication?"

It took the old man a moment, but in the end, he nodded and continued on to a table set up in the middle of the vault.

"My dear," he said, picking up a handheld black light and handing her a small screwdriver from a tool kit on the table.

Esme had already reopened the case, and now she used the screwdriver to undo the wooden frame holding the protective covering in place. When the frame was disassembled, she laid the painting out on the table, and then Nachman hit a switch on the side of the table, and the lights went out.

All the lights.

In an instant, it was completely, heavily, oppressively pitch-fucking-dark in the vault, which in

Johnny's mind had just been transformed into a tomb.

Extra perfect.

Now he couldn't breathe.

Geezus.

He'd never had any freaking phobias. He didn't have any phobias now, he was sure. He just couldn't breathe, because *suddenly* some *idiot* in a fucking *bathrobe* had turned off *all* the lights—off, out, extinguished—and they were God knew how far underground with the weight of the whole freaking world bearing down on them, and—

The black light came on.

It wasn't much, a purple glow falling on the Meinhard, but without anything to reflect. There wasn't any Day-Glo paint anywhere, which was probably a good thing in this room.

"No luminescence," Esme said, and he could just make her out, leaning over the painting, watching Nachman slowly run the light over the piece.

"Oh, my, Miss Esme, you are oh, so right," Nachman barely breathed the words, his attention rapt. "I believe we have the Meinhard."

He passed the black light over the painting two more times, with excruciating slowness, and all Johnny could think was "Dear God, man, get *on* with it, and get it *over.*"

But he kept those words to himself. To anyone in the room, which he knew made for a very small audience, had they been able to see him, which he knew they could not, he would have appeared perfectly normal, perfectly stoic, not a flicker of emotion, not a twitch of a muscle.

He was contained.

But he was on a countdown in his head, and he'd seen the switch Nachman had hit to turn out the lights, and when he got to zero, he was lunging for the switch and turning on the goddamn lights. It would be embarrassing, revealing, but not as bad as passing out.

He forced another breath into his lungs.

"Then, sir, I would appreciate payment," Esme said, in a tone of voice that was very clearly taking control of the situation, and all Johnny could think was *Thank God, somebody is taking control of this very dark situation*.

"As you wish," Nachman said, and in the next instant, the lights came on.

Johnny held himself back from collapsing in relief.

He was a Ranger, for God's sake.

He let out his breath and waited, watching Nachman shuffle over to a wooden Chinese cabinet with dozens of drawers. One by one, the old man opened drawers and pulled out stacks of cash. Bundle after bundle, stacking them in his arms, his lips moving as he quietly counted to himself.

"Five thousand, ten thousand, fifteen thousand, twenty thousand..."

Geezus, and just when Johnny had thought the night couldn't get any more bizarre.

He looked to Esme, to check his bearings, but for once, she didn't catch his gaze. She was busy,

damn busy, scanning the walls and the racks, looking at all the paintings, her expression one of intense focus, as if she was cataloging the hoard.

He looked back at Nachman. On, and on, and
on, the man counted, until he reached eighty thousand dollars, then he broke a bundle and counted
off two more thousand.

Eighty-two thousand dollars. Johnny tried to
think what the most cash he'd ever seen in one
place had been, and it fell far short of eighty-two
thousand dollars.

God, that was a lot of money, far more than he'd
anticipated. He doubted if Burt Alden would make
it through another day with that kind of money
on the line. He wondered if it was all going to
Bleak, or if there was a hefty commission in there
for Esme. A commission on eighty-two thousand
would sure explain her underwear—oh, hell, yeah.

He swept the vault with his gaze. He was standing in the middle of more than a fortune, more
than two or three fortunes. Esme had said the
Meinhard was worth two million, and it was no bigger than a piece of typing paper. The sheer volume,
the sheer square footage of all the other paintings
in the vault would probably put the value of the
vault's contents up into the hundreds of millions,
maybe even into the billion-dollar range.

A strange, strange night all around, he thought,
doubting if he would ever see its like again, and
pretty much hoping he wouldn't.

When Nachman was finished at the cabinet, he

brought all the money to the table and withdrew a folded piece of paper out of the pocket on his robe.

"Eighty-two, not one hundred thousand," he said, sliding the paper over to Esme. "Dear Burt still owed me twelve from a small loan we negotiated last April. With interest, the total is currently eighteen. He apparently found himself a bit short with another of his associates."

That was one way to put it, Johnny thought. And from twelve thousand to eighteen thousand in five months? Hell. Nachman wasn't a bathrobed wimp. He was a freaking loan shark, a great white.

"Yes, sir," Esme said, taking the paper. She opened it up, and Johnny saw her father's signature on the note—Burt Alden in big letters next to the hen scratches of Nachman's spidery hand. Then she started packing the money into the case. When it was full, she closed it up and put it back in the messenger bag still bandoliered across her chest.

He watched her stuff the remaining stacks of hundred-dollar bills on either side of the case in the bag, and when she had all the cash secured, he watched the subtle but profound relief that passed over her, the brief closing of her eyes, the slight softening of her shoulders—and without a thought, he reached out and stroked her cheek, letting her know that come hell, high water, or a hundred more goddamn tunnels, he was seeing this night through with her, all the way through. She wasn't alone.

Yeah, she'd had a tough night so far, but he could take care of that, too, whatever she wanted, and he was hoping with everything he had that it was more of what she'd wanted sitting in Solange.

Her lashes lifted, her gaze rising to meet his, and a slow wall of heat rolled straight through him. Unbidden, a smile curved his mouth. Yeah, they were on the same page here, and it was time to take her home.

CHAPTER TWENTY-THREE

What's love got to do with it? That's the question Dax had asked himself more times than he could count. *What in the hell did love have to do with it?*

Not much, had been the answer more times than he was willing to admit.

But this.

Standing just inside the entrance of Toussi Gallery, Dax knew this was crazy.

He tilted his head slightly to one side, looking through the crowd at the woman bent over a table writing something out on a small piece of paper.

What was that wrapped around her ass? Green shantung silk?

Yeah. That's what it was. Dax knew shantung when he saw it—jade green shantung.

There wasn't much of it, but he was going to go ahead and call it a skirt, for lack of a better term. And he was going to call her ass incredible, and her

legs heartbreaking, and the Chinese red stilettos
she was wearing—he was going to call those dangerous.

She straightened up from the table, and Dax
quickly retooled the whole deadly combination in
his head. The ivory satin halter top she was wearing
was the danger zone. The pale ivory breasts almost
spilling out of the top were the hot zone—a verifiable hot zone with a very elegant string of pearls
looping across it like a police line: Do Not Cross.

Yeah. He grinned.

Dax loved a challenge, and he was thinking going up against a string of pearls was a win-win situation, especially with a woman wrapped up inside
them. Women and pearls was one of his favorite
combinations, like tequila and a beach, like sunrise
and sex.

And yes, he was a great one for a wake-up call.

From the curvaceous mounds of her breasts it
was a short trip up the satiny skin of her throat and
the delicate angle of her jaw to a cherry lipsticked
mouth he didn't trust himself to stare at, and the
rest—smooth, pale cheeks, an elegant nose, and
thickly lashed and artfully made-up eyes, almond
shaped, sultry.

She was gee-fucking-gorgeous.

He felt it in his heart.

She reached back onto the table and retrieved a
small jacket, jade green shantung, and slipped it on
over the halter top. The jacket fit her like a glove,
and after it was on, she did one of those quintes-
sentially female things that no guy could resist—

she slid one perfectly manicured hand up around the back of her neck and with the utmost unconscious grace, lifted her hair out of the back of the jacket. The next move was also filled with so much fluid, female grace, the slight toss of her head to get her hair to settle back into a fall of silken auburn, he wondered for a second if someone was filming her. Who the hell else moved like that? Some movie star? Some model?

He didn't look around to see if there was anyone with a camera trained on her, though. He didn't want to miss anything, not a move.

Which proved to be his undoing.

Her next move, and so help him God, he never saw it coming, was to turn and look toward the door, and when she saw him, she smiled. It was a professional smile, not a personal smile, and yes, he knew the difference, intellectually. Emotionally, though, it was still a knockout. Then things got worse.

One long-legged, spike-heeled stride after another, she walked toward him, her smile in place, and he didn't know if she was going to sell him real estate or proposition him.

He was ready for either, and unbelievably, he found himself steeling his heart against the sound of her voice. If her voice in any way matched the sultry welcome of her whiskey-colored eyes, he was doomed.

"Hi," she said.

It did. He felt the slam-dunk with just one word.

"I'm Suzi Toussi." She held out her hand, and

like an idiot, he took it, shook it, and didn't let go—
so she did it for him, retrieving her hand and giving
him a very small, very aware smile that said she got
hit on every day of the week and twice on Sundays.
"Thanks for coming to the showing. Are you familiar with Nikki's work?"

"No." He looked around the gallery and changed
his mind. "Maybe." Some of the stuff looked familiar. The paintings were all angels like on the postcard, but the full divine being, instead of just the
partial view used on the invitation. Even a quick
look around showed that the artist had a couple of
models she used a lot, one guy with long blond hair,
and a guy with short dark hair, and from the looks
of some of the paintings, sometimes she put them
through hell.

"She did the Brad Pitt cover of *Esquire* magazine
a few years ago. You might have seen it."

Probably not. He didn't keep up with the
Pittster.

"Suzi," he said, bringing his attention back to
her face, especially her eyes, and there was a cor-
rection on the color. Whiskey didn't quite cover it.
They were darker than Scotch, richer, with a warm
undertone of amber, and like everything else about
her, they had an elegance that defied comparison.

He hadn't seen anyone like her, not anywhere,
and he'd seen a lot of women. They were kind of a
hobby with him, which he knew didn't throw him
in a very good light, but it did give him a certain
expertise, and one thing he knew beyond doubt

was that God made women like her for only one reason—to hurt men, to break their hearts and hurt them where they lived, which for Dax, currently, was just a little south of his belt buckle.

"So the gallery is yours?" Her name was on it— Toussi.

"Used to be." The luscious Suzi Toussi smiled. "Now I'm just the hired help."

"And what do you do when you're not hired to help out here? Take care of Mr. Toussi?" It wasn't fishing. He was dragging the ocean floor with a steel net.

"Mr. Toussi lives in San Francisco with Mrs. Toussi, and they manage to take care of each other without too much interference from me."

"Only child?"

"Two sisters and a brother," she said, obviously chatting him up, still so professional. She wasn't giving away anything...not yet.

He grinned. "I bet they were glad to get the boy."

She arched a delicate eyebrow. "In my experience, boys are nothing but trouble, but I bet you already knew that."

His grin broadened.

"So why did you sell out?" he asked. "This place looks like the place to be."

"I got an offer I couldn't refuse," she said, so cool.

"Early retirement and all that, but keeping your hand in on the side?"

"Not quite." The barest flicker of humor passed

through her gaze, and he was all but hypnotized with curiosity. "So, Mister . . . ?"

"Killian, Dax Killian."

"Dax," she repeated. "That's an unusual name."

"Daniel Axel," he explained. "About seventh grade, it got slammed together and stuck."

"I see, Dax." Her smile returned, perfectly professional, which simply wasn't going to do, not for him, not with her. "We have wine and *escabeche* and some other very nice . . . canapés and hors d'oeuvres for your pleasure. Feel free to look around, and if you need anything, don't hesitate to ask me, or one of my assistants. There are two or three still running about. Oh, just a moment." She lifted her hand and waved someone over.

Dax followed the gesture, and if his heart hadn't already been stolen, he might have been susceptible to the young woman heading in their direction.

Sweet lovin' Patsy. He'd never thought of a sweater dress as summerwear, but when it was cobalt blue, sleeveless, low-cut, and barely covered a very cute butt, he was going sweaters for summer. Yeah, sweaters and curves—slinky, slender curves, not like the lush, auburn-haired bombshell on his right.

"Jane," Suzi said, when the girl reached them. "This is Mr. Killian. He's interested in Nikki's work. Will you show him around, please?"

"My pleasure." Jane had silky dark hair falling straight to her shoulders, freckles and a small scar across the bridge of her nose, a wild pixie face, and the palest green eyes he'd ever seen. She also had a small scar along her left cheekbone, which in no way detracted from her beauty. If anything, it made her even more exotic-looking.

Esme was right. He needed to spend more time in Denver. He wasn't keeping up, especially in the old neighborhood. The chop shop where he'd moonlighted as a teenager wasn't too far north of the gallery, home of hot women and amazing angels.

"Thank you, Jane," Suzi said, then turned to him with another blindingly gorgeous smile. "Mr. Killian, my head assistant, Jane Linden, and my pleasure."

Given half a chance, he thought, watching her walk away.

"Mr. Killian," Jane said at his side.

"Dax," he offered, getting his mind back on his business, and he did have business here.

"Dax." The younger woman smiled with all the professional courtesy of her boss and gestured toward the far corner of the room. "We can start where Nikki McKinney started, with the Ascending Angel series. She was only sixteen when she won the prestigious Cooper-Lansdowne competition, which was the beginning of her brilliant career. She's had a meteoric rise in the art world since her first showing at Toussi when she was twenty-one, the youngest artist to ever have a solo show here, or at our sister gallery in Los Angeles."

"I can see why." The longer he looked at the paintings, the more intrigued he became. He pulled the invitation out of his back pocket. "I actu-

ally came here with a few questions, if you don't
mind."

"Not at all," the beautiful girl said.

Dax smiled back. "Well, I have a little sister,
about your age, I guess, and she's been correspond-
ing with this guy who asked her to meet him
here tonight, for this party, this showing, and I
thought—well, I thought I better meet him first.
From the invitation, it seemed like the artist knows
him. Nikki McKinney wrote him a note on the
card." He handed the postcard over, address side
up, so Jane would see it right off.

The girl took one look and let out a laugh, her
cultivated, professional smile turning into a real
grin.

"Johnny," she said, looking up and meeting his
gaze, her green eyes alight. "Johnny Ramos. Come
on over here, and I'll introduce you, so to speak."

She started weaving a path through the crowd,
and Dax followed, curiosity warring with concern.
Easy wasn't here. If she'd made it this far, she
would have called him. And if Easy wasn't here, he
didn't want to be meeting John Ramos in this room.
The kid had decked Kevin Harrell with a single
punch back when he and Easy were in school, and
Dax wanted the guy with those instincts to be with
her at Nachman's.

Dax didn't think Isaac Nachman would or could
do anything to Easy, but he'd always felt she was on
safer ground with the Otto Von Lindberg part of
the night's plan. Otto had a few sexual proclivities,
sure, but Easy had his number.

Nobody had Nachman's number, *nobody*, and the guy was way more than half a bubble off.

"So you know this Johnny Ramos?" he asked the lovely Jane.

"Very well," she said. "But I didn't know he had a girl he was seeing."

"The relationship is in its infancy. I think that's what tonight is all about, the first face-to-face meeting."

"Lucky girl," Jane said, her smile warming. "Come on."

She led him up a staircase to a catwalk that ran across the width of the gallery. At the top, she stopped and leaned against the rail, pointing at a twelve-foot-high piece of stretched canvas that dominated the western half of the gallery.

Geezus.

"That's him? John Ramos?" He didn't want there to be any misunderstanding.

"That's him, the Ironheart Angel."

Ironheart.

The guy had a tattoo. Actually, he had a few tattoos, but the heart-shaped one was prominent on the upper left side of his chest, a heart with wings, angel wings, like those sweeping in large graceful arcs from the guy's shoulder blades, but the wings on the tattoo were perfect, every feather in place, and the wings meant to keep him airborne were not—feathers were broken, some of them singed, some of them smoking, some of them on fire.

He was flaming out.

Burning in.

The angel's head was tilted back, exposing his throat, an incredibly vulnerable position that the painting made clear was nothing less than the beginning of the final end. Strength ebbing, his will proving not to be enough, not against the battle wounds marking his body, a long slice from beneath his right breast down the length of his thigh, the edges ragged, blood streaming, and the lesser wounds, numerous smaller cuts, all deep, the scrapes, and contusions, and burns.

The angel's left knee was bent, raised higher than the other, as if by some miracle of God, he would rally one more time and find the strength to push off and ascend. But Dax wasn't putting his money on it. This angel, Ironheart, had seen his last for this go-around. Simple fact.

Standing there, looking at the painting, Dax saw the violence of the attack that had destroyed him, and after another moment, he saw the whole attack, strike by parry, strike by failure to parry. It was there in the wounds. Ironheart was left-handed, a wicked-looking, modified drop-point blade with a skeletonized handle still in his grip, and he'd been taken down by a left-handed knife fighter.

John Ramos was left-handed.

He was also born and bred to the Locos and was safe with God—C/S, *con safos*. The gang tattoo ran down the inside of his right arm. Obviously, Nikki McKinney thought her street-fighting warrior angels actually came straight off the street, this one from Twenty-second, XX22ST. He was buck-ass naked in the painting, totally ripped, and the reason for that was made more than clear by the leading edge of another tattoo Dax could see gracing his left shoulder—the numbers and letters "75 RAN" on a scroll.

Suddenly, the whole night made more sense. There was a good reason John Ramos had been so effective at protecting Easy. He was a U.S. Army Ranger, 75th Ranger Regiment, and the iron in his iron heart? The letters "Fe," the chemical symbol for iron, were richly inscribed inside the winged-heart tattoo.

Ironheart—a good name for anybody from the 75th, though he couldn't say he'd ever met an angelic Ranger. Dax grinned. *Hoo-yah.*

He'd also never seen a knife-fighting angel. He looked around the gallery at the other paintings. They seemed to come in two basic flavors, dark angels and light angels, or as Jane had said, "Ascending Angels," and, he surmised, "Descending Angels."

Ironheart was definitely on the descent in the supersize painting, and of them all, John Ramos was the only one carrying a knife, using a knife. The drop-point blade in his hand was bloody.

"He's a Ranger," he said, and Jane nodded.

"Just back from Afghanistan, two weeks ago, his third combat tour," she said. "We were really hoping to see him tonight. Our guests really love meeting Nikki's models, especially the women."

Her smile said it all, not that Dax had needed the extra info. He was looking right at the guy.

A combat-hardened Ranger up against a seventy-nine-year-old nutcase was no contest. Dovey Smollett wasn't going to give this guy a run for his money either. Neither would Bleak.

Easy would, though. She would be running him hard for his money, and Dax figured the guy was loving it. Any Ranger who'd only been back for two weeks would still have women at the top of his . . . wait a minute.

His gaze shot back to the Ironheart Angel painting. Sure, the guy was like "enlarged." The painting was twelve feet high, but still . . . yeah, but still.

He shifted his attention back to Jane.

"This Ramos guy, how well do you know him exactly?" He wasn't a jerk about the question. He was just curious, and possibly a little concerned. Easy wasn't his sister, but he felt that way about her. He'd known her since she'd been in diapers. Hell, he remembered the day Aunt Beth had brought the little pink bundle home from the hospital, and he cared. A lot.

"We go to each other's birthday parties," she said, and Dax figured that was pretty well, and a pretty good way of putting it.

"And he's a—"

"Great guy," she filled in his blank. "You don't need to worry about your sister. I guarantee it. She couldn't be in safer hands."

Dax hoped the hell so.

CHAPTER **TWENTY-FOUR**

Phone in hand, Franklin stood in his office, looking down at Beth Alden in the room below. She was crumbling from the inside out. He'd seen it before, where the fear just ate the guts out of a person. That's what was happening down in his betting room. Fear was eating Beth Alden's guts out. Burt really should be ashamed.

He shifted his attention back to his phone and hit a number.

"Where the hell are you, Dovey?" he said, when the guy answered. He was just about finished screwing around with Dovey Smollett. "And why in the hell did I just get a call from goddamn Stu Abrams saying one of my boys just showed up at the goddamn Jack O'Nines in goddamn handcuffs? Why is that, Dovey?"

There was a long, appropriate pause on the other

side of the phone connection before Dovey came up with an answer.

"I don't know, Mr. Bleak, sir."

Fucking brilliant.

"It was Harrell, Dovey. Kevin Harrell. Your good buddy, right?"

Another long pause ensued.

"Yes, sir."

Like Franklin had said—fucking brilliant.

"One of my boys showing up at Abrams's club in handcuffs with a broken nose, that makes me look bad, Dovey. Real bad. And you're the guy who brought this douche on board. You're the guy responsible for this, Dovey. So what are you going to do about it?"

"I-I don't know, sir."

That's what Franklin had thought, that Dovey Smollett didn't know crapola about Shinola—and he was stuck with the guy, at least until the deal went down. He had guys running all over tonight, and Harrell was already a wash. Franklin wouldn't bet a rat's ass on Kevin Harrell getting out of the Jack O'Nines in one piece. The guy's timing was amazing. Amazingly bad. To show up at the club, mouthing off about working for Franklin Bleak, after Mitch and Leroy had just been there and worked Stu over a bit.

Bad news.

Real bad news.

And the guy had already been cuffed. *Christ.* Talk about just asking for it. Stu probably had him hanging upside down in the back room and was selling hits at twenty bucks a pop.

Shit. Harrell would be lucky to get out at all, let alone in one piece.

So Franklin was running shorthanded. He couldn't afford to let Dovey go, not on the manpower end of things, and not for the mess of letting a guy go, not when things were really starting to go his way—except for the damn money. He needed that damn eighty-two thousand dollars.

"And where are you, Dovey? Mitch and Leroy picked up that goddamn Cyclone at the Genesee entrance ramp onto the damn highway, but they didn't see you anywhere. So where the hell are you?"

The pause this time was interminable, until Dovey finally broke the silence.

"I don't know, sir."

That's exactly what Franklin had thought. It made him doubt his own judgment, that he'd handpicked Dovey Smollett to pick up Esme Alden. The girl couldn't be that goddamn elusive.

The girl wasn't that damn elusive.

Mitch and Leroy had her in their sights, streaking like a bat out of hell down the interstate, trying to keep up with a goddamn Cyclone that Mitch swore had a zero to a hundred of under twelve seconds, well under—*"Geezus, Frank. We almost lost her. The damn car hit the interstate and it was* Star Wars, *boss, a fucking jump into hyperspace."*

Franklin didn't want to hear about any jumps into hyperspace. He had a damn load of cocaine headed his way, and he needed that goddamn girl, and he needed her goddamn father. So where in the hell was Eliot? He should have had the Alden jerk here an hour ago, easy.

Eliot, dammit, Eliot could get out of hand, and if he'd accidentally "disabled" old Burt, then it was going to be damn hard for the man to get around and get the damn money. His next call, Franklin knew, had to be to Eliot. But he'd had kind of a busy night on the phone.

Good and busy. He grinned. Damn good and busy.

Katherine Gray had called him personally, and the sweet, husky sound of her voice had made all the trouble he was going to more than worthwhile. Graham Percy was aces, absolute aces. Percy was delivering on his promise, and Franklin needed Burt Alden to do the same. There was a lot on the line.

Katherine wanted to meet him. Percy had told her all about him, and she was intrigued. That's the word she'd used, "intrigued."

Hell, he understood it. He was a damned intriguing guy.

"Are you on a road, Dovey? Can you tell me that?" He turned away from the betting room and walked across the office.

"Yes, sir. We're on a road . . . a dirt road . . . in the woods, but it's damn dark up here, and—"

"And nothing, Smollett. Get your ass the hell out of there, and call me when you hit the goddamn suburbs. I want you over at the Commerce City Garage, where that Cyclone is usually parked, in case this Ramos guy shows up there."

The likelihood of Dovey getting lost in Commerce City was nil and none. If this Ramos guy headed home like a pigeon, Dovey could back up Mitch and Leroy, if he could get himself out of the woods. Franklin had his doubts.

"Yes, sir," Dovey said. "Bremerton thinks he knows how to get out of here."

The Chicago guy? Well, that was a good one, the damn guy from Chicago knowing how to get the hell out of Genesee. He was obviously a guy who paid attention. Dovey could learn a few things from a guy who knew how to pay attention.

"Then let him drive, Smollett, and get your ass back to Denver."

Franklin ended the call and had his finger on the speed dial to Eliot, when his enforcer entered the warehouse on the main floor.

With Burt Alden in tow—literally, *dammit*.

Franklin was kind of an expert in the broken bones department, and he knew at a glance that Eliot had broken Burt's arm. It was dangling at the man's side, looking useless.

God, that had to hurt.

Franklin had never had a broken bone, and he'd never had one for a good reason: He was smart.

Too smart to let some mope get ahold of him and break his goddamn arm.

He pushed open the window and hollered down into the warehouse, "Bring him up here."

Eliot nodded and headed toward the stairs, hauling the guy with him. He had a grip on the older man's good arm and was practically lifting Burt off his feet. Eliot was a big guy, six four, two hundred and eighty pounds of pure stupid mean. Dovey had it all over Eliot in the brains department, which wasn't saying much, but Eliot knew how to execute an order. He never failed. Give Eliot an order and count on results; that's what Franklin did, what he'd been doing for fifteen years, ever since Eliot's last heavyweight fight had put him in a coma for a week and a half. The guy hadn't come out of it quite right, and he'd been Franklin's boy ever since.

He wasn't much in the looks department, but for what Franklin used him for, his looks worked, scaring money out of people more often than not, before Eliot ever got a chance to use his fists on them. His years in the ring had left him with a disfigured left ear, a general puffiness in his face, and one drooping eyelid, not to mention a few scars.

Franklin went back to sitting at his desk and waited. When Eliot brought Burt into the office, he could see right off the bat that his man had gone too far, too early in the game. Sweat was rolling off the older man, and his skin was pale, his glasses askew, his thin sand-colored hair sticking up all over. Burt Alden wasn't a big man. He had a narrow build and a narrow face, and he looked more than half sick with pain. Of course, anyone would look sick dressed in brown corduroy pants and a ratty green striped shirt.

Style wasn't that hard to come buy. Franklin had it by the boatload—quality slacks, black in color, dark blue silk shirt, a quality shirt, and a sharp vest, also in black, to match the slacks. Add a gold pocket watch, and bodda-bing bodda-bang, instant style.

Style was easy, except for guys like Burt Alden, who just never got it.

"Look at you, Burt. You look like hell." Franklin didn't understand it, why anyone would let themselves get in such a state. "Where the hell is my money?"

"Th-the money's good, Bleak," Burt said, wincing.

"I know it's good, but *where* is it?" He was mad enough to do some real damage if Burt didn't pony up. Katherine Gray wanted to meet him, but Graham Percy would pull the plug if Bleak didn't get his hands on the cocaine, and the Chicago boys weren't going to be giving it away. They were going to want the cash sitting in their hands, all the cash.

"My girl's got it. She's bringing it." Burt sucked in a breath. "She had a deal tonight."

That was news.

"Up in Genesee?"

"Yeah," Burt said, his face growing even paler, if that was possible. "H-how'd you know about Genesee? You, you d-don't have my girl, do you?"

"No, Burt," Franklin reassured the man. "I don't have your girl."

Now your wife, asshole, that's a different story, and she's sweating almost as badly as you.

But Beth Alden's life was looking up. She didn't know it yet, but her husband had just delivered some very good news. Little Esme Alden had made it to Genesee and back, and if she'd gone there to get the money, well, then Burt's life was looking up, too.

"She got the whole eighty-two thousand? Is that what you're telling me, Burt?"

The older man nodded, one, slow, short nod—and even that hurt. Franklin could tell.

He looked at his watch—coming up on midnight—and looked back at Burt Alden. Five hours was a lot when a guy's arm was broken, but Franklin figured the guy would hold on. He'd seen guys hold on for an ungodly amount of time, guys who'd been hurt a lot worse than old Burt. Franklin knew, though, that old Burt could be hurt a lot worse than just a broken arm. Something about the way the guy was hanging there from Eliot's grip made Franklin think there had been some internal damage.

Eliot usually did some internal damage.

But if old Burt didn't hold on, well, it wasn't really Franklin's loss, not as long as he had the eighty-two thousand, which just kept bringing him back to the same place he'd started out tonight. He needed the girl.

He'd known it. So help him God, he'd known it. That was why he'd sent goddamn Dovey over to LoDo in the first place, to pick her up.

"Where were you supposed to meet her to get the money, Burt?" It would be easy enough for Eliot to make the meeting. Hell, maybe Franklin would go himself. Esme Alden was a looker. She was no Katherine Gray, not nearly as much pizzazz, but she had her share, and from all accounts, she was real smart. Valedictorian, Dovey had said, and yet she'd ended up dating one of Baby Duce's boys, so how smart was she, really?

Franklin was sure proud of his little girl. Lindsey was no valedictorian. She was an athlete, varsity, which was even better in Franklin's book. His little Lindsey was real popular, too. Dovey had said Esme Alden hadn't had a date in high school. Lindsey had lots of dates, and she sure as hell would never end up with some damn gangbanger from the Locos.

Pure class, that was his little girl.

"I . . . I wasn't meeting her," Burt said, every word sounding like it cost him. "She's coming here, to do . . . do the deal."

Now Burt had shocked him. Franklin wouldn't have sent his mother-in-law, a coldhearted, double-crossing bitch Franklin hated down to his socks, to deal with a guy like him, and Burt had planned on sending his daughter to the warehouse in his stead?

Unfuckingbelievable. Nobody in their right mind was that careless.

"So you're telling me, that if I just stay put here tonight, your daughter is going to walk through my door at five A.M. with eighty-two thousand dollars?"

"Yes." Burt nodded. "Yes. She'll be here. I promise."

What a lying sack of crap. Franklin didn't believe him.

"And you'd let her do that, Burt? Show up here on her own with that kind of money?"

"Sh-she won't be alone. Her cousin is coming with her."

"Her cousin?" Franklin couldn't believe it. What a joke. Hell, if he gave Burt enough time, the old guy would probably have his whole damn family in on this. Maybe Franklin could sell them all wholesale as a single unit or something.

Burt was struggling, his breath coming hard, his body starting to shake.

Franklin gave Eliot a look, a hard look, and Eliot shrugged.

Internal damage, Franklin thought, and hell, wasn't that just the way it went sometimes. But the night was definitely looking up. With Esme Alden having already made her run to Genesee, all Franklin needed was for Mitch and Leroy to get her and bring her to the warehouse. This whole deal could be tied up well before five A.M.

He pulled out his phone and was scrolling down for Mitch's number, when Burt collapsed flat-out on Franklin's New Zealand wool rug.

"Get him out of here," he said to Eliot, without looking up from his phone. "Take him down to the betting room and let his wife look at him for a while." And that ought to be a happy reunion.

Franklin shook his head. People led such screwed-up lives.

"And Eliot?"

"Yes, Mr. Bleak?"

"Take the woman's gag off. I bet she's gonna have a few things to say to her husband."

"Yes, Mr. Bleak."

Burt was such a loser.

"Mitch," he said when his second in command answered. "You still got that Cyclone in sight?"

"Yes, boss."

"Good. Burt Alden is here, Mitch, and he told me the girl picked up the eighty-two thousand up there in Genesee. So go get it. Whatever it takes."

"Yes, boss. What about the girl? You still want her, too?"

Franklin gave the question a moment's thought. "If you get the money, I don't need the girl." He had enough Aldens cluttering up his warehouse. "But if she doesn't have that money on her, bring her in chains, if you have to. I don't give a damn."

"And the guy with her? Duce's boy?"

"Get rid of him, Mitch, no witnesses, understand?"

"Yes, boss."

"Duce doesn't ever need to know what happened to his boy, if you do it right. So do it right."

"Yes, boss."

Franklin ended the call and walked over to the window overlooking the betting room.

Eliot was just depositing a limp and unconscious Burt Alden on the floor in the betting room, and from what Franklin could see, it didn't look like Beth was any too happy to see him.

Wives, Franklin thought. He hadn't seen his in fourteen years. As soon as Burt came around, Franklin would bet the whole eighty-two thousand that the guy was going to wish he hadn't seen his either—not in this place.

CHAPTER TWENTY-FIVE

Harold's Gas-N-Go was on the west side of Denver, hell and gone in the suburbs, a block off the interstate. Johnny finished pumping gas into Solange's tank and reracked the nozzle. Esme had gone inside the small convenience store to use the facilities.

He was surprised she'd lasted as long as she had. It was nearing midnight—and Johnny could feel his clock ticking. Five A.M. wasn't nearly far enough away for what he had in mind.

Waiting for his receipt, he checked both ends of the street. It was pure rustbelt, lined with auto parts stores and metal buildings rented out to machine shops and car repair guys. Poorly lit, grim, like a place where trouble happened—like that damn tunnel at Nachman's.

What in the hell had that all been about? he wondered. He'd never had any trouble coming back from a tour of duty before—hadn't had any trouble this time, until that damn elevator door had opened.

The receipt rolled out of the gas pump, and he tore it off and tucked it in his shirt pocket, his fingers brushing against the envelope.

Oh, yeah—the realization hit him. Just like every other time over the last two weeks, he conveniently kept forgetting about the envelope. Except it wasn't so damn convenient, not when it crept up on him in the dark and made him break out in a sweat.

He hadn't read what was inside. The actual letter was none of his business. His job was to deliver it. That was all, just deliver it. Take it up to Cheyenne, Wyoming, and give it to a girl, Lori Heath, whose husband was never coming home. He'd made the promise. He could do the deed. He'd almost driven up there tonight, but had ended up at the Blue Iguana instead.

Because there was more than one girl in Cheyenne, and if he got close enough to do his duty by Lori Heath, he had to face the other one, a girl named Cassie McAllister, and there was no neat and tidy letter to hand to Cassie. No, he'd have to talk to her, face-to-face. He'd have to stand there in her double-wide trailer sitting in its patch of dust and tumbleweeds and tell her what had happened to that rodeo cowboy who'd come through Cheyenne a year ago, riding in Frontier Days, his last go-round before he'd shipped out— the one who'd fathered her baby, the one she hadn't heard from in months, the one who said he'd be coming back.

John Paul Cooperman had come back, and he wasn't anywhere near Cheyenne, and he didn't plan on ever getting within a hundred miles of the place ever again, and Johnny was going to have to explain why to a twenty-two-year-old girl with a brand-new baby.

Hell. He wasn't sure he could explain it to himself. Or maybe he was, and that's what was keeping him out of Wyoming.

Fuck.

In a couple of days, Johnny promised himself. He'd make the run up to Cheyenne in Solange, and he'd take care of business.

Getting back in the Cyclone, he pulled the car up to the front of the store, then leaned over and knocked the jockey box open. He didn't smoke very often, but he always had a pack of Faros in the car. He bought them off the bartender at Mama Guadalupe's, an old guy named Rick. He had to dig deep to find them, and by the time he sat back up in the driver's seat, another car had pulled up a couple of spaces over.

A few cars had come and gone since he and Esme had gotten there, gassing up or people running into Harold's for something—but this car was different.

It looked like all the others, a regular late-model sedan, a Crown Victoria, a real tuna boat. It had a couple of guys in it, like any number of the previous vehicles.

But it was different.

It made the hackles rise on the back of his neck, and he never second-guessed that particular buzz of warning.

He pushed in the Cyclone's lighter, then knocked a cigarette out of the pack of Faros. When he was lit, he settled back into the driver's seat and waited for somebody in the Crown Vic to make a move.

He didn't have to wait long.

The guy in the passenger seat, a short, stocky redhead with male pattern baldness, got out of the Vic and headed into the store. The other guy, gray-haired, older, taller, stayed in the car.

Johnny took a long drag off the cigarette, watching the redhead scan the aisles. When the guy started toward the bathrooms, Johnny made his move, getting out of Solange and heading inside.

"Hey, hey," the clerk behind the counter said. "You can't smoke in here. Take it back outside."

Dream on, *cholo*.

Johnny gave him a punk-ass stare and flashed the Locos sign with the fingers of his right hand.

As he passed the counter, he reached out and snagged a couple of candy bars and a lighter.

"You should leave, man," he said, keeping his voice low. Combined with the hand sign, it was a clear threat, and if it got the clerk calling the cops, so much the better. Johnny knew Loretta wouldn't want to see him dragged in for smoking in a convenience store and stealing candy bars and a Zippo. When the lieutenant swung her weight around for SDF, she liked to do it for something worthwhile, but if that's all this turned out to be, fine. He'd take the dressing-down.

It was a short-lived hope.

Behind him, he heard the main door open again. Perfect.

He glanced back, and sure enough, the gray-haired guy had followed him in. This was starting to look like exactly what Johnny had thought it might be—an ambush.

The clerk had disappeared.

Good. Considering how close Harold's was to the interstate, the poor guy probably got robbed once a week. He wasn't going to take a chance on three guys casing his store.

Down at the end of the aisle, into a hallway, Johnny could see the red-haired guy cozied up to the bathroom door, wiggling the handle.

And it pissed him off, royally.

That sonuvabitch—rattling the door of the women's rest room, when there was a woman inside, Johnny's woman.

"Eh! Cabrón!" he called out. "Back the *fuck* off that door."

The guy looked up and flipped him off.

Johnny was impressed. The guy had more balls than he would have guessed—more than was good for him, that was for damn sure.

"Come on out of there," the red-haired guy was saying, keeping his attention focused on Johnny, giving him a look that said he was the one who had better back off.

Right. Like that was going to happen.

"I've got some news about your father, Esme," the red-haired guy continued. "Come on."

Esme? News about her father? Oh, man, that guy couldn't have come up with anything worse to say if he'd had all year. Any doubt Johnny might have had in his mind about the guy maybe being a random pervert was gone—not that he'd had much of a doubt.

The sound of the lock being released from inside drew the guy's gaze back to the door, and that was all she wrote. In that one moment of inattention, Johnny moved in and decked the guy. One punch, hard, like a fucking pile driver. To his credit, the guy almost managed to block the blow, but no forty-year-old asshole was fast enough to beat a Ramos left hook. The redhead dropped like a stone, out cold, and Johnny leaned down and quickly frisked him for a piece. He found a Beretta 9mm, grabbed it, and turned to meet the threat he could hear coming down the aisle at a run.

This asshole was even older than the redhead, and Johnny would bet his socks that neither of them had ever been U.S Army Rangers.

Hubris. That's what hit him, and sent him rocking. The old guy had clocked him.

Geezus. Stars. Yeah, he was seeing them, but he was still scrambling, still moving, knowing he couldn't afford to let the old gray-haired geezer lay another hand on him.

Geezus. He'd lost the 9mm on the floor somewhere.

Okay, that hadn't been his smartest move

tonight—but it was one move smarter than what happened next. The old guy did get ahold of him, moving like lightning. Johnny elbowed him hard and twisted out of his grip, grabbing hold of the old guy and slamming him into the wall. Then found himself facedown on the floor with the old guy on top of him.

Geezus. What the fuck was this?

He reached back and grabbed a handful of whatever he could reach, pants, shirt, whatever, and jerked hard, dislodging the gray-haired guy enough for him to move and twist—and go totally mannequin on command, just like the old guy.

"Freeze, sucker."

That's what she said—*Freeze, sucker,* her voice glacial. And she was backing it up with the muzzle of her .45 pointed straight at the old guy. He couldn't miss it. From this angle, with Johnny and the old guy close enough that the gun was almost pointing at him as well, the barrel of a .45 looked humongous, like a bottomless pit, a large, gaping black hole leading straight to hell.

For an instant, the old guy looked like he might try something, another move.

"He's got a gun inside his waistband, right side," he said.

"Take it, Johnny," Esme said, moving a step closer, holding the old guy's gaze. "If you so much as twitch, it's all over for you. I won't miss."

It wasn't the words, it was the tone of voice that sent the message. She was dead serious. Only a fool would mistake her, and the old guy proved not to be a fool.

Johnny released the guy's gun from its holster and leveled it at the bastard. "Get off me, *pendejo*, very, very slowly."

As soon as the old guy was off him, Johnny rose to his feet, and Esme gave him a handful of flex cuffs she'd pulled out of an outside pocket on her messenger bag. It took him and the hog-tying queen of LoDo less than a minute to secure Bleak's two guys and be heading back out the door.

He grabbed a cold drink as they passed the coolers, and left a ten on the counter.

Hell, he'd been saved by a girl.

"Thank you," he said as they dropped into the seats in the Cyclone. It was the only appropriate thing to say.

He fired the car up and wheeled her in reverse, until they were heading back out onto the street.

"You're welcome," she said.

He cast her a quick glance. She was secretly gloating. He could tell. The *Mona Lisa* smile on her face was a dead giveaway.

"Burt?" Beth said, staring down at her husband. He was practically at her feet, having been dropped there by the Hulk, which is what she'd been calling the guy who'd kidnapped her. "Burt?"

If he was smart, and he could hear her, he'd be wise to answer. Her mouth hurt so badly from where the Hulk had ripped away the tape holding her gag in place, and yet she was so grateful to be able to talk, especially to the man on the floor.

"Burton Aaron Alden?"

This was his fault. She knew it. This wasn't a random act of violence. This was a not-so-random Burt-Alden-hadn't-paid-his-bookie act of retribution. She'd seen it a hundred times in their marriage, just never so seriously, never so dangerously. The truth was so demoralizing, it made it hard to breathe.

"Are you okay?" she asked. He didn't look okay.

"No," he mumbled, the word barely a breath of sound.

"Is your arm broken?" It looked broken.

"Yes."

"I'm leaving you for this, Burt," she said. "I mean it this time. If we get out of this alive, I'm leaving you."

"I'll quit," he said, still so quietly she could barely hear him. "I swear."

She didn't even bother to answer. She was leaving him, and this time she meant it.

CHAPTER TWENTY-SIX

Esme remembered the summer Dax had set the pure stock Plymouth drag title up at Bandimere with an 11.897-second time at 119.46 miles per hour in his Hemi 'Cuda. The two of them had toasted his success with a couple of her mother's homemade root beers. It had been a big day, sharing a cool moment with her cool cousin.

Today had been a big day, and Johnny had been going faster than Dax coming down out of the mountains. Thank God he had an upgraded suspension on the Cyclone. She didn't mind fast, and she hadn't felt unsafe, but neither had she taken her eyes off the road or her hands off the car. Her right hand had been holding onto the door, and her left had been wrapped around the edge of her bucket seat, in case they'd gone airborne.

He'd cut it down a notch now that they were in Denver, and her hands were in her lap, trying not to wring each other. Damn. She knew what made her feel unsafe—a couple of armed and dangerous guys trying to grab her in the middle of a simple bathroom pit stop.

"Who were those guys, do you think?" she asked. "Bleak's?" They had to be Bleak's. She was beginning to think that somehow she, and Dax, and her dad had completely underestimated how serious Franklin Bleak was about collecting his money. It seemed a little crazy, how all these guys were after her, chasing her all over the damn state.

"You tell me," he said, lifting his hips off the seat and pulling two wallets out of his back pocket. He handed them over to her, and all she could do was look at him and be a little amazed.

Then he reached in his front pockets, one after the other, and produced two cell phones, and handed them over.

"That's . . . uh, good work." Why in the hell hadn't she thought of that? Frisking. She should have thought of that, or at least noticed what he was doing. He'd taken their weapons. She'd noticed that. He'd also unloaded both pistols before dropping them in the backseat. She'd definitely noticed that. He'd been very fast about it, very efficient, like it was something he did all the time.

She opened the first wallet and read the name on the driver's license. "Mitch Hardon, that was the old guy, the one who almost ate your lunch."

He cast her a narrowed glance across the car, being such a guy about it.

"He's got two hundred and fifteen dollars in

cash, a couple of credit cards, and stuff," she said, setting it aside and opening the other wallet. "And we've got Leroy Fitzer, twelve bucks, somebody else's credit cards—some guy named Jason L. Davidson—two condoms, and a Bleak Enterprises business card, listing him as a production manager."

"Mystery solved," he said, then cleared his throat. "You were good back there." He had both hands on the wheel, his gaze straight ahead.

"So were you." It was true. "Thanks. I think that's about the third time you've saved me tonight. We make a good team."

"I think that time it was you who saved me, so we're close to even, and we haven't even gotten to the main event."

She gave her head a small shake. "Well, you're not on for the main event. You've already gone beyond the call of duty here tonight." She still didn't know why, not exactly, but she was grateful.

"Five A.M. at Bleak's warehouse," he said clearly. "I'm going to be there, with you and your partner, if he ever shows up."

"Oh, hell." Dax. She'd forgotten to call Dax. She'd listened to his message, but then lost cell reception again. She quickly pulled her phone out of her messenger bag and keyed in his number.

"Dax," Esme said into her phone, when he answered. "We just hit the city limits."

Over on his side of the car, she heard Johnny choke a bit on a swallow of the drink he'd gotten at Harold's. When she looked, he was staring at her with an odd expression on his face—concern, maybe, or disbelief. It was hard to tell.

"Did you get the cash?" Dax asked, and she put her attention back into the phone call.

"Yes."

"Are you still with Ramos?"

"Yes."

"Good, don't let yourself get out of his sight, not for an instant."

"Warner and Shoko." She understood. Down to the marrow of her bones, she understood. "What in the hell are they doing in Denver?"

At the worst, she'd figured Warner would realize Otto had screwed up the deal after the fact, not practically in the middle of it, and not where she'd be within striking distance.

"If Warner authorized the sale of the painting, then he was here to collect his half a million."

"And if he didn't authorize it?" Otto had done a little moonlighting in Bangkok, making some cash on the side with bits and pieces of Warner's enormous collection, but unloading the Meinhard on his own was an unprecedented risk. Warner would notice that the Meinhard was missing, and yes, she could imagine that he would come after it fast and hard. Later, though, after she was long gone.

"Then Otto got off easy," Dax said.

"Is he dead?" With Shoko in the mix, sometimes dead wasn't such a bad option. And oh, holy crap, was she going to be in it up to her neck, if Warner's dragon lady had killed Otto Von Lindberg. An anonymous hooker turning an anonymous trick in a hotel room and nobody was the wiser. An anonymous hooker leaving a dead trick in that hotel room, and suddenly she wasn't anonymous. Suddenly everybody knew who she was; suddenly everybody remembered talking to her—starting with the parking valet.

"No. He's not dead. He'll be sporting 'Nazi hero' for a while, so whatever the reason is that Warner keeps him around, that reason is still holding."

The relief she might have felt failed to materialize. Being in the same country as Warner was enough to tighten her gut. Add Shoko, and her gut was tying itself in knots.

Nazi hero. Goddammit. She had half that mark, and the only thing that had saved her from the whole abomination was Dax. Eighteen months later, and she could still feel the tip of the bitch's blade. It woke her up sometimes, always in a cold sweat, and the demon from that bad dream was here, in her hometown. So help her God, she'd never imagined Denver could be so damn full of so many badass felons out to grease her.

"Johnny and I left two of Bleak's guys hog-tied in a convenience store off I-70 near Sixth Avenue." And she was definitely pegging those two as felons. Hell, they worked for Bleak.

When Dax didn't say anything, she knew she was hearing his "oh, for the love of God and Patsy Cline" silence, his unhappy silence.

"You were followed." His words were flat when he finally spoke.

"Yes, but we did good," she assured him.

"The two of you should have done good," Dax said. "You're you, and Ramos is a Ranger."

Esme felt her eyebrows lift up.

"He just got back from Afghanistan two weeks ago, his third combat tour," Dax said. "I'd guess he's still pretty sharp."

"Like a tack," she said, all the pieces falling into place. She slanted Mr. U.S. Army Ranger a glance. Only one word came to mind, and she wasn't shy about saying it. "Hoo-yah."

Johnny didn't look over, made no acknowledgment whatsoever of her revelation, except for the big grin that spread across his face.

Johnny Ramos a Ranger; it made perfect sense.

"You should have told me," she said, still looking at Johnny.

"I did tell you," Dax said on the phone. "What I haven't told you is that the cops are looking for the blond hooker who was in Otto's room, and my guess is that by the time they lift the prints off the prepaid phone you used, they'll know your shoe size and your horoscope. So lay low."

Crap. "I was wearing gloves, Dax. There won't be any prints, but how in the hell did they find the phone?"

"Followed the emergency GPS signal straight to the B and B bathroom, babe. It was a piece of cake."

And they had Shoko to thank for this. If she'd left Otto alone, no one would even have a clue what had gone on in the Oxford. No one would have cared.

"So where are you going to lay low?" Dax asked.

"Where are we going?" she asked Johnny.

"My place," he said.

"No good," Dax said, before she could relay the information. "Somebody at the Oxford gave them Ramos's description, and they've got his name."

Oh, hell. "Your place is no good," she said to Johnny. "The cops are onto you at the Oxford."

He didn't say much to that, just one word under his breath, and it rhymed with luck.

She didn't blame him.

"Tell Dax I've got a safe house in my neighborhood," he said after a moment. "If he shows up at the corner of Vine and Hoover in Commerce City, I'll come down and bring him in. Ask him what time he thinks he'll get there."

"An hour, maybe two," Dax said, obviously able to hear everything in the car. "I've picked up a tail. When I shake it, I'll show."

"I still haven't heard from my dad, about the name," she said.

"Don't worry. I got the name. Thomas called back and left it on the machine."

"So we're good to go?" she asked.

"You've got the money, and I've got the name," Dax said. "We're good to go. Just stay out of trouble until five o'clock. We'll sort out this mess with the Denver cops once we're back in Seattle. I'll send them the file on Shoko. If they ask around, somebody at the Oxford will undoubtedly remember seeing the dragon lady tonight. Case solved. Everybody happy."

"We're going to run?"

"Like hell, bad girl." He ended the call, leaving Esme to stare at her phone and wonder how in the hell she was supposed to stay out of trouble trapped in some safe house alone with Johnny Ramos for two hours.

Two hours was a long time.

Damn long.

CHAPTER TWENTY-SEVEN

"Ouch."

"Baby."

"You're being too rough."

She let out a little snort and kept dabbing away at his cheek. She'd taken her shoulder holster off and left it in the bedroom, where she was planning on taking a nap before they went to Bleak's.

Johnny understood the concept. Rangers slept when they could. It was just good standard operating procedure, but he was pretty damn sure he wouldn't be napping.

"You should probably have a stitch put in this, maybe two," she said.

He'd been cut on his face, fairly deep, where Mitch Hardon had hit him. The guy must have been wearing a ring.

"If you want to do it, get a suture kit out of the pack."

She leaned back and gave him a look. "You're kidding, right?"

"No." Johnny wasn't kidding, he was dying. Esme was standing in front of him at the kitchen table in the safe house, doing her Florence Nightingale impersonation, and all he could think about was her cleavage, the soft shadow between her breasts, the soft curves at the V of her jacket.

He wanted to touch her so badly, he hardly dared move.

It had been quiet on the corner of Vine and Hoover since they'd arrived. The blue neon sign for the Commerce City Garage was lit up across the street, and that's where his apartment was, on the ground floor. One of the other SDF operators had the second-floor apartment, Red Dog, Gillian Pentycote.

The building he and Esme were in had started out thirty years ago as a restaurant with a few office suites on its upper floors. Since SDF had bought the place last year, the restaurant had been gutted and converted into a garage for storing cars, and the two upper floors had been redesigned into working and living space. Steele Street Annex, it was called, with some talk going on about building another team. General Grant wanted it. The world situation needed it, and Johnny wanted more than anything to be part of it.

Except for right now. For right now, there wasn't anything he wanted more than Easy Alex.

He'd pulled Solange into one of the bays on the ground floor, and the whole place was locked up tighter than a drum with all the building's security systems up and running.

Esme was safe from everything in Denver except him, and he was safe from everything except the tightness in his chest that got worse every time she bent over and dabbed at his cheek with an antiseptic-saturated cotton ball. It stung like hell, and he didn't feel a thing. He was completely removed from the minor pain of having his face cut open in a fight, and completely, totally fascinated with the cut of her jacket—low.

He knew what was underneath it, the red lace bra, the one that matched her panties, which was all that was under her skirt, except for her black satin slip.

There had to be a way to get her out of all that stuff, but he'd been enduring her tender care for half an hour and was down to four and a half hours before they left, and he hadn't gotten anywhere.

Four hours, if he included drive time over to Bleak's warehouse—much less than that, if this Dax guy shook his tail and showed up.

Great. He had two hours he could count on, max, and he was sucking air.

Dax. The name had thrown him for a second there. He'd only ever heard of one guy named Dax—Dax Killian, the Gunfighter. But where he'd heard about him was over in the Sandbox, never anyplace in the States.

Esme leaned over him again, this time with a small gauze bandage and a couple of pieces of first-aid tape, and he had to remind himself to breathe.

His heart was pounding deep in his chest, and he knew if she'd had any idea how much he wanted her, she'd be running in the other direction.

And he didn't want that, so he kept himself still. If all he got was her company until five o'clock, he'd take it and be glad. Nothing in Afghanistan smelled like her. Nothing in Afghanistan looked like her. She was soft curves and golden hair, strands of it slipping loose and curling along her cheek. She was high heels and a tight skirt, and everything about her got him hot.

She laid the gauze on his cheek and oh, so carefully smoothed the tape down with the tips of her fingers.

It was crazy, and he wondered why it always had to be like this, with a woman so cool and calm and going about her business, and a guy driving himself nuts thinking about that hot, sweet place between her legs and how much he wanted to touch her there with his tongue, and his fingers, and be with her there, so deep inside her.

Geezus. The way she smelled made his head swim. It made it hard to think, made him hard . . . harder than Chinese arithmetic.

The sound of a car door being slammed shut on the street below had him reaching for her. He closed his hand around her wrist, stopping her from finishing with the bandage. Another door slammed shut, and he quickly rose to his feet and headed toward the bedroom that looked out onto the Commerce City Garage.

Okay, maybe he did have a brain left in his head. That was very reassuring.

And he had an erection.

And maybe that was reassuring, too, though to date, that hadn't been a problem for him. His problem was the exact opposite.

Standing at the window in the darkened room, he watched two men approach the garage where he normally would have been for the night, if he could have stood the place on his own.

"Dovey," she said, stopping beside him, her gaze angled toward the street.

"And the other guy, the one from O'Shaunessy's, do you know him?"

She shook her head.

Below them, Dovey Smollett and the guy in the Chicago Bears jacket walked back and forth in front of the garage, trying the doors, and looking in the windows. Dovey stepped back and looked up at the second floor, but like the first floor, all was dark, quiet, empty. With Solange parked inside this building, there was nothing there to make anyone think he and Esme had run for home.

Dovey pulled out a phone and made a call, and after a few more minutes of wandering around, both he and the Chicago guy got back in the Buick LeSabre and hunkered in—stakeout.

"Looks like we're going to have company for a while," he said, glancing down at her, and for an instant she was looking up at him, but only an instant, before she looked away, a soft casting downward of her eyes, a lowering of her lashes.

And that was it, the one missing piece in all his heated lust and yearning, the one admission of awareness that she had any clue of what he was feeling, and that maybe she was feeling it, too—a guy needed that. Just because she'd kissed him twice in the car didn't mean she wanted to kiss him here, where the distance between a kiss and the bed was shorter than a shift worker on payday.

Geez, she was so beautiful.

The blue glow of neon washed over her face, deepening shadows, highlighting curves, like the curves of her mouth, the soft fullness of her lower lip, the sweet dipping curve of her upper lip. Her face was more contoured as a woman than it had been as a child, even as a teenager. She was far more alluring, far more lush. He'd wanted her so desperately at eighteen, it was hard to imagine that he would have ever come to want her more—but he did. At sixteen, seventeen, eighteen, it had all been hormones and whatever ideas of love he'd managed to comprehend at the time.

Tonight the need was deeper. She'd been there with him during that firefight, only her out of all the people he'd ever known. He'd never claim to understand why, but he knew his tie to her was strong. It had happened in an instant, at first sight, a long time ago, and what he wanted from her was a chance to see where it all went.

Just a chance to lay himself up against her, to connect with her, mouth to mouth, body to body, to see if she could save him just a little bit, just enough to take the sharp edges off his dreams, to take the tension off his mind.

No. He didn't have PTSD. He had what everybody else over there had, three tours of combat and a lot of rough living in between, and there had to be a break in there somewhere. When he'd seen her on Seventeenth, that's exactly what he'd seen: a worn-out little hooker and a safe harbor all wrapped up in one blonde.

He'd been home for two weeks without being with a woman, and the need for her was running through him hard, cutting deep, straight to his core. There were other girls. There were always other girls, but the whole damn night had been about this girl, about winning her for himself, and the win was to have her sweet and naked beneath him, wanting him, her mouth parted, her legs spread, letting him push up into her, take her, fuck her, make her his.

It was primal. It was real. It was what he wanted. Hell, he'd been wanting it, or some version of it, since seventh grade, and there was no damn explanation for that. Or if there was, he wasn't sure he could face it. Esme Alexandria Alden, *geezus*, she had always been the one—the only one who turned him inside out. He wanted her, and she was standing next to him in a dark, and quiet, and private place, knowing it.

Arousal didn't wash down through him. It had already arrived between his legs, hard, and hot, and heavy. She wasn't running anywhere. Not moving an inch—and she was blushing. He couldn't see the color of it staining her skin, not in the blue light, but it was there, in the downward tilt of her head, as if she had something to hide. It was there in her stillness beside him, the same stillness he'd felt in himself sitting at the table.

She knew what the two of them were about, and without another worrisome thought, he slid his hand around the side of her neck, cupping her face, and he lowered his mouth to hers.

Her response was to melt against him with a soft groan, her mouth open, welcoming him, her hands going to his chest, and that felt so good, to have her touching him.

But take it slow, he told himself. Don't devour her, and whatever you do, *pendejo*, do not . . . do not scare her off. So for a long, endless minute, he kissed her, his tongue sliding deep, his mouth slanted over hers, just letting the taste and softness of her seep into him.

Yeah, this was all going to go just great.

Breaking off the kiss for a moment, he unsnapped and shrugged out of his holster and set the whole rig on a nearby table. Then he kissed her, picking the whole marvelous thing up again.

Her hand came up around the back of his neck, drawing him closer, and he gave in to it, letting her run this show, until she rocked her hips against him. It was a small move, just a brush of her pelvis up against his—and it was like getting plugged into a 220-volt outlet.

He stood perfectly still, holding her, his tongue

making a slow foray across the inside of her mouth—his brain on fire.

God, it had been too long since he'd done this. She had no idea what she was doing to him—because she did it again, rocked against his cock, and his hands tightened on her, going to her hips. Slowly, inexorably, he started pulling up her skirt, hauling it hell and gone up over her ass, because he had to get his hands on her, on her skin, between her legs, under those panties.

And when he did, she felt like heaven. She was so wet and soft, his fingers sliding through her silken folds and into her vagina. His kiss got harder, his body pressing against her, and when she groaned, her legs widening, he knew she wanted exactly what he wanted. With one hand, he undid his belt buckle, no sooner getting it open than she was helping unsnap his jeans, unzip them, and push them down off his hips, so she could take him in her hand.

It was sweet, he couldn't deny it, but what he wanted wasn't sweet. What he wanted was to ride the edge she was putting him on and take it home. With his hand in her hair, holding the back of her head, kissing her, he pushed the scrap of red lace down—down to her thighs, then farther. He lifted her leg to get one side of her panties down off her calf and over her high heel, and with her leg wrapped around him, and her body so hot and warm up against him, everything in his world started coming together.

Hauling her back up against the wall, he pushed

into her, one long slick slide of heated sex with her head going back, and her arms around his shoulders holding on for dear life. Nothing had ever been sweeter than to thrust into her again, and again, and again.

She had her tongue halfway down his throat, her little groans echoing in his mouth every time he pushed into her. *Oh, geezus.* He was so into her, driving deep, hot and hard and fast, and just feeling her come apart all over him.

"John . . . Johnny . . . *Johnny*—" She strained against him, riding him, and when she tightened around him, he went straight over the edge, pumping into her one last time, and *oh, God*, it felt so good to come inside her.

So amazingly good.

He held himself still, letting it all roll over him, her sweet, sweet softness, the way she smelled, the smell of them together, the sound of her breathing in his ear. She tightened around him again, a small contraction of her inner muscles, and he let out a soft laugh, nuzzling the side of her neck.

"Keep your legs wrapped around me," he said, carefully pulling himself free and repositioning his arms around her to keep her close.

She sighed, and he kissed her ear.

"*Esme,*" he whispered her name and nuzzled her neck again. This was heaven. Easy, easy Alex in his arms, making love with him. He'd had a few girls. Once, he'd even thought he was in love—but this, with Esme, it felt different to be with her, different and better, more complete.

He kissed her again, his mouth partly open on the tender place below her ear. She responded by sliding her fingers up into his hair, and it felt so good.

"Come on, baby," he said, carrying her over to the bed. "Let's go do this right."

CHAPTER TWENTY-EIGHT

Picked up a tail—Dax guessed that was one way to put his problem, and it was true. He did have a guy on him, no doubt one of Lieutenant Loretta's, but then there was this other part of his problem, the bigger part, the "trying to pick up a tail" part of his problem, or at least trying to pick up a piece of it. He was going to give it another five minutes, and then he'd head out, lose the cop, and make straight for Commerce City. The corner of Vine and Hoover, where Johnny Ramos had taken Easy, was a good location, within striking distance of Bleak's warehouse without being too close for comfort.

From up on the catwalk, he checked the whereabouts of the plainclothes cop. The guy wasn't bad at his job. He just wasn't good enough not to tip off Dax. By far, the more interesting person working the room was Suzi Toussi. According to his reckoning of the sale tags, she was close to selling a quarter-million dollars' worth of naked angels here tonight.

He was impressed and even thinking of buying one of them himself. The Johnny Ramos paintings were very cool, stark, very hard-edged, and Dax liked that. He wanted a coolheaded, hard-edged guy watching over Easy. But the other model, the blond-haired guy—the paintings of him were different, somehow more profoundly involving, more emotionally complex. One on the west wall, in particular, kept drawing Dax's attention. It was one of the most transcendent paintings he'd ever seen, the kind of piece he wouldn't mind looking at for the next fifty years, the kind of piece that might help a guy get through the night sometime—and God knew, every now and then a guy needed a little help getting through the night. Nikki McKinney's process for her art included photography and paint, and for this piece she'd printed a life-size, high-contrast photograph of the angel in a creamy sepia tone on canvas and painted over the top of that in incredibly luminous, sheer colors, more like glazes, in a dozen shades of yellow, gold, and blue. The angel seemed to be in the act of lifting off the canvas, and in Dax's eyes, there was no doubt about where he was going: straight to Paradise.

And there was something about him that said he could take you there, too.

He felt Jane come up beside him, from a moment spent talking to another guest. "I used to pray to that angel," she said.

Dax nodded. He definitely understood the impulse.

"How much is it?" he asked.

"It's not for sale."

He gave her a curious look.

"I think we've all prayed to it at some time or another over the last few years, since Nikki painted it," she explained. "So the other angels come and go, but we keep that one."

And Dax guessed he understood that, too.

"Thanks for showing me around," he said, and she smiled.

"You're welcome. If I see Johnny tonight, I'll be on the lookout for your little sister."

That was sweet, he thought.

"Thanks."

The lovely, wild Jane went back to talking to the other party guests, and Dax set his sights on the real wild thing in the gallery, Ms. Suzi Toussi.

She was easy to find—dark auburn hair and jade green shantung silk. There wasn't anyone else like her, probably not in five states.

At twenty feet and closing, she looked up and caught his eye, and he grinned. She'd been watching out for him.

Good thing. She needed to watch out for him.

"Ms. Toussi," he said.

"Mr. Killian." She turned from another man to greet him—and he liked that. It felt right, like the way things ought to be.

"I was hoping you might have a back way out of here," he said, not mincing words.

A small moue of humored understanding curved her lips and lit the hazel depths of her eyes.

"You do seem the sort," she said, lightly crossing her arms over her chest, which just did amazing things underneath her halter top.

"Sort?" He wasn't at all sure that was a compliment.

"The sort who needs a back way out of most things," she said, and his grin broadened.

"The more discreet, the better."

"Of course." She did a quick glance around the gallery. "Is it the man in the poorly fitted gray suit and the intriguingly nondescript navy blue tie?"

She was good, very good, absolutely nailing the plainclothes cop, and his grin got even broader.

"Come on, then," she said. "Let me show you the etchings I keep on the second floor."

She led the way up the stairs, chatting to him the whole time, pointing out paintings as she spoke, giving a darn good impression of someone doing a hard sell. At the top of the stairs, instead of taking the catwalk, she directed him to a door at the west end of the landing, and once they were through it, his estimation of her went up another twenty points. They'd passed through to the building next door, an architectural firm, and in under a minute, they were standing in the firm's foyer, and she was keying in the security code in order to open the front door and let him out.

"You must know these guys pretty well," he said.

"Well enough to have their security code," she agreed, tossing him a smile over her shoulder.

Yeah, he just bet she did, which didn't really set as well as it should have, considering how convenient it was proving to him.

"Thanks for helping me out."

"My pleasure, I'm sure," she said, concentrating on the keypad.

"Can I buy you a cup of coffee? To show my appreciation?"

She finished with the code and turned to face him with her hand on the doorknob, ready to let him out.

"I'm a little busy right now," she said.

"I meant later." Light from the streetlamps on Seventeenth was doing the loveliest things to her skin, casting it in warm ecru and soft shadows.

"How much later?"

He wanted to kiss her, but even by his rather loose standards, that was probably rushing things.

"I'm going to be in Singapore at the end of this month," he said. "I know a great coffee shop on Licho Street."

"I'm sure it's charming," she said. "But I don't think I'll be in Singapore at the end of the month."

"Bangkok in September?"

She shook her head, a small smile playing about her mouth. "Not likely."

"How about the patio at Duffy's Bar at seven o'clock."

"In the morning?"

He looked at his watch. "About six and a half hours from now. I won't have long, about half an hour. I've got an early flight to catch out of here. But I'd like to see you."

"That's, um, very sweet."

Sure it was. That was him—sweet. It seemed to be going around.

"Duffy makes great coffee."

She let out a soft laugh. "I know."

"It's a date, then?"

She laughed again, and opened the door. "Good night, Mr. Killian."

He wanted to touch her, just once, to see if her skin was as soft as it looked, and to sort of imprint her, he guessed. But he didn't. He kept his hands to himself.

"Good night." That's all he did—say good night, and look at her mouth, and walk out the door, and wonder if she would show up at Duffy's.

He'd be there. That was for damn sure.

Well, if this wasn't the craziest, most soul-searingly sensual thing she'd ever done, getting hot and naked and tearing up the sheets with Johnny Ramos, Esme didn't know what would be, not that Esme the Wanton gave a damn.

Oh, my, God . . . she arched her back, and he pushed into her again. *Oh, my, God.*

The temperature in the bedroom had risen fifteen degrees since they'd started taking each other's clothes off. He'd turned on a bedside lamp, and she could see the flex and give of his muscles with every move he made. She could feel the matching rhythm of his body inside hers.

He did it again, thrust into her, and her eyes drifted closed on a wave of pleasure.

Oh, my, God ... they should have been doing this years ago. She'd been wrong that long-ago night in Roxanne. She should have ... should have ... *oh, my, God* ... He was so deep inside her, pressing into her, short, hard thrusts, winding her up, taking her higher, pushing her closer, until she ... until he slowed it down again, pulling out of her, kissing her, and slowly working his way down her body with his mouth.

She moaned in frustration and pleasure, and then just in pleasure as his mouth found her breasts, and his fingers slipped inside where his cock had been and he started the whole cycle again, the teasing of her until she thought she'd die of it.

Johnny ... she opened her eyes on a soft breath and threaded her fingers through his silky dark hair, watching him tease her nipples ... *Johnny.*

He was everywhere, skin to skin with her, his hands on her, large and strong, holding her, one on her upper arm, the other under her hips, pulling her tight against him. When his mouth slid even lower, her breath caught in her throat. She wanted his tongue on her, knew how magical that could feel, and he didn't disappoint her.

With every languorous stroke, she sank deeper into a well of pure sensation, until she couldn't even think. Her fingers tightened in his hair, holding him to her. She felt the crest of her release rising toward her, and she waited, breath held, loving the soft, wet heat of his tongue, the pressure he applied, and loving it oh, so very, very much when he oh, so very gently . . . sucked.

The crest inside her rose and crashed, flooding her with the most intense pleasure, moment after endless moment, his tongue still on her as she came, holding her in thrall to his mouth . . . *Johnny.*

He'd been so bad, the baddest boy in school, to have turned out so very, very good.

When her hips relaxed back into the bed, he raised his head, and the look in his eyes was almost her undoing. She'd been claimed, the intensity and fierceness of his gaze said it clearly—she'd been claimed, and she was his.

Another, completely different kind of thrill went through her on a deep, visceral level. Without releasing her gaze, he moved up her body and thrust into her again, and the pleasure was so hot and sweet, she felt herself falling into a state of utter and complete acquiescence. She didn't mistake his action for anything other than what it was—the putting of his mark on her while she was still throbbing from the pleasure he'd given her, no one else, only him.

From the day they'd met, he'd always been there, watching over her, wanting this, to be so close to her, a part of her, and he'd been right to want it, understanding better than her what was possible between them. From the day they'd met, he'd been a constant in her life, never getting too far away, her own guardian angel.

And, oh, God, her angel knew his way around a woman.

Pleasure rolled through her with his every move.

His mouth came down on her cheek, kissing her, and moved to her mouth, consuming her. His hands were in her hair, her bobby pins long gone, and she was coming undone again, her release powered by the force of his body, rock solid and honed.

He tilted her head back and slid his mouth down to the side of her neck, and holding her, his breath echoing harsh and fast in her ear, he came, stiffening above her, his pleasure triggering her own. She was sinking and floating and couldn't seem to hold him tight enough. Her mouth was open on his shoulder, tasting him. She was filled with the scent of him, with the hard length of him, feeling the strength and heat of his body covering her, and she never wanted it to end.

He was doomed. Johnny had never felt it more surely in his life. When a woman felt this good, a guy was doomed. He'd do anything. He'd seen it before, when his friends had fallen in love, and yes, that was the "L" word. It made men crazy.

But what was a guy going to do? There was no walking away from this, and that meant he wasn't in charge anymore. It meant this slip of a female with the soft voice, and the soft skin, and the divinely soft piece of heaven between her legs was in charge. It scared the hell out of him. This was more danger than he'd signed on for tonight.

Curiosity had gotten him into this. He'd been as curious as a goddamn tomcat about her, and look where it had led him—straight into Doomsville. Suddenly, he needed her.

He needed the wonder of this, of being inside her, of being so consumed by her. He needed one place where he could let down his guard, one safe place, and he'd found it with her. Carefully, he eased himself free and pulled her close into his arms. Somewhere, though, sometime, somehow, she'd needed the same thing, a safe place, and she hadn't found it.

Facing her, both of them on their sides, he smoothed his hand gently up her back and over her shoulder. He'd felt the scars while they'd made love. He'd seen them, and he knew exactly what it was he'd seen—a kanji, of all the damn things. Someone had cut a kanji into her shoulder. It was healed, but it was there. Undeniable.

He smoothed his hand over her again and brought it to rest on the scar, then gently ran his fingers down the length of it. A tattoo he would have almost understood, but not scarification, not on Esme Alden, not by choice. No, Easy Alex hadn't asked for this to be done to her—which begged a whole lot of questions.

"Hero?" he asked. He'd recognized the character, knew it from his friend Skeeter's artwork.

SDF's resident kick-ass blonde wrote and illus-
trated the Japanese-style comic books known as
manga, and heroes were always part of her stories.

In his arms, Esme sighed and moved closer, her
body softening against his.

"I ran into a woman in Bangkok who had a
knife."

Well, that sent a chill down his spine.

"This is Japanese, not Thai."

"So is she." She said it like it was the end of the
discussion, but it wasn't, not by a long shot.

"And she did this to you because?"

The question was met with silence. She was
thinking, though, thinking hard. He could almost
hear the gears grinding in her head.

"Why don't you just tell me what happened," he
suggested. "That'll be the easiest."

And still she kept thinking, not talking.

Okay, fine. She didn't need to talk, not really. He
was putting it together all on his own, remembering her on the roof of the Wazee Warehouse—so
calm, so cool, so skilled.

"It was like at the Oxford, wasn't it," he said.
"Except things went bad. You were 'recovering'
something, weren't you?" She was a damn cat burglar, a thief.

"A fourteenth-century gold Buddha," she admitted after another long silence. "It was stolen from
the ordination hall of the Wat Pho temple in
Bangkok. It's an important piece, a sacred object,
and the monks pray every day for its return. They've
been praying for over twenty years for its return.

Dax and I got a line on it, and figured we could add some actual recovery expertise to their prayers, so we went for it. I just got a little ahead of him, ended up in a tight spot."

Okay, a legitimate cat burglar.

"What happened to the Buddha?" It was obvious what had happened to her, and the thought of her being in a "tight spot" scared the hell out of him.

"Still missing. I blew that one."

And gotten herself cut and scarred for life by some psycho Japanese bitch with a knife.

"This business you're in, this private eye, put your ass in a sling thieving and impersonating god only knows what besides cheap hookers—have you really given this career path the thought it deserves?" He didn't think so, not really. "Seems to me there's an awful lot of risk involved." Too much damn risk. It was crazy. She needed another job.

"I'd say I'd given it about as much thought as you've given your job. U.S. Army Ranger seems to have an awful lot of risk involved in it, too."

Touché.

If anyone had told him back in high school that he and Esme Alden had anything in common besides a lot of unresolved fascination and lust, mostly his, he'd have told them they were nuts. But here they were, both a little battle-hardened, both putting themselves on the line for what they believed in. Of course, he'd take combat over psycho, knife-wielding Japanese women any day of the week.

Geezus.

The urge to protect her, which had always been ridiculously high in his book, was now through the roof.

Goddammit. Love. He should have seen this coming. What in the hell had he been thinking? That all these years he'd just wanted her because he hadn't been able to get her? That it had just been some sort of conquering caveman instinct?

No such luck. It had been love, and he was doomed. He knew it, and yet he knew if he looked really deep in his heart, if he looked beyond the stark-edged danger of the thing, the truth was that he didn't give a damn. If he'd known being doomed felt this good, he'd have thrown himself over the edge of it a long time ago.

CHAPTER TWENTY-NINE

Something was wrong.

Sitting at his desk, Franklin looked at his phone for the tenth goddamn time in as many minutes and knew he had a problem—two of them. Mitch and Leroy had disappeared off the goddamn planet.

Mitch would have answered his phone with the last breath he had, which made Franklin wonder if his guys were dead, and really made him wonder who in the hell Johnny Ramos was in real life. He sure as hell wasn't just some damn north-side Loco, not if he'd gotten the drop on Mitch and Leroy. Those two boys had been street-fighting men since the day they'd been born, and the streets they'd been fighting in were Denver's. Bleak owned this damn town, and he'd lost two men somewhere between Genesee and Commerce City? He didn't think so, not to one gangster and a girl.

So who the hell else was out there gunning for

him tonight? Somebody sure as hell had beat up and handcuffed Kevin Harrell. Who was that?

Goddamn cocaine. So help him God, he'd known better.

But the deal had been so sweet, no fail, a sure shot—and that should have been his first goddamn clue. There was no such thing as a sure shot.

Coming to a decision, he speed-dialed another number, and then waited through seven long rings before somebody answered.

"Yo."

"Rollo? It's Franklin."

"Franklin, you pussy, what the fuck are you doing calling me at two o'clock in the goddamn morning?"

"I've got a job for you."

There was a slight pause.

"How much?"

"A thousand bucks."

"Fuck you." Rollo hung up the phone, and Franklin gritted his teeth.

Then he dialed the number again.

"Two thousand," he said when Rollo answered.

"Double it, and tell me what you want."

Four thousand dollars. Franklin usually had that much lying around in his "who gives a fuck" box, but not tonight. He needed every damn last dollar he'd been able to get his hands on to close the Chicago deal. He was tight, his balls in a goddamn vice, but only for tonight. By tomorrow afternoon, he'd be rolling in dough and on his way to meet Katherine Gray.

But he had to get through this night and his five o'clock meeting, and his nine o'clock meeting, and for that, he was going to need Rollo and two of his guys to replace goddamn Mitch and Leroy. He wasn't going into anything with just Dovey and Eliot at his back. Dovey was a lightweight, and Eliot was...just Eliot, damaged goods, and Bremerton belonged to Chicago.

"You, and Greg, and Sammy at my warehouse at four o'clock this morning, packing. I'll need you until noon."

"Packing? Double it again, Bleak, and if me or one of my boys has to actually shoot somebody, the price goes to fifty in a heartbeat."

Fucking Rollo.

"Be here, four o'clock sharp." God, Franklin thought, some of the people he had to deal with were such assholes. But his back was against the wall. Esme Alden was showing up at his place with eighty-two thousand dollars, her cousin—whoever in the hell that turned out to be, and maybe he better send Eliot back down into the betting room to find out—and probably this goddamn Johnny Ramos, who even if he was just a damn member of the Locos meant Franklin was really, really screwed. Gang members tended to stick together, that was the whole goddamn point of them, and if Ramos brought a few of his homeboys with him, or a couple of those damn Crazy Spiders—well, hell, if that's the way it was going to go down, he might even be so goddamn bold as to bring Baby Duce— and if that's the way it was going to go down, well, hell, Franklin might as well throw himself out the goddamn window right now, head fucking first, just to make it easy on himself.

And now he was going to be short eight thousand dollars.

Where in the hell was he going to find another eight thousand dollars before nine A.M.? He had four hundred and eighteen thousand dollars sitting in his safe, and Alden's eighty-two on the way, and that was it. He'd squeezed every lime, shaken every tree, gotten all the juice out of everybody.

And he'd borrowed the rest, borrowed it from guys who would chop him up into little pieces and feed him to their goldfish if he didn't pay it back on time, guys in New Jersey who made the Chicago boys look like amateurs.

He was so far out on a fucking limb here.

He dropped his head in his hands and took a deep breath. There was no fooling himself on the deal. The Chicago boys would notice the missing eight thousand and have his head on a platter. He knew Chicago boys. He'd been one, and it had been a bloody fucking business. The guys in New Jersey would never lay a hand on him. He'd be dead long before they figured out he'd welshed on their deal.

Fuck.

How had this happened? Five hours ago, he'd had everything under control, completely under control. And now . . . now—

Christ.

John Ramos. That was it. That was the problem.

For whatever reason, Ramos had walked into the middle of Franklin's deal and everything had gone straight to hell. *Everything*.

He was going to kill the bastard. If John Ramos showed up at Franklin's warehouse, he was going to kill him. And he was going to fuck the girl, tie her up and fuck her, and then sell her to the highest bidder, over and over again, until he had his eight thousand dollars.

Or maybe Rollo would take her in payment. That would save a lot of time and effort on Franklin's part. Let Rollo, and Greg, and Sammy have her in lieu of a cash payment. There wouldn't be much left of her by the time Rollo's crew ran through her, but that wasn't Franklin's problem.

His problem was having half a million dollars in cash on hand at nine o'clock.

Goddamn Johnny Ramos.

Franklin didn't deserve this. He really didn't.

Sex.

And plenty of it.

Dax looked at the two kids standing in front of him, and he wondered if Easy knew that her hair was sticking out on one side, and that her exquisite Karan suit jacket was snapped incorrectly. The jacket was cattywampus and gaping, and he could tell that somehow, she'd lost her bra.

Dax let his gaze drift over the luxurious apartment Johnny Ramos had brought him to, the one across the street from the Commerce City Garage, and he noticed the low-lit bedroom on the other side of the loft.

Fifty bucks said Esme's bra was in that room.

"So," he said, bringing his gaze back to the two of them. "Did you count the cash?"

Standard operating procedure—always count the cash.

Always.

But from the look on Easy's face, that vital detail had somehow gotten overlooked.

"You didn't count it at Nachman's?" She should have counted it at Nachman's.

"There, uh, wasn't time," she said—also incorrectly. There was always time to count the cash. "Johnny was, uh, in a bind."

A bind?

U.S. Army Rangers did not get themselves into binds that overrode standard operating procedures, not unless there was gunfire involved, and Nachman was a pacifist, in an odd manner of speaking, as long as a person wasn't a Nazi.

"And you didn't do it when you got here?"

"Um, no, Johnny was hurt, and I thought we should stop the, uh, bleeding," she said.

She was, he assumed, referring to the scratch on Ramos's face.

He got the picture, loud and clear, and he was fascinated. Easy was not easy, and in less than five hours, Johnny Ramos had caught her, wooed her, and tumbled her hard.

He checked his watch.

"We should leave here about four-thirty, which

gives us a couple of hours. If somebody would like to start a pot of coffee, I think we should go over our plan for the meeting and count the cash," he said. "I can guarantee you that Bleak is going to count it. Is that Dovey Smollett I saw in the Buick LeSabre?" When he'd gotten to the corner of Vine and Hoover, he'd noticed the stakeout and called Esme for further directions to the safe house. Charo was currently safely parked in the building's garage, with Smollett none the wiser.

"Yes, sir," Ramos said, nearly snapping to attention.

Okay. Time for a little attitude adjustment, so to speak. Three tours of combat in Iraq and Afghanistan, Dax guessed he wasn't surprised the kid had heard his name. He'd certainly seen recognition on the young guy's face when Esme had introduced him as her partner, Dax Killian.

"You can forget any of those stories you heard in the Sandbox, Ranger," he said. Hell, if even half the stories had been true, Dax might have been impressed himself—but more than half of them weren't. Only a couple were true, but apparently, a couple were more than enough.

"Yes, sir."

"Tonight we're just a couple of guys with a job to do."

"Yes, sir."

Rangers, Dax thought. *You had to love the Rangers.*

CHAPTER THIRTY

Five A.M., *party time,* Esme thought, sliding out of the Cyclone's front seat. Johnny had parked Solange on the east side of the warehouse by the loading docks, per Bleak's instructions. She and Dax had been told someone would be waiting for them in the docking area, and there was—a huge, hulking guy standing by the building's rear entrance.

Dax followed her out of the car, coming from the backseat, carrying a small duffel bag loaded with the eighty-two thousand dollars. Exactly eighty-two thousand dollars—they'd counted it twice.

Charo had been parked two blocks over with the key under her front seat, safely snugged rear-end-first into a loading dock at the long abandoned Geiss Fastener building, a backup escape, if things didn't exactly go according to plan.

It happened—like in Bangkok, where her perfect

plan for recovering a small fourteenth-century gold Buddha had gone awry and she'd ended up face-to-face with Erich Warner. Unfortunately, Shoko hadn't been far behind. She of the one name and the many knives hated other women with a cold and ruthless passion—and she was here in Denver, unless Otto had been a hit-and-run, and she and Warner were already gone, headed back on Warner's private jet to any one of half a dozen elaborate mansions he owned around the world. Warner wouldn't be happy, not about losing the Meinhard, but as long as Esme's name stayed out of it, she didn't give a damn if Warner was happy or not.

Somebody else wasn't very happy this morning, and even though she cared very much about that person, there wasn't a damn thing she could do about it. Johnny was getting out of the other side of the car, and his expression could only be described as grim.

She had overruled his plan to leave her behind in the safe house and have just him and Dax go into Bleak's with Baby Duce and a couple of Locos, and bring in some guy named Sparky Klimaszewski to pull strings and jerk Bleak's chain on the side.

To her amazement, Dax had grinned at Johnny's suggestion to bring in this Sparky guy and been all on board with bringing in Duce, but hell, it hadn't even been a plan, not really, just a knee-jerk guy thing—"Leave the girl out of it and let's get some guys and go do this thing." And yes, she'd had to remind Dax, very clearly, that they didn't work that way, and that this was her deal. She'd been working it for a month, her dad even longer, and that was the crux of the matter. More than her deal, this was her responsibility. It was her father they'd come to save.

She glanced at the duffel bag and hoped to hell that eighty-two thousand hard-earned dollars and the name Lindsey Larson were enough to do the job.

Eighty-two damn thousand dollars—what in the hell had Burt Alden been doing to get himself into Franklin Bleak for eighty-two thousand dollars? Johnny wondered, pulling his phone out of his pocket for one last-ditch effort to sell his soul to Sparky. Alden must have been operating every which way from Sunday to get that kind of money out of one of Bleak's bets. Or, if it had been more than one bet, why had Franklin let him get in so deep before he paid off? The only reason Johnny had was that Alden must be one of Bleak's high rollers, a real boom-or-bust kind of guy who played a lot of cash. If so, this wasn't the end of it. Alden would be back in the game as soon as he got the scratch, and this whole damn night and all of Esme's efforts and laying herself on the line would have meant nothing.

So here he was, trying for the fourth time to make a call that was really going to cost him, and instead of negotiating to get Franklin off his ass, he was going to be working a deal to get Franklin off Alden's. For his trouble, he could count on owning the top slot on Sparky's short list for a long time and being on Bleak's until hell froze over, a price he was more than willing to pay if Klimaszewski would just wake the hell up and answer his damn phone.

"This better be my wife," Sparky finally answered on the third ring, sounding half asleep and maybe hung-over, with a real crabby edge to his voice.

"What's the matter, old man, did Carol Ann leave you again?" Johnny said, trying not to sound so damn relieved he could spit.

"Johnny, you jerk," Sparky said. "You must be in a whole helluva lot of trouble to be waking me up at—*geezus*—it's five o'clock in the morning, boy."

"I'm at Franklin Bleak's warehouse."

"Why?" Sparky asked. "You know better than to lay a bet with Bleak."

"I'm not laying a bet. You had it right the first time. I've got some trouble that needs clearing up."

"Then you need Superman, boy, not me," Sparky said.

Superman? Christian Hawkins? Johnny hoped to hell not. The last thing he wanted was for any-one at Steele Street to know what he'd been doing all night. This deal with Esme and Bleak was so far under the table, there was no way to bring it out into the light of day and make it look good. Drugs, illegal gambling, prostitution—if they'd missed a vice here tonight, Johnny didn't know what the hell it might be.

"No, Sparky. I just need you."

"For what?" The old man sounded damn suspi-cious, and Johnny didn't blame him.

"I've got a friend who's into Bleak real deep. We've got the cash to clear the debt, but Bleak's threatening payback with interest. I need you to call him off."

His request was met with a long moment of silence, and then another, and another. Johnny was beginning to think Sparky had dozed off, when the old guy spoke.

"I've got some stuff I can use on Bleak, sure, but it isn't going to come cheap." Sparky didn't sound half asleep or hung-over now. Oh, no. The chop-shop king of Denver was wide-awake and firing on all cylinders.

"How bad are you going to hit me?"

"Three cars," Sparky said without hesitation. "I've already got them scouted. All you have to do is go and pick them up. Piece of cake for you, Johnny."

Yeah, Johnny just bet. Stealing cars was never a piece of cake, even if the keys were in the ignition and the doors weren't locked. Stealing anything took a mind-set Johnny had backed off from a long time ago. No, it wasn't going to be easy for him to steal three cars for Sparky, no matter how good he was at it.

"What have you got on Bleak?" he asked.

"You don't want to know, boy," Sparky said. "It's dirty business. Let me give him a call. That's all it'll take."

Sparky was right. Johnny had a good enough imagination to imagine he didn't want to hear what lousy information the chop-shop king had on the bookie—and yeah, for a second, Johnny had to wonder what knowing all these guys said about him. But then he looked up ahead, at Esme climbing the concrete steps into the warehouse, and figured he was in good company, skirting the edge of Denver's underworld with the girl of his dreams.

God, he was such a sap. He'd finally had her, twice, no less, and three hours later, he already wanted her again. But mostly he wanted her out of here. He didn't know why she couldn't have just stayed put at the safe house. Everyone would be so much happier if she wasn't in the middle of this. He sure as hell would be.

"Can you make that call in about fifteen minutes, Sparky?"

A pair of headlights at the end of the Bleak parking lot announced another arrival, a big-ass black Escalade that all but had Baby Duce's name painted on the door panels.

Both Dax and Esme glanced back at him, and Johnny gave a short nod. They'd seen the Escalade, too.

"Sure, Johnny. I can have Bleak eating out of my hand in fifteen minutes."

"Thanks, Sparky."

"You call me when you're done with this, and I'll let you know about those cars."

Hell.

"Sure, Sparky. I'll give you a call." He pressed his end button.

At the top of the stairs, Esme came to a stop, and the brute waiting for them at the back door got a confused look on his face.

"The boss wants you inside," he said.

Fighter, Johnny thought, looking the guy over. He looked like he'd spent a lifetime getting hit in the face.

Johnny looked down at the guy's hands and made a mental note not to end up on the receiving end of a right hook. It would put him into next week, guaranteed.

"We've got company," Dax said, gesturing at the Escalade being parked at the next dock over.

The fighter looked, and Duce and his boys got out of the big SUV.

"He ain't s'posed to be here," the guy said.

"Well, why don't we let Mr. Bleak tell him that," Dax said, walking by the fighter and into the warehouse.

The big guy looked even more confused. Then he looked at Esme and his face cleared, like he suddenly remembered what he was supposed to do.

"You," he said, pointing at her. "You come on inside."

Asshole. Johnny had his number. He took the last two stairs in one step, hearing Duce and the Locos coming up behind him, and within a couple of minutes, he, Esme, Dax, Duce, two *Arañas Locos,* and eighty-two thousand dollars were cruising into Bleak's warehouse.

Baby fucking Duce.

Franklin couldn't believe he was looking at Baby

fucking Duce standing in the middle of his warehouse at five o'clock in the morning.

"Yeah, sure, I get it," he said into his phone, not quite believing what he was hearing coming at him from the other end of this call, either.

There was no justice.

He was screwed.

Goddamn Sparky Klimaszewski was playing hardball to keep Burt Alden in one piece, and Burt Alden was already broken, at least his damn arm if nothing else, and Franklin knew there was something else broken on the guy, probably more than one something else.

But hell, he wasn't going to tell Sparky that.

"Yeah, sure, I remember, Sparky. I remember how it used to be." This was all just so goddamn bad. How in the hell had this happened? he wondered. How in the hell had his back gotten shoved so hard up against the wall?

Five guys and a girl—that's all that had come in through his loading dock, but he'd done nothing but sweat since they'd arrived, and then his phone had rung. Bad news on top of bad news, like the two gangsters with Duce, one of them with vampire caps on his teeth. *Geezus*. Franklin had heard a few things about the *Arañas Locos*, the Crazy Spiders, and none of it was good.

"Sure, Sparky. There'll be no heat on the guy. Once I'm clear with a guy, I'm clear with him, you know that."

Goddamn Sparky. How in the hell had the chop-shop king of Denver gotten into his deal? What the hell was Burt Alden to Sparky Klimaszewski? Some long-lost brother or something?

And Duce, goddamn Baby Duce wanted a cut of the deal, of the cocaine, and if Franklin didn't deliver, things were going to happen—bad things, to him, personally, with Duce throwing him to the Parkside Bloods.

Old news, now, and Duce didn't know it, but he and the Bloods were going to have to get in line behind Sparky Klimaszewski if they wanted a piece of Franklin's ass. Sparky, Duce, Bloods, the Chicago boys, the guys from New Jersey—hell, he needed a goddamn dance card to keep track of everyone who wanted a piece of him. If he lived 'til Christmas, it would be a miracle.

Baby Duce, the two *Arañas*, Johnny fucking Ramos, Esme Alden, and "the cousin"—five guys and a girl, that's all he was looking at, and he was in it up to his eyeballs.

Franklin had six guys at his back, six mean sons-a-bitches packing plenty of hardware, and he was still sweating. Johnny Ramos, who had screwed the whole deal for him in the first place, didn't look like he'd be all that damn easy to kill, and if that wasn't bad enough, the damn cousin Esme Alden had brought with her looked like he could drop them all on a dime. Dax was his name, and Franklin didn't know what in the hell kind of name that was.

The only damn bright spot of the whole damn morning was Esme herself.

Dovey was such an idiot. He'd gotten it all wrong, and the photos Franklin had seen simply had not done the young woman justice.

She was exquisite—fine-boned, elegant, gorgeous, classy, every square inch of her, and stupid him, he'd already made his deal with Rollo.

Hell, he could get a fortune for her in this certain Middle Eastern market he had done business with a few times. He needed to think this through, figure out the win for himself. With the eighty-two thousand to finish his cocaine deal, and the girl, he could come out okay.

That's all he needed, half a million dollars' worth of cocaine with a ready market in Aspen and Vail, and one drop-dead gorgeous girl worth ten times those two young whores he'd sold five years ago. By the time he unloaded all that, he'd be sitting back on top. Of course, from the looks of things, he'd need to be sitting someplace other than Denver.

Goddamn cocaine.

Keep your head down, lay low, work your bets—those were his rules, and he'd broken them all for a damn drug deal and a shot at Katherine Gray, who wasn't going to find him all that damned intriguing if he was dead.

He needed to put Rollo off, that was all. Offer him more money if he'd wait until the coke was delivered and sold. Hell, that's all he needed to do, hold everything together until he could get the coke sale money in his coffers.

Of course, he was running a tight margin on the

cocaine sale, damn tight, what with the exorbitant interest rates charged by the Jersey guys, and having to buy off Duce, and now to buy off Rollo.

But damn Sparky didn't want cash or cocaine. Damn Sparky wanted Burt Alden.

"That's old news, Sparky. Nobody cares about two runaway whores who disappeared off the face of the earth five years . . . well, yeah . . . sure, Sparky, the cops care, but nobody is going to be dragging the cops into our business, are they?"

Klimaszewski was insane. Nobody in their right mind would drag the cops down on Commerce City just to save Burt Alden.

"That's a bad decision, Sparky. I mean it. You—" Sparky interrupted him, and Franklin listened with growing unease—hell, as if he wasn't uneasy enough.

This lawyer guy Klimaszewski was talking about was no good. Franklin bent his head into the phone, holding it closer. Sparky couldn't really be serious about dragging this guy up out of the past. One dead lawyer who had been into cheap whores, big bets, and premium cocaine, who had bought the farm one night in kind of a gruesome manner, and Sparky was going to hold that over his head?

Nobody could tie Franklin to that deed—but the more Sparky talked, the more uneasy Franklin got.

"Yeah, yeah, I get it," he said, reaching the end of his rope—like he needed blackmail on top of every other screwup he'd had to contend with tonight. "My guy is counting the cash now. If it comes up right, Alden is off the hook. I won't touch him. He can walk away."

In theory, Burt Alden could walk away, but only in goddamn theory. In truth, Alden hadn't budged since Eliot had dropped him on the betting-room floor.

Franklin turned and looked halfway down the length of his warehouse, where Esme and her knights in shining armor were waiting for him to accept payment and clear the debt. Shifting his gaze to Dovey, he watched the kid count the last of the bills out of the duffel.

When Dovey gave him the "okay," he made his decision—he would roll over for Sparky. Burt had already had the crap beat out of him. Nothing was going to fix that, except a trip to the hospital, but if he handed the guy over, that's where his buddies would take him. Sparky Klimaszewski didn't make idle threats. Guaranteed, by this time tomorrow, if Burt Alden didn't get put back together, the Bleak warehouse was going to be swarming with cops looking to hang the guy who had offed one lousy lawyer and sold two whores.

Christ. Like the world didn't have enough lawyers and whores. Sure, he and Eliot had gone a little overboard with the lawyer guy, but so what? What was one lousy lawyer in the scheme of things?

"Sure, Sparky. I'm reading you, and we're clear." Clear as mud. "My guy kind of wrenched Alden around a bit, but I'm gonna take care of that right now. If I'd known he was important to you, I'd have told Eliot to be more careful with him. But you know how these things happen . . . sure, sure, Sparky. Alden won't see my guys again. Hands off. Right."

Bullshit. All of it. Franklin was going to do whatever it took to get out of this with the most he could get, which he was afraid was not going to include lunch with Katherine Gray.

He ended the call and stared down the main aisle of the warehouse. The answer to his problems was watching him with her big gray eyes, her cute little suit fitting her just so, her blond hair twisted up in a real sophisticated style. She had diamonds in her ears, and high heels on her feet, and all he needed to do was get rid of her father, get rid of her goons, and keep her with him, and for that, he only needed one thing—her mother.

CHAPTER THIRTY-ONE

Esme stood carefully and quietly in the bottom of a canyon of paper-filled pallets—paper towel pallets, paper napkin pallets, and towering pallets of toilet paper. It was damned crowded on the floor, with a baker's dozen of mostly very bad guys variously arranged around a small table, including the three gangsters on the home team.

No, sirree, having three of the worst gang-bangers in the history of Denver on her side was not a comfort, not when Franklin Bleak was headed their way. Six or eight Locos might have done the trick, but she only had three, and it was all she could do not to bolt.

The bookie had his damn money. Dovey had counted it and given him the sign. All was well. All was as it should be, and yet Esme had a very strong feeling that the deal wasn't even close to being over, and she wanted it over. She wanted out of this damn warehouse, and the closer Franklin Bleak got, waddling his short, overweight, gimpy body down the aisle toward the table, the more she wanted out.

She consciously deepened her next breath to keep from jumping straight into full-blown panic. Even with Johnny on one side of her, Dax on the other, and an auto-loading .45 closer than both of them, Bleak scared the hell out of her. The photographs she'd seen of him, a couple of stills taken in a Denver restaurant, did not do him justice. He'd looked almost normal, smiling, raising a glass of wine in a toast, a heavily made-up bimbo on each side.

But he wasn't normal. Not even close.

It wasn't his slightly misshapen body, his right leg obviously shorter than the other and giving him an odd limping gait, that made him look so strange. It wasn't his hair, worn in a dark, greasy comb-over long enough to be tucked behind his ears. It wasn't his clothes, a disco turn of electric blue silk and badly tailored black polyester with the looping chain of a pocket watch crisscrossing the front of his mismatched vest. It wasn't even his shoes, shiny bright black patent-leather elevator shoes with taps—freakin' taps. Every step he took down the concrete floor was an announcement—"I'm coming. I'm coming. I'm coming." And every step made her want to run like hell.

No, what made Franklin Bleak so damn scary was his face, every part of his face, the low widow's peak of sparse dark hair backed up by the comb-over, the beakish nose, his eyes too round, the irises too dark, like bottomless pits, fixated on her, and his mouth. It didn't close, but stayed partly open, his tongue sliding across his lips. She was creeped out to the max and had to force herself to hold her ground—carefully, quietly, nothing show-ing, not giving her fear away. But sweat was bead-ing on her upper lip and running down the middle of her back.

He stopped at the table, his gaze still riveted to her, and he stood there, staring, until she under-stood this was personal between them. That what-ever was going through his head was more than the debt her father owed—and all she could think was that he was damn lucky she didn't draw down on him, anything to get the bastard to back the fuck off. She wasn't going to play this game with him, and yet it was only when he broke eye contact with her that she realized Dax had said something.

"Yes. The money's good, but it's late," Bleak said, his gaze shifting to Dax for a brief couple of sec-onds before returning to her.

"Eighty-two thousand clears the debt, no reper-cussions, no blood revenge, no breaking anybody, no shakedown," Dax said, his voice slow and calm and sure without an edge in sight. "That's the deal, nothing more." He made it sound like they were ex-changing calling cards, but what he put on the table was the Lindsey Larson file.

Bleak picked it up, took one look inside, and turned beet red, color and anger infusing his face in equal measures. Those too-round, bottomless black eyes landed on Dax with the force of a train wreck, but Dax had faced down a helluva lot worse than a psycho bookie.

"That's the deal, nothing more," he repeated, still very calm, very matter of fact, and Esme breathed a little easier. As weird as Bleak was, Dax wasn't fazed by the crooked little man. She was overreacting, that was all.

His fist tightening around the file, crushing it, Bleak turned to the huge guy who'd met them at the loading dock door, "Bleak's beast," she was calling him. The guy bent his head to Bleak's, and the bookie said something too softly for her to hear. The big guy nodded and turned and left, heading toward a door at the rear of the warehouse.

"This is a mistake," Bleak said, raising the fistful of crumpled papers. "You would have been better off leaving her out of this."

Dax nodded his head. "Absolutely. You're right, and I have no intention of ever going to Folton Ridge again . . . unless you give me a reason to go."

No one with half a brain would mistake Dax's calmness for anything other than what it was— complete and utter control of himself and the situation.

"A smart man would forget what he knew," Bleak warned.

At the end of the warehouse, the huge guy had opened the door and disappeared inside.

"A smart man would take the money and call it good," Dax said. "Take the money, Bleak."

Take the damn money, Esme thought, her attention shifting from Bleak to the door at the end of the warehouse and back again. *Take the damn money, so we can get the hell out of here.*

This had dragged on too long already. Nothing good could come from staying any longer. All Bleak had to do was pick up the duffel bag, or give some sign of acceptance. Any damn sign would do.

But this damn standing there, giving everybody the evil eye, that wouldn't do at all. That was indicative of some unforeseen problem, and Esme didn't want there to be any unforeseen problems. Straight deal, that's what her father had arranged with Bleak.

A movement at the end of the warehouse drew her gaze down the length of the aisle, and with the shift in attention came a horrifying sinking of her hopes.

Her feet moved of their own volition, everything inside her telling her to run, while at the same time telling her it was too late. Bleak's beast had a bundle of rags by the scruff of the neck, an old green striped shirt and a pair of worn brown corduroys, and inside the rags, hanging slack from the beast's hands, was her father.

Dead. He looked dead, and even with everything inside her telling her to run to him, she was frozen, held in place by a sudden wash of emotion and Johnny's hands catching her and dragging her up against him, keeping her from moving any closer.

Her father's arm had been broken. The way it was hanging, the angle, was bizarre, and for a moment, all she could think about was the pain he must have felt.

It was the beast, the damn beast who had hurt him. Bleak wasn't big enough to have done the deed. The beast had beaten her father and broken his arm. Her breath started coming faster, and she began to struggle.

"Let go of me," she said under her breath, the words meant for Johnny. "Let *go* of me."

"No, babe." His voice was not slow and calm. It was harsh and hard, and full of the same serious intent she felt in his body. He wanted out of there, too, and he was taking her with him.

"He's not dead," Bleak said, and nodded at Dovey, who immediately trotted down the aisle to the beast and took hold of her father's head, tilting it back so she could see that his eyes were open—and filled with agony. "Not yet."

"What have you done to him?" she demanded.

"Go see for yourself," Bleak said, but when she and Johnny started forward, he held up his hand. "Just the girl. No one else."

"No," Johnny said immediately.

"Let me go. I have to see if he's okay. I have to help him." She lifted his hands away, peeling them off from around her waist, feeling his reluctance to let her go, and when she was free, she started forward, her gaze riveted to her father.

He was breathing, with each breath costing him in pain, and every step she took closer to him took her another step away from the safety of Johnny's arms, from the safety of Dax and the Locos.

A hospital, that's all she could think. She had to get her dad to a hospital. When she was within twenty feet, Bleak's beast dropped him and headed back toward the rear of the warehouse, letting her father crumple into a pile on the concrete. A terrible cry of pain came out of her father, an expulsion of air edged in acute distress, and she ran the last few feet, before dropping to her knees by his side.

"We're done here," she heard Bleak say behind her.

Her father's skin was pale and clammy, his every breath coming ragged and hard. She didn't know where to touch him, hardly dared to touch him.

"Dad, Dad..." She lightly smoothed his hair back off his brow. "It's Esme, Dad. I'm here, and I'm going to take care of you, get you to a hospital."

"Your friends can take him," Bleak said, appearing at her side. "You're coming with me."

She looked up, her gaze drawn by a sickening awareness, to find him standing between her and the rest of the men in the warehouse, blocking her view, blocking her from their view. A wave of dread sluiced down through her body. He was crazy. She wasn't going anywhere with him, and she had enough guys on her side to enforce that plan. She could overpower him herself, if it came to that.

He was close enough to touch, mere inches from her, the duffel bag in his right hand. With his left, he handed her something small, a piece of hard plastic, a quick exchange accompanied by a dire warning.

"Come with me, or my man Eliot will snap her neck."

The words were so cruel, so unexpected, it took a second for them to sink in, and she still didn't understand, until she looked at the small thing he'd given her.

Beth Alden, R.N.—that's what it said, the blue letters printed on a white base. Her mother's name tag, her identification badge.

Behind him, she heard the commotion of Johnny moving forward and being blocked by Bleak's other men.

Eliot, she thought. Bleak's beast was named Eliot, and he had her mother.

"Bleak!" She heard Dax call the guy's name, but she was watching the bookie, watching him limp his way to a set of stairs crawling up the side of the warehouse and leading to a door one floor above the door where Eliot had disappeared again.

She looked over her shoulder at Johnny and Dax, the small name tag grasped in her hand.

"It's okay," she said. "I've got everything under control. I'll be back in a moment." Then she turned to her dad and let the name tag drop to the floor as she rose to her feet.

Suddenly, she wasn't afraid.

Johnny was terrified, his blood running cold, watching her follow Franklin Bleak up the stairs. The only thing keeping him in place was Dax.

"Leave her be, Ranger." The guy's voice was right

behind him, a softly spoken command of unmistakable authority, but it wasn't the command keeping him from starting World War III in this damn warehouse and going after her. It was knowing Dax wouldn't take an unnecessary risk with her life. It was knowing Dax understood her skill levels better than he did, knew her internal resources. And it was knowing how she'd drawn down on Mitch Hardon in the Gas-N-Go, with absolute precision, and absolute certainty.

It was knowing she had a Para-Ordnance .45 caliber pistol tucked into a shoulder holster and that she most definitely knew how to use it.

Not even Patsy could save this goatfuck.

Dax let his breath out, slow and easy, watching his bad girl climb those damn stairs, which more than likely led to Bleak's office. Of all the possibilities of what could happen in that room, he was sure of only one—the guy was unlikely to come out ahead of Easy.

But something was up.

She'd strayed from the plan, big time.

"Do you mind?" he said to Dovey, gesturing at the pile of crumpled humanity on the floor.

Dovey gave him the go-ahead with a short nod, and Dax walked over and knelt down by his uncle.

Damn Burt—he'd really gotten into it this time.

Dax lightly pressed his fingers to the side of the guy's neck, feeling his pulse.

Fluttery, he decided, which was just so damn bad.

He picked up a small piece of plastic lying next to his uncle and turned and looked back at Baby Duce.

"He needs a hospital. Can you send him with your boys?"

The shot caller for the Locos gave a nod, and the two *Arañas* and Johnny moved forward to pick up a very limp Burt Alden, leaving just him and Duce to face off Bleak's remaining five guys. Duce, Dax figured, could at least be counted on not to accidentally shoot him, and Dax had certainly been up against worse odds than five to one, hence those stories that had made his name in Afghanistan. As far as Johnny, Dax hadn't always had a partner who so instinctively understood a good plan when it was thrown out on the stage without any explanation.

Getting the Ranger out of the warehouse, where he could scout the building and find Esme, was precisely what they needed. Getting Burt out of the warehouse was simply the best Dax could do for his uncle under the current circumstances. There was no calling an ambulance down into this mess. He wasn't too concerned about losing the two gang members. If anything started to happen, he would just as soon not have two unknown shooters at his back. And if anything started to happen, there was going to be shooting.

Bleak had his Aunt Beth.

It was her name tag Easy had left on the floor.

Dax was guessing Beth was being held in the

warehouse somewhere, probably through the door where that big guy had gone to get Uncle Burt, and that real big guy was undoubtedly still with her, and that was the threat Bleak had used to get Easy to go up those stairs with him.

His bad girl could take Bleak. The problem was his sweet Aunt Beth. She couldn't take anybody, and Dax didn't know what kind of shape she might be in after a night of Bleak's hospitality. Judging by Uncle Burt, his hopes weren't too high.

This was bad.

CHAPTER THIRTY-TWO

This was horrifying, Esme thought, looking down into Bleak's betting room from his office and seeing her mother handcuffed and taped to a chair. She'd been hurt, and it was all Esme could do to keep from pounding on the window and yelling that she'd be okay, her girl was here to save her.

But Esme was currently frozen in place, and she needed just a second to pull herself together.

Franklin Bleak had his hand on her ass.

There they were, the two of them standing at the window, and Bleak opening up the blinds to show her his big surprise, and in her first moment of shock at seeing her mother so poorly mistreated, the bastard had grabbed her ass.

He was still grabbing it. She could feel all five of his fingers and his palm pressing into her. It was his fourth mistake, and the whole thing was just lose, lose, lose for him from here on out.

"Take her out to the van. We'll meet you there in a couple of minutes." Bleak was on the phone to Eliot, who Esme could see crouched behind her mother, cutting away at the tape holding her to the chair. He'd already uncuffed her arms, which tactically wasn't the advantage it should have been. Her mother was either in shock, or her arms had fallen asleep, because she wasn't moving, not until Eliot finished with the tape and hauled her to her feet, and even then, she wasn't exactly moving, just swaying, until she started to collapse. Eliot caught her, threw her over his shoulder, and headed out a door leading to the outside on the south side of the building.

"So where are we going?" she asked, though she already knew the answer—nowhere. Whatever was going to happen, she was going to make damn sure it happened right here, where she still had backup and a chance.

"Mexico," Bleak said, giving her ass a little pat before he turned away and started across the office. "I've got a place down there on the beach."

"I like Mexico," she said, not taking her eyes off her mother until the door closed behind her and Eliot.

"You'll really like my place." Bleak gave a little chuckle, and Esme turned. "I've got maid service and a pool."

He really was crazy. He'd kidnapped her mother, and he thought she'd like his place on the beach?

He knelt down in front of a very large floor safe and started dialing in a combination, and she tallied it up as mistake number five, right after kid-napping her mother, beating her father, blackmail-ing her, and assuming she either wasn't armed or didn't have the sense to take the initiative. He glanced back once, but the only possible reason he could have for taking his eyes off her for even one second was that he didn't consider her a threat.

He was wrong.

She moved and had her gun jammed up against the back of his skull before he had the safe door open, exactly where it would have been if he'd taken his eyes off her or not.

"Get facedown on the floor."

He started to splutter, and she pushed the gun harder against him. He'd either get the picture, or he wouldn't. The choice was his.

He chose to lie down on the floor, exactly as she'd ordered, which saved his life. She didn't have time to mess around with him, not with her mother outside and in Eliot's clutches. She didn't have any handy restraints on her, either, but it didn't slow her down.

With the gun still pressed against the bottom of Bleak's skull, she slipped her knife off her skirt and thumbed it open. She made two quick cuts, slicing the backs of each of his sleeves and a little bit of him in the bargain.

He squirmed and squealed, and she'd had enough.

"I'd just as soon blow your brains out here, Bleak, as turn you over to the cops, so shut up and put your hands together." He'd either obey, and she'd tie him, or he wouldn't, and she'd shoot him. He seemed to get the message.

He held his hands together, and she wrapped one slit-open sleeve around both his elbows, the silk tightening as it twisted. Then she cold-cocked him with her pistol, knocking him out.

In seconds, she was through the door leading to the room where her mother had been held, and she was running down the stairs.

The minute Johnny got through the door to the outside, he peeled off from the "Let's Rescue Burt Alden" group and started down the loading docks. Burt Alden was on his own with two Crazy Spider boys, and Johnny wished him the best of luck. From the looks of him, he was going to need it.

All Johnny needed was Esme.

There were no outside windows on the warehouse, except for in some of the doors, and what Johnny was looking for was a door on the south side, the side Esme was in.

Now that they'd met face-to-face, so to speak, that bastard Bleak was at the goddamn top of his freaks and perverts list, and his skin was crawling just thinking about her being alone with the guy.

At the corner of the building, he slid up next to the wall and looked to see what was on the other side. Lights from the parking lot in front didn't reach back this far, and it was dark except for one bare bulb hanging over a closed door.

He avoided looking at the light and instead looked beyond it. He could hear someone walking, but didn't hear any taps, so he knew it wasn't Bleak. Silently, he dropped off the side of the docking bay and crouched low to the ground. One of Bleak's white vans with his logo on it was parked about ten yards from the door with the light above it, and once Johnny slipped into the shadows away from the building and along a fence enclosing Bleak's property, he could look back and see the man heading toward the van.

It was the fighter, and he was carrying something, a woman, but it wasn't Esme. This woman was heavier, not by much, but she was definitely rounder and more softly built than Esme, and she was dressed in scrubs. The fighter opened the back doors on the van and unceremoniously dumped the woman inside. Johnny didn't know who she was, but she hadn't been struggling, and wasn't moving, which made him think she was out cold, and there was just something about putting an unconscious woman in the back of a panel van that didn't set right with him, especially by a guy the likes of the fighter.

He moved quickly and silently along the fence, getting into position, when the back door of the warehouse swung open.

"*Eliot!*" Esme yelled, her gun drawn and aimed. He didn't know at what the hell what. Standing in the light, looking out into the darkness, she couldn't be seeing a damn thing. It was just too damn dark, a new-moon night with the sun not quite breaking the horizon.

The fighter stopped and turned. Johnny could see the expression on his face, and it was one of confusion again.

"Let my mother go!" Esme said, her voice carrying across the lot, her steps carrying her down the side of the building.

Her mother, Beth Alden? Franklin Bleak had been damn busy tonight.

"Where's Mr. Bleak?" the fighter, Eliot, asked, his confusion turning into belligerence.

"He's on his way down, but he wants my mother to stay here. He's not taking her to Mexico with us."

Oh, hell, no, Johnny thought. No women from here were going to Mexico tonight.

"Walk away from the van, Eliot," Esme said, continuing to move away from the light, he was sure in an effort to see her opponent more clearly. "Mr. Bleak wants you back up in his office. He needs help with the money."

Nice try, but actually, Esme was not a very convincing liar.

"No," Eliot said, a little unsurely. He was facing Esme, but reached back into the van and threaded his fingers through Esme's mother's hair before taking a strong, one-handed grip on her head. "Mr. Bleak told me to snap her neck, if things went wrong, and I think this is wrong."

And that's what came from thinking—trouble.

Johnny raised his pistol, lining up on Eliot's head and moving forward. If the bastard made another move, he was dead.

And the bastard did, but it wasn't to snap Beth Alden's neck. With his attention on Esme, the fighter slowly slid his other hand to his waist, thumbing aside his jacket, his hand open. The instant Johnny saw the guy's gun, he fired.

Eliot dropped like a stone, his pistol never leaving its holster.

Inside the warehouse, three of Bleak's guys scattered like rats at the sound of gunfire, all of them heading in some fashion toward the loading docks door, leaving Dax and Duce squared off with Dovey Smollett and some big guy in a Chicago Bears jacket. But it wasn't a contest. Within a split second of the gunshot, Dax had drawn his pistol, getting the drop on everybody, and was moving toward the back of the warehouse.

"Duce, you cover them."

"I'm cool," the Locos shot caller said, drawing a big, old, unwieldy but intimidating "Dirty Harry" .357 Magnum out of the back of his pants.

Gangsters, Dax thought.

White boys, Duce thought, barely holding off from a grin. He had two of them in his sights, two of Bleak's. That jerk, to think he was going to pull off a coke deal in Duce's backyard with the Parkside Bloods looking on.

Bleak was fucking nuts.

And he'd gone up those stairs with a duffel bag full of eighty-two thousand dollars.

Duce liked that. He liked it a lot. He liked it so much, he was going to take his .357 and go give Franklin asshole Bleak a little visit.

But he owed Dax Killian, so he stayed put right up until Dax went through that back door, and then Duce moved out, running about half sideways to keep his gun leveled at the two white boys.

The big guy lifted his hands with a phone in one, which was nice, real polite. Little old Dovey Smollett was shaking so bad, Duce doubted if he'd be raising anything for a while.

"Hey," the guy in the damn Chicago Bears jacket said. Didn't he know he was in Bronco country? "Can I call my girl? I'm running late, and uh, she gets real mean if I'm late."

Jerk white boys, couldn't even keep their women in line.

"Sure, *cabrón*, call your woman."

The guy hit a speed dial, and man, his woman must have been sitting on her phone, she answered so fast.

"Loretta," the guy said. "Honey baby, this party is almost over, been some real noise out here. If you want to see me, you better be ready now…sure, baby. See you soon."

Honey baby? Duce liked that. He thought his

Carmelita might like honey baby, too. He knew she'd like the eighty-two thousand.

When he reached the bottom of the stairs, he started sidestepping up, keeping his gun on those two white boys the whole way.

CHAPTER **THIRTY-THREE**

Oh, my, God—Esme moved even faster down the side of the building, heading for the corner, which she hoped would provide her with some cover. She'd just gotten Eliot lined up in her sights, when the other shot had been fired and Eliot had disappeared from her field of view.

"Esme," a voice called out, and she stopped cold.

Oh, my, God—relief flooded through her. It was Johnny.

She started forward, running toward the van, when his voice stopped her.

"Go get Solange, bring her around. I'll get your mom."

"Is she—"

"Fine," he said. "She's fine, but we need to leave, now. Oh, hell."

"What?" she called out, backpedaling for a moment, but still heading around the corner for the

Cyclone. With Bleak out cold and Eliot dead, she couldn't imagine that Dovey or those other guys were going to give them too much trouble about getting her dad and getting the hell out of here.

"I can *smell* the cops coming, that's all. Come on, Esme, *move*."

She did, breaking into a run. He'd left the keys in the ignition, and she didn't have any trouble firing the Cyclone up and finding reverse. She hit the lights, and after a few feet, spun the wheel and eased back around the corner, until she came to a stop at the van. She threw the shifter into neutral and pushed down the parking brake.

Eliot was everywhere, literally, but she didn't dwell on it. Snap her mother's neck? She didn't think so, and she was oh, so grateful to Johnny for keeping that from happening. If he hadn't, she would have—and there still would have been Eliot everywhere.

Between the two of them, they got her mom into the passenger seat, and Esme was about to crawl into the backseat, when the warehouse door opened and another shaft of light fell out on the Cyclone.

"Are we clear?" Dax asked, his gaze catching hers.

"Clear," she said.

"And the money?"

"Up the stairs behind you. In a duffel on the floor in Bleak's office, next to him."

The door closed again, and she and Johnny both got in the rumbling Cyclone.

"Where's my dad?" she asked.

"On his way to the hospital in Duce's Escalade."

Thank God. Esme allowed herself another moment of relief. Now all they needed was Dax and to get the hell out of here.

Dax ran up the stairs, burst through the door, and immediately saw Bleak bleeding and tied on the floor, out cold.

He couldn't help but grin. His bad girl was so good, and he was so proud of her.

He snatched up the duffel and turned to leave, when the other door in Bleak's office opened, and suddenly, there he was in a true Mexican standoff. Duce stood in the doorway, his .357 in his hand, and a whole lot of "what the fuck am I gonna do now" on his face.

"You let those guys go?" Dax asked, and Duce shrugged, but he still had his .357.

Yeah, that's the way this was going to go down. Goatfuck all the way. He didn't want to kill Duce, not for money, and he sure as hell wasn't going to let Duce kill him.

"Let's call it good," Dax suggested, unzipping the bag and without a moment's hesitation or even bothering to look, he reached in and pulled out ten thousand dollars. He'd counted it. He knew exactly what was in each bundle and he had four bundles of twenty-five hundred in his hand.

He put the cash on the floor.

"Let's call it good," he repeated, and at Duce's short nod, he turned and left—a done deal.

He all but slid down the stairs, crossed the betting room on a running stride, and hit the door with enough force to knock it back on its hinges, and he no sooner cleared the door than he heard two things—the rumbling roar of Johnny revving up the Cyclone, and the sound of sirens closing in.

CHAPTER THIRTY-FOUR

Esme hurt all over from lack of sleep, and lack of food, and a whole damn night spent running around in a pair of three-inch heels, and yet she had a smile on her face. Her father wasn't close to dying. Other than a broken arm and three cracked ribs, he was going to live long enough for her to personally kill him, unless her mother got to him first.

Johnny's driving had revived her mother while they'd still been on their way to the hospital. About the second rubber-burning, tire-squealing turn, she'd come out of her faint enough to grab onto the console, and by the time they'd hit eighty miles an hour on a Commerce City street, she'd had enough blood and adrenaline pumping through her to talk, though she hadn't said much beyond "Slow down!" and "Watch out!" and "God save me!"

The doctor had checked her out anyway, and given her a clean bill of health, and as soon as Dax came back to get them, Esme was taking her mother home.

And when she went back to Seattle, she was taking her mother back with her, at least for a couple of weeks. Her father was either going to have to figure out his gambling problems or go it alone, and Esme didn't have a clue which way it would all end up. But she was never going through this again. She hoped her mother decided the same.

She checked her phone—7:25 A.M. Johnny had gone to a meeting, of all things, and promised he'd call her when it was over. God, she was thinking about him. Johnny Ramos, U.S. Army Ranger. The night had been wild, the sex amazing, and it all felt so right. It felt like love, which was crazy in one night, except he'd been a part of her life since she'd been thirteen years old, the part she'd longed for, and to be with him had felt so right, so easy.

She'd already told Dax she was staying in Denver for a week or two, just taking some time off. She needed to see where this all went. To bed, for sure, but maybe someplace else as well.

She checked her phone again—7:26 A.M. Johnny had thought his meeting would wind up by nine. Dax had said he'd be back before eight, and after dropping her and her mom off, he was headed to the airport, where he was going to see if he could track down Warner's jet, see when it had come in and when it had left, then back to Seattle, and from there to Singapore.

But she was staying in Denver.

She took another quick glance at her watch—7:27 A.M. She felt like an idiot for wanting to see him again as soon as possible, like maybe this morning, about nine-oh-five or so, right after his meeting—but there she was, Esme the Impatient, Esme the Insatiable, Esme Maybe in Love.

Duffy's made great coffee, and it was a great summer morning in the Mile High City after one helluva night, but it was 7:28 A.M. and Dax's time was running out.

He had the place to himself, and that hadn't been his plan, or his wish. One of Duffy's cooks had just finished watering the pots and pots of flowers filling every corner of the outside patio, geraniums and petunias still fresh with morning dew, and another cook had brought out the coffee pot to give him a refill and another chocolate croissant to fill him up, and it was all just great, but damn he'd hoped to be sharing it with her, the *her*, Suzi Toussi.

He hadn't been hit that hard by a woman in a long, long time. It wasn't something a guy was going to forget.

He pushed back from the table and tossed a ten next to his plate. The next time he ran into Suzi Toussi, he wasn't going to let her get away. All he had to do was make sure there was a next time.

He could do that.

He could make *damn* sure there was a next time.

Suzi slipped out of her black 1955 Porsche Speedster, the one she'd bought off Kid Chaos, Nikki's husband, over at 738 Steele Street, and quickly walked to the side door of Duffy's Bar. Everybody used the side door if they wanted into Duffy's before eleven o'clock in the morning, except for those brave souls who hazarded the alley, and the crumbling brick steps, and the wrought-iron gate into the patio. She hurried down the hall past the bathrooms, and ducked behind the coat closet to get to the door leading to the patio from inside the bar.

For a second, her heart soared ridiculously high. There was a cup of coffee on a table, a plate with a half-eaten chocolate croissant—and a ten-dollar bill lying between the plate and a small bouquet in a vase.

He'd already paid and gone.

Her smile faded, and she just stood there and stared at the empty table, the sense of loss she felt completely out of proportion with the circumstances. But there it was, taking the air out of her.

She was late, and he was gone. Dax Killian. God, what a name.

She looked to either side of the patio, just in case...just in case—but no luck. She'd missed him.

Don't be ridiculous, she told herself. He probably

hadn't even shown up. The coffee could have been anyone's, and even if it was his, by any test of reason, it was impossible to feel a sense of loss over missing someone a person didn't even know, or had barely met.

And yet it was there, weighing on her in an odd, sad way.

She looked around the patio again, then walked over to the iron gate leading into the alley. There was no one, only the bricks of the surrounding buildings warming up with the morning sun, the damp alley where one of Duffy's busboys would have hosed it down—and a table where someone had been just minutes before she'd arrived.

She went over to the table and sat down in the chair where that someone had been sitting, and told herself she'd never been this ridiculous in her life.

She touched the coffee cup. It was still warm.

Oh, hell, she really had just missed him, or someone.

They'd barely met, she assured herself. She'd spent more time talking to the surveillance cop last night than she'd spent talking to Dax Killian.

He shouldn't matter, not to a reasonable woman, not at all. Yet she found herself running one finely manicured finger along the edge of the croissant plate, and when she looked at the flowers in the vase, she saw the note.

Duffy, it said. *If she doesn't show, would you see that these get to Suzi Toussi at Toussi Gallery on Seventeenth.* And it was signed—*Dax.*

Unbidden, a thrill went through her, and a very pleased, cat-in-the-cream smile curved her lips. The flowers were gorgeous, fresh and dew-kissed, picked right out of Duffy's pots, a bright red geranium surrounded by a dozen or more purple and white double petunias, but the vase—ah, the vase. Upon closer inspection, it was exquisite, and she had to wonder where in the world Dax Killian had found a Chihuly vase between one and seven-thirty on a Saturday morning?

The only reasonable answer was that it was his, and he'd left it, this lush little piece of art, on a patio table for her.

He'd come into her gallery last night looking for Johnny, and that connection was more than enough.

With a name and a connection, she could find anybody.

CHAPTER THIRTY-FIVE

Dylan Hart's office always left Buck Grant cold. It was so damned austere, like the man himself, coldly efficient, everything expensive and in its place. A guy didn't feel good even bringing a cup of coffee into the room. As a matter of fact, he didn't think he'd ever seen anybody drinking coffee in Dylan's office. He'd sure as hell never seen anybody set a coffee cup on Dylan's desk.

Which was Buck's problem. He'd brought a cup of coffee with him into Dylan's private lair, already slopped a little over the edge, and now he didn't know what in the hell to do with his cup. The finish on the damn desk probably cost more than the wood to build it. Buck was no connoisseur of anything that didn't have a caliber and require a cartridge, but he was no cretin either.

"Sir," Dylan said, setting an extra chair down in

front of the desk and taking the cup out of his hand.

Hawkins brought his own chair in, too, and shut the door behind him.

Buck got the good chair, and Dylan put his cup on the desk, sloppy drips and all—problem solved. That's what a second in command did, solve the commander's problems, and nobody was better at it than the two men in front of him.

Good. They were going to need to be better—better than they'd ever been if they were going to solve the problem he'd brought with him from Washington, and even better than that if they were going to do it without losing the team.

He dropped a pair of files on the desk and sat down. Nothing about the damn thing was going down any easier this morning than it had yesterday afternoon when he'd first seen it. If anything, the longer he'd had to think about it, the more disturbing it had become.

In half an hour, the rest of the team would be assembled in the main office, but Grant had wanted to see Dylan and Hawkins first. They needed to be told first, and there was no easy way to do it.

"We've been tagged for an assassination in South America," he said. Nothing unusual there; that was all in the normal course of SDF's business, of any Special Ops business. "If you can bring him in, the powers that be would like to talk to the guy, but bringing him in is secondary to retiring him. Four agents have been lost trying to do one or the other, so the idea has been put forth to send in a team, your team."

Still business as usual—SDF often got tasked with missions other entities had failed to successfully accomplish.

Grant pushed the top file across the desk, but kept his hand on it.

"No matter what you think, this guy is not who you think he is," he said, and after a moment, during which he hoped to hell those words sunk in, he removed his hand.

He saw the look that passed between the other two men, and he was glad of it. His guys didn't get paid to be delicate, but the file was asking a lot of anyone—a goddamn helluva lot.

Dylan reached for the file and opened it without hesitation—and then he froze, turned to absofuckinglutely stone. Not a flicker of emotion showed on his face. Nothing. But within that complete stillness, Buck was reading a maelstrom. Dylan's breathing had missed a beat and started back up too shallow, too fast. Buck didn't have to guess what his subordinate was struggling with. He knew—utter disbelief, total denial, and fast on its heels, confusion, and in about thirty more seconds, it was all going to coalesce into anger—cold, glacially cold anger.

And then fury, hot, and dangerous, and unacceptable.

Hawkins leaned over, took a look at the photograph stapled inside the folder, and sat back in his chair. After a couple of quiet seconds, he brought his hand up and rested it on his chest, open, relaxed, as if he was feeling the beat of his heart.

He well could be. It was a lot to take in.

Dylan was looking at the photograph, frozen in his chair, and Hawkins was looking at the floor, his hand over his heart—and Grant could have heard a fucking pin drop in the room.

The next move wasn't his, and he had to wonder why in the hell he'd brought a cup of coffee with him. Hope, he guessed, that somehow this wouldn't be so goddamn awful that he wouldn't even be able to drink a goddamn cup of coffee.

Fat chance, and he couldn't remember a time when he'd hated the politicos in Washington, D.C., more than this moment. He was pretty sure the two men in front of him were feeling the same way, and he could A1 guarantee they were both contemplating assassination—but not of the guy they'd been tasked with killing. No, they'd both be wanting the one who had dreamed up this goatfuck in the first place.

They could do it. Grant's job was to make sure they didn't.

Their gazes met again on the other side of the desk, and this time, Grant didn't have a clue what was passing between them.

When Dylan's gaze returned to the folder, and he started reading, Grant guessed the coast was nominally clear for a discussion of the situation, or at least a recap of the information he'd already read three times.

"The guy's name is Conroy Farrel, which, as you

will both remember, was one of J. T. Chronopolous's code names, a situation which was carefully created by one of our government's darker agencies. It's a case of identity theft, if you can call it that when it reaches this level and has been sanctioned by the government. He was put into Paraguay by the CIA, though they aren't the ones who created him. Although, as you may well suspect, I have reason to doubt that denial."

Neither of his guys was talking, which was the exact situation Grant wanted to avoid. He wanted them to talk, a lot, to figure out how to explain to the rest of the team—to Kid, who'd lost his brother; to Creed, who had almost died losing J.T.—how and why Conroy Farrel had been set in J.T.'s place by their own government, with J.T.'s connections, and J.T.'s clearances, and worst of all, with what looked very much like J.T.'s face. The similarities were eerie, not complete, but eerie. For most dealings, Conroy Farrel could undoubtedly pass as SDF's first dark angel without batting an eyelash.

Dylan finished reading the first page of the file and handed it over to Hawkins, silently—and so it went, page after page.

"Farrel has gone rogue," Grant continued. "And the CIA is having a helluva time trying to take him out. The prevailing opinion is that SDF, who knows more about the real J.T. than anyone on the planet, is the team to go get this guy."

Dylan shook his head. "Not the team," he said.

"No," Hawkins agreed, accepting the next page.

Well, that was the last thing Grant had expected,

that they would out-and-out refuse to take the mission.

"Hawkins and I will go in and get him for you," Dylan said, finally lifting his gaze from the folder and meeting Grant's eyes with his own. "Just the two of us."

Grant looked to Hawkins, who nodded. "Nobody else needs to be involved."

Grant knew what they were doing, trying to protect the rest of the team, and he couldn't fault them for it, but neither could he allow it.

"The CIA has already lost four other agents. I can't authorize sending another two guys in, when it was the team that was tagged for this. Success is mandatory."

Dylan's gaze grew very cold.

"They'll get their success," he said.

"But we go in alone," Hawkins added.

"If funding is an issue—"

"We'll use the CHF," Hawkins finished Dylan's sentence for him.

Oh, hell, the CHF.

"You mean the Contraband Holding Facility?" Grant asked. "That coffee can full of diamonds in Quinn's kitchen?"

A mission a few years ago involving a load of contraband dinosaur bones had netted the team a cache of diamonds nobody had bothered to officially report, and the windfall had gone into their emergency fund, the CHF.

"No," he said. "It's not a funding issue, unless we fail. Then, as usual, we'll be left to pick up the pieces and pretend we never went anywhere or did anything."

Another glance passed between the two men.

"Nobody needs to know we went in alone," Dylan said. "Let Hawkins and me do the recon on this thing. That's all, just the recon. We'll report back to you with what we find, and the three of us can decide what to do from there."

"You know that's the best way," Hawkins said, seconding the plan. "We can't use CIA intel to catch a rogue CIA agent. We need boots on the ground. Two people, not a team, not at this stage."

Grant considered the compromise and knew he'd just been handed a solution to his biggest problem with the tasking. He wasn't likely to lose his whole team, if the whole team wasn't involved. He didn't have to figure out how to control Creed and Kid, if Creed and Kid didn't know about Conroy Farrel.

On the other hand, he couldn't think of a better way to get the guy killed than to put his fate in the jungle boy's and Kid's hands—and yes, he knew that might have been exactly why this thing had landed on his desk. Plenty of folks in Washington didn't think he kept a tight enough rein on his SDF operators. Some of those folks might be counting on them to run wild, do the deed, and then take the fall for good.

"I'll expect a report in eight weeks," he said, coming to his decision. He didn't have to worry too damn much about controlling Dylan Hart and

Christian Hawkins. He'd never seen either one of them not in control of themselves.

"We need twelve, minimum, for an initial evaluation," Dylan said. "Especially if we're going in cold. We'll need time to set up a network."

"Prade?" Grant asked, and Hawkins nodded.

"Is connected from Tijuana to Tierra del Fuego."

"Then you've got twelve weeks," Grant said. "And I've got the whole team waiting out there for something."

"Did you get us Ramos?" Dylan asked.

In answer, Grant slid the second folder across the desk. "He's all yours." And he was another one who was nothing but trouble, another independent thinker. SDF was full of them, and Grant wouldn't have had it any other way, but by any standards, according to some information he'd gotten, Johnny Ramos was coming off of one helluva night.

Something was up, something big. Johnny felt it as strongly as anyone else in the room when General Grant, Dylan, and Hawkins came out of Dylan's office.

Sitting on top of the snack table, Skeeter stopped with a Sugarbomb doughnut halfway to her mouth. Standing next to her, Creed shoved the last bite of his in his mouth, and Kid set his back on the tray, uneaten.

Smith and Quinn were sitting at a table with a chessboard between them, and though they stopped playing the game, they both kept eating, and Zach was sitting at Cherie Hacker's desk, smoking with the window open and drinking coffee, and specifically not eating a Sugarbomb doughnut.

Johnny chewed and swallowed and rose to his feet.

Something was up.

He couldn't read Dylan very well, but the guy looked a little gray. Hawkins he could usually read a little better, but Superman wasn't giving anything away, other than the seriousness of his expression.

General Grant, Johnny couldn't read at all. No matter what catastrophe hit, the guy was always the same. He always moved at the same pace, talked at the same pace, and both of those could be a little on the slow side. He was a measured guy, and when the general's gaze landed on him, Johnny felt measured, too—measured up.

"I heard you had a busy night last night," General Grant said to him, and Johnny felt his heart drop all the way to the soles of his feet. It took everything he had not to look at Skeeter, who'd been called by the cops last night, questioning his whereabouts.

Hell, if he got arrested while Grant was in town, he could damn well forget about being part of SDF, and there was a damn good chance he was going to get arrested. He had a call in to Lieutenant Loretta. He'd saved a couple of women from being kidnapped to Mexico, but he'd killed a guy while doing it, and the lieutenant was going to want a full accounting, if not his ass in her jail, before this was finished.

"Yes, sir," he said.

"I heard you and Dax Killian can both be placed at the scene of a cocaine sting set up by the Denver Police Department this morning."

Oh, shit.

"Yes, sir."

The old man looked him over again. Everybody else was looking at him, too, Skeeter looking like she wanted to bust the tar out of him for being an idiot.

"If you have any other civilian sins on your head, Ramos, you better confess it all to Lieutenant Loretta, and if you can manage to keep your name out of the paper, you'll report here to Dylan, Wednesday morning."

That sounded like good news.

He angled a glance over at Hawkins, who gave him a nod, and although Johnny felt the thrill of that acceptance go all the way through him, he felt the gravity of Superman's thoughts even more strongly.

He shifted his attention back to Grant.

"Yes, sir," he said. This was what he wanted, a chance to be part of all this, and that's what he'd be, one part. The team was the thing, the whole of it. The parts could come and go, but the work of the team was what mattered. It stretched out in the years of missions behind them, and it stretched forward in the years of missions ahead of them, and for a while, if he could keep his name out of the paper, he was going to get to be a part of it.

He would never tell a soul, but in his heart, he was just so goddamned proud of himself, he could bust.

CHAPTER **THIRTY-SIX**

"Hey, baby."

"Hey."

"This is your idea of fun, right?"

"Not quite," Esme admitted, feeling the mud and the rain soak into her pants where she and Johnny were huddled together under a makeshift shelter he'd lashed together out of sticks and branches in the middle of the woods. "Actually, I'm kind of a city girl at heart."

"You don't like playing Army Ranger?" He sounded surprised.

She shook her head. "I like playing *with* Army Rangers. I don't like playing at *being* an Army Ranger."

A gust of wind sent another showering of rain into their shelter, soaking her where she was already double soaked.

"Hoo-yah," he said.

And she punched him, hard, right on the arm.

"Does this mean you don't want to cook up our MREs and eat dinner out here?"

"Roger that, Ranger boy."

"You look cute in camo," he said, and she hit him again.

"I look cute in Vera Wang. *You* look cute in camo."

"The hot tub looks nice and warm from here," he said.

Yes, it did. Quinn and Regan Younger had offered them their home up in the mountains west of Denver, in Evergreen, for a week, while they were in Hawaii, and she and Johnny had jumped at the chance. From where he'd been teaching her survival skills, his specialty, along with a whole lot of weapons skills, demolition skills, communications skills, and even some newly acquired medical skills, they could see Quinn and Regan's back deck, and the hot tub was definitely steaming.

"If we go back to the house, we could play doctor again," he suggested. "Or we can stay out here and weather the storm in real Ranger fashion."

"If I freeze to death, you're going to have to play by yourself." It was a warning, nothing less.

"Last one in the hot tub gets to take the other one's clothes off."

More rain blew into the shelter, and she started to shiver.

"You always cheat, when that's the bet," she said, not really minding the cold too much, not when the mountains smelled so good, so green, and the hot tub was only a hundred feet away, and not when she was in love.

Five months of flying back and forth between Seattle and Denver; trying to maintain a long-distance relationship was taking its toll. When he was gone, he was really gone, incommunicado, and he was never anyplace he could tell her about, off on some mission he couldn't tell her about, add the distance part of the long-distance relationship, and she wasn't sure how much longer they could keep it going. And yet, the more she was with him, the more she wanted to be with him. She wasn't even close to getting enough of Johnny Ramos, so she'd started looking at making some changes, starting with location, location, location, starting with taking over her dad's office. She'd talked to Robert Bainbridge, and the lease was hers, if she wanted it, if she wanted to go out on her own. Her dad didn't need the Faber Building property anymore. After the disaster of the Bleak deal, he was finished, and so was her parents' marriage. At least it looked that way to Esme. Some lines, once crossed, couldn't be uncrossed.

"Okay, babe, let's practice our fireman's carry," Johnny said to her, scooting out from under the branches and offering her his hand.

"What? You're quitting?" she said, really starting to shiver now. "You wimp. I was just getting warmed up."

She took his hand, and just by leaning down, he was able to swing her up onto his back.

"You were just starting to get really cold, sweetheart," he said, starting down the trail to the house. "It's hot tub time."

"And steak. You promised me a steak."

An hour later, soaking in a steaming hot tub with the rain turning to snow and drifting down around them under a night full of stars, Esme finally pushed her plate away.

"I'm stuffed."

"You're gorgeous. Come here," he said, taking her hand and pulling her over onto his lap.

She straddled him, and his mouth came down on hers in an instantly drugging kiss.

"I love you, Esme," he said against her lips, pulling back from the kiss just enough to speak.

"I know." And she did. She felt his love with every call, every e-mail, every letter and gift that arrived in her mailbox. She felt it with every text message that blinked onto her phone, and she felt it every time they made love, but she wanted more.

He was already so hot and hard, and with the warm water lapping against their skin, he held her close and pushed up inside her.

"*Johnny...*" She melted against him, his name feeling like a benediction, his body feeling like heaven.

He moved inside her, and she leaned back so she could see his face. He was so beautiful, his hair much longer than it had been last summer, dark and silky. She ran her fingers through it, and his eyes came open, his gaze holding hers. She loved watching the pleasure in his eyes, how every move she made on him was reflected in their depths. Sliding down on him, she leaned forward again and took his mouth with hers, her kiss so hot.

His hands moved to her hips, and he held her to him, guiding her in the rhythm of their joining.

She leaned back again, watching him. He was so hard everywhere, his body like a slab of granite to the touch. She dreamed about him at night. Every time she lay down to sleep, her thoughts drifted to this, to him being inside her, rocking into her, and some nights she thought it would drive her crazy not to have him.

"Ironheart," she whispered, sliding her hand over the tattoo on his chest. He was the angel Nikki had painted, the dark angel, the warrior angel with the bloody knife in his hand. He never talked about his work, but Dax knew, because he'd done it, and Dax talked to her, telling her things without ever telling her too much.

This warrior code, it ran so deep, and it ran deep in her lover.

She bent over him again, taking him in another kiss as he slid in and out of her. This bond ran deep, too, this lover bond. He was such a part of her.

She had to tell him she wanted more.

He kissed her, and he teased her, and he made sweet, hot love to her, until the fire lit deep inside her, and when she came, her soft cries of pleasure in his ear, his arms locked around her, he pushed

into her one last, hard, deep time, and came undone with her.

Sex in hot tubs, right, that could kill a guy, if he
wasn't careful, and yet Johnny had never seen that
in any of his training manuals. Of course, other
guys weren't having sex with Easy Alex, and she was
just so freaking hot. He'd never had a woman like
her, and he never had her enough. Some changes
needed to be made. Five months of hit-and-miss
hot sex, and missing her way too damn much, just
wasn't cutting it.

He needed her close more, needed to taste her
more, smell her more, be with her more. She was
such a safe harbor for him, and God, sometimes
he needed a safe harbor, especially when he was
home.

She'd gone to Cheyenne with him last August
and helped him deliver that letter, and it had
been so good to have her there, good for Lori
Heath. The other girl had been harder to face,
Cassie McAllister. When a guy was injured so badly
that he turned away from people he loved, it was a
hard thing to explain, even to himself. What had
happened to John Paul Cooperman, Johnny's best
friend through three tours of combat, could happen to any soldier—the debilitating injury, the
deeply scarring wounds—and Johnny hadn't had
any words of solace for the young woman going it
alone out on the Wyoming prairie. He'd check on

her again, though, and let Cooperman know how she was doing. He'd promised.

He had managed to keep his name out of the paper, with Lieutenant Loretta's deep understanding and help, and what he'd learned over the last five months was that no matter how long he'd lived at Steele Street and the Commerce City Garage, no matter how much he'd thought he'd known about Special Defense Force, being on the inside was far, far different than being on the outside. The missions took everything he had and then some. Hell, keeping up with Creed was damn near impossible, and the guy had years on Johnny. *Years.* He hadn't even worked with Red Dog and Travis yet, and quite frankly, he knew he wasn't ready. Skeeter and he made a good team, because they'd spent ten years in each other's faces. They could almost literally communicate telepathically. Hawkins and Dylan still intimidated the hell out of him, trying to meet their standards, but the two of them hadn't been around much since he'd come on board, so a lot of his training had been supervised by Kid, and a lot of his missions had been with C. Smith Rydell. Johnny literally loved working with the guy. Rydell was like a wall of titanium, sixteen feet long, eight feet high, twelve inches thick. It didn't matter how you washed up against him, he was so fucking solid, the experience was always the same. Not even Hawkins had that going for him. And because it was always the same, because Rydell was more consistent than an atomic clock, Johnny learned, and everything he learned from Rydell, he learned right, and every time he did something, he did it right, and that's what made Rydell happy, and if Rydell was happy, a guy's chances of surviving were damn good.

But this thing with Esme, this had to change. This was fluid, and growing, and becoming so important to him. She was his, and he wanted to make those ties that bound even closer.

"Baby?"

"Hmmm," she sighed in his ear, her warm, wet body so soft and lovely in his arms.

"I've got something for you," he said, reaching behind him into one of the cargo pockets on his BDUs.

She lifted her head from his shoulder, curious as he rummaged around in the pocket until he found what he wanted.

It always looked so sappy when guys did this on some reality television show, and it always sounded so sappy when some guy was talking about doing it, and it looked sappy when some guy put his big moment up on YouTube.

But when a guy was doing it himself, it felt, and looked, and sounded so profound, so different from what a guy had imagined. For one thing, he'd never imagined he'd be proposing to a naked woman in a hot tub unless there had been quite a bit of tequila involved.

Go figure. Here he was, stone cold sober, and she was as beautifully naked as a woman could get, which in his book was pretty well summed up by the word "completely."